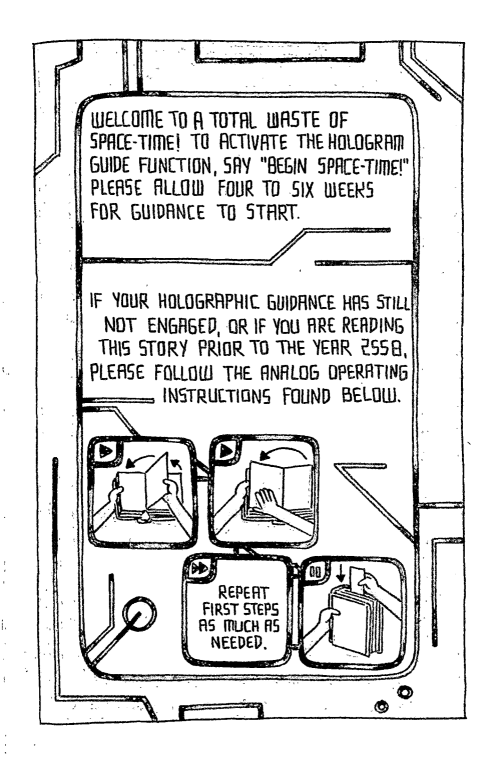

WELCOME TO A TOTAL WASTE OF SPACE-TIME! TO ACTIVATE THE HOLOGRAM GUIDE FUNCTION, SAY "BEGIN SPACE-TIME!" PLEASE ALLOW FOUR TO SIX WEEKS FOR GUIDANCE TO START.

IF YOUR HOLOGRAPHIC GUIDANCE HAS STILL NOT ENGAGED, OR IF YOU ARE READING THIS STORY PRIOR TO THE YEAR 2558, PLEASE FOLLOW THE ANALOG OPERATING INSTRUCTIONS FOUND BELOW.

REPEAT FIRST STEPS AS MUCH AS NEEDED.

OUR STORY SO FAR...

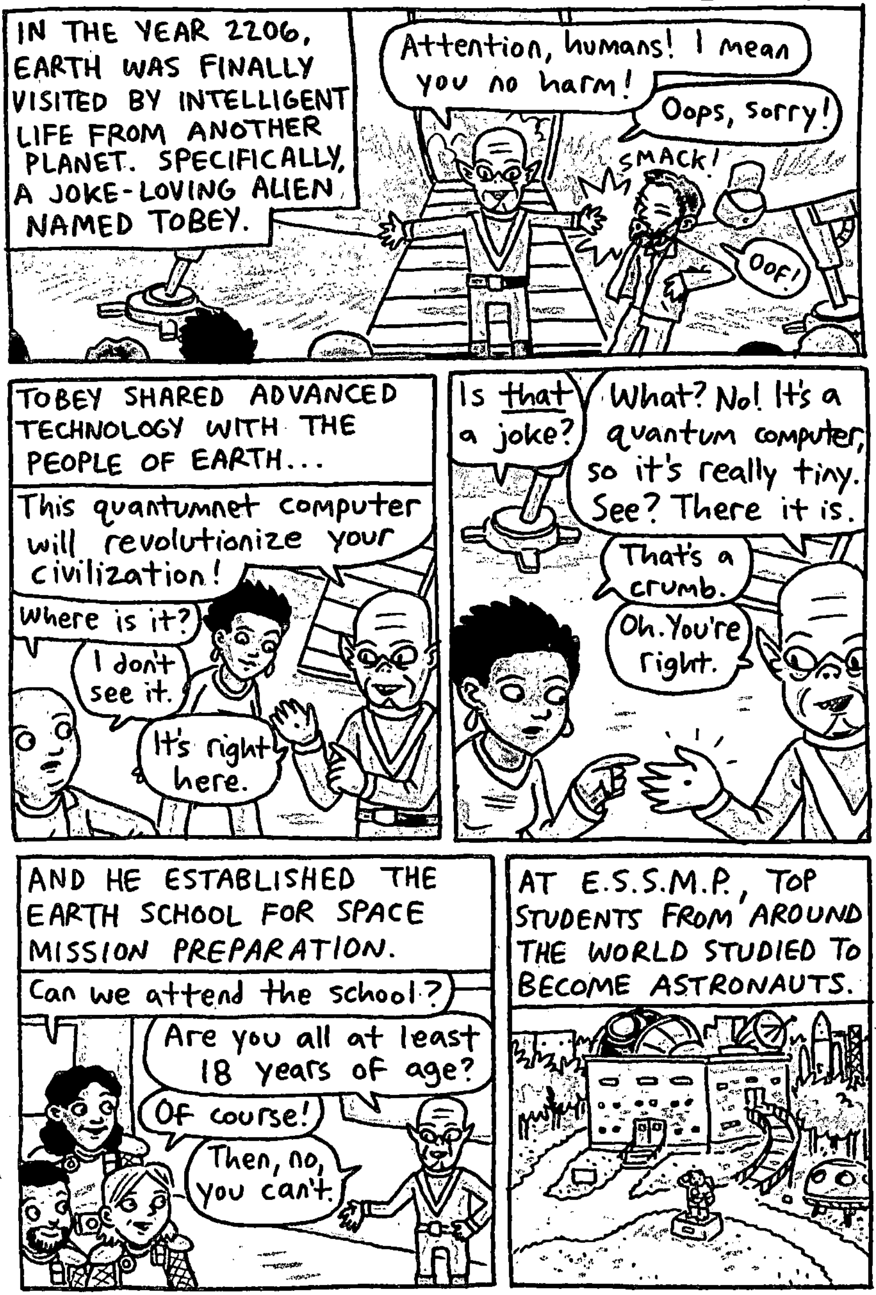

IN THE YEAR 2206, EARTH WAS FINALLY VISITED BY INTELLIGENT LIFE FROM ANOTHER PLANET. SPECIFICALLY, A JOKE-LOVING ALIEN NAMED TOBEY.
Attention, humans! I mean you no harm!
Oops, sorry!
SMACK!
OOF!
TOBEY SHARED ADVANCED TECHNOLOGY WITH THE PEOPLE OF EARTH...
This quantumnet computer will revolutionize your civilization!
Where is it?
I don't see it.
It's right here.
Is that a joke?
What? No! It's a quantum computer, so it's really tiny. See? There it is.
That's a crumb.
Oh. You're right.
AND HE ESTABLISHED THE EARTH SCHOOL FOR SPACE MISSION PREPARATION.
Can we attend the school?
Are you all at least 18 years of age?
Of course!
Then, no, you can't.
AT E.S.S.M.P., TOP STUDENTS FROM AROUND THE WORLD STUDIED TO BECOME ASTRONAUTS.

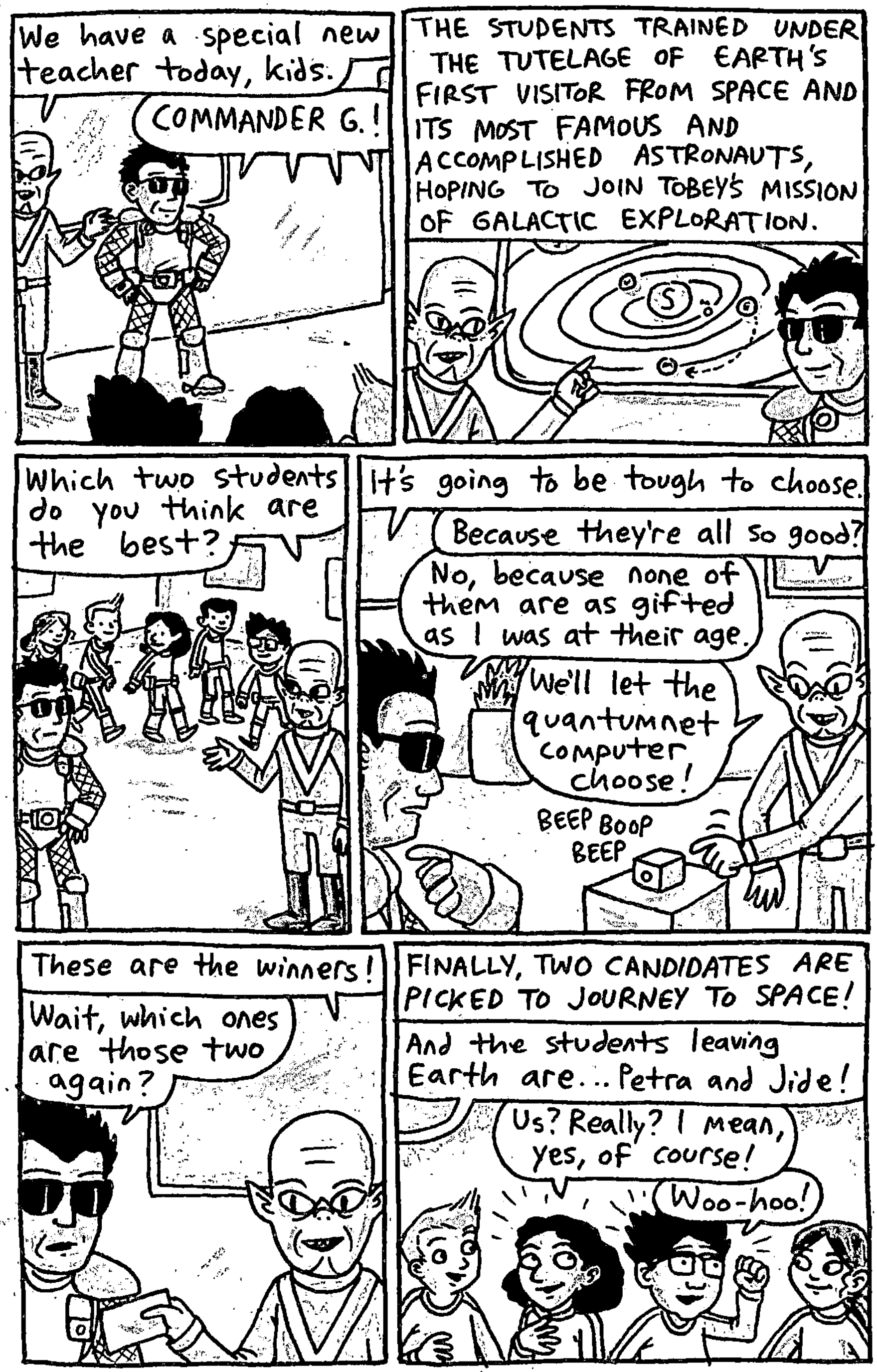
We have a special new teacher today, kids.
COMMANDER G.!
THE STUDENTS TRAINED UNDER THE TUTELAGE OF EARTH'S FIRST VISITOR FROM SPACE AND ITS MOST FAMOUS AND ACCOMPLISHED ASTRONAUTS, HOPING TO JOIN TOBEY'S MISSION OF GALACTIC EXPLORATION.
S
Which two students do you think are the best?
It's going to be tough to choose.
Because they're all so good?
No, because none of them are as gifted as I was at their age.
We'll let the quantumnet computer choose!
BEEP BOOP BEEP
These are the winners!
Wait, which ones are those two again?
FINALLY, TWO CANDIDATES ARE PICKED TO JOURNEY TO SPACE!
And the students leaving Earth are... Petra and Jide!
Us? Really? I mean, yes, of course!
Woo-hoo!

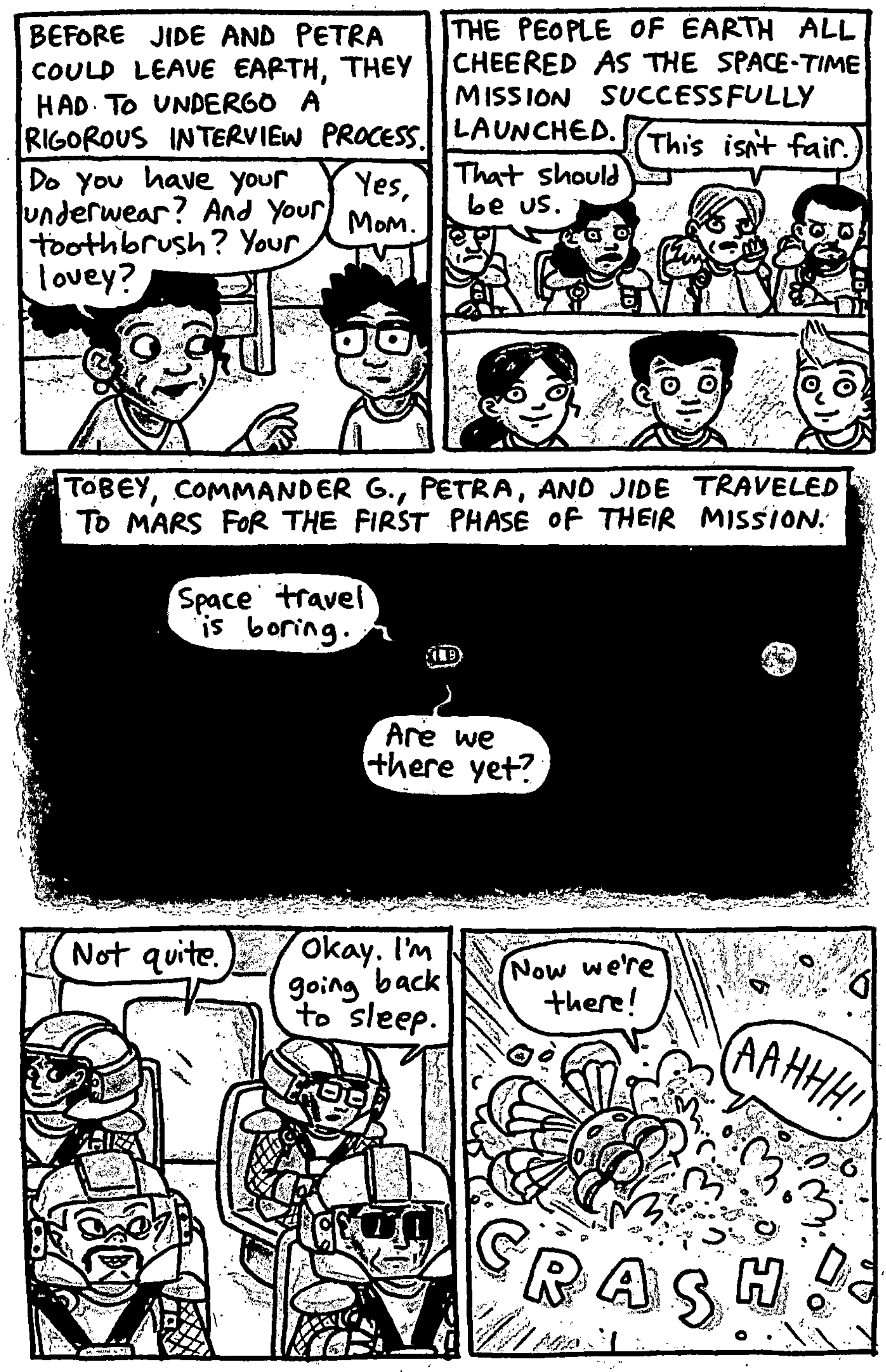
BEFORE JIDE AND PETRA COULD LEAVE EARTH, THEY HAD TO UNDERGO A RIGOROUS INTERVIEW PROCESS.
Do you have your underwear? And your toothbrush? Your lovey?
Yes, Mom.
THE PEOPLE OF EARTH ALL CHEERED AS THE SPACE-TIME MISSION SUCCESSFULLY LAUNCHED.
That should be us.
This isn't fair.
TOBEY, COMMANDER G., PETRA, AND JIDE TRAVELED TO MARS FOR THE FIRST PHASE OF THEIR MISSION.
Space travel is boring.
Are we there yet?
Not quite.
Okay. I'm going back to sleep.
Now we're there!
AAHHH!
CRASH!

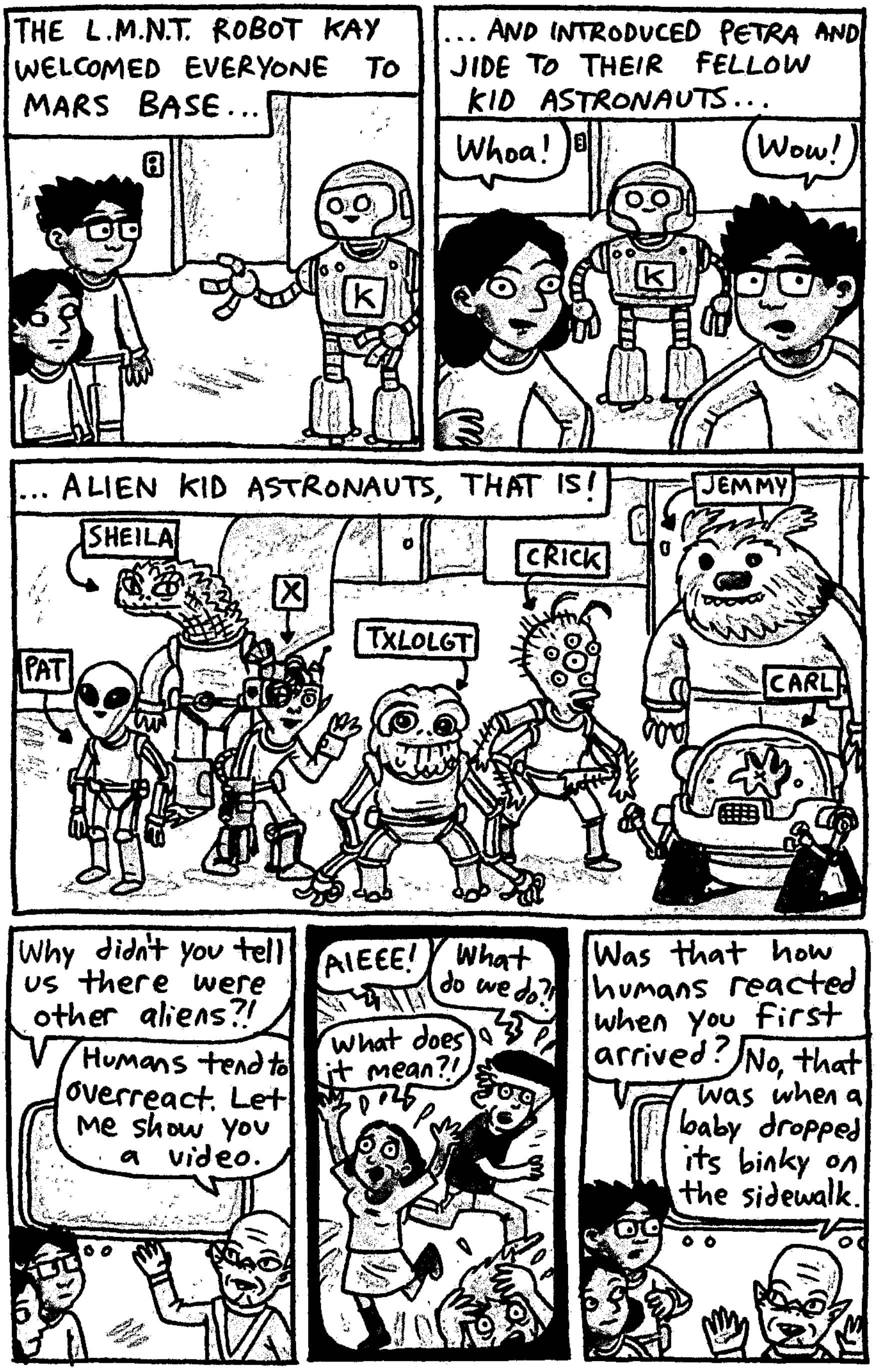
THE L.M.N.T. ROBOT KAY WELCOMED EVERYONE TO MARS BASE...
... AND INTRODUCED PETRA AND JIDE TO THEIR FELLOW KID ASTRONAUTS...
Whoa!
Wow!
K
... ALIEN KID ASTRONAUTS, THAT IS!
SHEILA
X
PAT
TXLOLGT
CRICK
JEMMY
CARL
Why didn't you tell us there were other aliens?!
Humans tend to overreact. Let me show you a video.
AIEEE!
What do we do?!
What does it mean?!
Was that how humans reacted when you first arrived?
No, that was when a baby dropped its binky on the sidewalk.

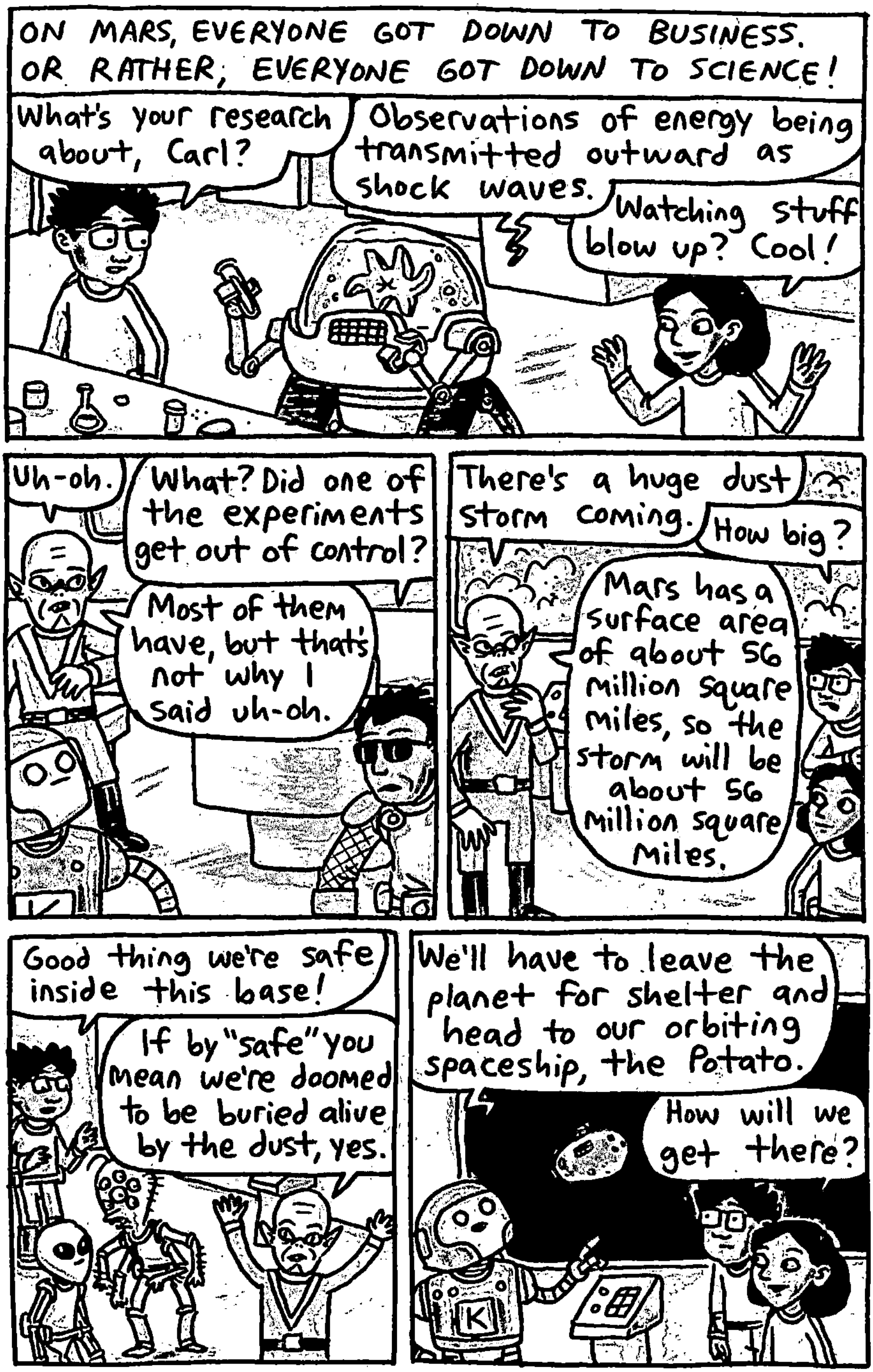
ON MARS, EVERYONE GOT DOWN TO BUSINESS. OR RATHER, EVERYONE GOT DOWN TO SCIENCE!
What's your research about, Carl?
Observations of energy being transmitted outward as shock waves.
Watching stuff blow up? Cool!
Uh-oh.
What? Did one of the experiments get out of control?
Most of them have, but that's not why I said uh-oh.
There's a huge dust storm coming.
How big?
Mars has a surface area of about 56 million square miles, so the storm will be about 56 million square miles.
Good thing we're safe inside this base!
If by "safe" you mean we're doomed to be buried alive by the dust, yes.
We'll have to leave the planet for shelter and head to our orbiting spaceship, the Potato.
How will we get there?
K
K

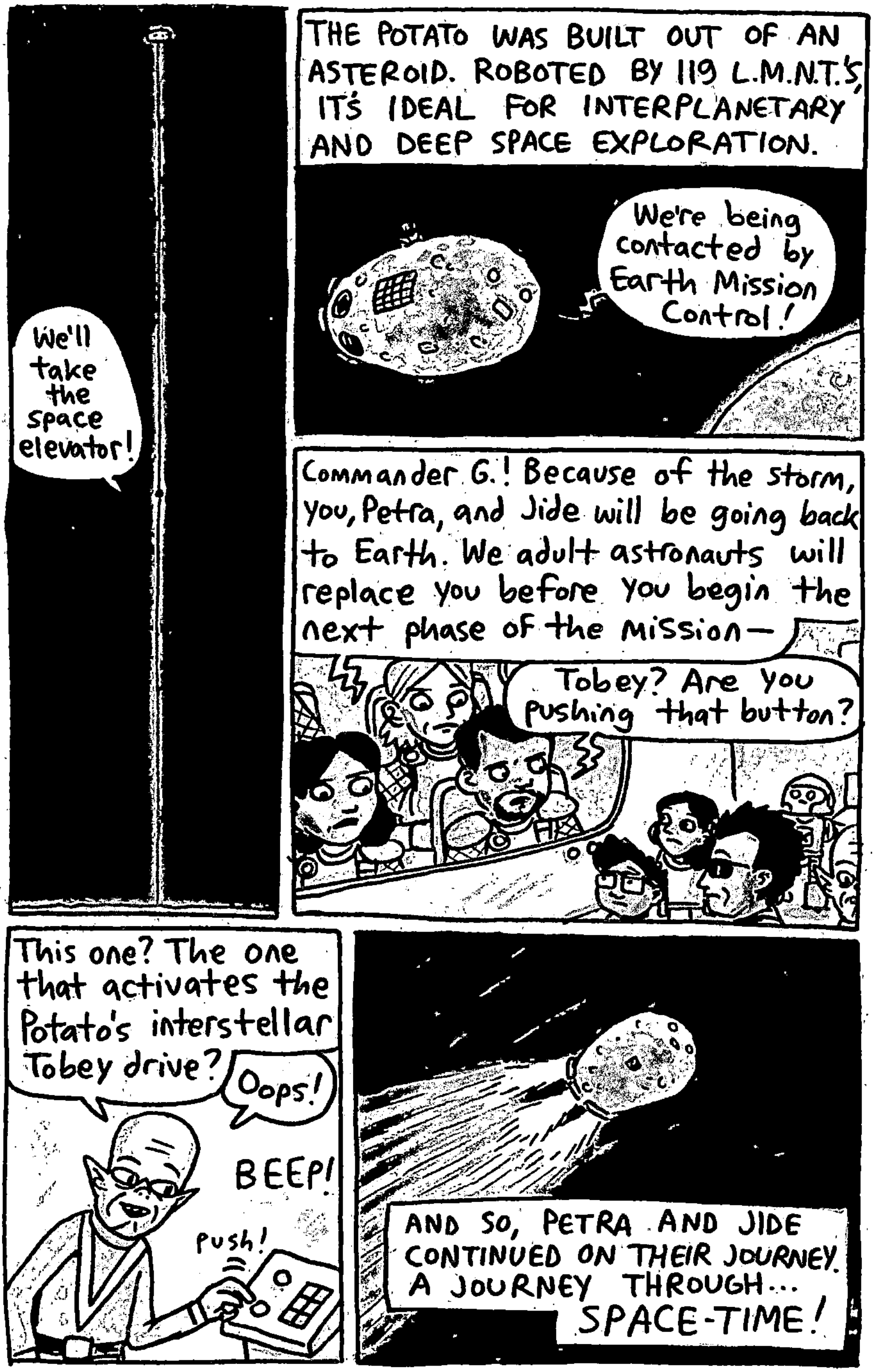

THE POTATO WAS BUILT OUT OF AN ASTEROID. ROBOTED BY 119 L.M.N.T.'S, IT'S IDEAL FOR INTERPLANETARY AND DEEP SPACE EXPLORATION.
We're being contacted by Earth Mission Control!
We'll take the space elevator!
Commander G.! Because of the storm, you, Petra, and Jide will be going back to Earth. We adult astronauts will replace you before you begin the next phase of the mission—
Tobey? Are you pushing that button?
This one? The one that activates the Potato's interstellar Tobey drive?
Oops!
BEEP!
Push!
AND SO, PETRA AND JIDE CONTINUED ON THEIR JOURNEY. A JOURNEY THROUGH...
SPACE-TIME!

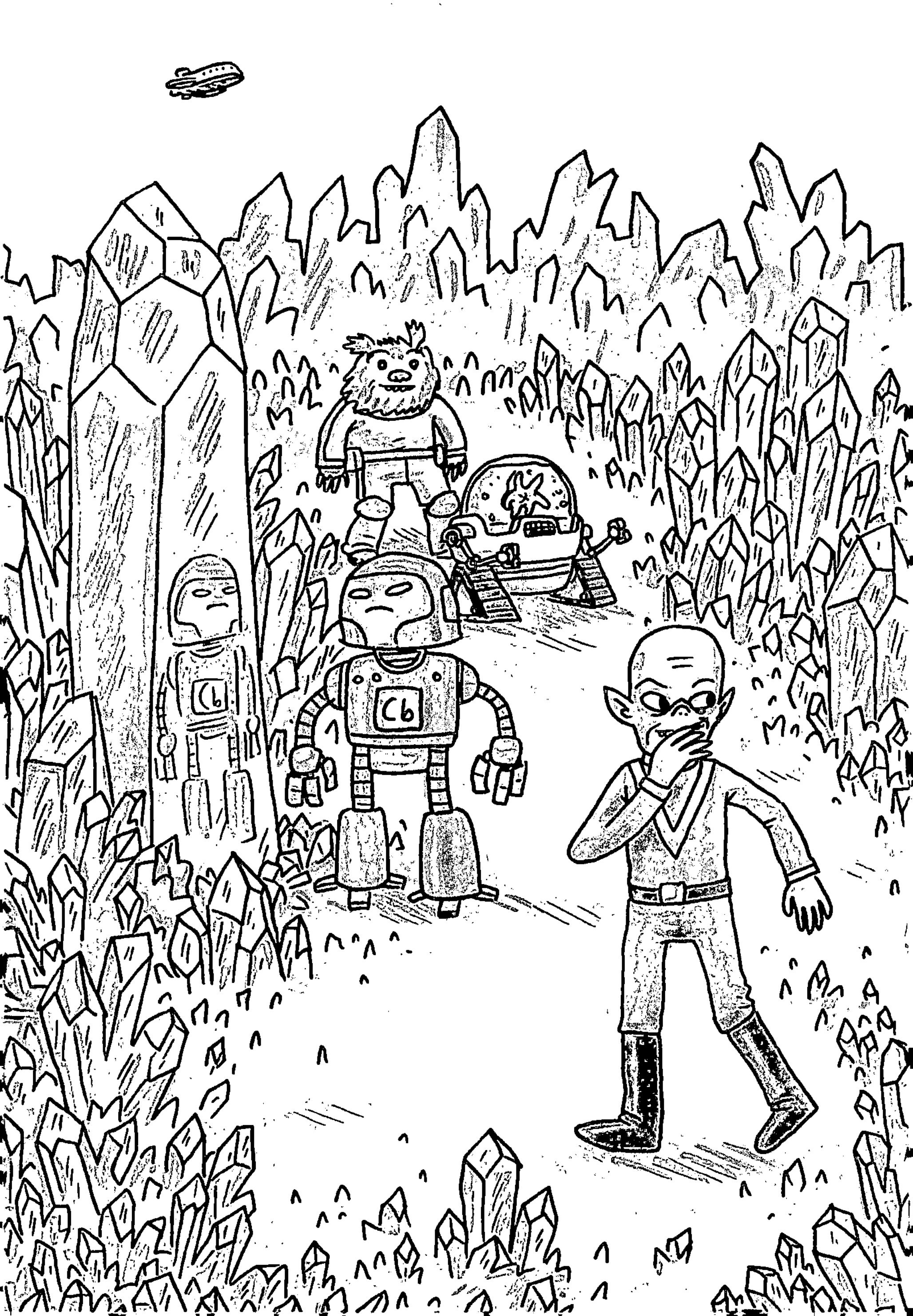
Cb
Cb

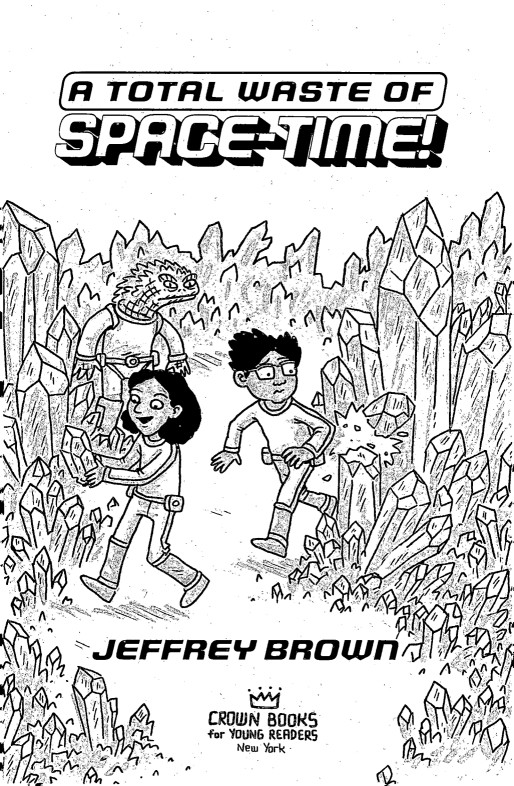

A TOTAL WASTE OF SPACE-TIME!

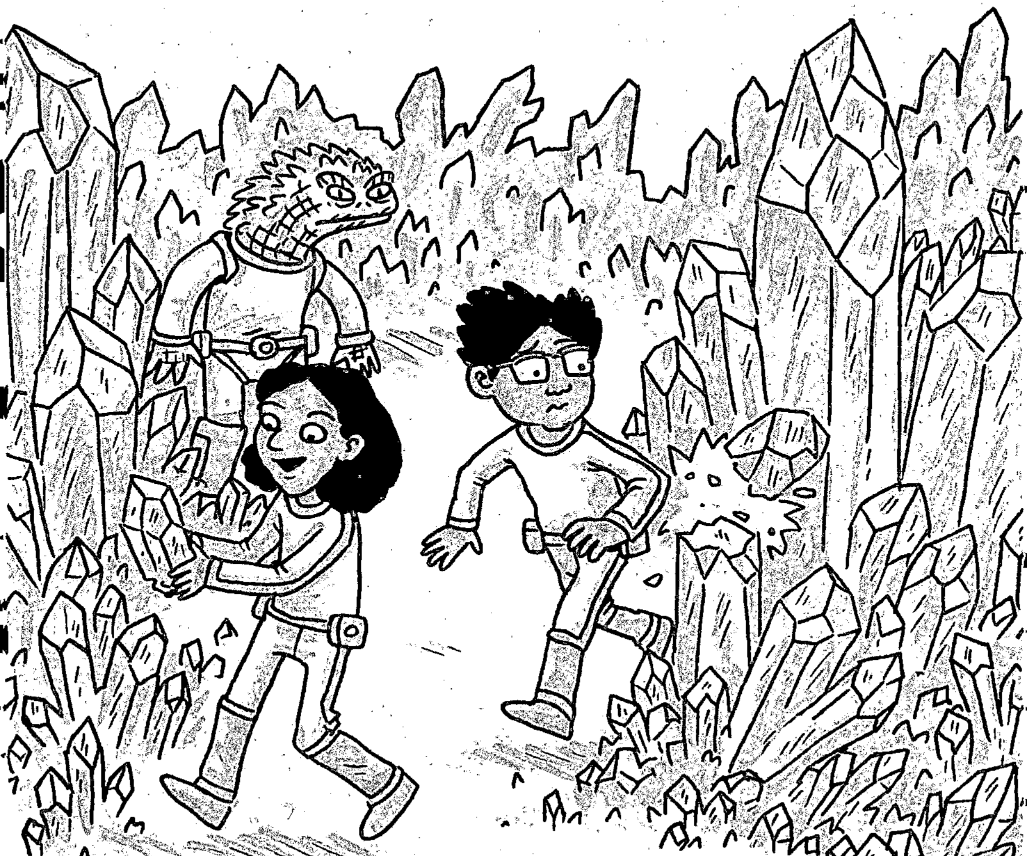

JEFFREY BROWN

CROWN BOOKS
for YOUNG READERS
New York

THE FOLLOWING TECHNICAL DATA CAN BE USED TO IDENTIFY THE SECOND ANALOG VOLUME OF SPACE-TIME! WITHIN HUMAN INFORMATION SYSTEMS.

Copyright © 2021 by Jeffrey Brown

All rights reserved. Published in the United States by Crown Books for Young Readers, an imprint of Random House Children's Books, a division of Penguin Random House LLC, New York.

Crown and the colophon are registered trademarks of Penguin Random House LLC.

RH Graphic with the book design is a trademark of Penguin Random House LLC.

Visit us on the Web! rhcbooks.com

Educators and librarians, for a variety of teaching tools, visit us at RHTeachersLibrarians.com

Library of Congress Cataloging-in-Publication Data is available upon request.

ISBN 978-0-553-53439-9 (hardcover) — ISBN 978-0-553-53440-5 (lib. bdg.) — ISBN 978-0-553-53441-2 (ebook)

Printed in the United States of America

10 9 8 7 6 5 4 3 2 1

First Edition

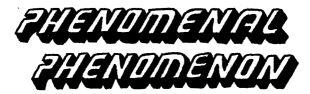

PHENOMENAL PHENOMENON

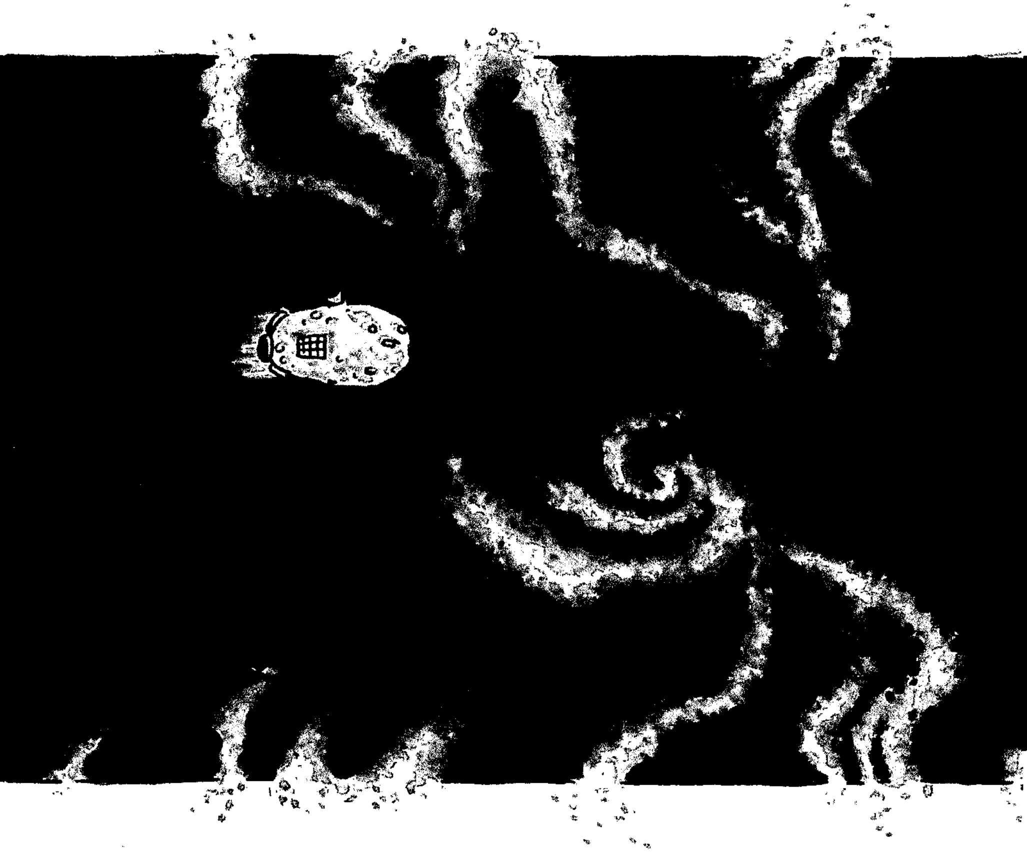

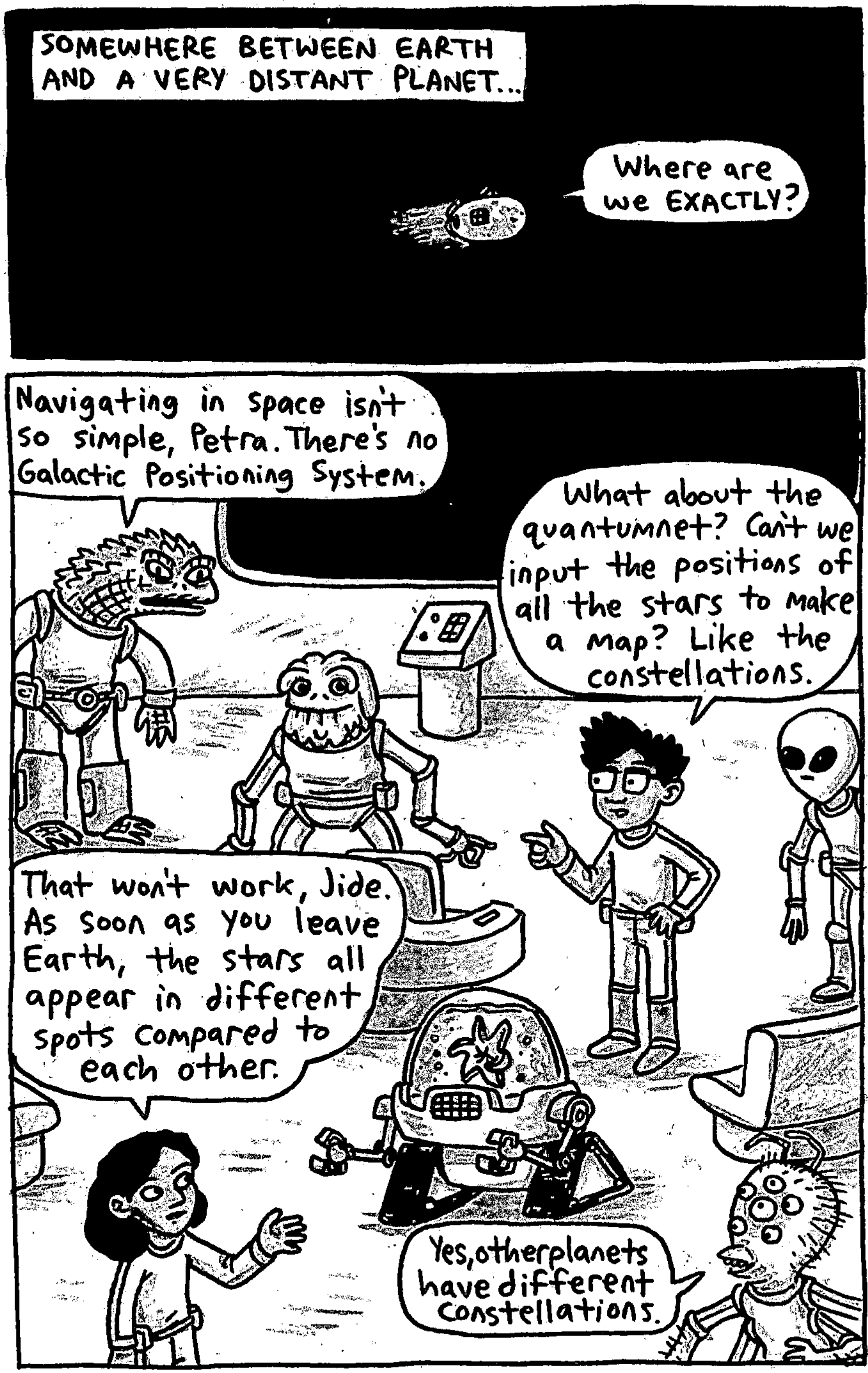
SOMEWHERE BETWEEN EARTH AND A VERY DISTANT PLANET...
Where are we EXACTLY?
Navigating in space isn't so simple, Petra. There's no Galactic Positioning System.
What about the quantumnet? Can't we input the positions of all the stars to make a map? Like the constellations.
That won't work, Jide. As soon as you leave Earth, the stars all appear in different spots compared to each other.
Yes, other planets have different constellations.

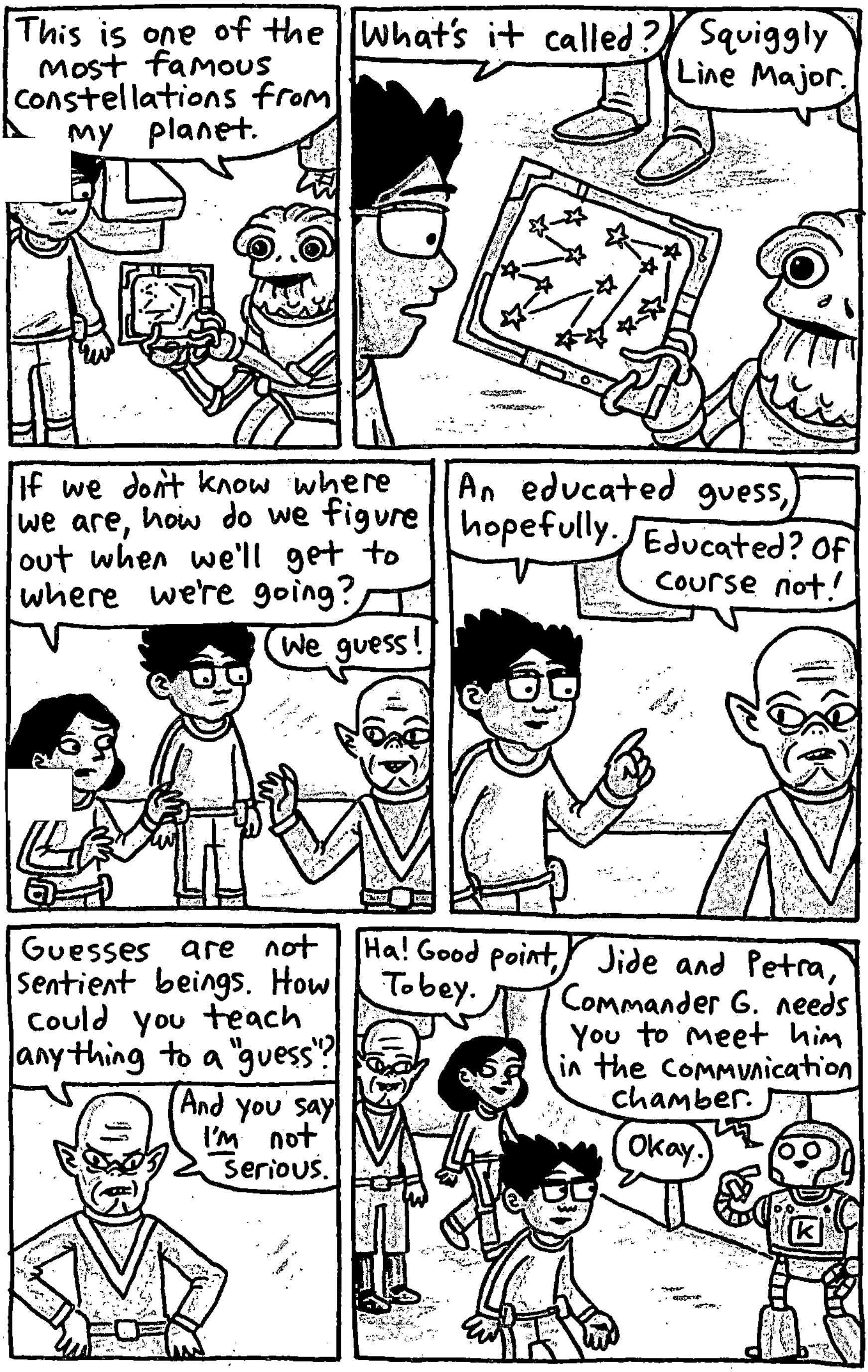

This is one of the most famous constellations from my planet.
What's it called?
Squiggly Line Major.
If we don't know where we are, how do we figure out when we'll get to where we're going?
We guess!
An educated guess, hopefully.
Educated? Of course not!
Guesses are not sentient beings. How could you teach anything to a "guess"?
And you say I'M not serious.
Ha! Good point, Tobey.
Jide and Petra, Commander G. needs you to meet him in the communication chamber.
Okay.
K

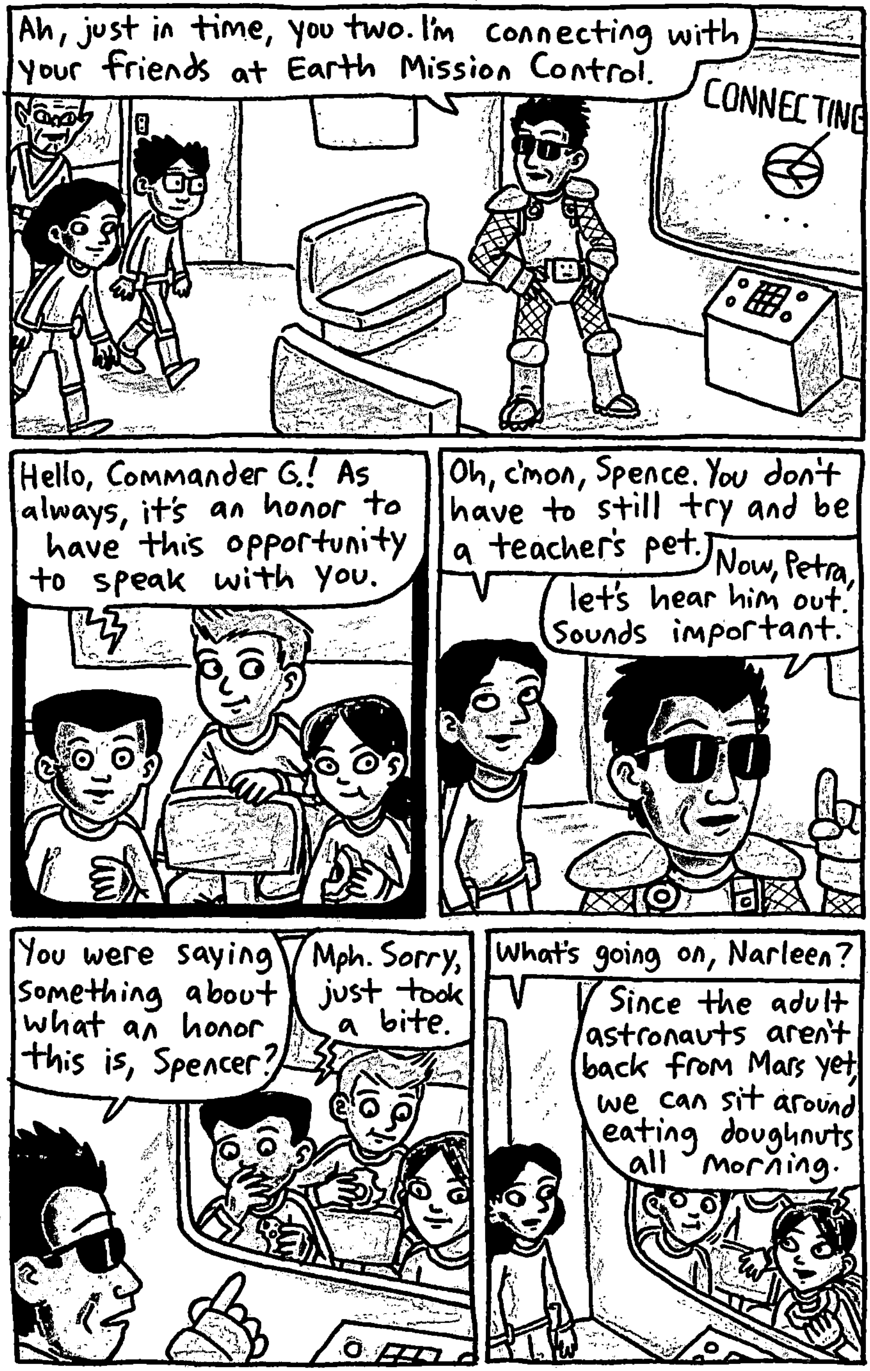
Ah, just in time, you two. I'm connecting with your friends at Earth Mission Control.
CONNECTING
Hello, Commander G.! As always, it's an honor to have this opportunity to speak with you.
Oh, c'mon, Spence. You don't have to still try and be a teacher's pet.
Now, Petra, let's hear him out. Sounds important.
You were saying something about what an honor this is, Spencer?
Mph. Sorry, just took a bite.
What's going on, Narleen?
Since the adult astronauts aren't back from Mars yet, we can sit around eating doughnuts all morning.

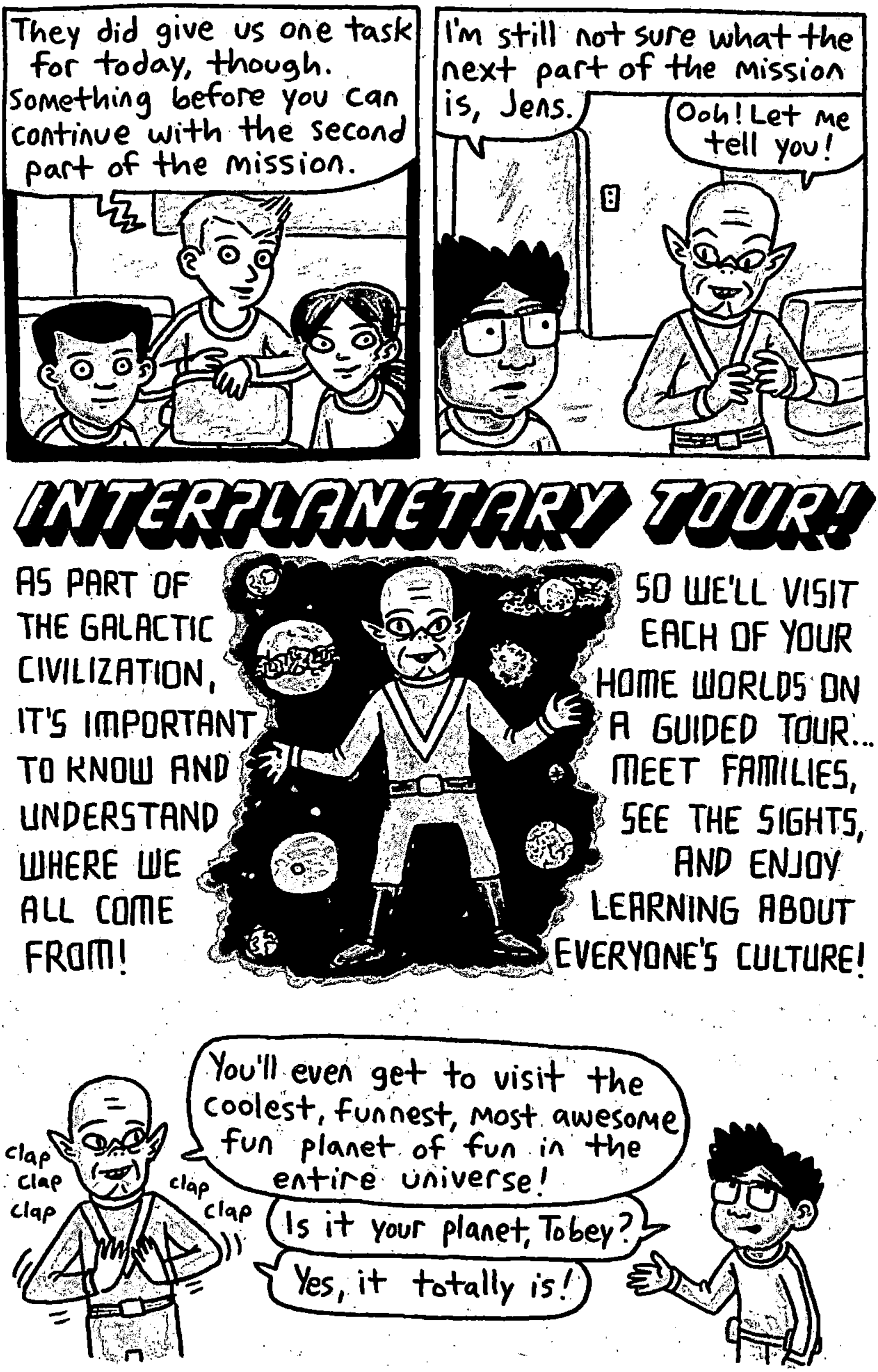
They did give us one task for today, though. Something before you can continue with the second part of the mission.
I'm still not sure what the next part of the mission is, Jens.
Ooh! Let me tell you!
INTERPLANETARY TOUR!
AS PART OF THE GALACTIC CIVILIZATION, IT'S IMPORTANT TO KNOW AND UNDERSTAND WHERE WE ALL COME FROM!
SO WE'LL VISIT EACH OF YOUR HOME WORLDS ON A GUIDED TOUR... MEET FAMILIES, SEE THE SIGHTS, AND ENJOY LEARNING ABOUT EVERYONE'S CULTURE!
You'll even get to visit the coolest, funnest, most awesome fun planet of fun in the entire universe!
clap clap clap
clap clap
Is it your planet, Tobey?
Yes, it totally is!

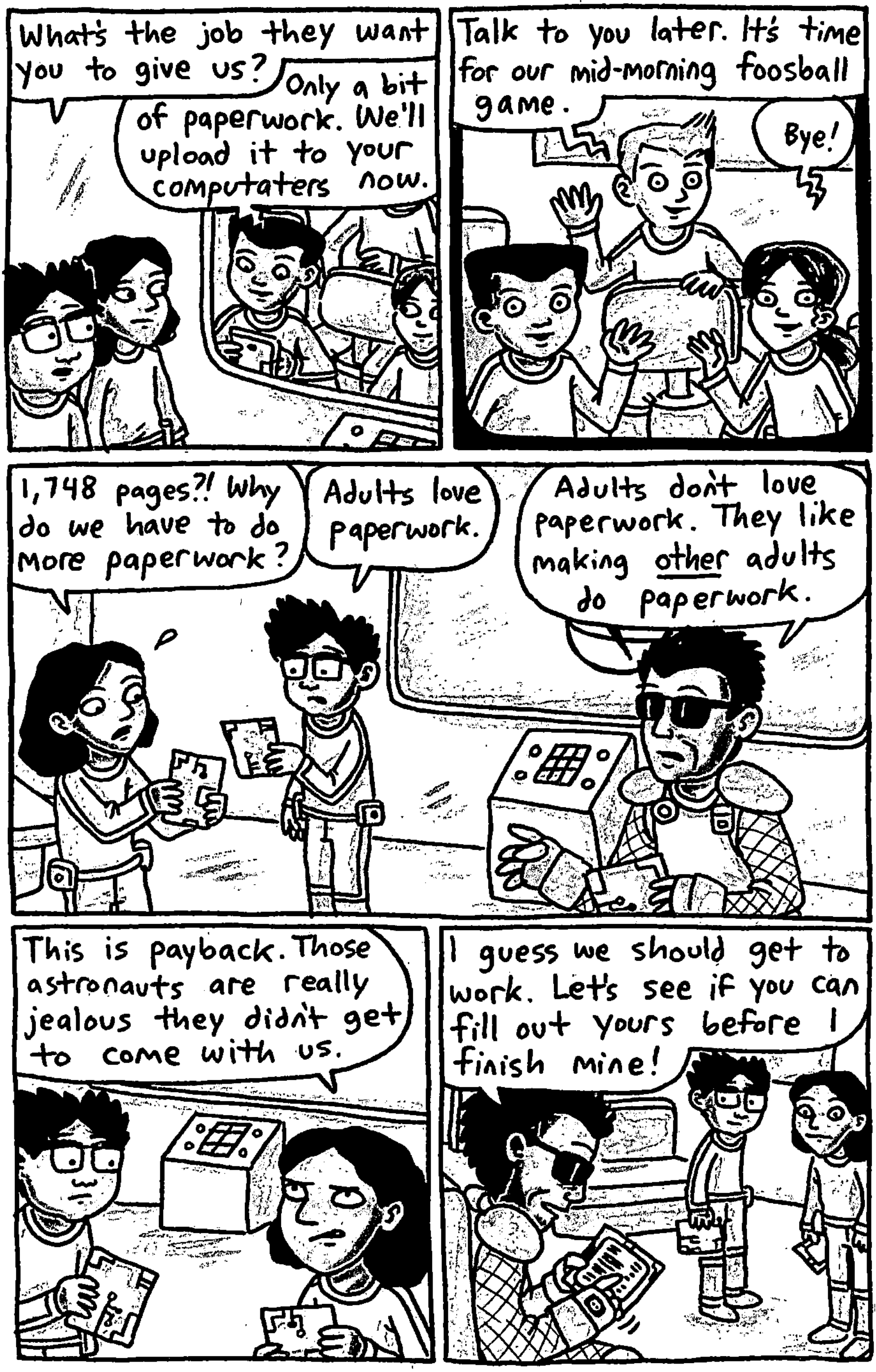

What's the job they want you to give us?
Only a bit of paperwork. We'll upload it to your computaters now.
Talk to you later. It's time for our mid-morning foosball game.
Bye!
1,748 pages?! Why do we have to do more paperwork?
Adults love paperwork.
Adults don't love paperwork. They like making other adults do paperwork.
This is payback. Those astronauts are really jealous they didn't get to come with us.
I guess we should get to work. Let's see if you can fill out yours before I finish mine!

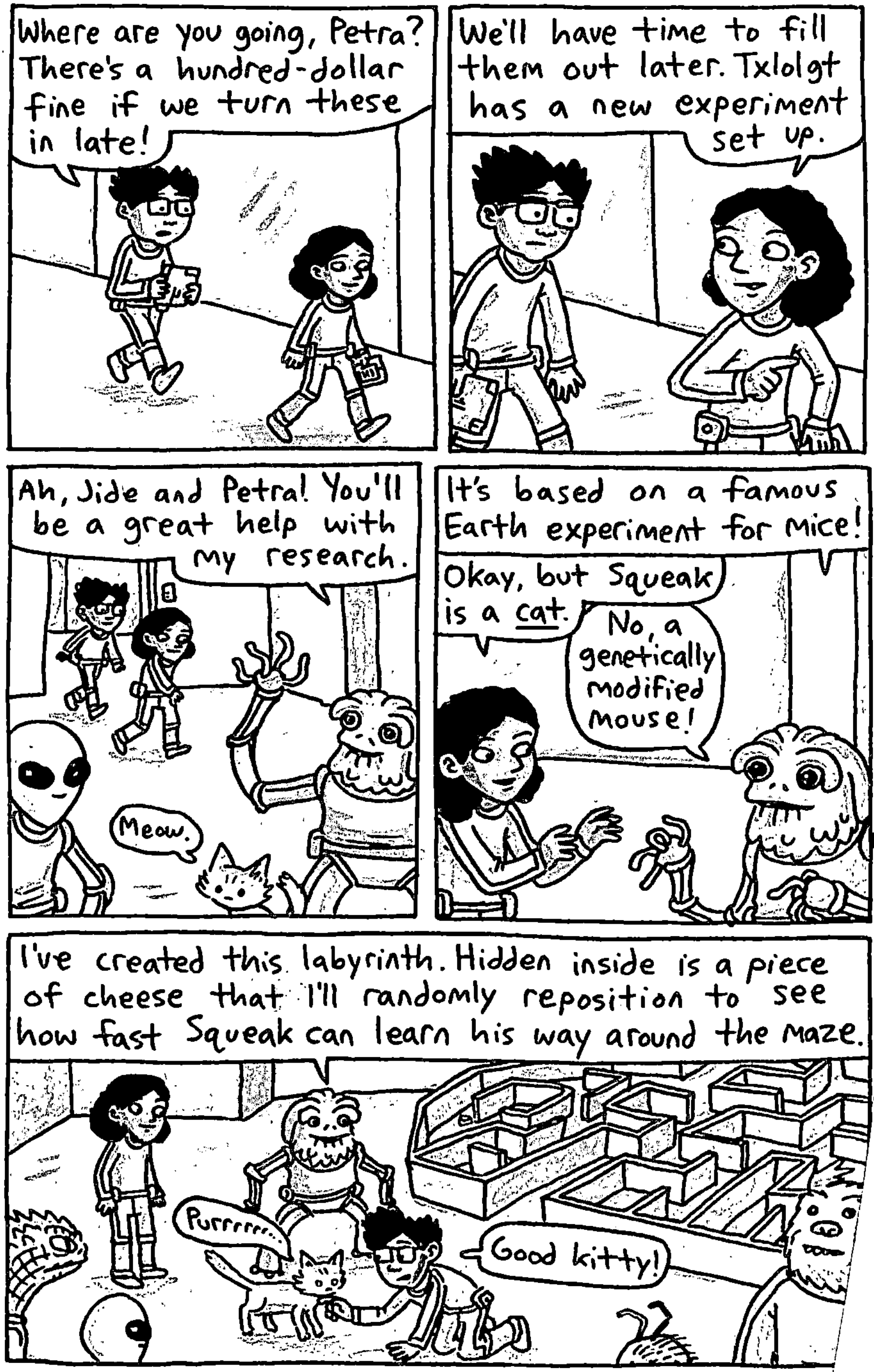

Where are you going, Petra? There's a hundred-dollar fine if we turn these in late!
We'll have time to fill them out later. Txlolgt has a new experiment set up.
Ah, Jide and Petra! You'll be a great help with my research.
Meow.
It's based on a famous Earth experiment for mice!
Okay, but Squeak is a cat.
No, a genetically modified mouse!
I've created this labyrinth. Hidden inside is a piece of cheese that I'll randomly reposition to see how fast Squeak can learn his way around the maze.
Purrrrrr...
Good kitty!

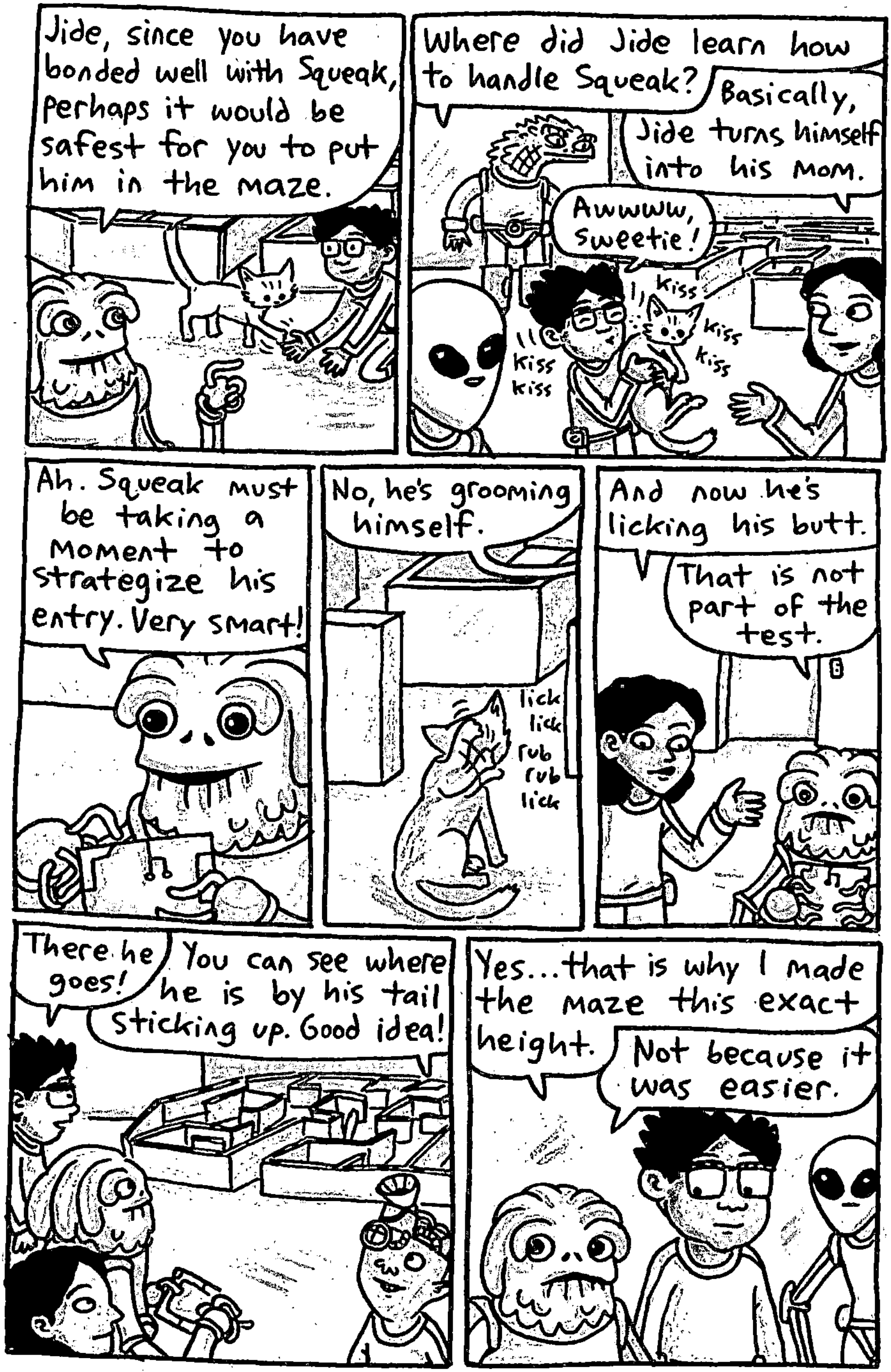
Jide, since you have bonded well with Squeak, perhaps it would be safest for you to put him in the maze.
Where did Jide learn how to handle Squeak?
Basically, Jide turns himself into his mom.
Awwww, sweetie!
kiss
kiss
kiss
kiss
kiss
Ah. Squeak must be taking a moment to strategize his entry. Very smart!
No, he's grooming himself.
lick
lick
rub
rub
lick
And now he's licking his butt.
That is not part of the test.
There he goes!
You can see where he is by his tail sticking up. Good idea!
Yes...that is why I made the maze this exact height.
Not because it was easier.

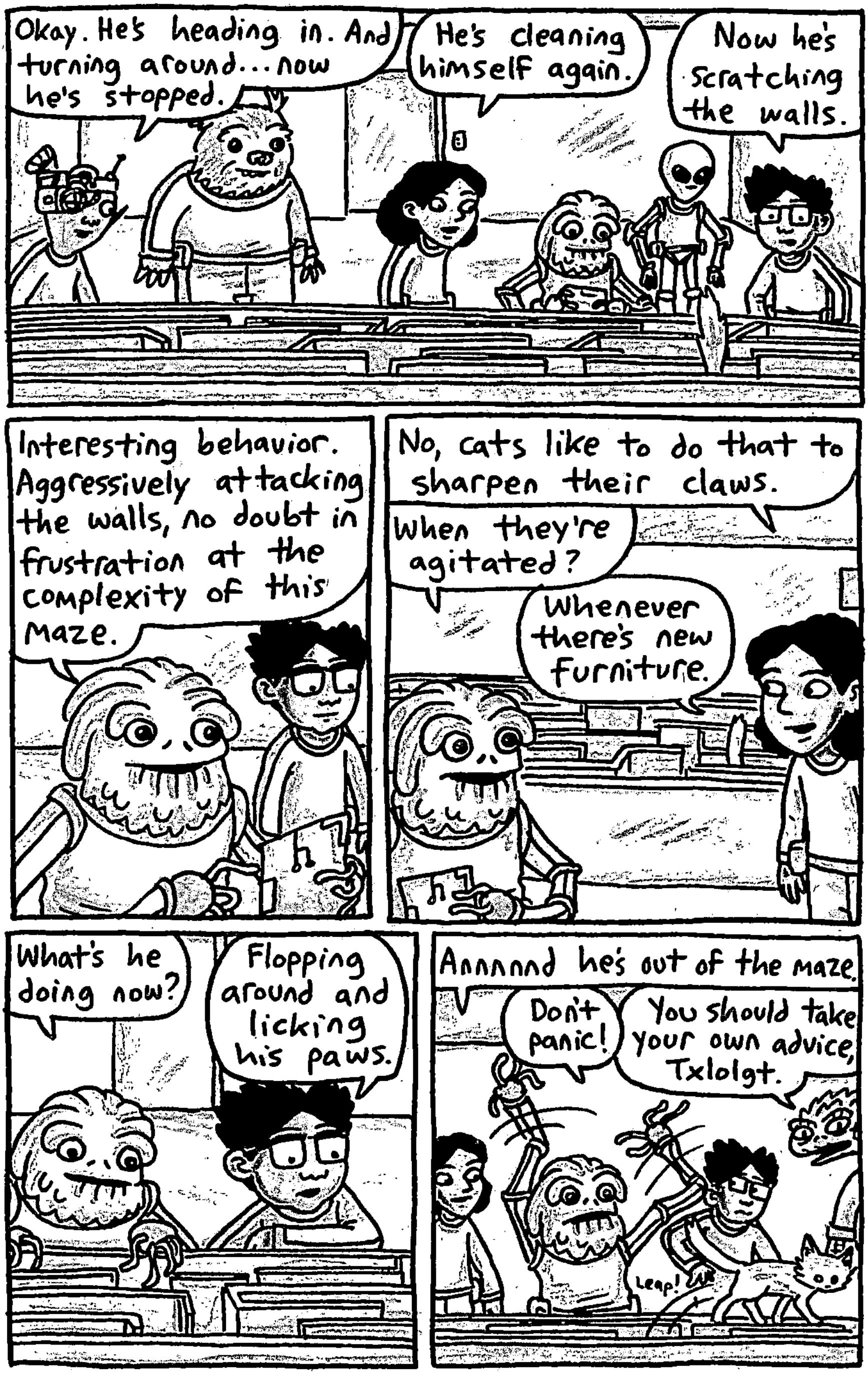
Okay. He's heading in. And turning around... now he's stopped.
He's cleaning himself again.
Now he's scratching the walls.
Interesting behavior. Aggressively attacking the walls, no doubt in frustration at the complexity of this maze.
No, cats like to do that to sharpen their claws.
When they're agitated?
Whenever there's new furniture.
What's he doing now?
Flopping around and licking his paws.
Annnnnd he's out of the maze.
Don't panic!
You should take your own advice, Txlolgt.
Leap!

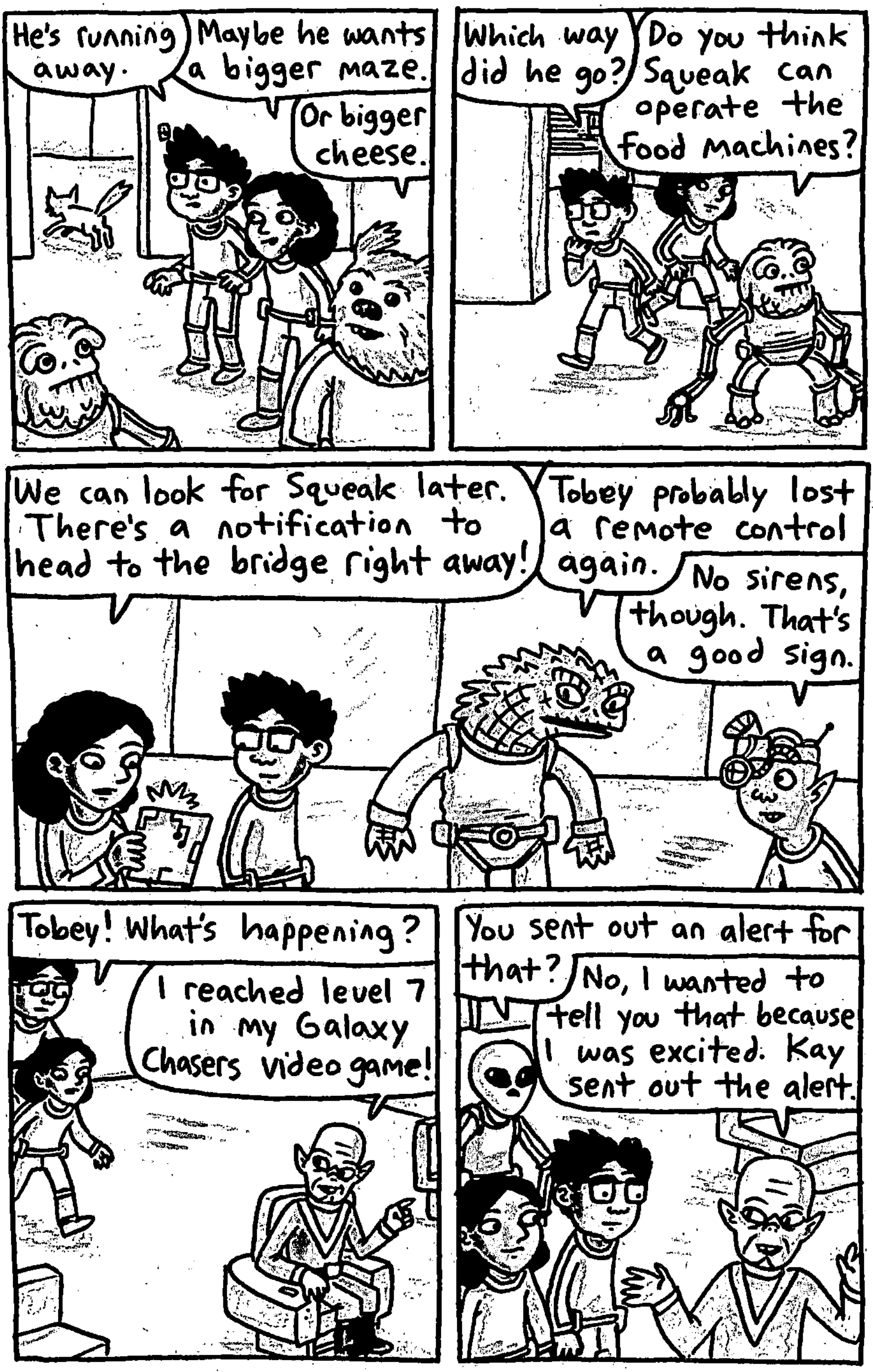
He's running away.
Maybe he wants a bigger maze.
Or bigger cheese.
Which way did he go?
Do you think Squeak can operate the food machines?
We can look for Squeak later. There's a notification to head to the bridge right away!
Tobey probably lost a remote control again.
No sirens, though. That's a good sign.
Tobey! What's happening?
I reached level 7 in my Galaxy Chasers video game!
You sent out an alert for that?
No, I wanted to tell you that because I was excited. Kay sent out the alert.

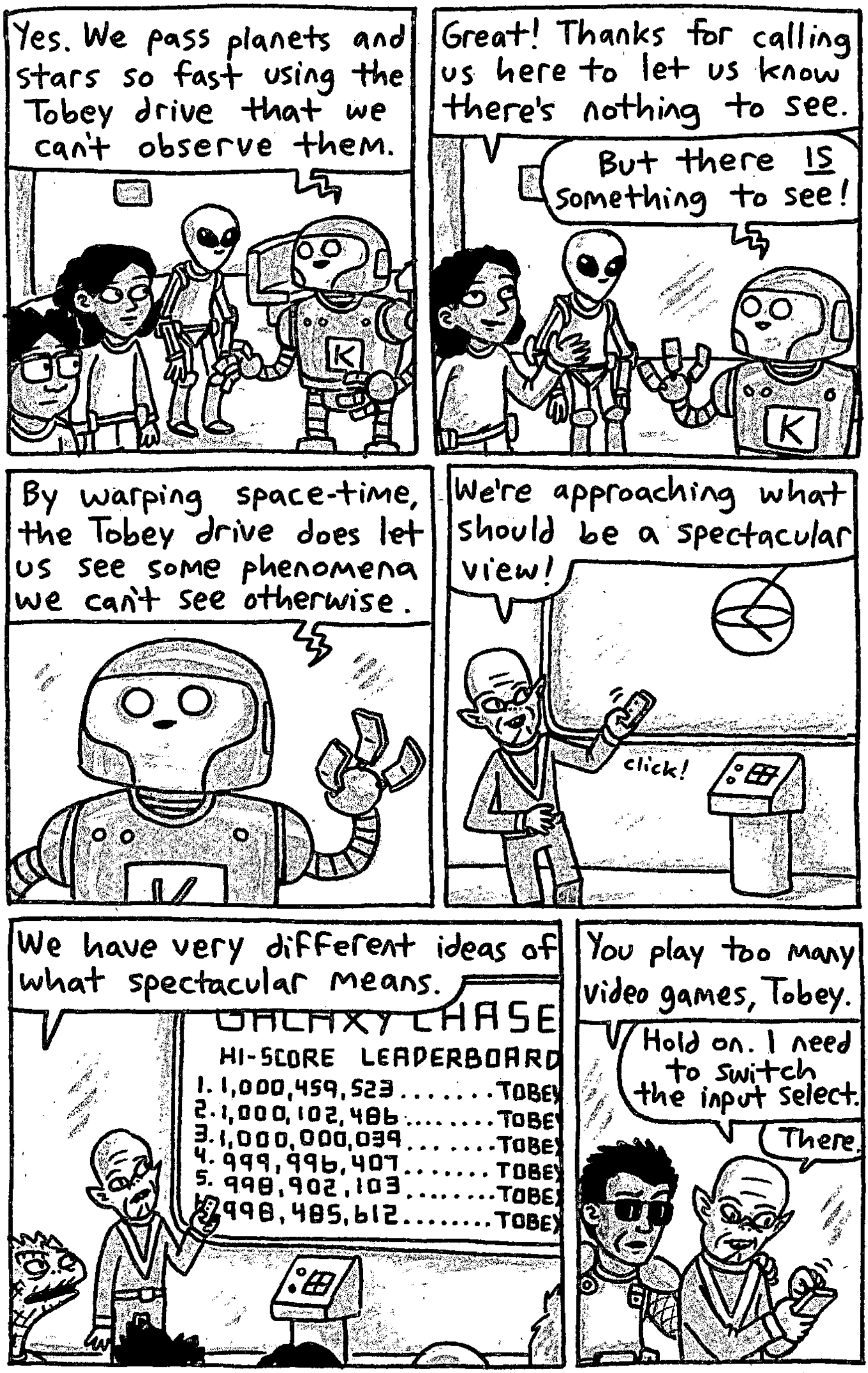

Yes. We pass planets and stars so fast using the Tobey drive that we can't observe them.
Great! Thanks for calling us here to let us know there's nothing to see.
But there IS something to see!
K
By warping space-time, the Tobey drive does let us see some phenomena we can't see otherwise.
We're approaching what should be a spectacular view!
click!
We have very different ideas of what spectacular means.
GALAXY CHASE
HI-SCORE LEADERBOARD
1. 1,000,459,523.......TOBEY
2. 1,000,102,486.......TOBEY
3. 1,000,000,039.......TOBEY
4. 999,996,407.......TOBEY
5. 998,902,103.......TOBEY
998,485,612.......TOBEY
You play too many video games, Tobey.
Hold on. I need to switch the input select.
There.

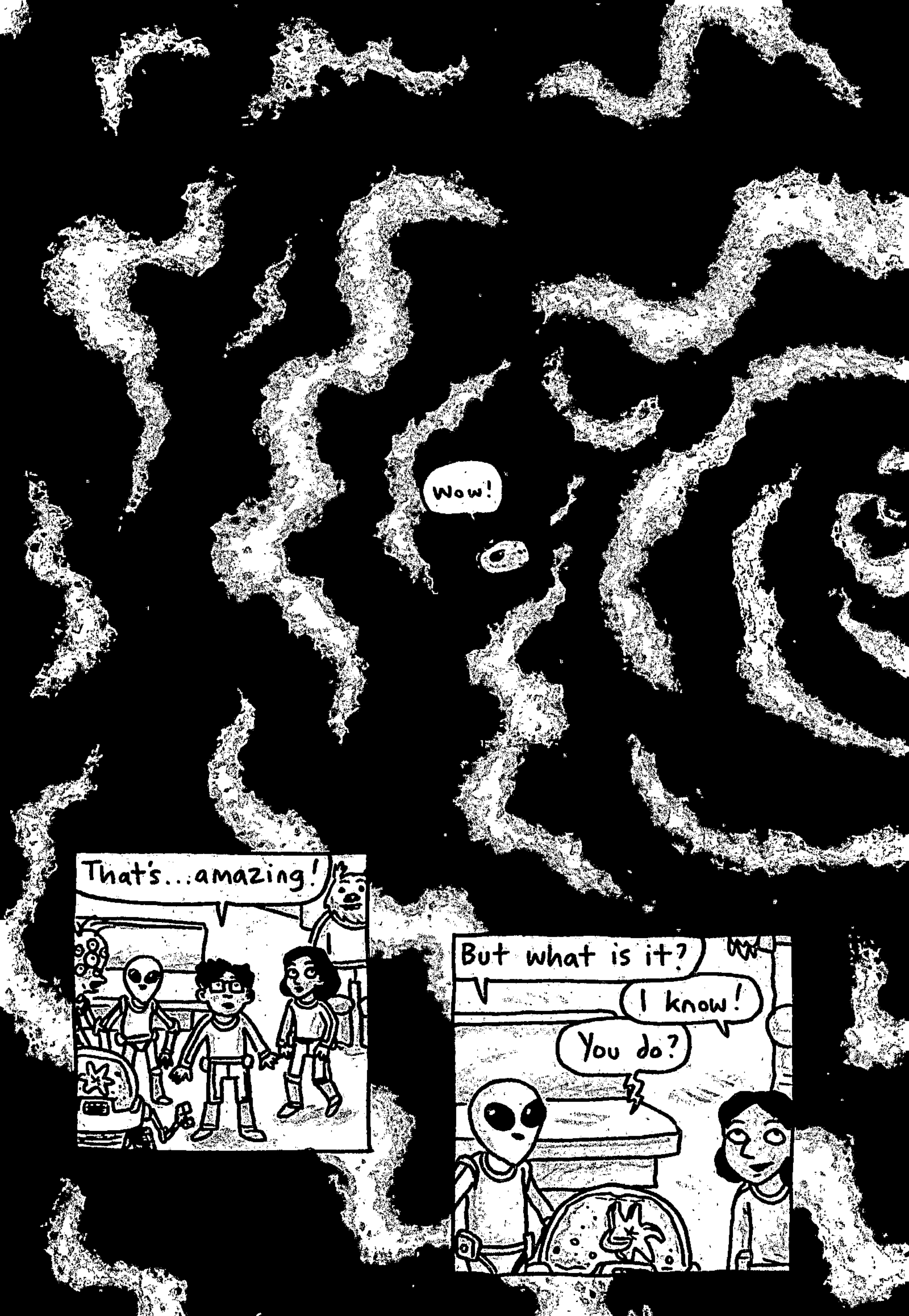
Wow!
That's...amazing!
But what is it?
I know!
You do?

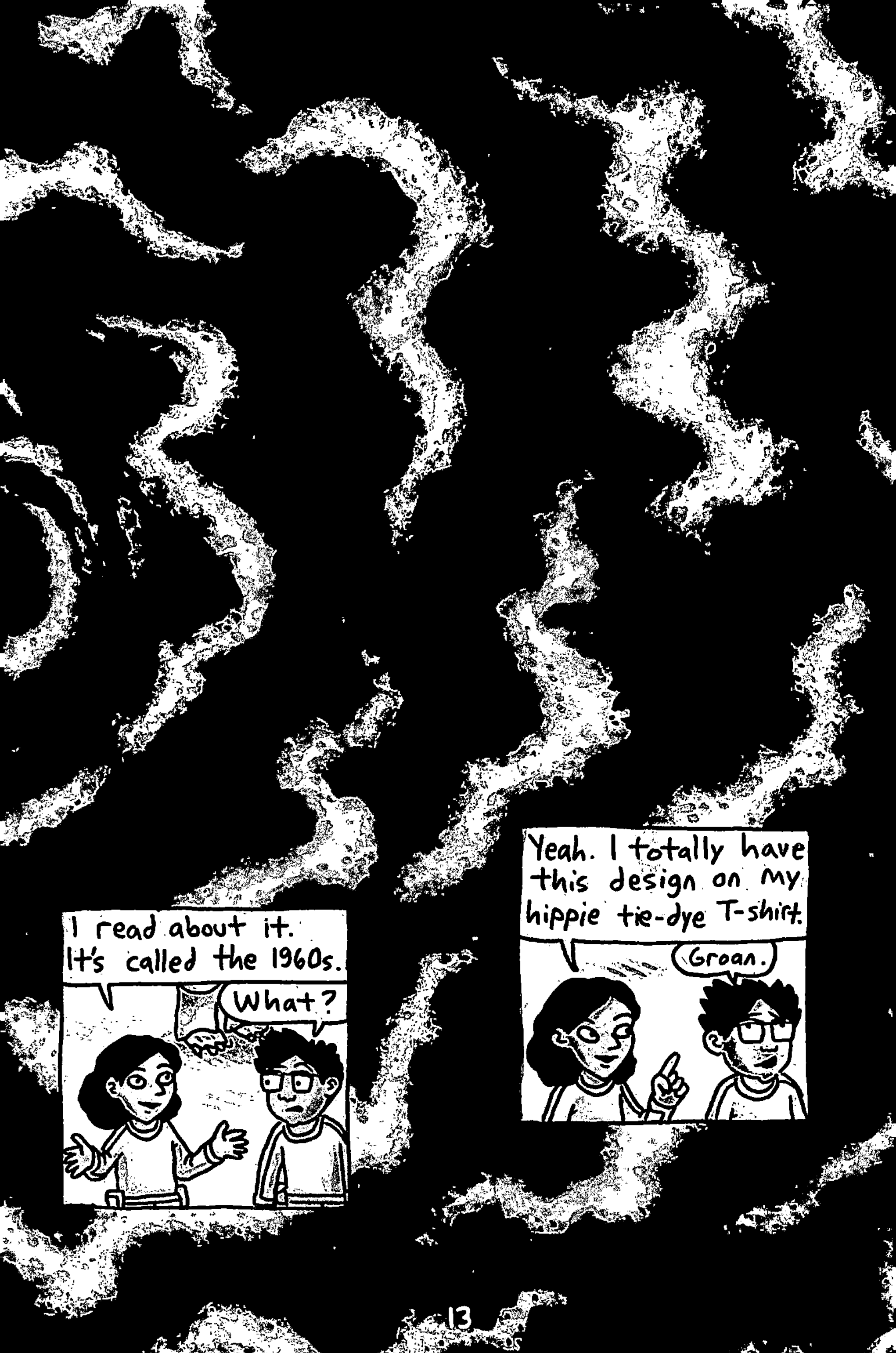
I read about it. It's called the 1960s.
What?
Yeah. I totally have this design on my hippie tie-dye T-shirt.
Groan.

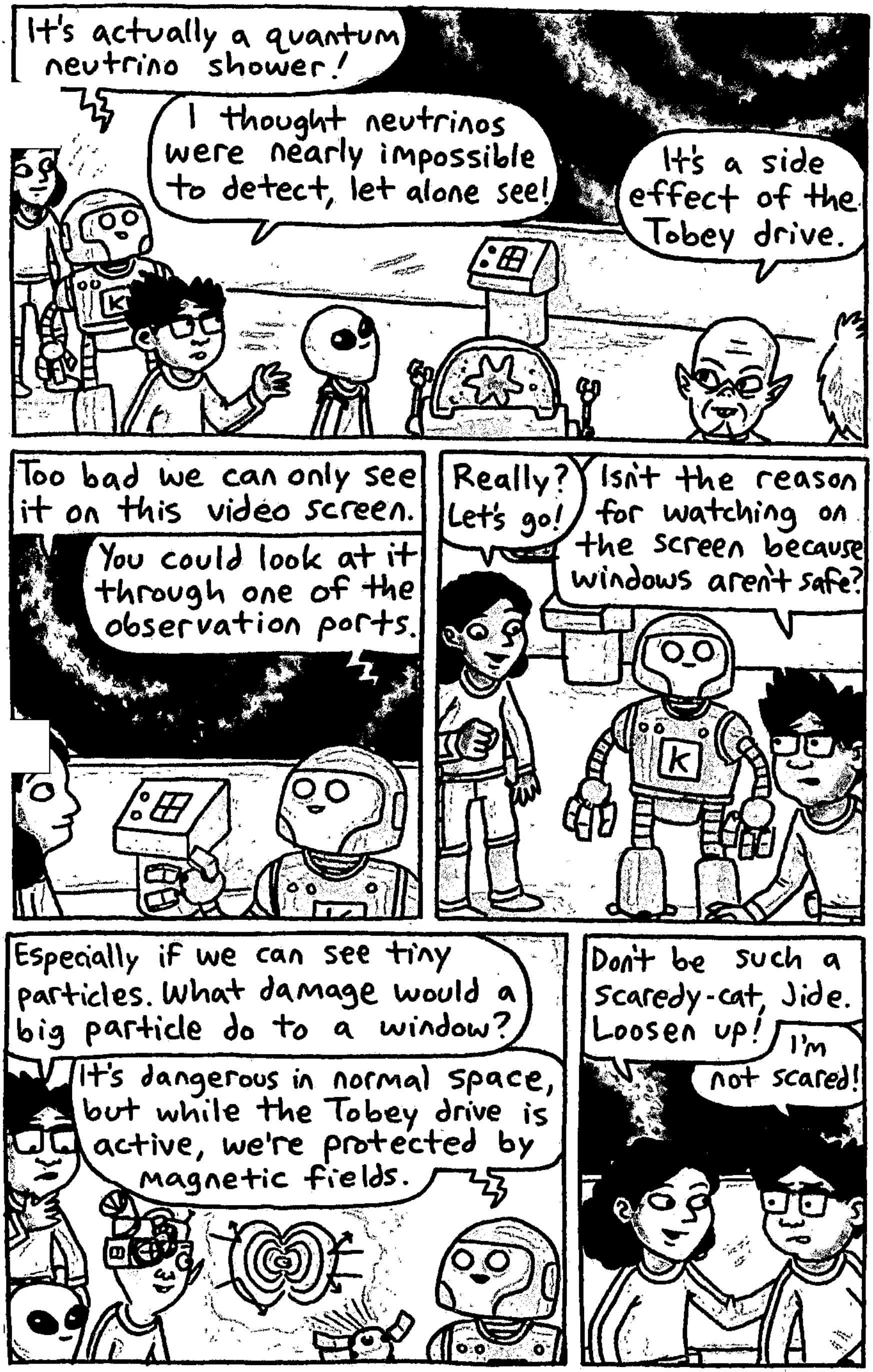
It's actually a quantum neutrino shower!
I thought neutrinos were nearly impossible to detect, let alone see!
It's a side effect of the Tobey drive.
Too bad we can only see it on this video screen.
You could look at it through one of the observation ports.
Really? Let's go!
Isn't the reason for watching on the screen because windows aren't safe?
Especially if we can see tiny particles. What damage would a big particle do to a window?
It's dangerous in normal space, but while the Tobey drive is active, we're protected by magnetic fields.
Don't be such a scaredy-cat, Jide. Loosen up!
I'm not scared!

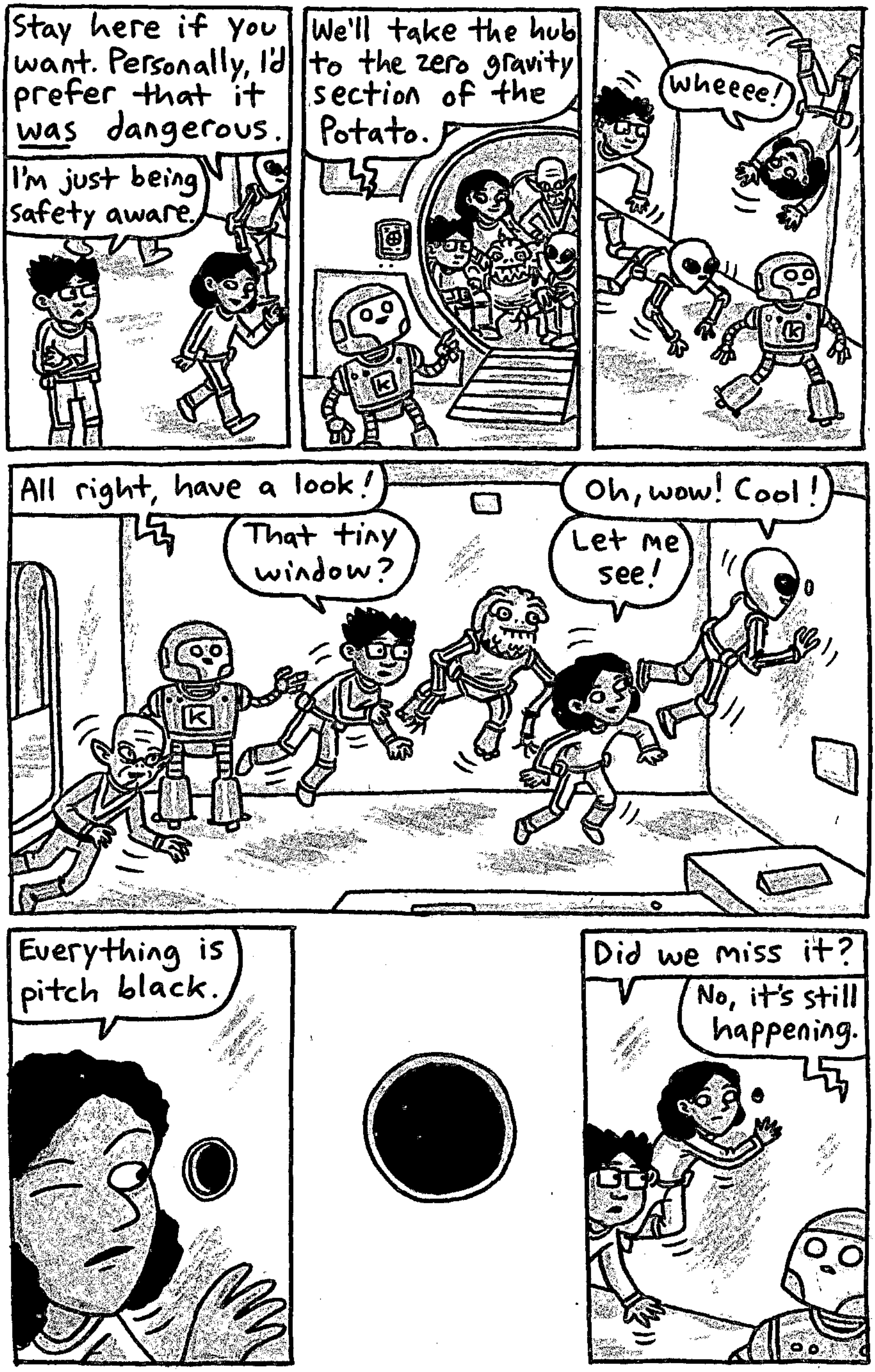
Stay here if you want. Personally, I'd prefer that it was dangerous.
I'm just being safety aware.
We'll take the hub to the zero gravity section of the Potato.
Wheeeee!
All right, have a look!
That tiny window?
Let me see!
Oh, wow! Cool!
Everything is pitch black.
Did we miss it?
No, it's still happening.

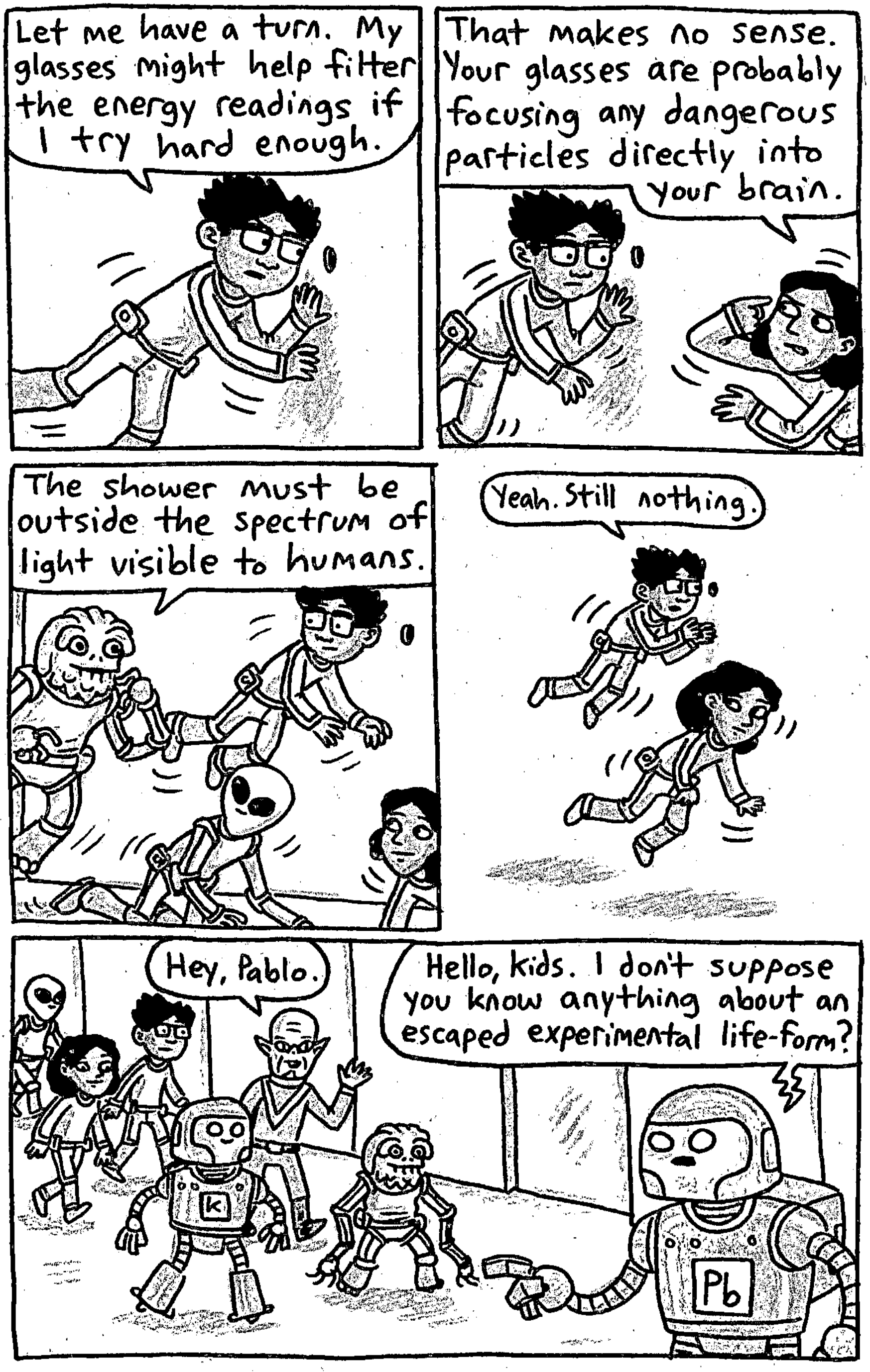
Let me have a turn. My glasses might help filter the energy readings if I try hard enough.
That makes no sense. Your glasses are probably focusing any dangerous particles directly into your brain.
The shower must be outside the spectrum of light visible to humans.
Yeah. Still nothing.
Hey, Pablo.
Hello, kids. I don't suppose you know anything about an escaped experimental life-form?
K
Pb

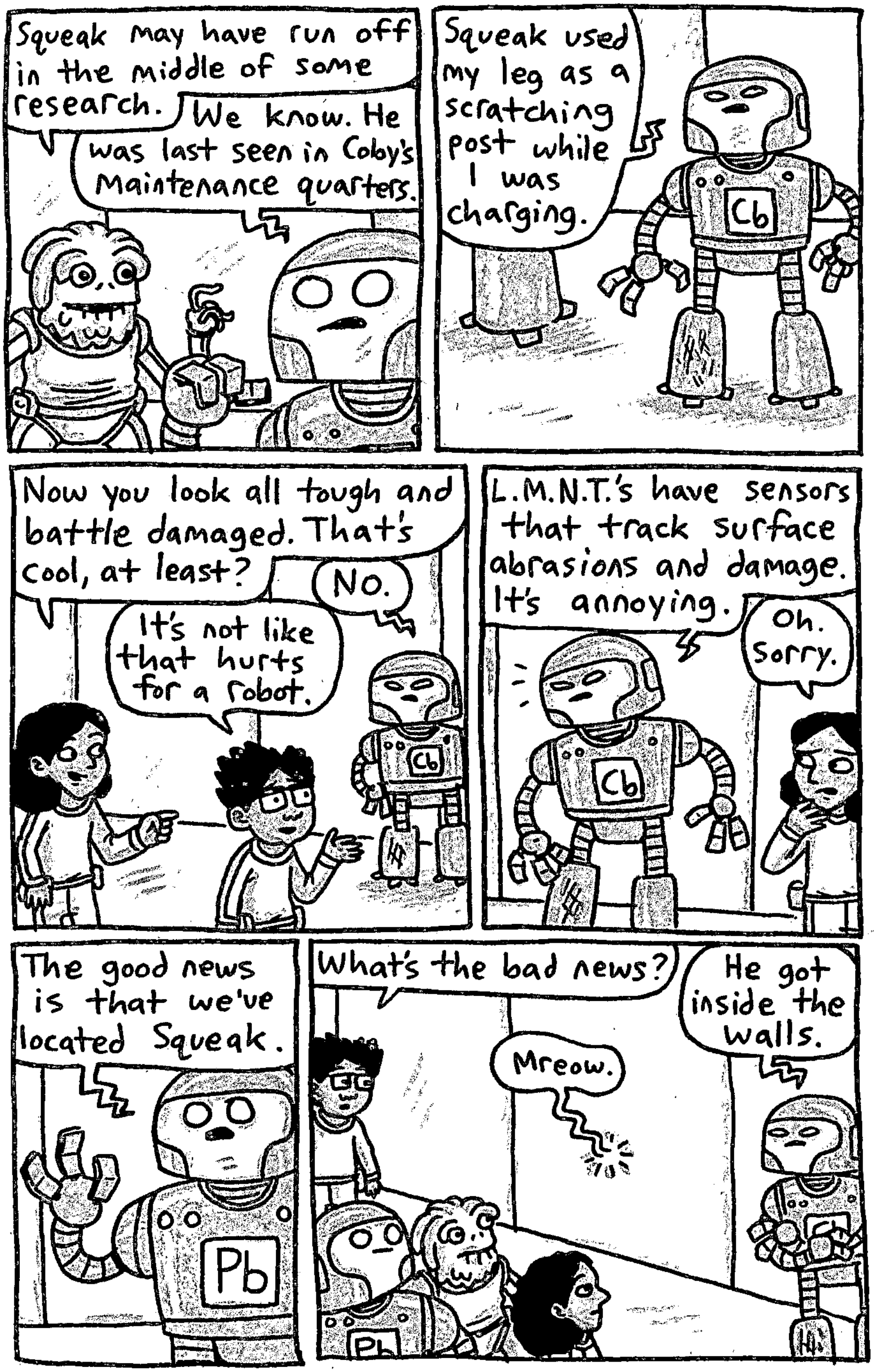
Squeak may have run off in the middle of some research.
We know. He was last seen in Coby's Maintenance quarters.
Squeak used my leg as a scratching post while I was charging.
Now you look all tough and battle damaged. That's cool, at least?
It's not like that hurts for a robot.
No.
L.M.N.T.'s have sensors that track surface abrasions and damage. It's annoying.
Oh. Sorry.
The good news is that we've located Squeak.
What's the bad news?
He got inside the walls.
Mreow.

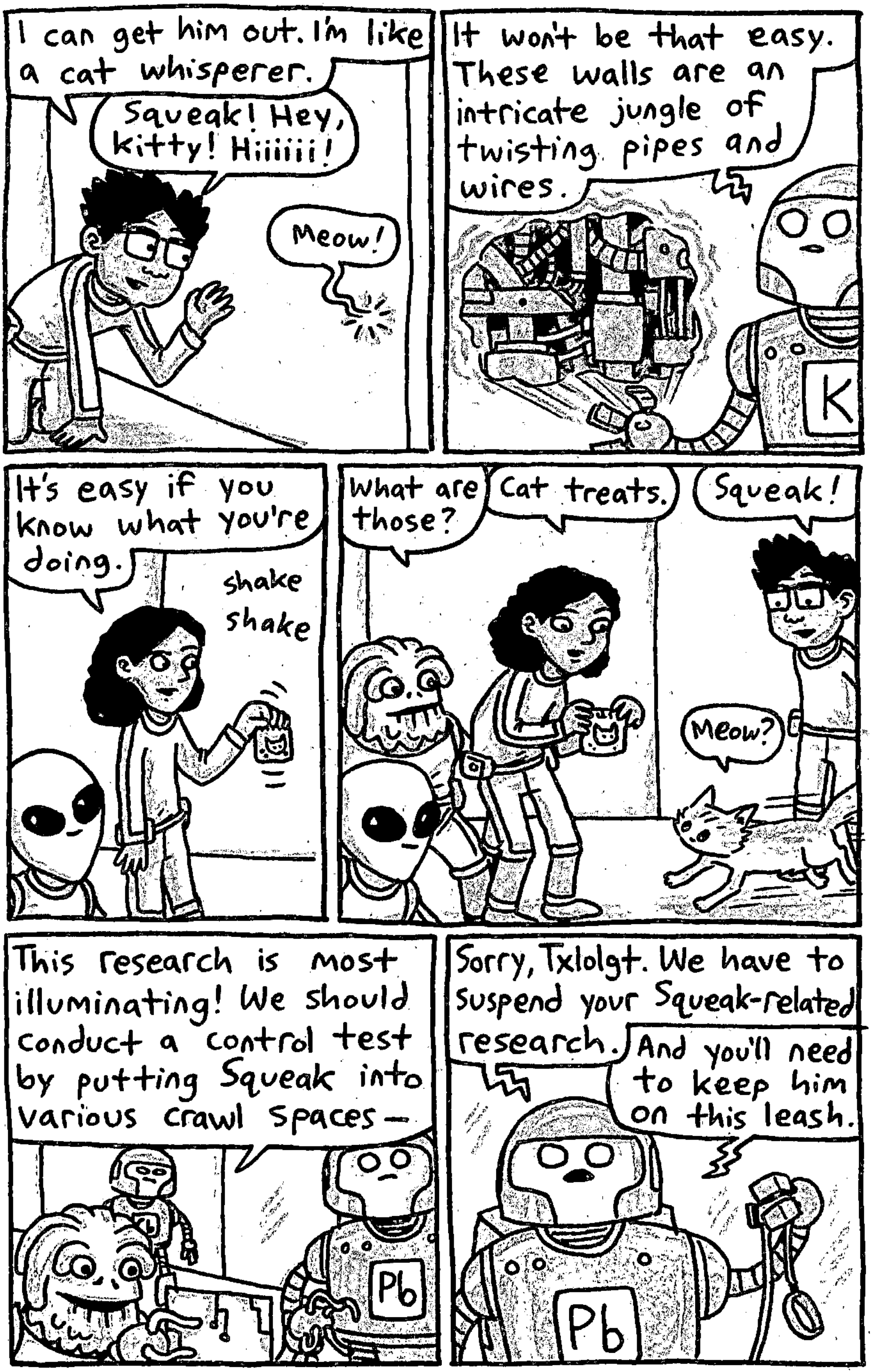
I can get him out. I'm like a cat whisperer.
Squeak! Hey, kitty! Hiiiiii!
Meow!
It won't be that easy. These walls are an intricate jungle of twisting pipes and wires.
It's easy if you know what you're doing.
shake shake
What are those?
Cat treats.
Squeak!
Meow?
This research is most illuminating! We should conduct a control test by putting Squeak into various crawl spaces—
Pb
Sorry, Txlolgt. We have to suspend your Squeak-related research.
And you'll need to keep him on this leash.
Pb

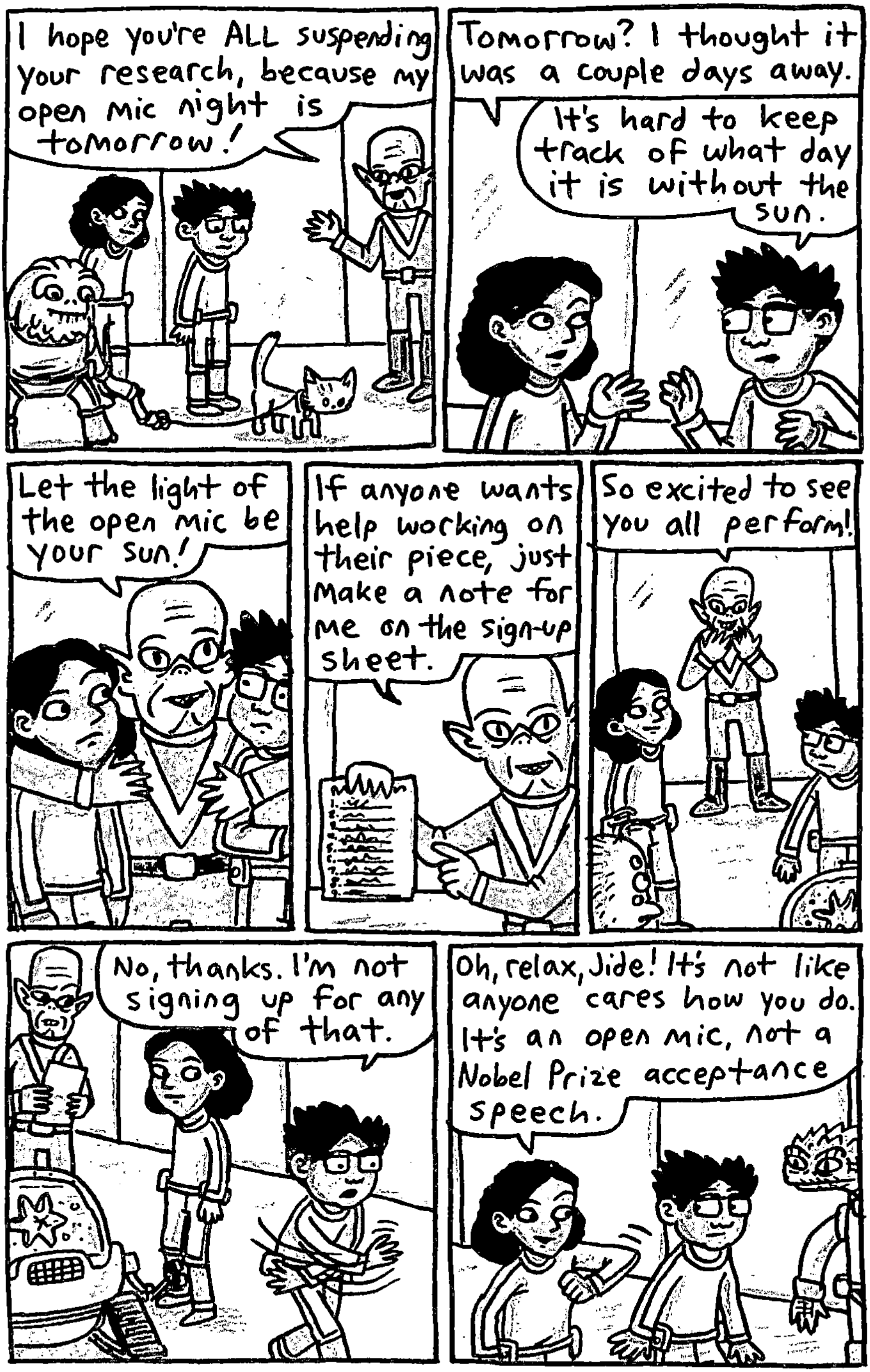
I hope you're ALL suspending your research, because my open mic night is tomorrow!
Tomorrow? I thought it was a couple days away.
It's hard to keep track of what day it is without the sun.
Let the light of the open mic be your sun!
If anyone wants help working on their piece, just make a note for me on the sign-up sheet.
So excited to see you all perform!
No, thanks. I'm not signing up for any of that.
Oh, relax, Jide! It's not like anyone cares how you do. It's an open mic, not a Nobel Prize acceptance speech.

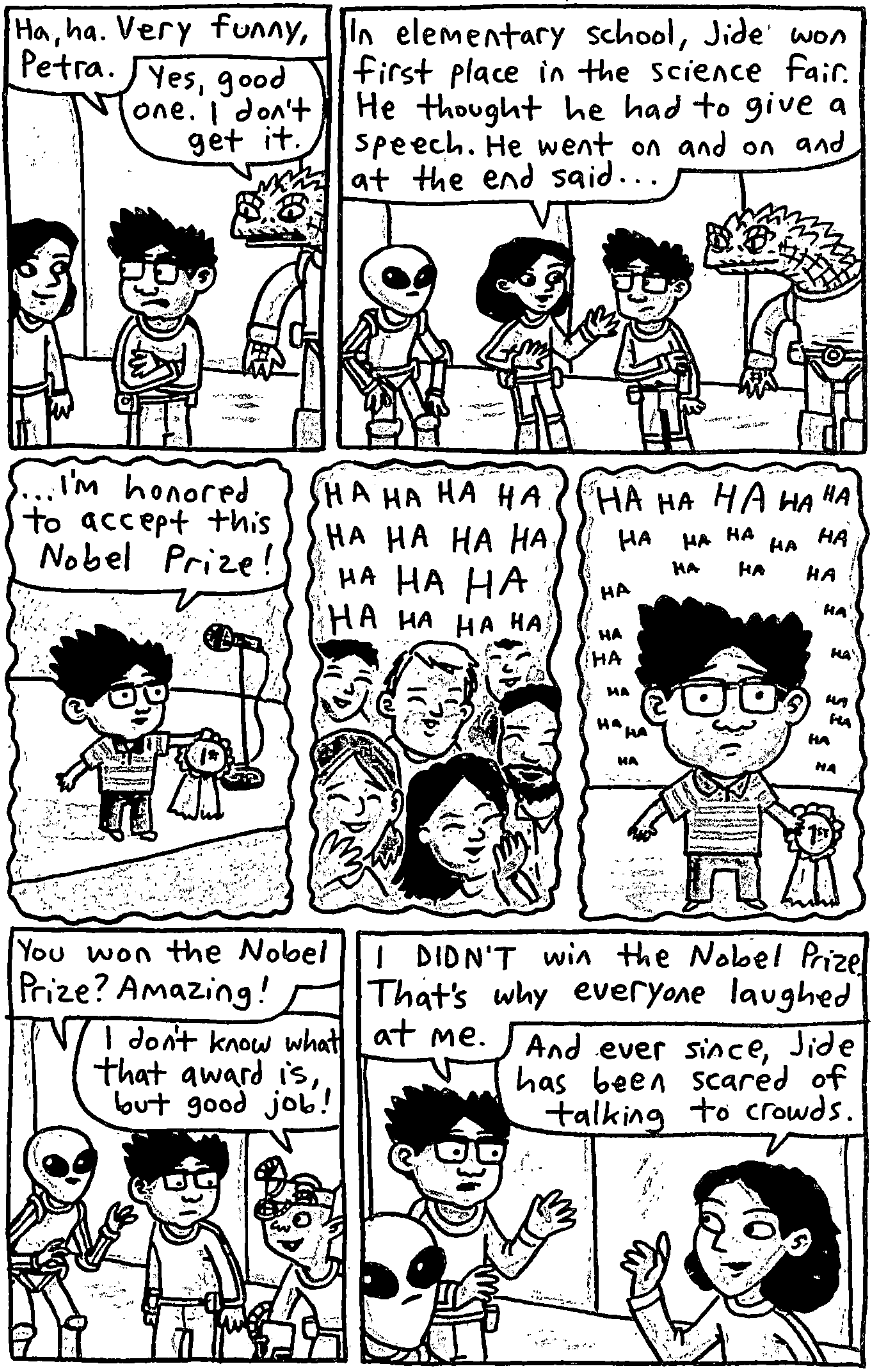

Ha, ha. Very funny, Petra.
Yes, good one. I don't get it.
In elementary school, Jide won first place in the science fair. He thought he had to give a speech. He went on and on and at the end said...
...I'm honored to accept this Nobel Prize!
HA HA HA HA
HA HA HA HA
HA HA HA
HA HA HA HA
HA HA HA HA HA
HA HA HA HA HA
HA HA HA
HA HA HA HA HA HA HA HA HA HA HA HA HA HA HA
You won the Nobel Prize? Amazing!
I don't know what that award is, but good job!
I DIDN'T win the Nobel Prize. That's why everyone laughed at me.
And ever since, Jide has been scared of talking to crowds.

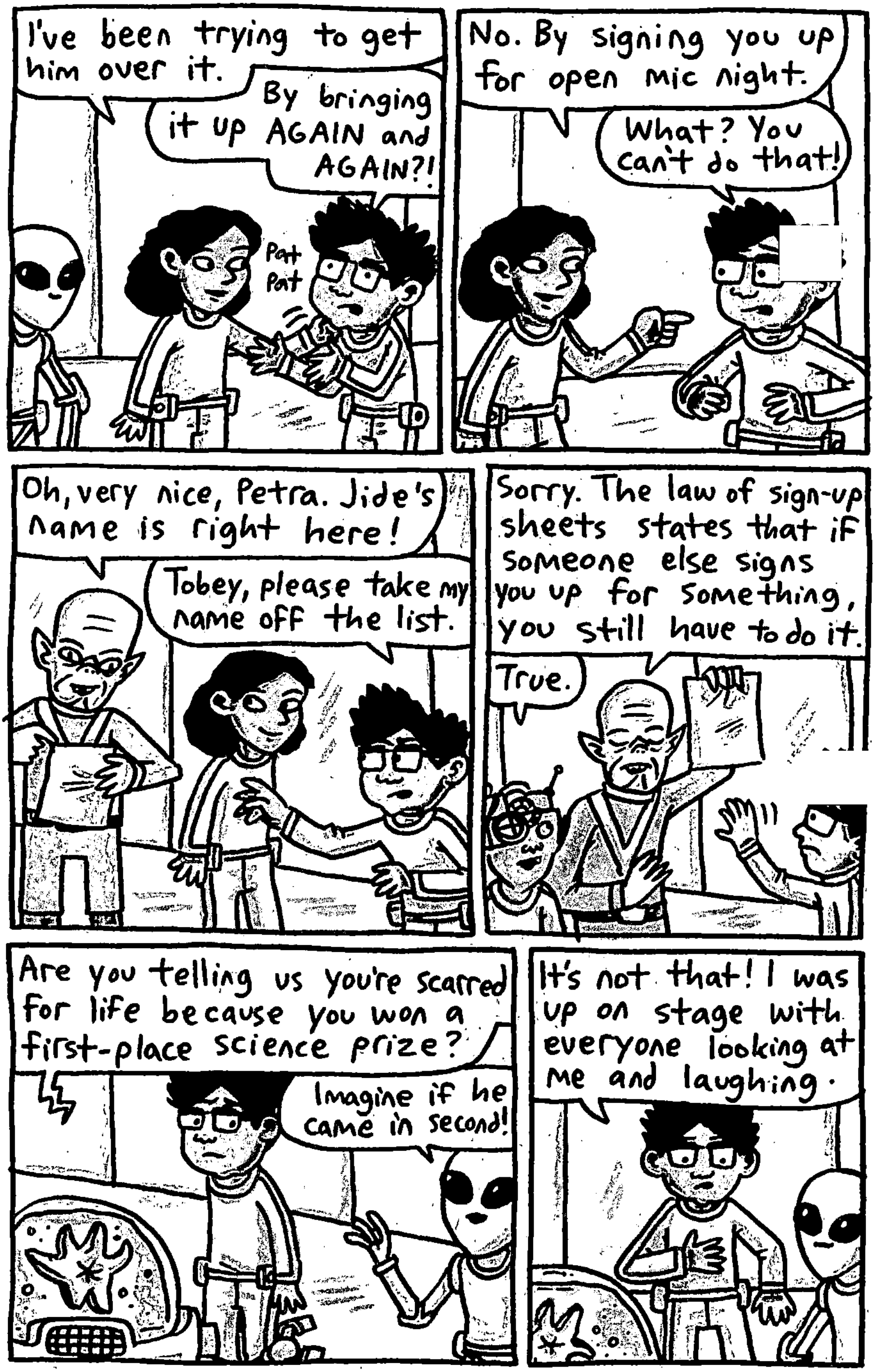
I've been trying to get him over it.
By bringing it up AGAIN and AGAIN?!
Pat Pat
No. By signing you up for open mic night.
What? You can't do that!
Oh, very nice, Petra. Jide's name is right here!
Tobey, please take my name off the list.
Sorry. The law of sign-up sheets states that if someone else signs you up for something, you still have to do it.
True.
Are you telling us you're scarred for life because you won a first-place science prize?
Imagine if he came in second!
It's not that! I was up on stage with everyone looking at me and laughing.

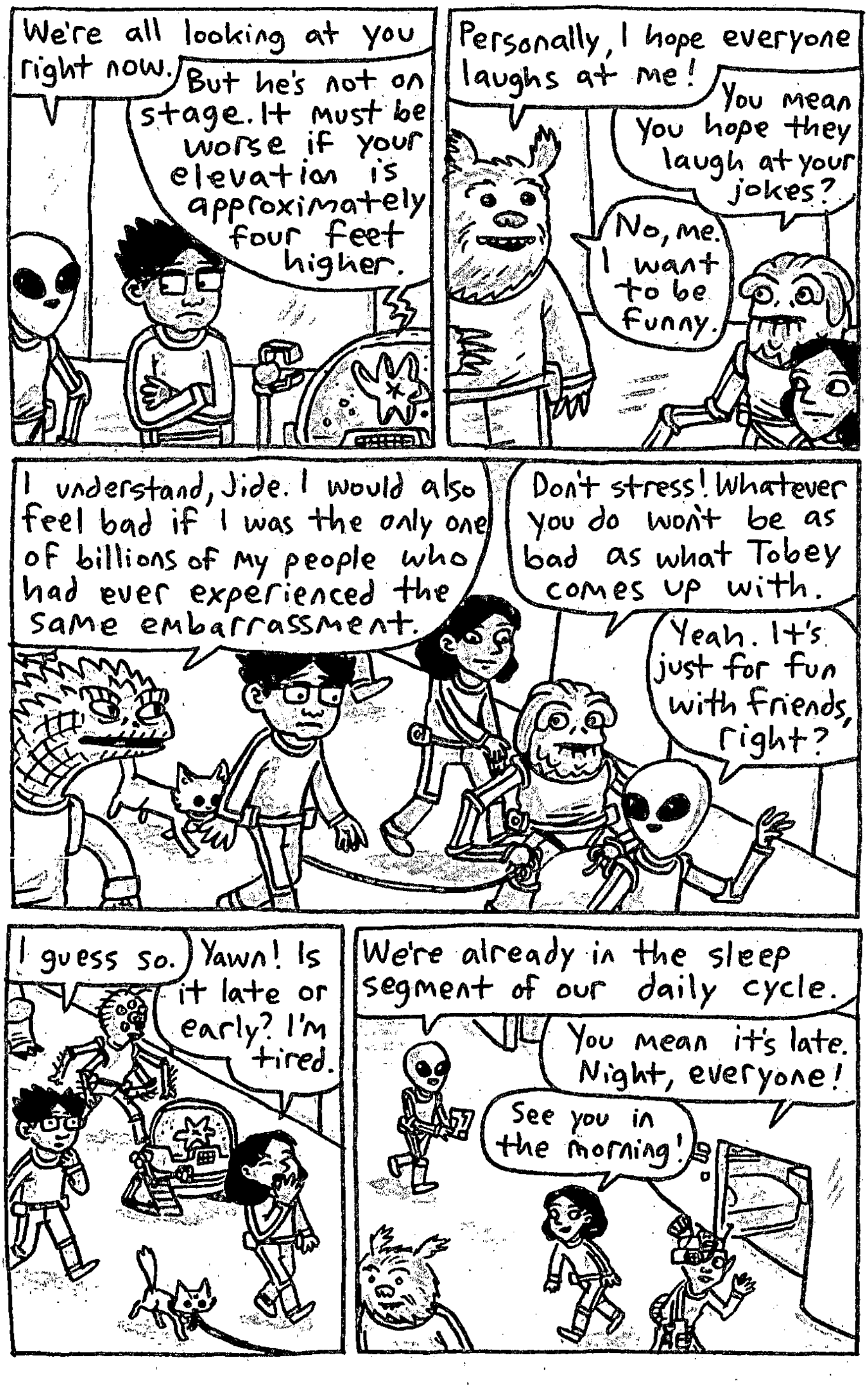
We're all looking at you right now.
But he's not on stage. It must be worse if your elevation is approximately four feet higher.
Personally, I hope everyone laughs at me!
You mean you hope they laugh at your jokes?
No, me. I want to be funny.
I understand, Jide. I would also feel bad if I was the only one of billions of my people who had ever experienced the same embarrassment.
Don't stress! Whatever you do won't be as bad as what Tobey comes up with.
Yeah. It's just for fun with friends, right?
I guess so.
Yawn! Is it late or early? I'm tired.
We're already in the sleep segment of our daily cycle.
You mean it's late. Night, everyone!
See you in the morning!

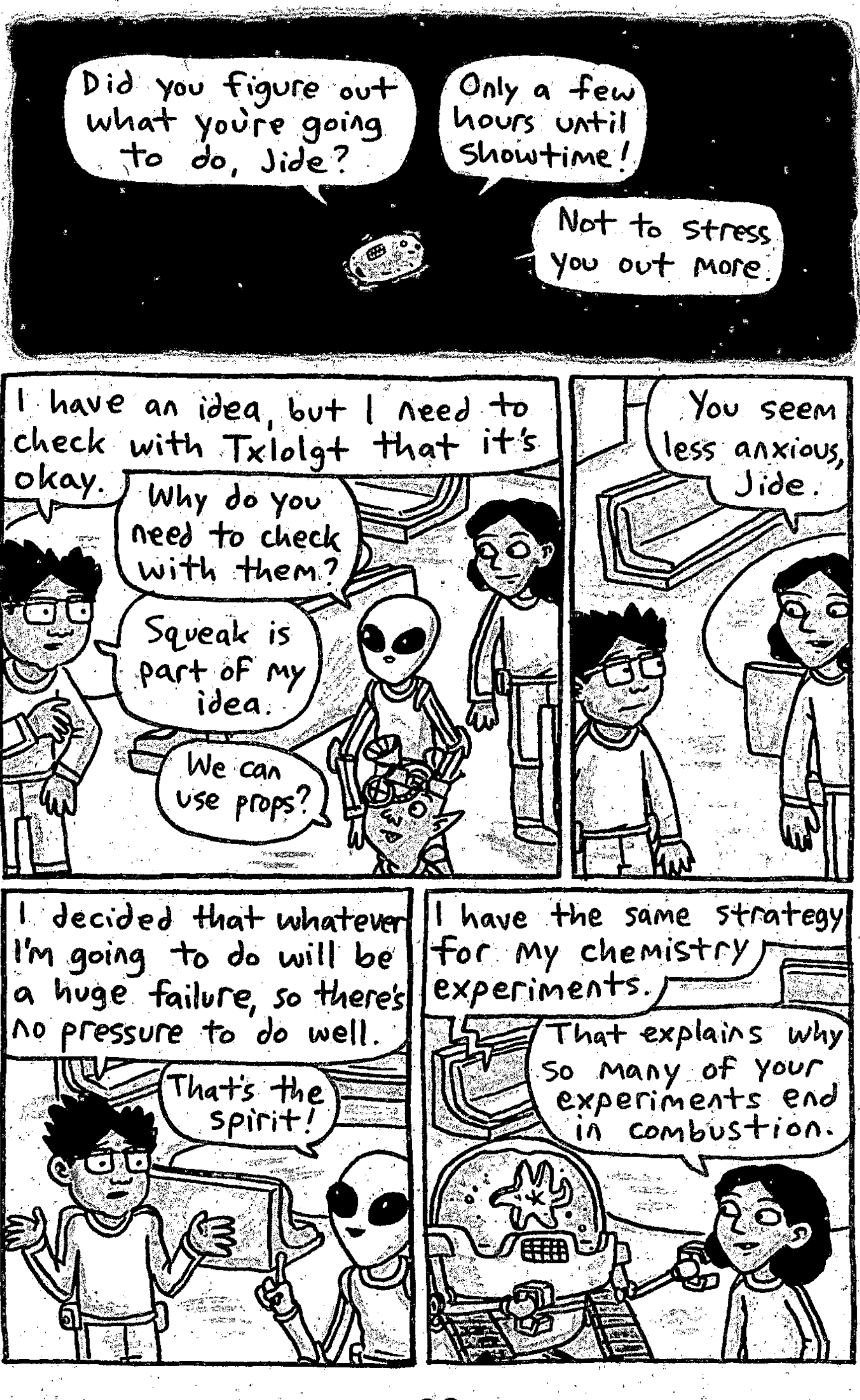
Did you figure out what you're going to do, Jide?
Only a few hours until Showtime!
Not to stress you out more.
I have an idea, but I need to check with Txlolgt that it's okay.
Why do you need to check with them?
Squeak is part of my idea.
We can use props?
You seem less anxious, Jide.
I decided that whatever I'm going to do will be a huge failure, so there's no pressure to do well.
That's the spirit!
I have the same strategy for my chemistry experiments.
That explains why so many of your experiments end in combustion.

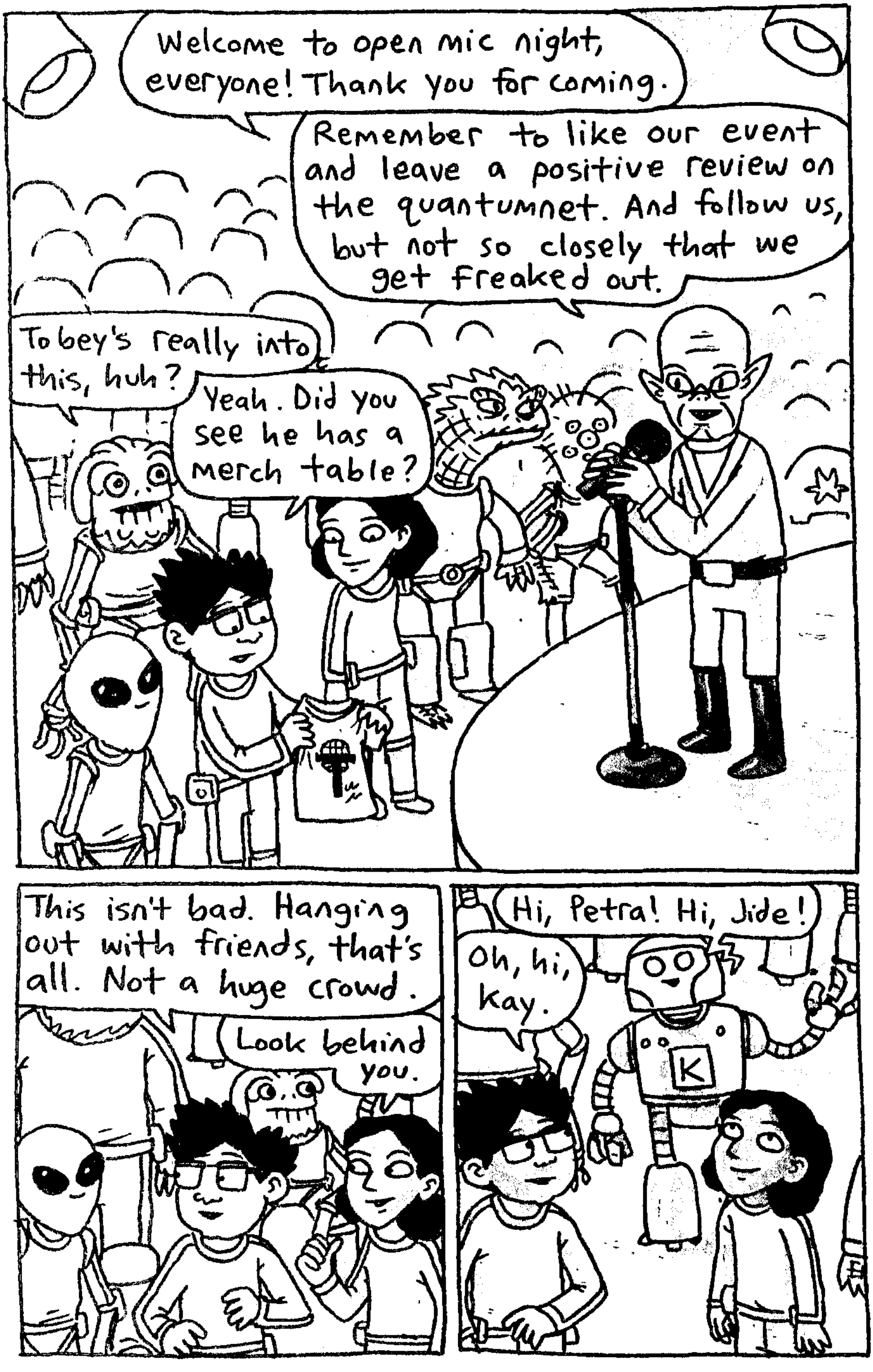
Welcome to open mic night, everyone! Thank you for coming.
Remember to like our event and leave a positive review on the quantumnet. And follow us, but not so closely that we get freaked out.
Tobey's really into this, huh?
Yeah. Did you see he has a merch table?
This isn't bad. Hanging out with friends, that's all. Not a huge crowd.
Look behind you.
Hi, Petra! Hi, Jide!
Oh, hi, Kay.

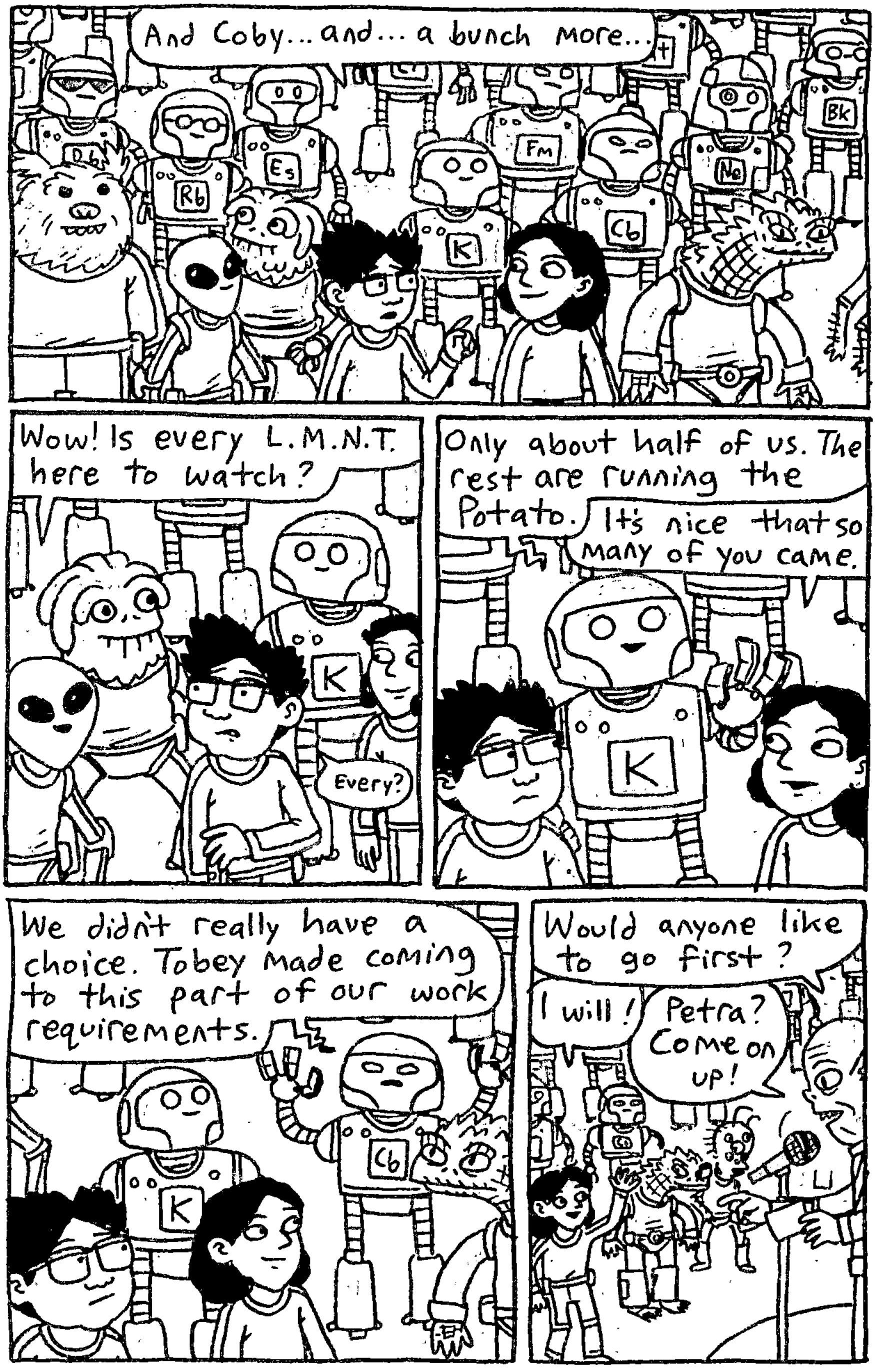
And Coby... and... a bunch more...
Wow! Is every L.M.N.T. here to watch?
Every?
Only about half of us. The rest are running the Potato.
It's nice that so many of you came.
We didn't really have a choice. Tobey made coming to this part of our work requirements.
Would anyone like to go first?
I will!
Petra? Come on up!

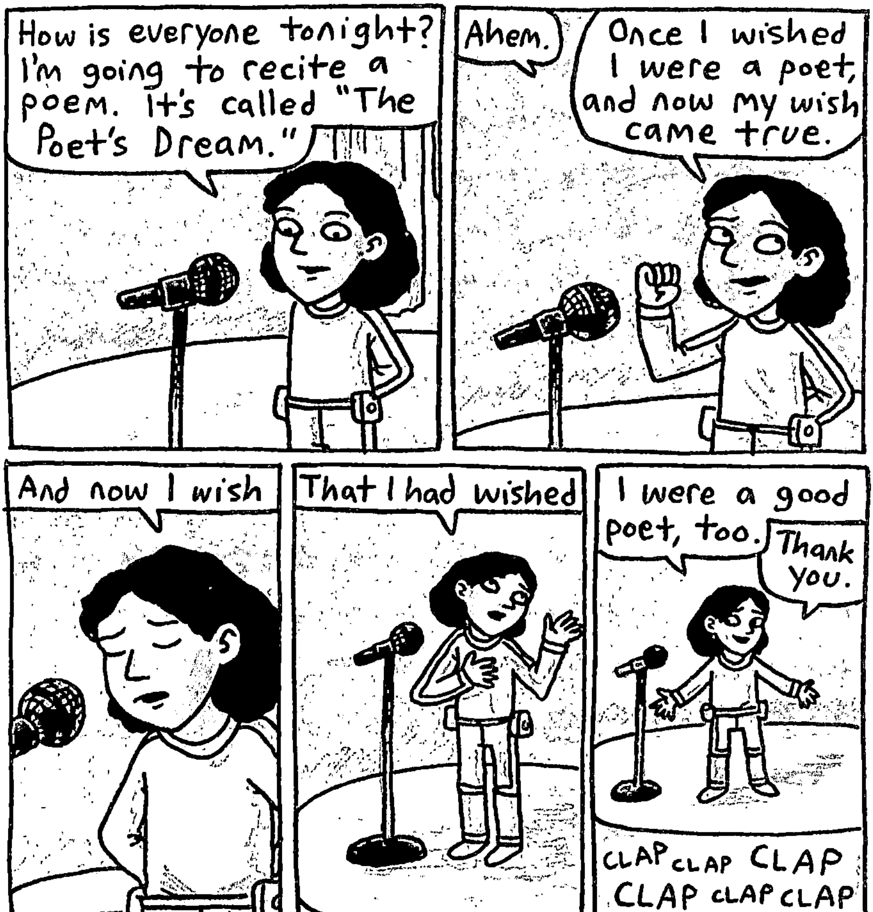
How is everyone tonight? I'm going to recite a poem. It's called "The Poet's Dream."
Ahem.
Once I wished I were a poet, and now my wish came true.
And now I wish
That I had wished
I were a good poet, too.
Thank you.
CLAP CLAP CLAP
CLAP CLAP CLAP
Very nice, Petra. As a courtesy reminder, please silence your computater notifications.
That was funny, Petra.
Yes. It was my favorite so far.

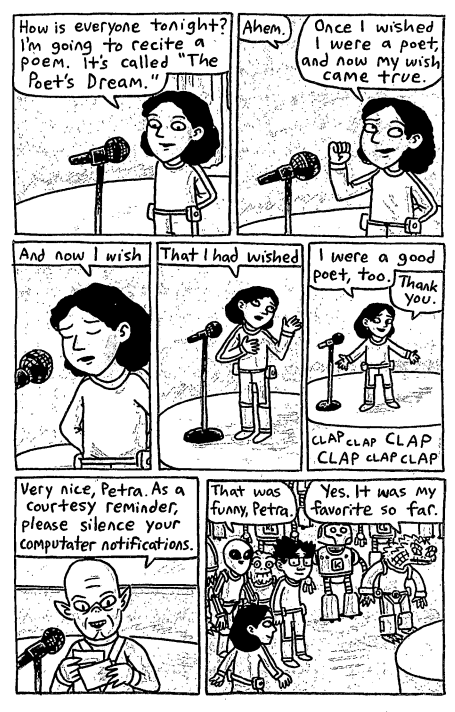

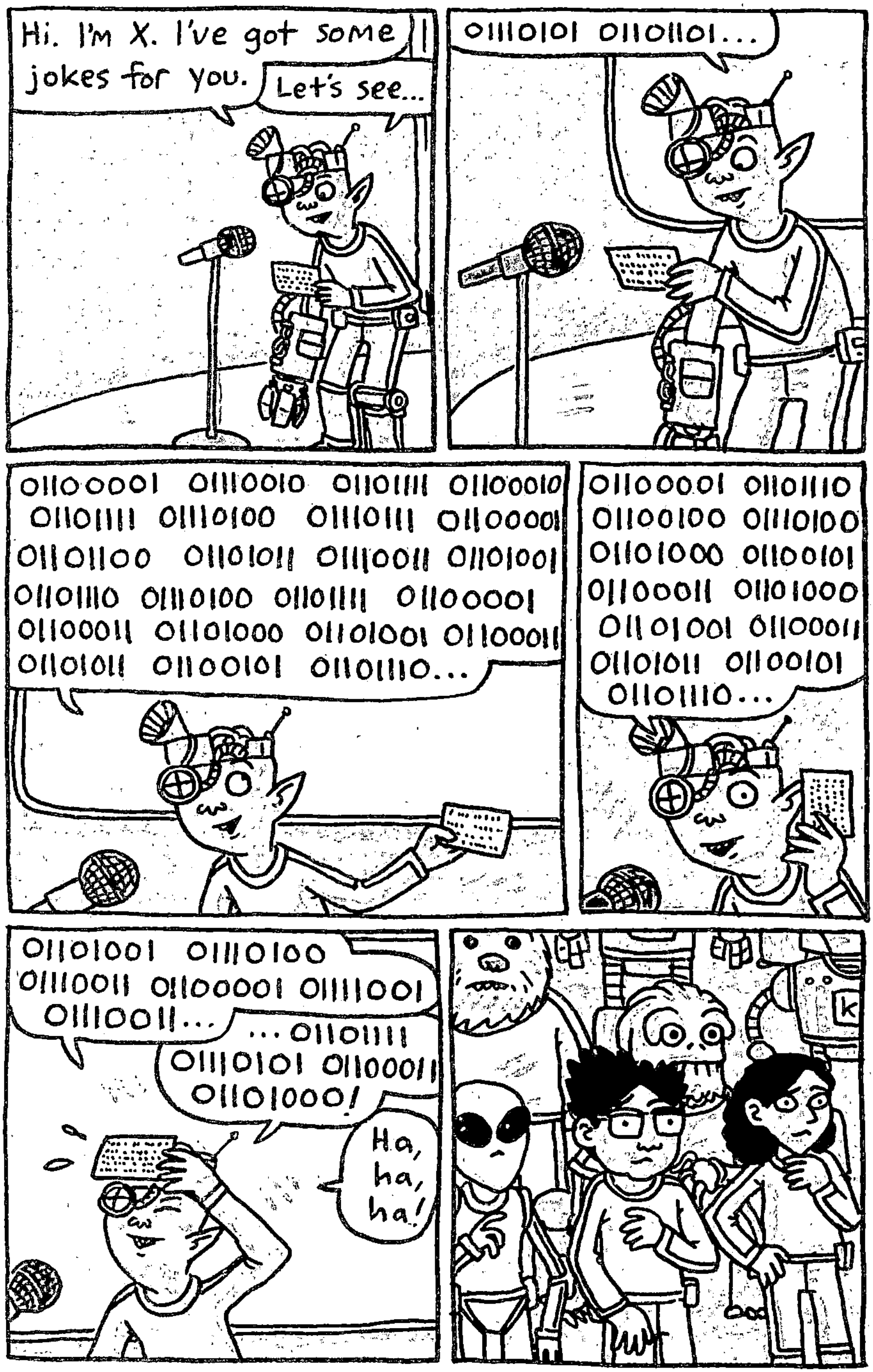

Hi. I'm X. I've got some jokes for you.
Let's see...
01110101 01101101...
01100001 01110010 01101111 01100010 01101111 01110100 01110111 01100001 01101100 01101011 01110011 01101001 01101110 01110100 01101111 01100001 01100011 01101000 01101001 01100011 01101011 01100101 01101110...
01100001 01101110 01100100 01110100 01101000 01100101 01100011 01101000 01101001 01100011 01101011 01100101 01101110...
01101001 01110100 01110011 01100001 01111001 01110011...
...01101111 01110101 01100011 01101000!
Ha, ha, ha!

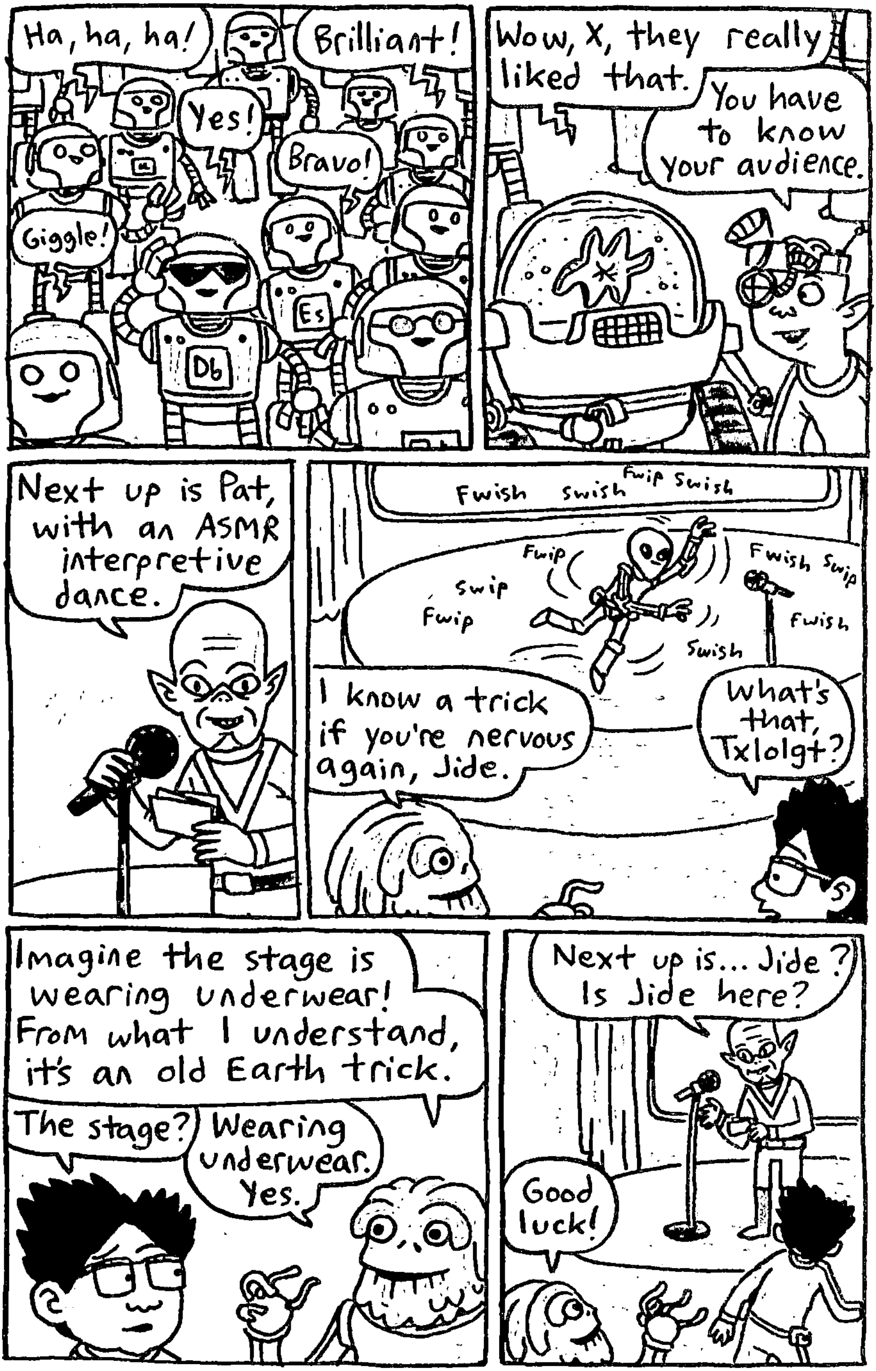
Ha, ha, ha!
Brilliant!
Yes!
Bravo!
Giggle!
Es
Db
Wow, X, they really liked that.
You have to know your audience.
Next up is Pat, with an ASMR interpretive dance.
Fwish swish Fwip Swish
Fwip
Swip
Fwip
Fwish Swip
Fwish
Swish
I know a trick if you're nervous again, Jide.
What's that, Txlolgt?
Imagine the stage is wearing underwear! From what I understand, it's an old Earth trick.
The stage?
Wearing underwear. Yes.
Next up is... Jide? Is Jide here?
Good luck!

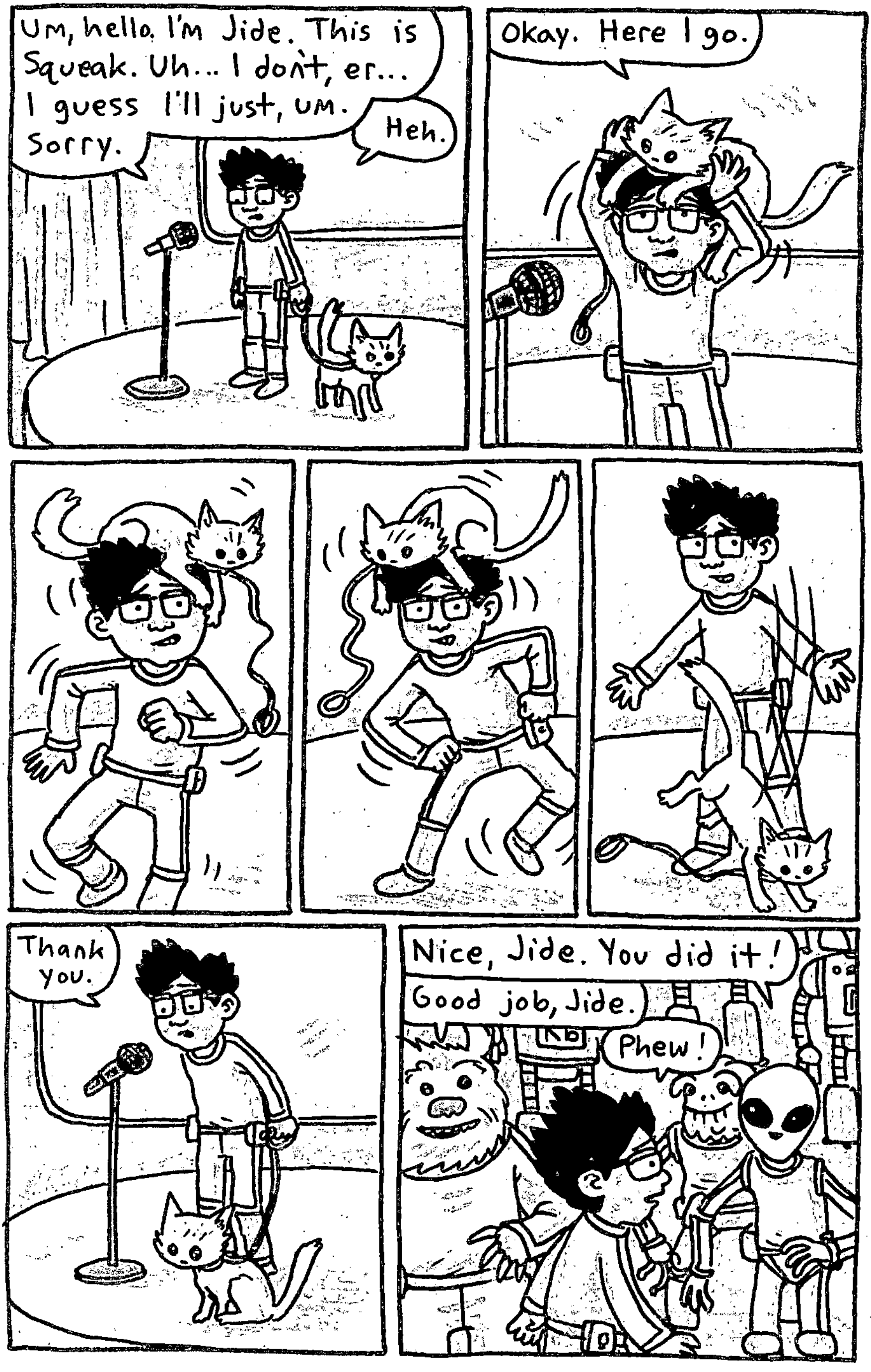
Um, hello. I'm Jide. This is Squeak. Uh... I don't, er... I guess I'll just, um. Sorry.
Heh.
Okay. Here I go.
Thank you.
Nice, Jide. You did it!
Good job, Jide.
Phew!

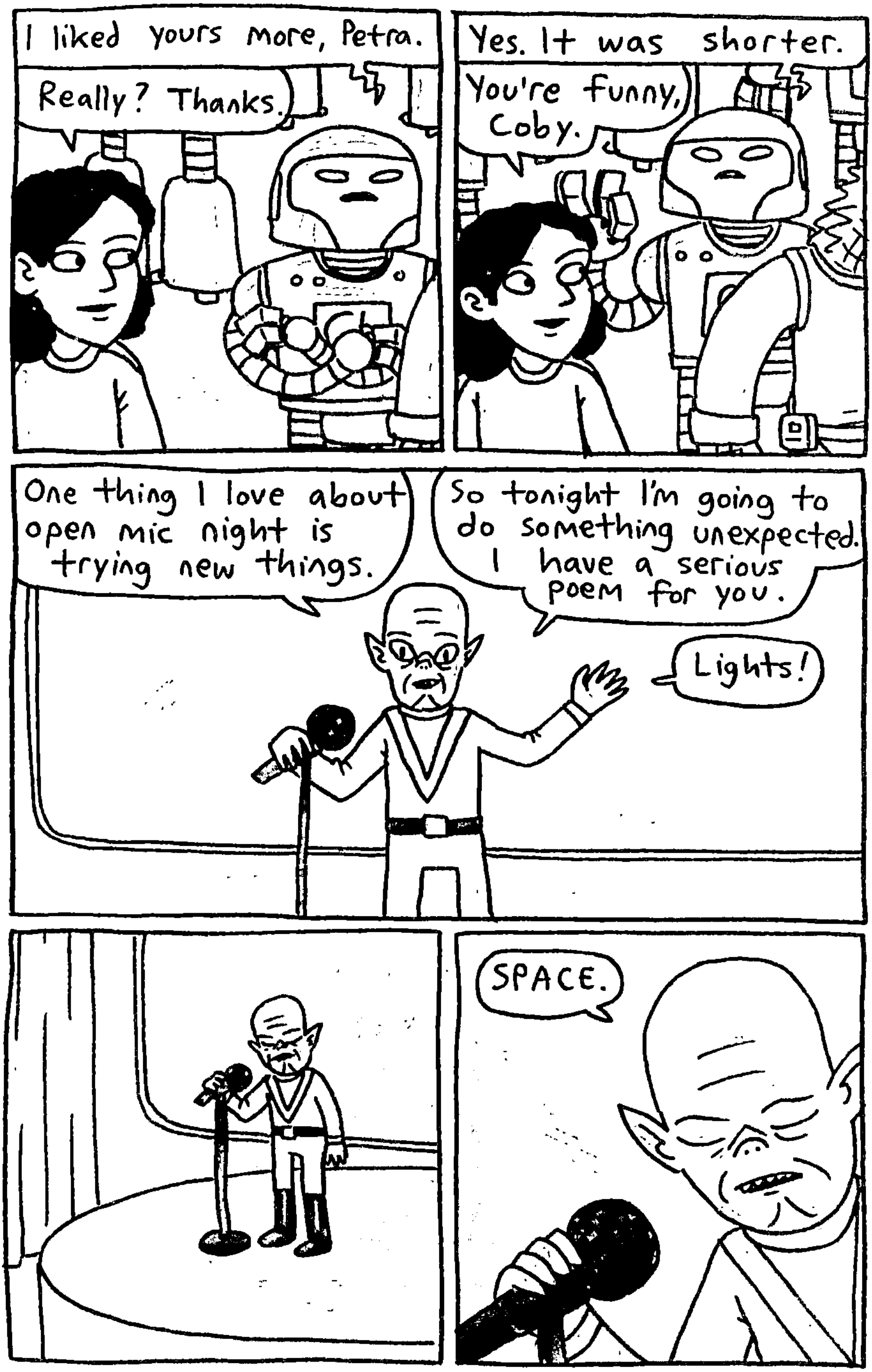
I liked yours more, Petra.
Really? Thanks.
Yes. It was shorter.
You're funny, Coby.
One thing I love about open mic night is trying new things.
So tonight I'm going to do something unexpected. I have a serious poem for you.
Lights!
SPACE.

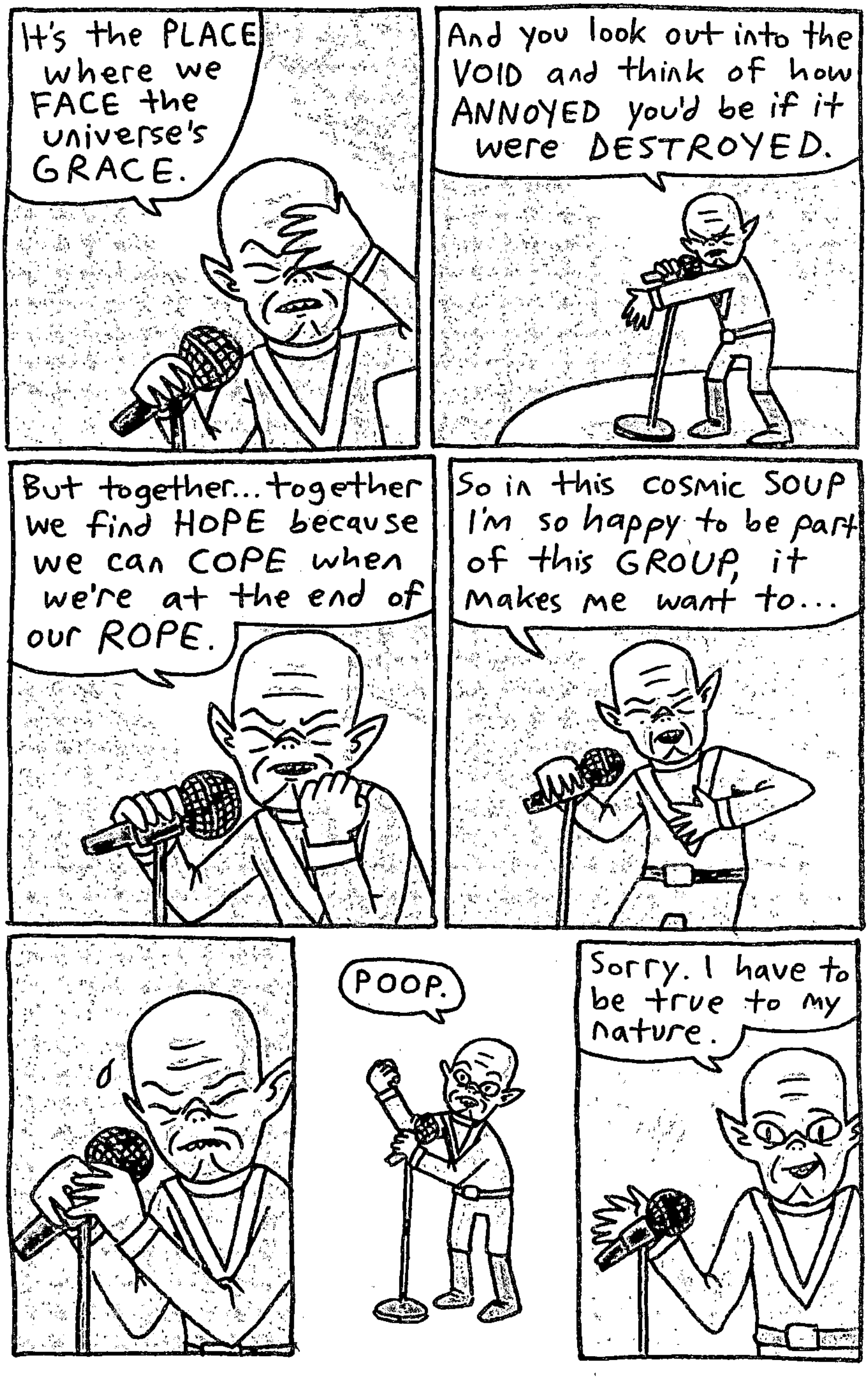
It's the PLACE where we FACE the universe's GRACE.
And you look out into the VOID and think of how ANNOYED you'd be if it were DESTROYED.
But together... together we find HOPE because we can COPE when we're at the end of our ROPE.
So in this cosmic SOUP I'm so happy to be part of this GROUP, it makes me want to...
POOP.
Sorry. I have to be true to my nature.

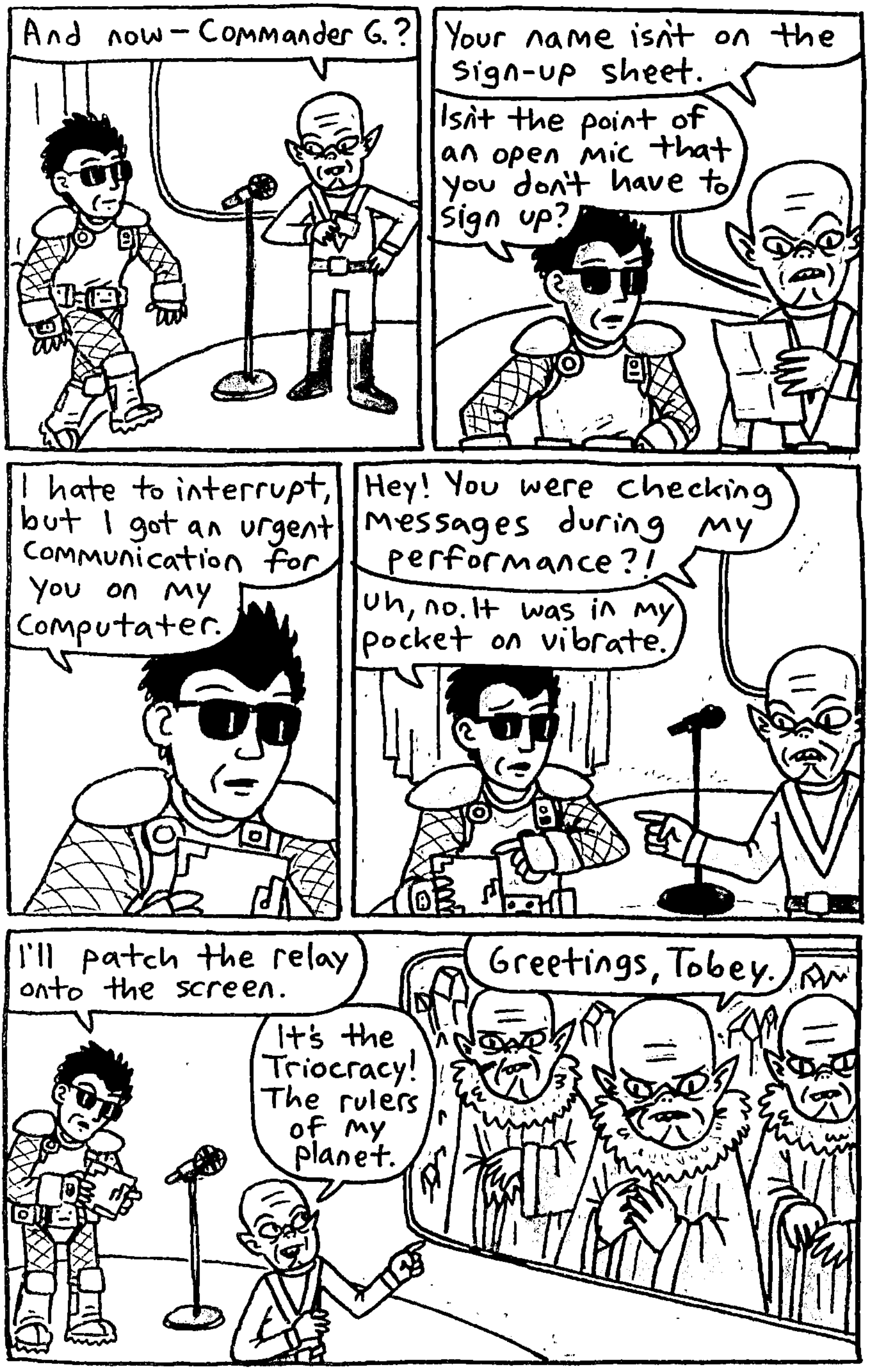

And now—Commander G.?
Your name isn't on the sign-up sheet.
Isn't the point of an open mic that you don't have to sign up?
I hate to interrupt, but I got an urgent communication for you on my Computater.
Hey! You were checking messages during my performance?!
Uh, no. It was in my pocket on vibrate.
I'll patch the relay onto the screen.
Greetings, Tobey.
It's the Triocracy! The rulers of my planet.

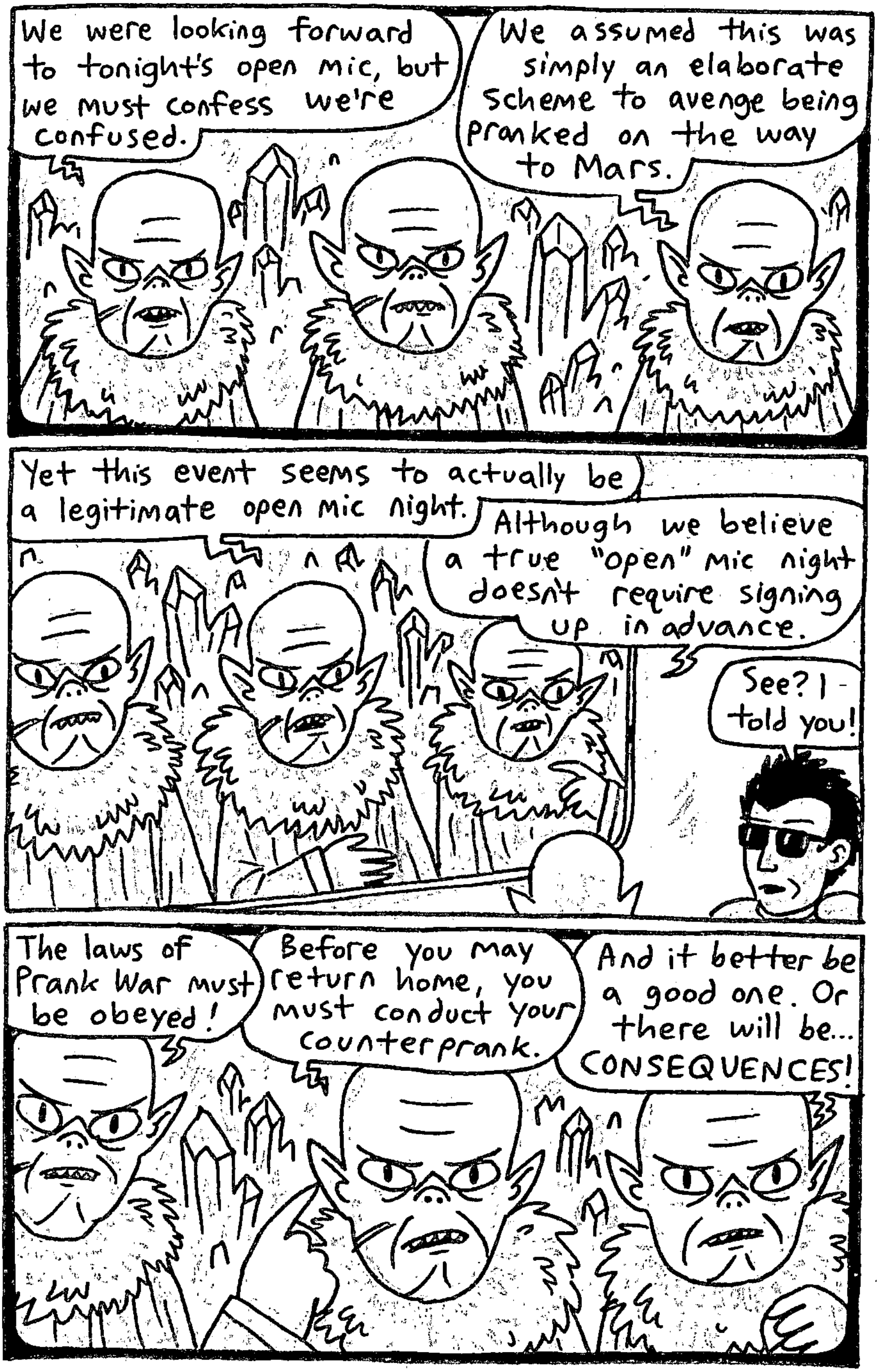
We were looking forward to tonight's open mic, but we must confess we're confused.
We assumed this was simply an elaborate scheme to avenge being pranked on the way to Mars.
Yet this event seems to actually be a legitimate open mic night.
Although we believe a true "open" mic night doesn't require signing up in advance.
See? I told you!
The laws of Prank War must be obeyed!
Before you may return home, you must conduct your counterprank.
And it better be a good one. Or there will be... CONSEQUENCES!

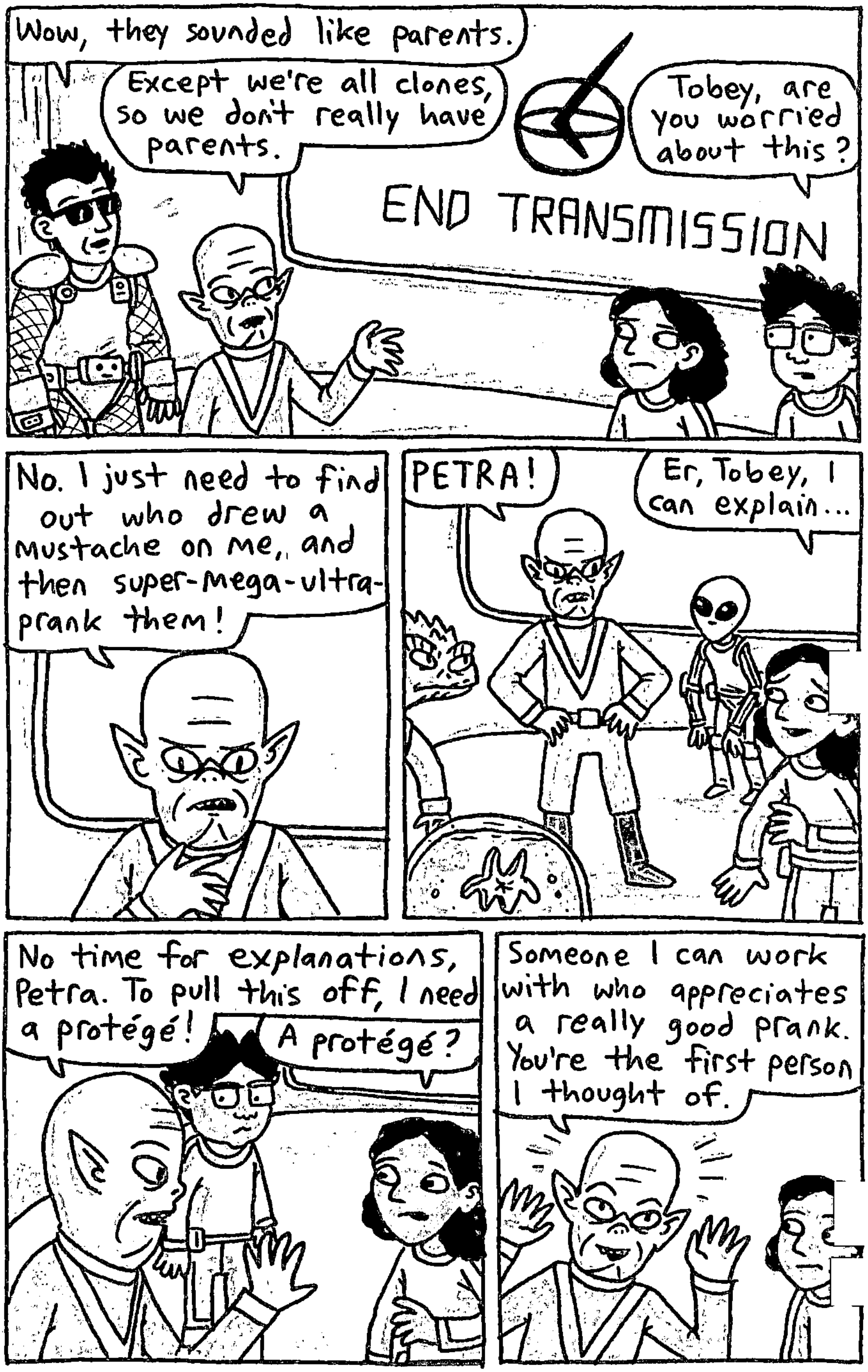
Wow, they sounded like parents.
Except we're all clones, so we don't really have parents.
Tobey, are you worried about this?
END TRANSMISSION
No. I just need to find out who drew a mustache on me, and then super-mega-ultra-prank them!
PETRA!
Er, Tobey, I can explain...
No time for explanations, Petra. To pull this off, I need a protégé!
A protégé?
Someone I can work with who appreciates a really good prank. You're the first person I thought of.

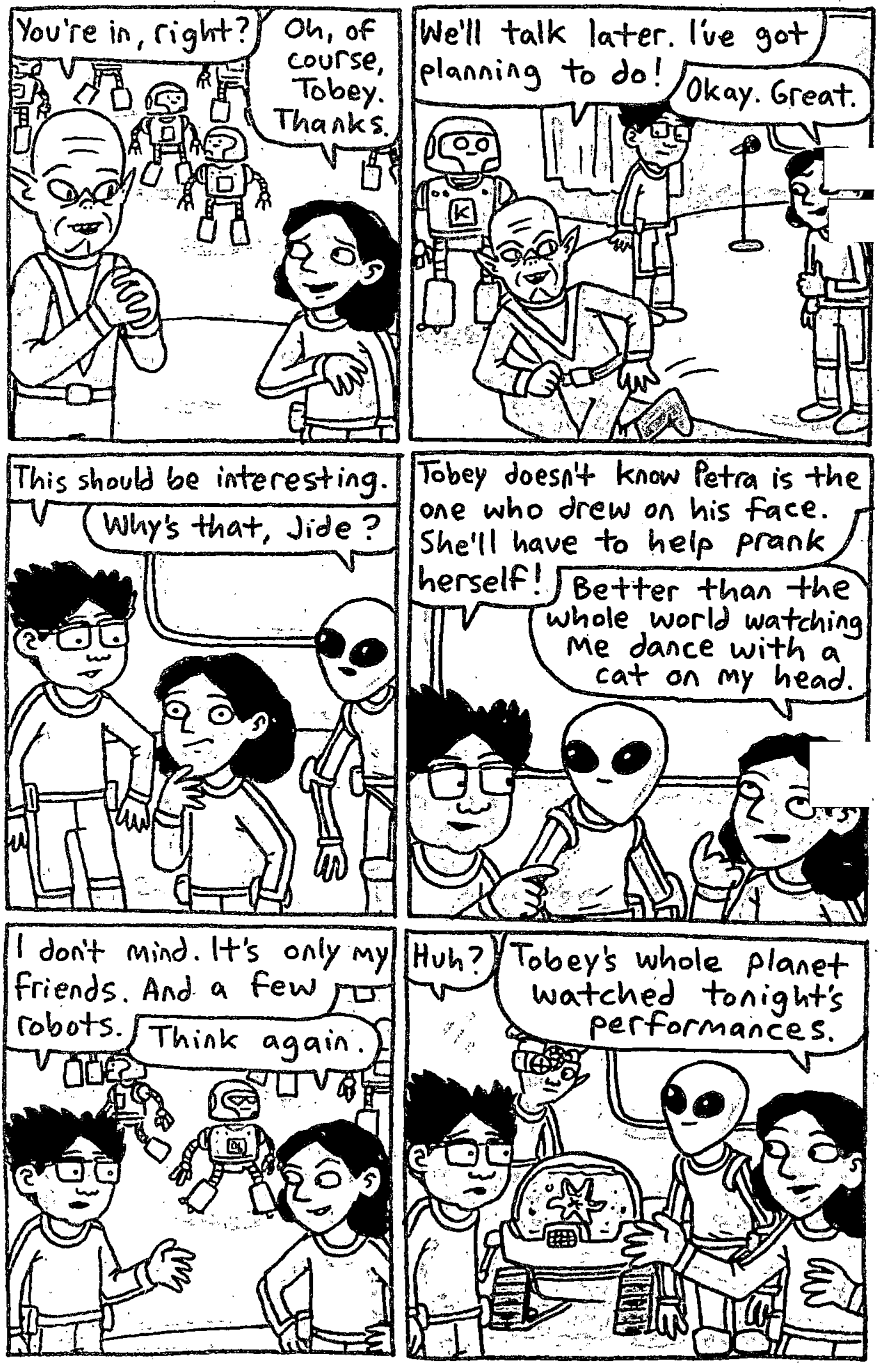
You're in, right?
Oh, of course, Tobey. Thanks.
We'll talk later. I've got planning to do!
Okay. Great.
This should be interesting.
Why's that, Jide?
Tobey doesn't know Petra is the one who drew on his face. She'll have to help *prank* herself!
Better than the whole world watching me dance with a cat on my head.
I don't mind. It's only my friends. And a few robots.
Think again.
Huh?
Tobey's whole planet watched tonight's performances.

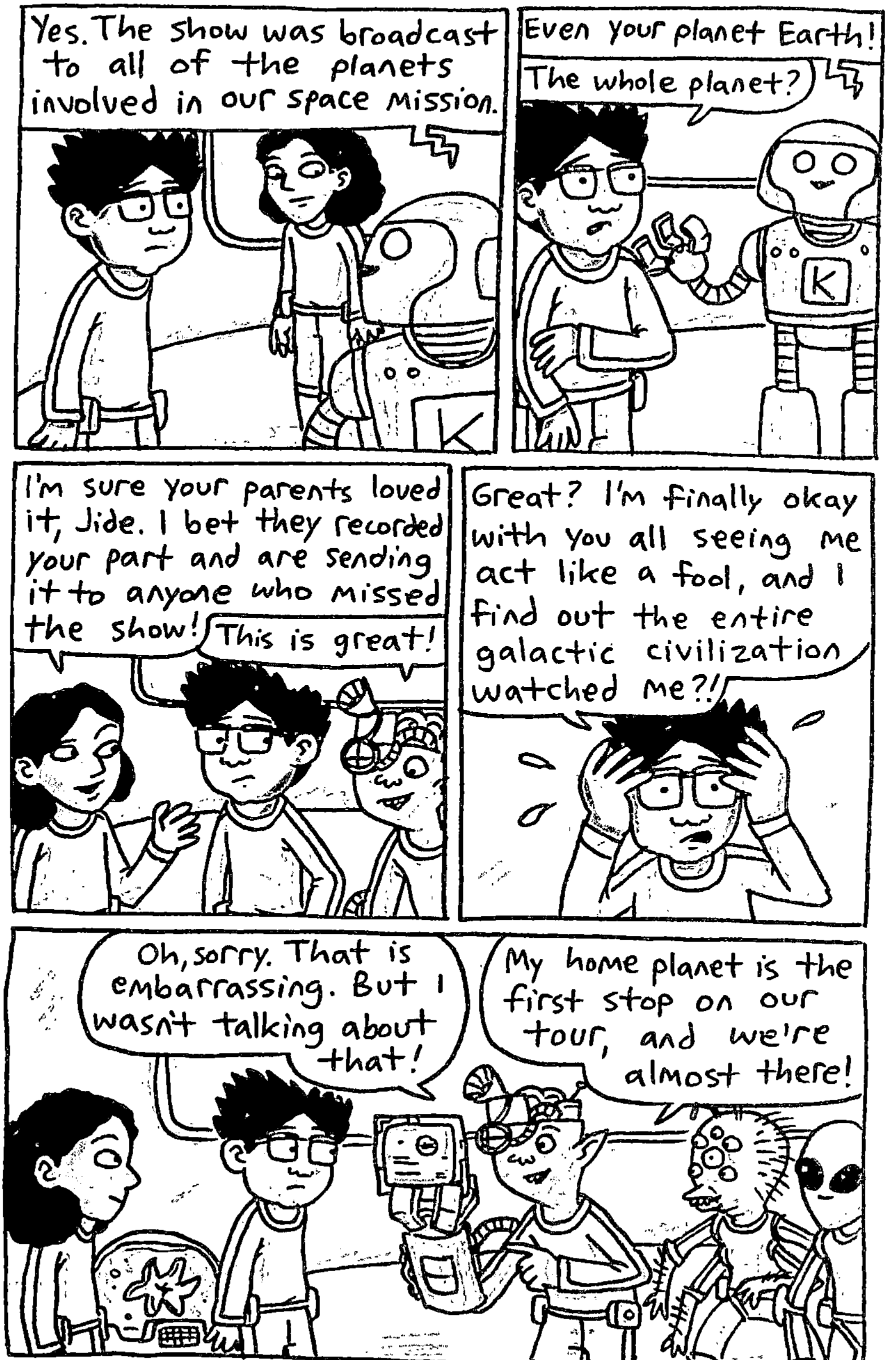

Yes. The show was broadcast to all of the planets involved in our space mission.
Even your planet Earth!
The whole planet?
I'm sure your parents loved it, Jide. I bet they recorded your part and are sending it to anyone who missed the show!
This is great!
Great? I'm finally okay with you all seeing me act like a fool, and I find out the entire galactic civilization watched me?!
Oh, sorry. That is embarrassing. But I wasn't talking about that!
My home planet is the first stop on our tour, and we're almost there!

DIGITOTALLY AWESOME

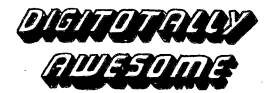

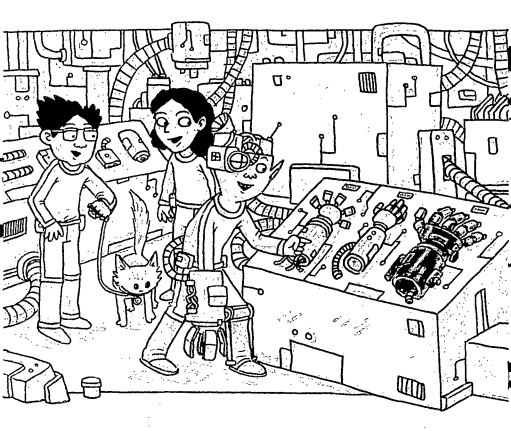

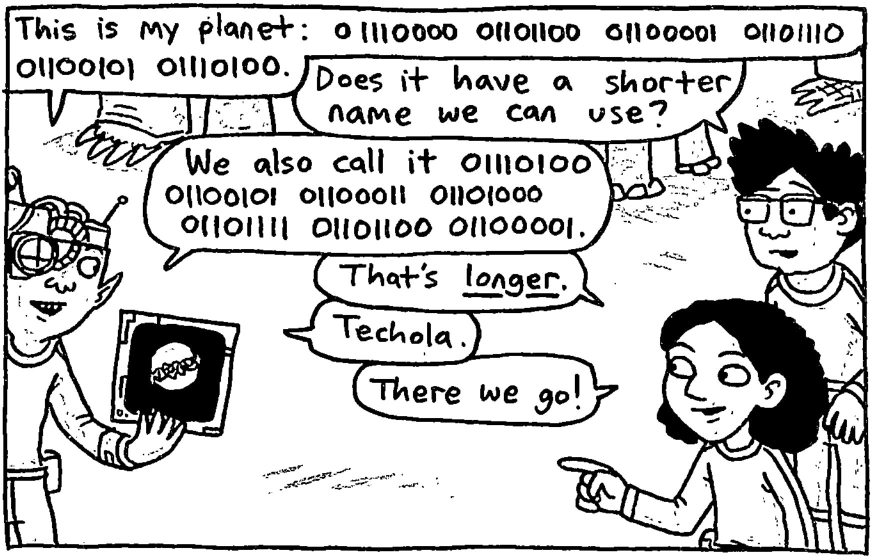
This is my planet: 01110000 01101100 01100001 01101110 01100101 01110100.
Does it have a shorter name we can use?
We also call it 01110100 01100101 01100011 01101000 01101111 01101100 01100001.
That's longer.
Techola.
There we go!

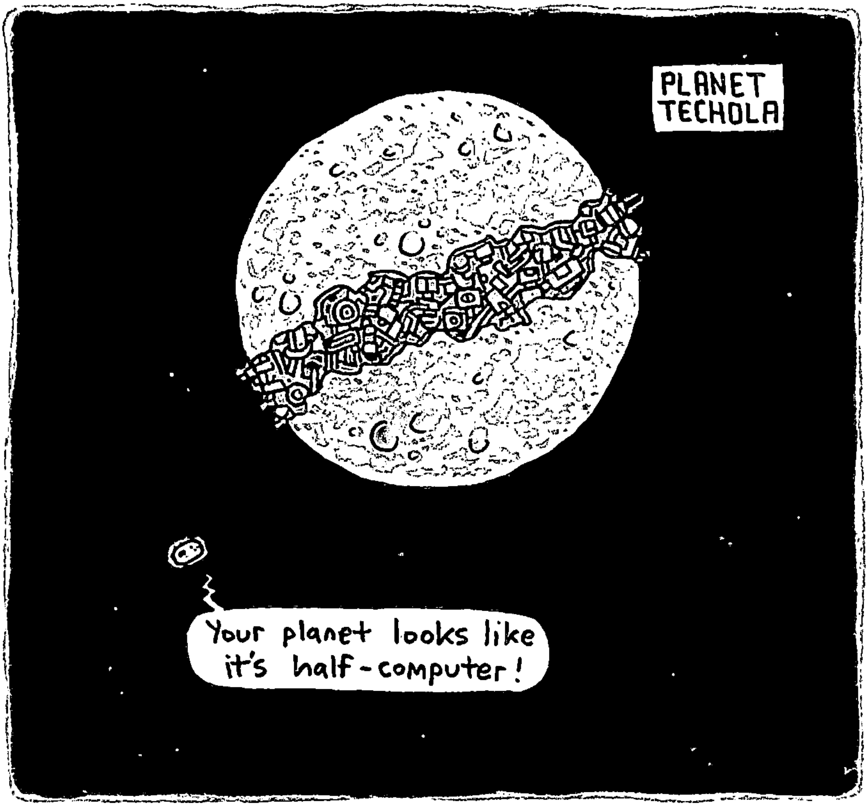
PLANET TECHOLA
Your planet looks like it's half-computer!

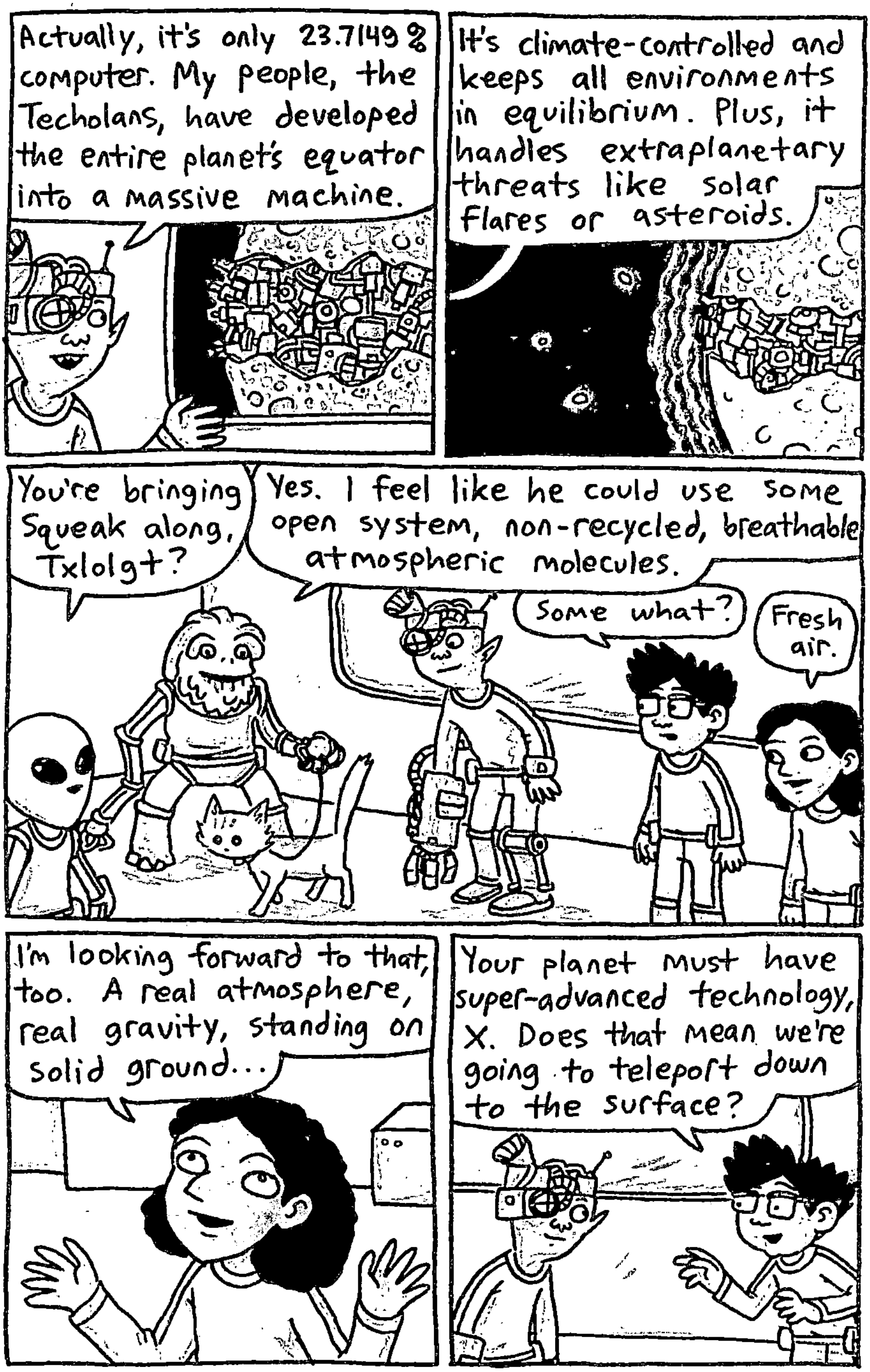
Actually, it's only 23.7149% computer. My people, the Techolans, have developed the entire planet's equator into a massive machine.
It's climate-controlled and keeps all environments in equilibrium. Plus, it handles extraplanetary threats like solar flares or asteroids.
You're bringing Squeak along, Txlolgt?
Yes. I feel like he could use some open system, non-recycled, breathable atmospheric molecules.
Some what?
Fresh air.
I'm looking forward to that, too. A real atmosphere, real gravity, standing on solid ground...
Your planet must have super-advanced technology, X. Does that mean we're going to teleport down to the surface?

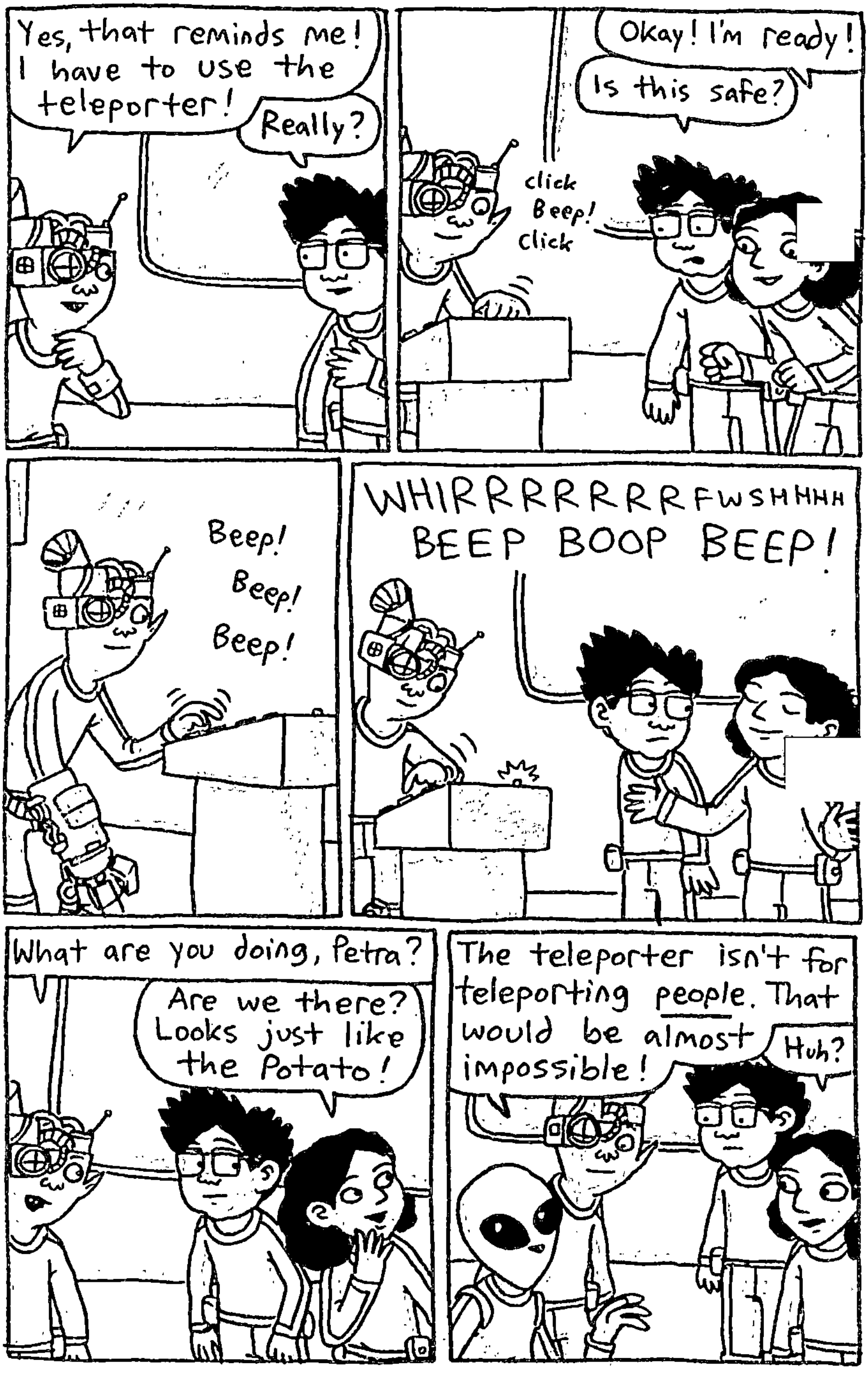
Yes, that reminds me! I have to use the teleporter!
Really?
Okay! I'm ready!
Is this safe?
click
Beep!
Click
Beep!
Beep!
Beep!
WHIRRRRRRRFWSHHHH
BEEP BOOP BEEP!
What are you doing, Petra?
Are we there? Looks just like the Potato!
The teleporter isn't for teleporting people. That would be almost impossible!
Huh?

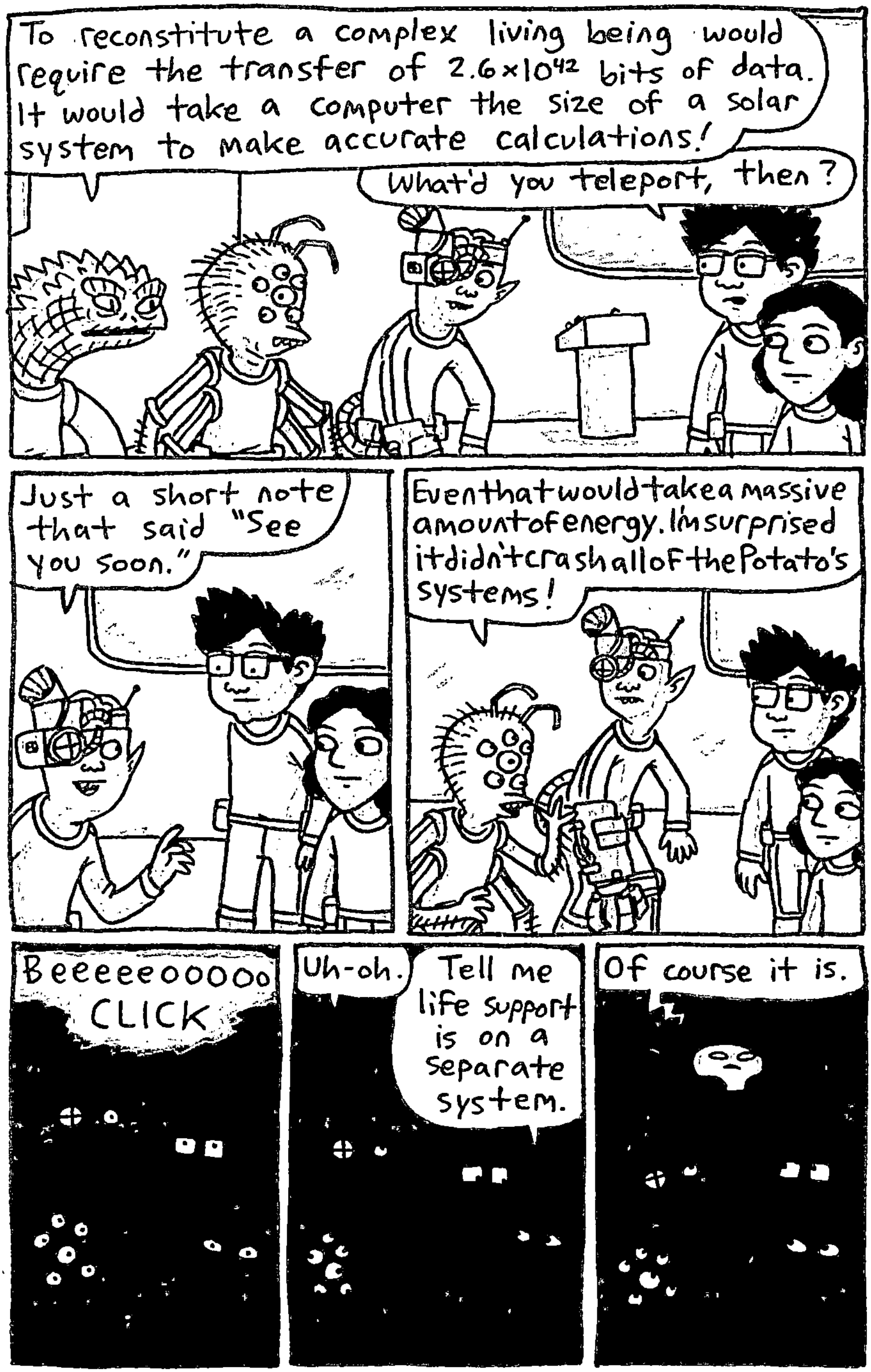
To reconstitute a complex living being would require the transfer of 2.6×10^{42} bits of data. It would take a computer the size of a solar system to make accurate calculations!
What'd you teleport, then?
Just a short note that said "See you soon."
Even that would take a massive amount of energy. I'm surprised it didn't crash all of the Potato's systems!
Beeeeeeooooo
CLICK
Uh-oh.
Tell me life support is on a separate system.
Of course it is.

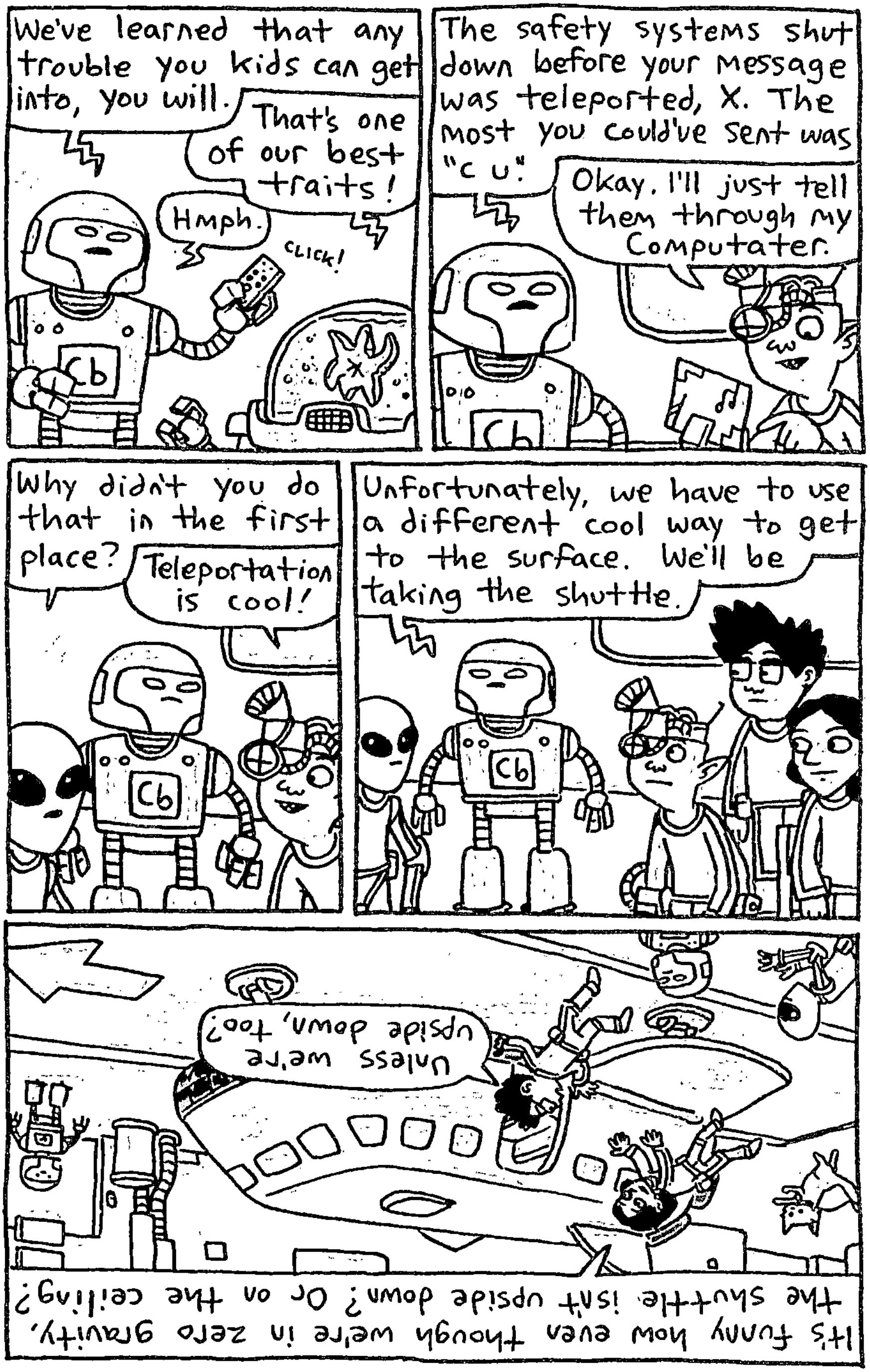
We've learned that any trouble you kids can get into, you will.
That's one of our best traits!
Hmph.
CLICK!
The safety systems shut down before your message was teleported, X. The most you could've sent was "c u."
Okay, I'll just tell them through my Computater.
Why didn't you do that in the first place?
Teleportation is cool!
Unfortunately, we have to use a different cool way to get to the surface. We'll be taking the shuttle.
Unless we're upside down, too?
It's funny how even though we're in zero gravity, the shuttle isn't upside down? Or on the ceiling?

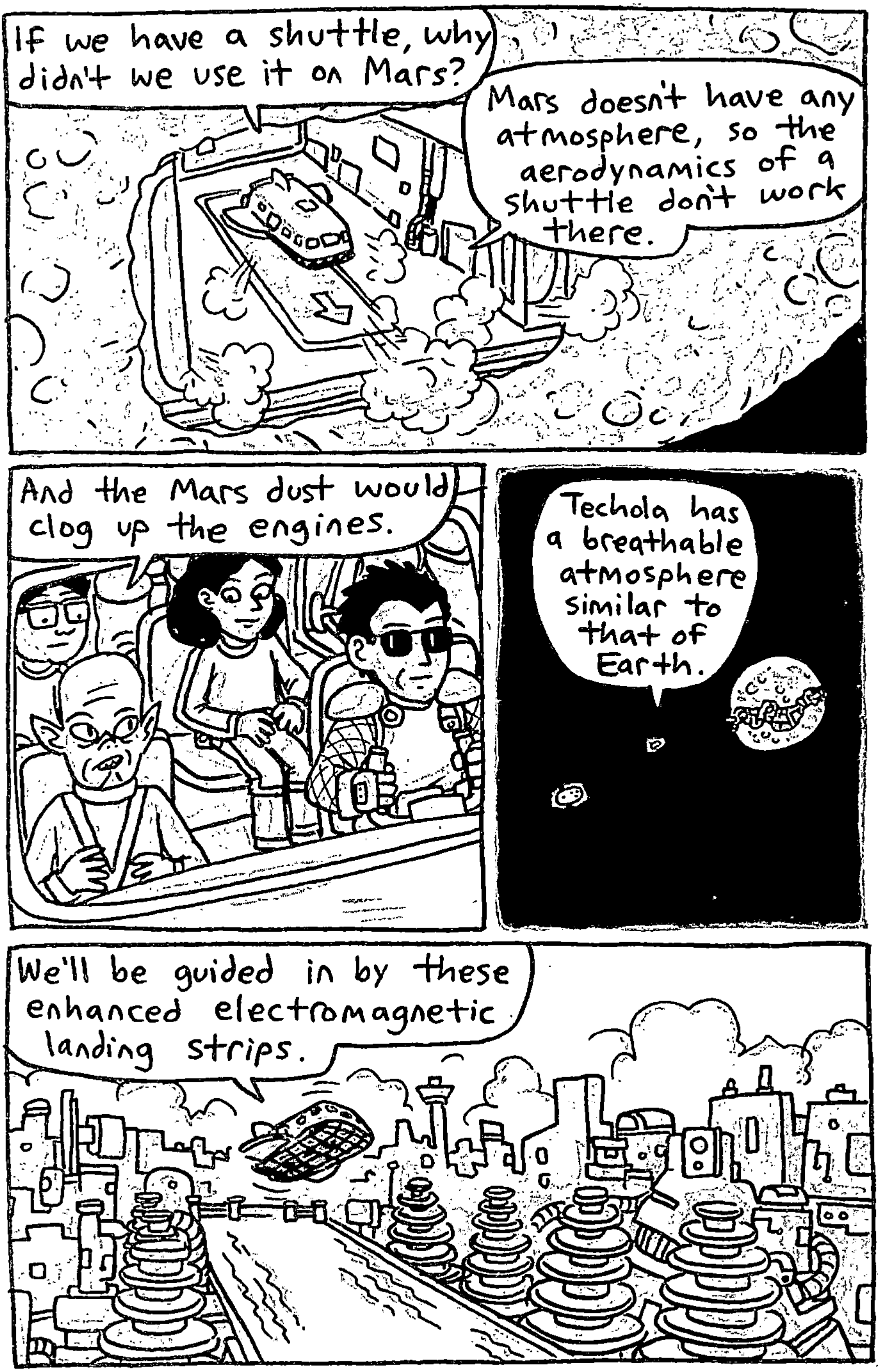
If we have a shuttle, why didn't we use it on Mars?
Mars doesn't have any atmosphere, so the aerodynamics of a shuttle don't work there.
And the Mars dust would clog up the engines.
Techola has a breathable atmosphere similar to that of Earth.
We'll be guided in by these enhanced electromagnetic landing strips.

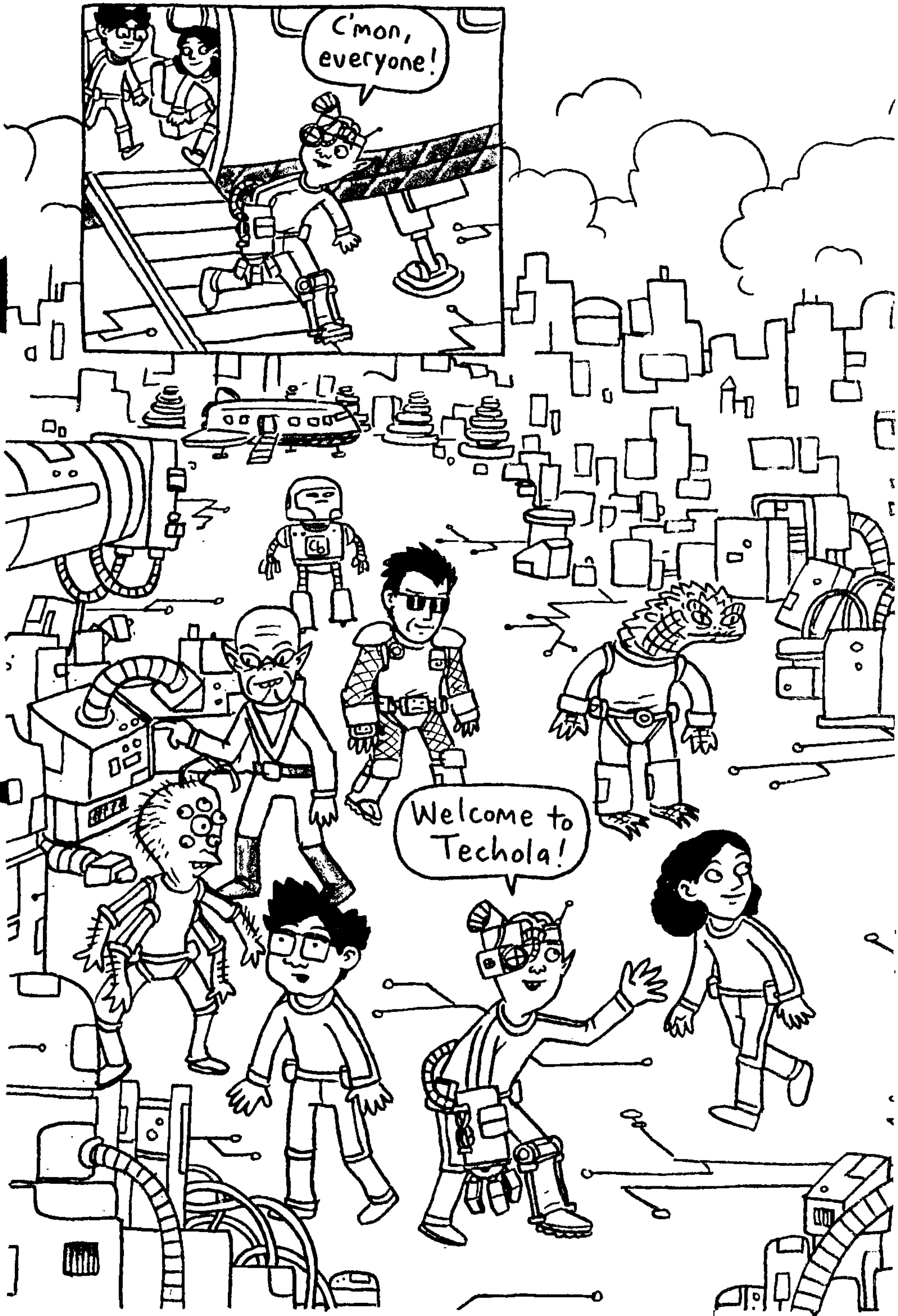
C'mon, everyone!
Welcome to Techola!

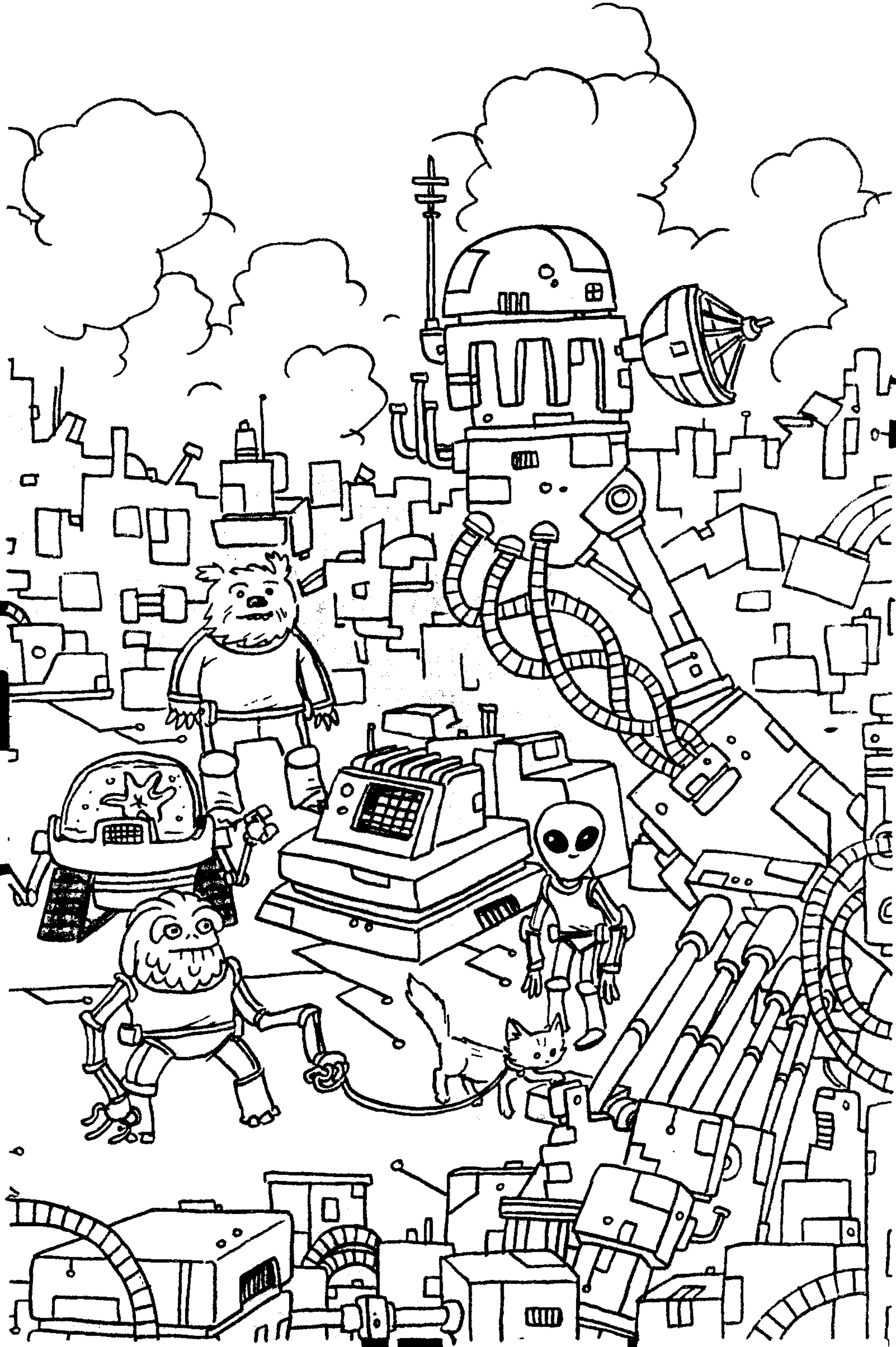

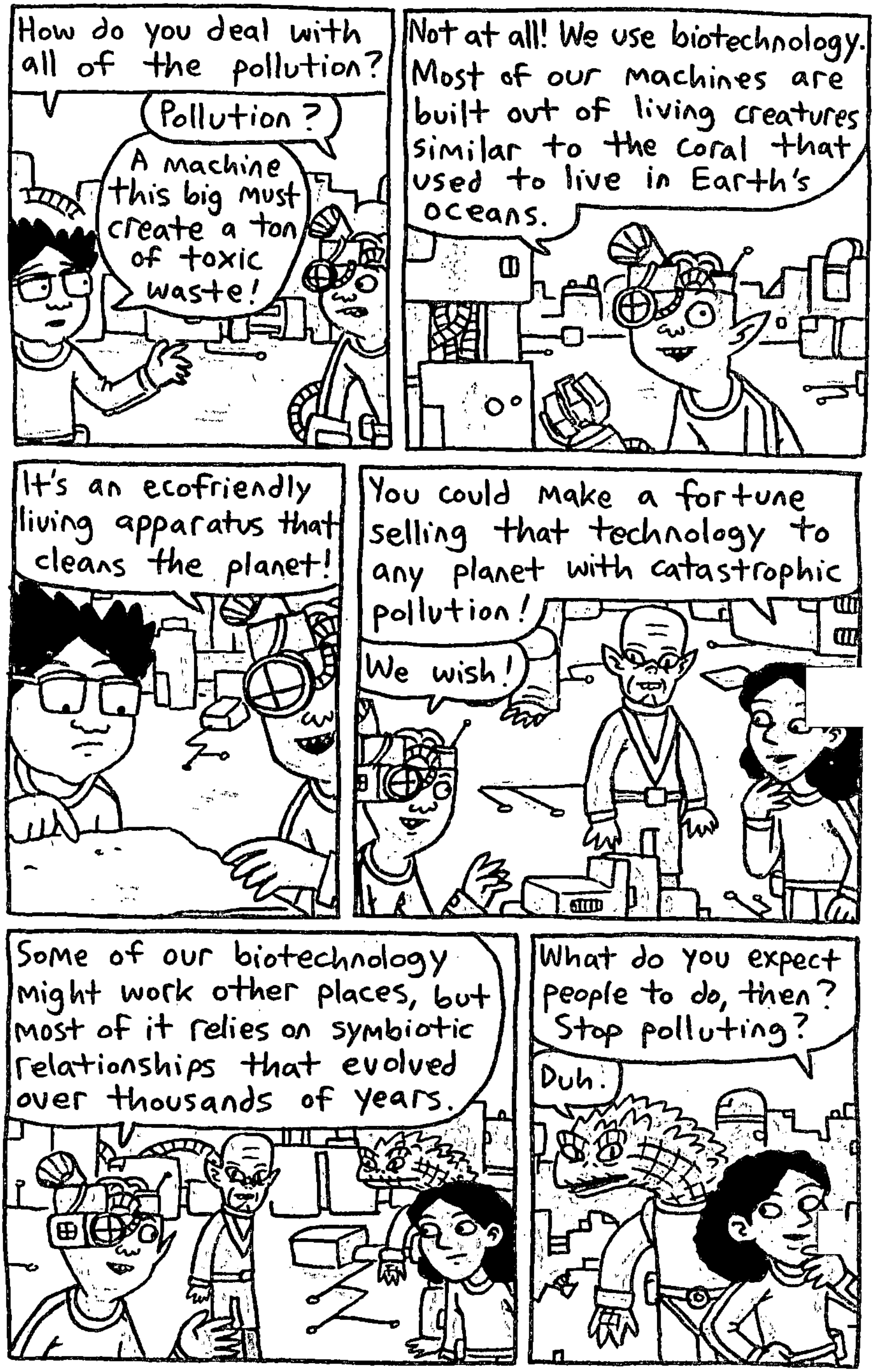
How do you deal with all of the pollution?
Pollution?
A machine this big must create a ton of toxic waste!
Not at all! We use biotechnology. Most of our machines are built out of living creatures similar to the coral that used to live in Earth's oceans.
It's an ecofriendly living apparatus that cleans the planet!
You could make a fortune selling that technology to any planet with catastrophic pollution!
We wish!
Some of our biotechnology might work other places, but most of it relies on symbiotic relationships that evolved over thousands of years.
What do you expect people to do, then? Stop polluting?
Duh.

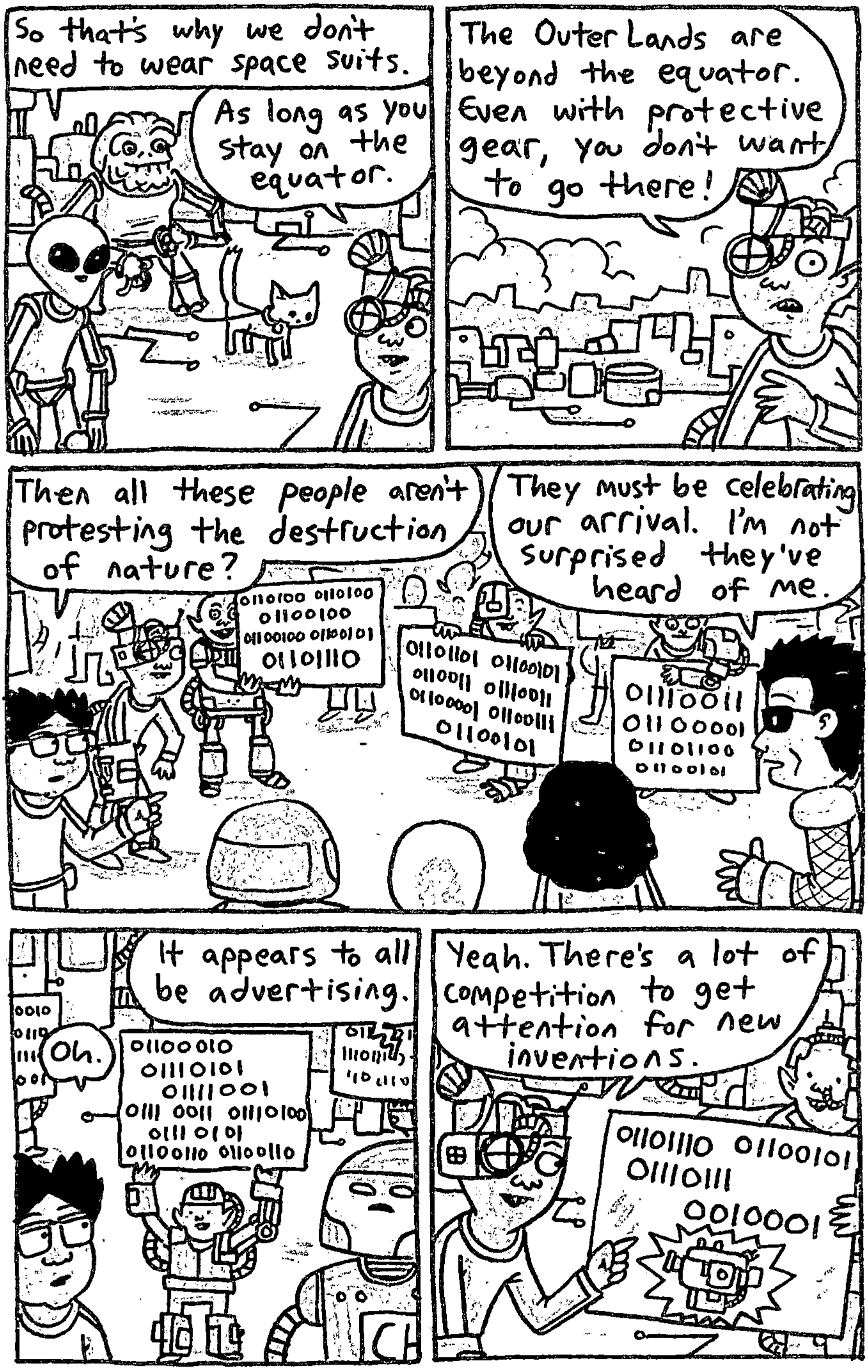

So that's why we don't need to wear space suits.
As long as you stay on the equator.
The Outer Lands are beyond the equator. Even with protective gear, you don't want to go there!
Then all these people aren't protesting the destruction of nature?
They must be celebrating our arrival. I'm not surprised they've heard of me.
01110011 01100001 01101100 01100101
It appears to all be advertising.
Oh.
01100010 01110101 01111001 0111 0011 01110100 0111 0101 01100110 01100110
Yeah. There's a lot of competition to get attention for new inventions.
01101110 01100101 01110111 00100001

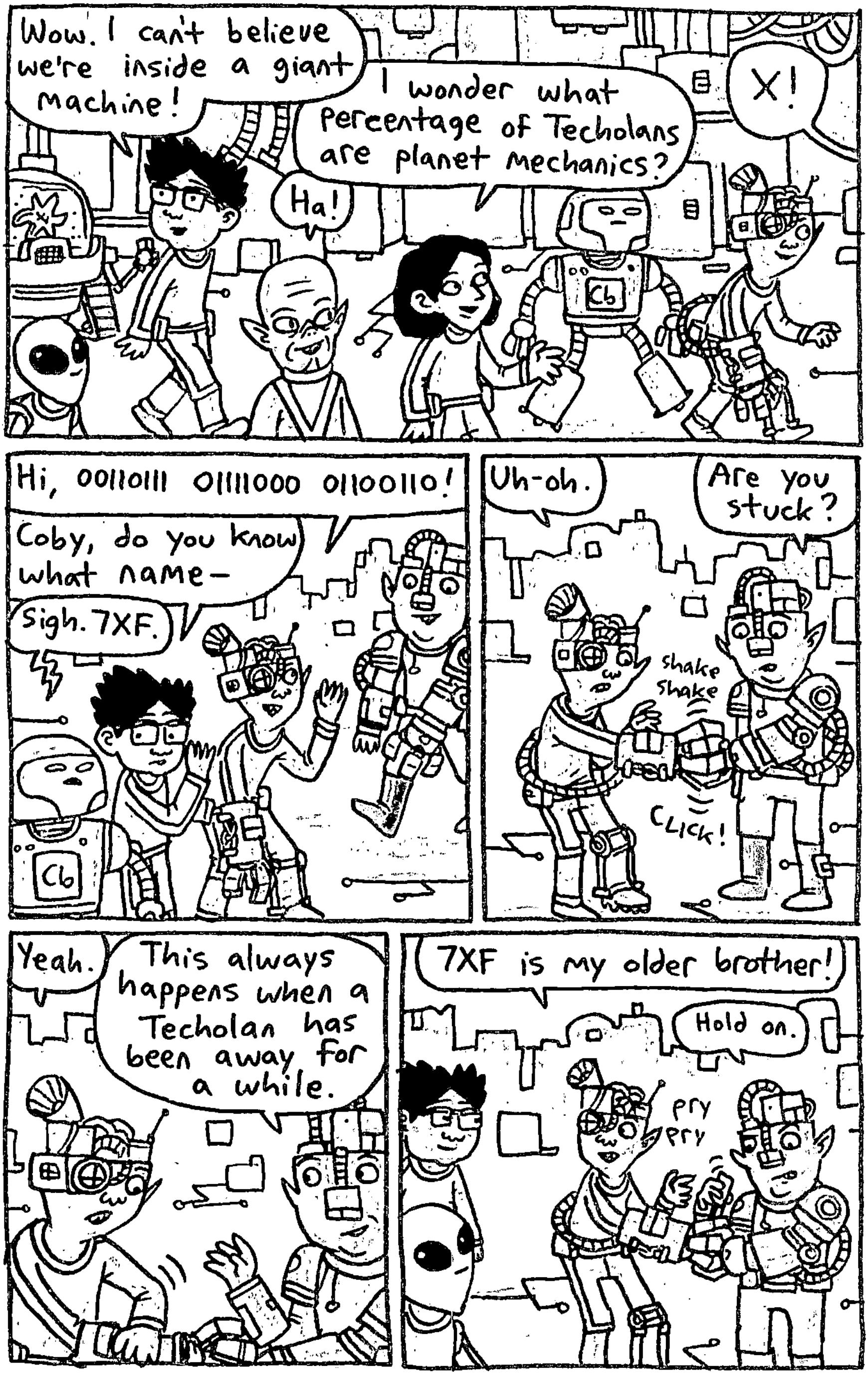

Wow. I can't believe we're inside a giant machine!
Ha!
I wonder what percentage of Techolans are planet mechanics?
X!
Hi, 00110111 01111000 01100110!
Coby, do you know what name—
Sigh. 7XF.
Uh-oh.
Are you stuck?
shake shake
CLICK!
Yeah.
This always happens when a Techolan has been away for a while.
7XF is my older brother!
Hold on.
pry pry

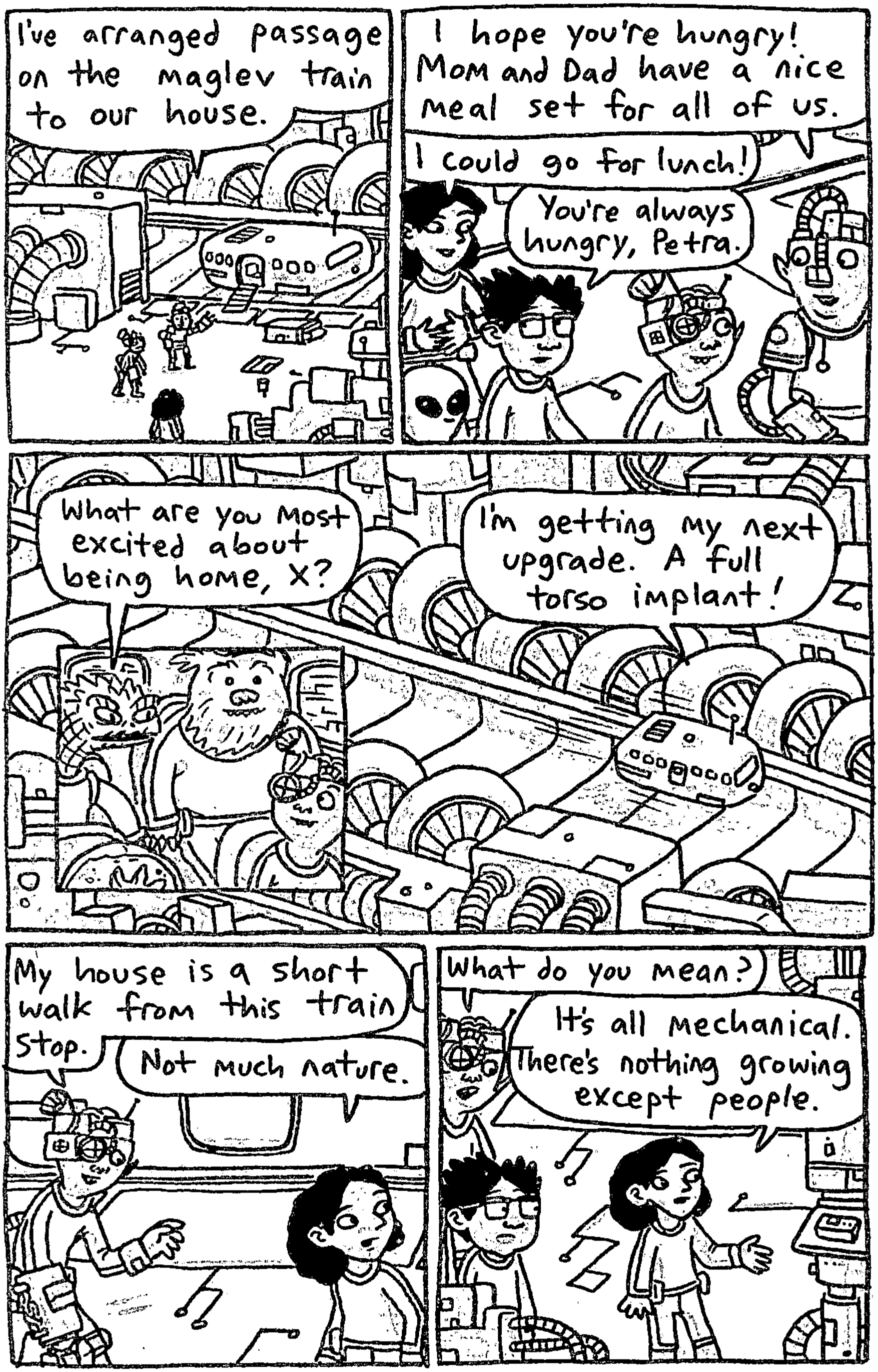

I've arranged passage on the maglev train to our house.
I hope you're hungry! Mom and Dad have a nice meal set for all of us.
I could go for lunch!
You're always hungry, Petra.
What are you most excited about being home, X?
I'm getting my next upgrade. A full torso implant!
My house is a short walk from this train stop.
Not much nature.
What do you mean?
It's all mechanical. There's nothing growing except people.

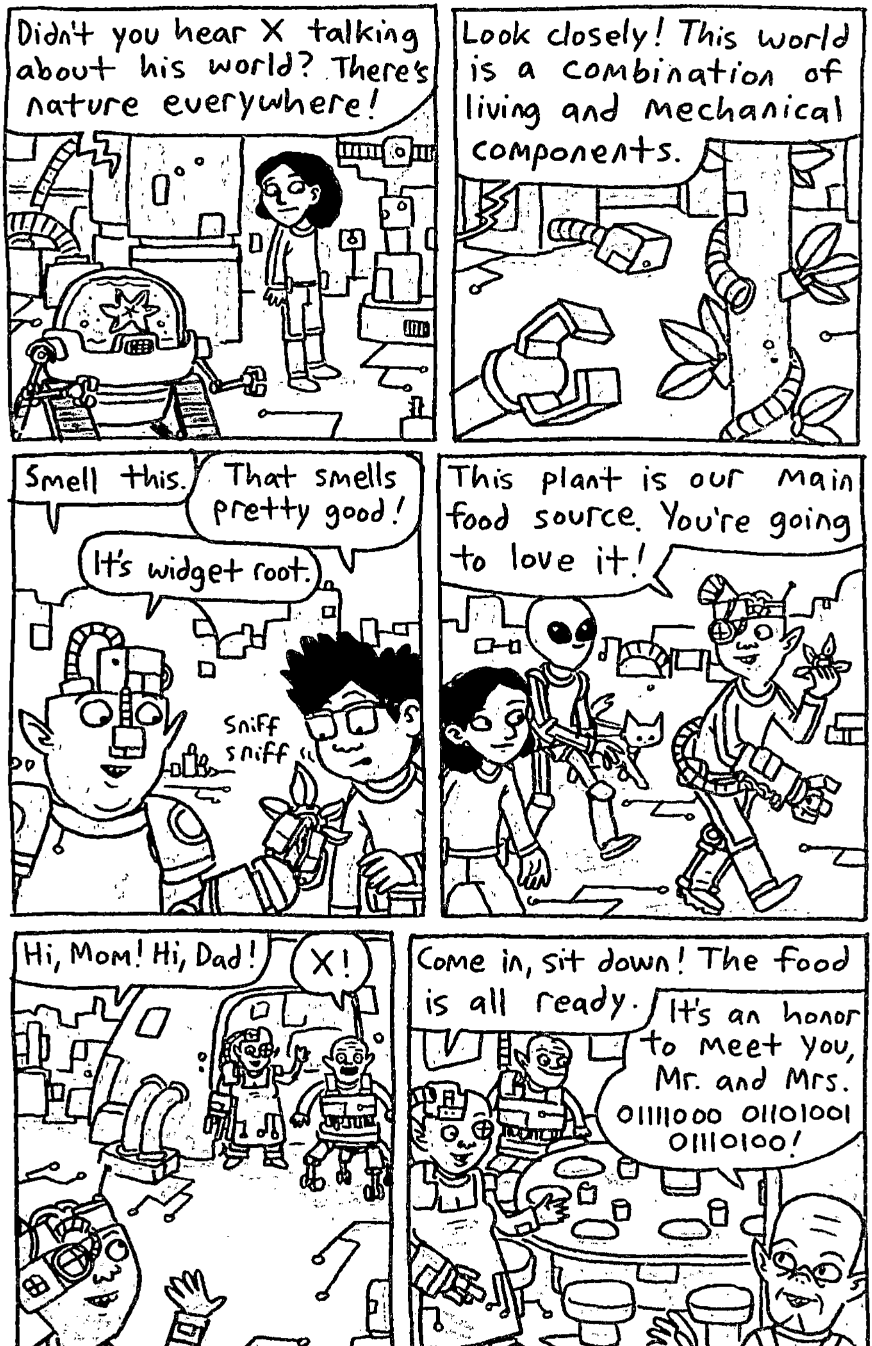

Didn't you hear X talking about his world? There's nature everywhere!
Look closely! This world is a combination of living and mechanical components.
Smell this.
That smells pretty good!
It's widget root.
Sniff sniff
This plant is our main food source. You're going to love it!
Hi, Mom! Hi, Dad!
X!
Come in, sit down! The food is all ready.
It's an honor to meet you, Mr. and Mrs. 01111000 01101001 01110100!

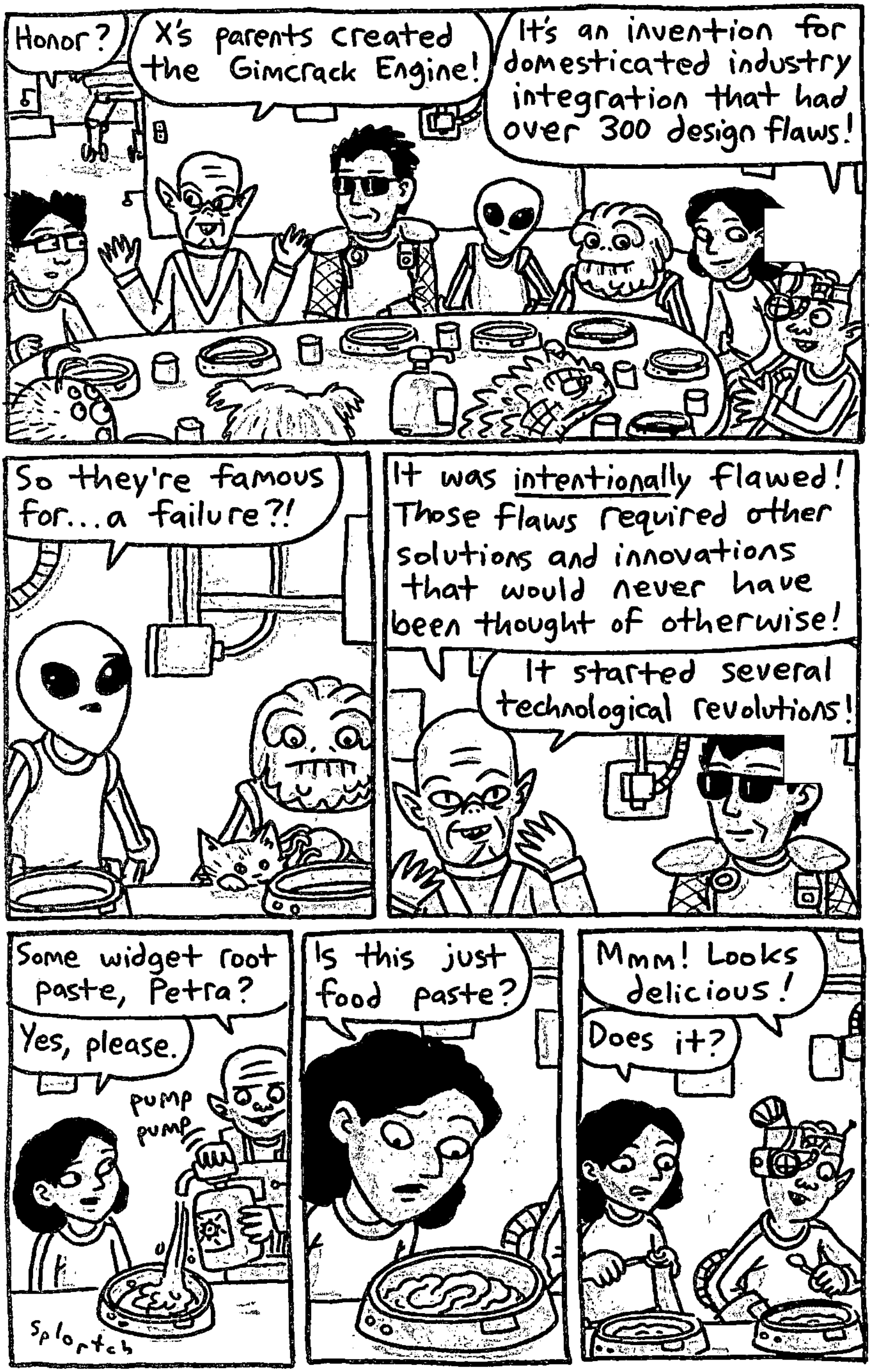
Honor?
X's parents created the Gimcrack Engine!
It's an invention for domesticated industry integration that had over 300 design flaws!
So they're famous for...a failure?!
It was intentionally flawed! Those flaws required other solutions and innovations that would never have been thought of otherwise!
It started several technological revolutions!
Some widget root paste, Petra?
Yes, please.
pump pump
splortch
Is this just food paste?
Mmm! Looks delicious!
Does it?

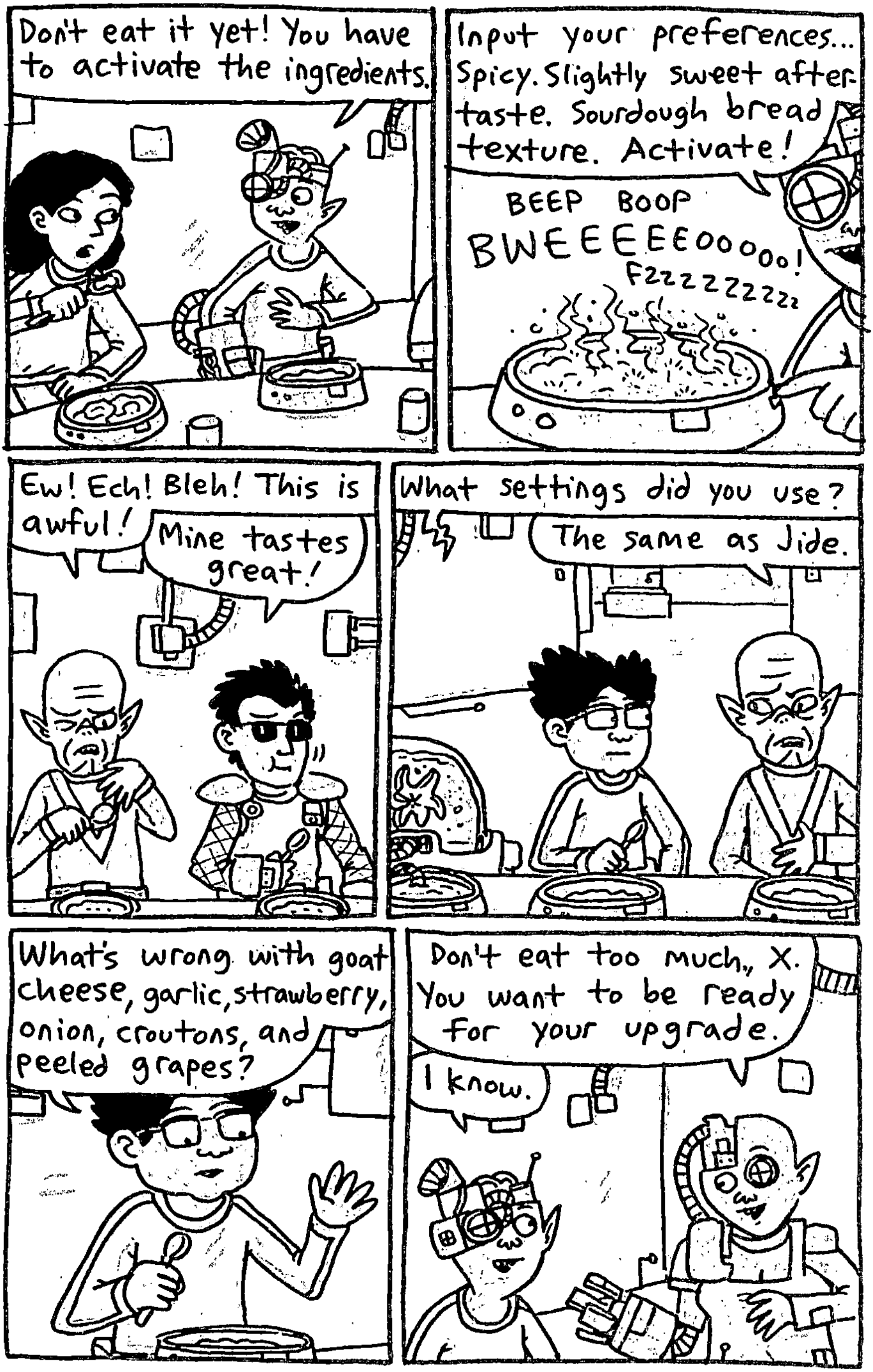
Don't eat it yet! You have to activate the ingredients.
Input your preferences... Spicy. Slightly sweet after-taste. Sourdough bread texture. Activate!
BEEP BOOP
BWEEEEEEoooooo!
Fzzzzzzzzz
Ew! Ech! Bleh! This is awful!
Mine tastes great!
What settings did you use?
The same as Jide.
What's wrong with goat cheese, garlic, strawberry, onion, croutons, and peeled grapes?
Don't eat too much, X. You want to be ready for your upgrade.
I know.

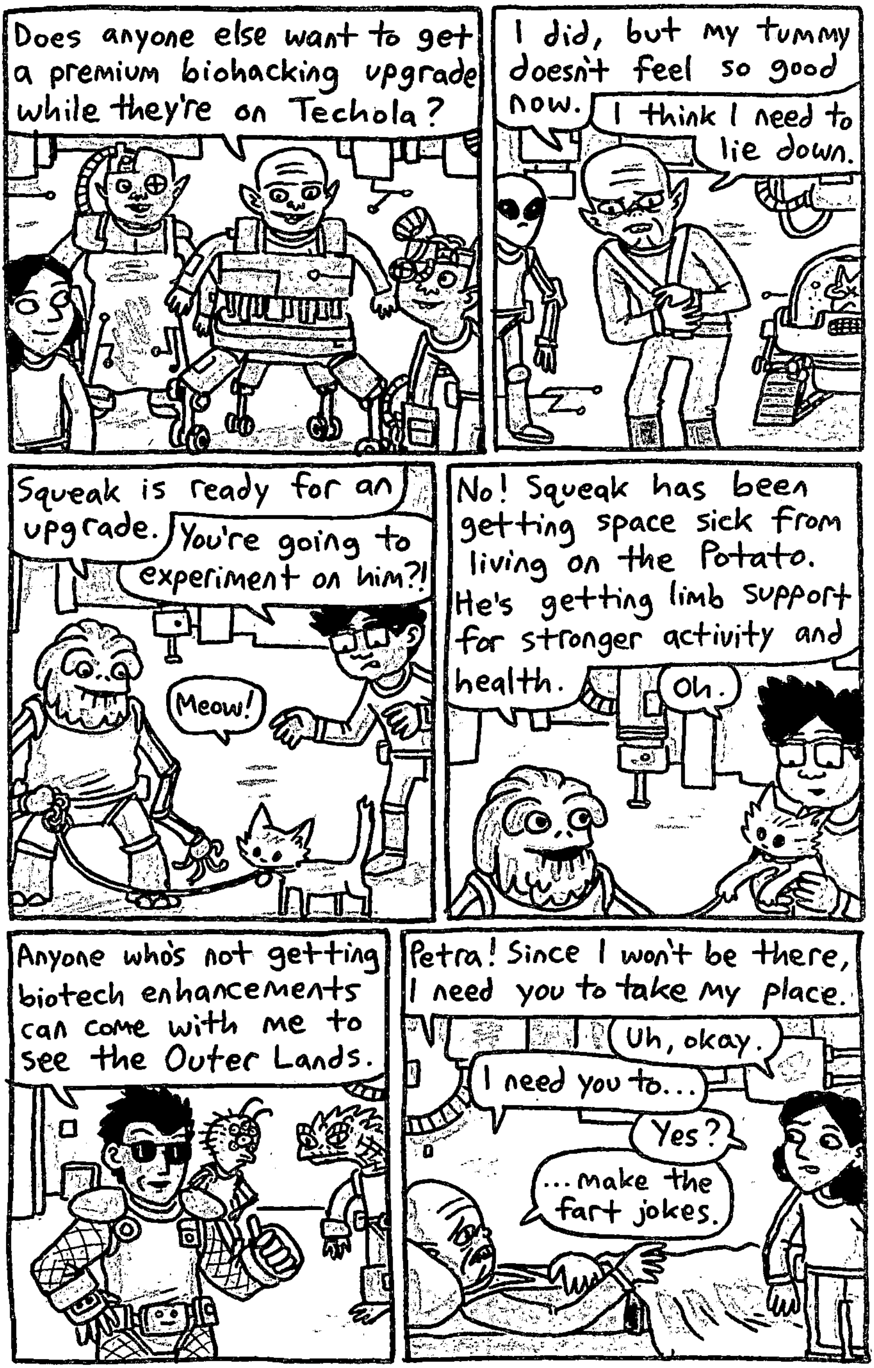
Does anyone else want to get a premium biohacking upgrade while they're on Techola?
I did, but my tummy doesn't feel so good now.
I think I need to lie down.
Squeak is ready for an upgrade.
You're going to experiment on him?!
Meow!
No! Squeak has been getting space sick from living on the Potato. He's getting limb support for stronger activity and health.
Oh.
Anyone who's not getting biotech enhancements can come with me to see the Outer Lands.
Petra! Since I won't be there, I need you to take my place.
Uh, okay.
I need you to...
Yes?
...make the fart jokes.

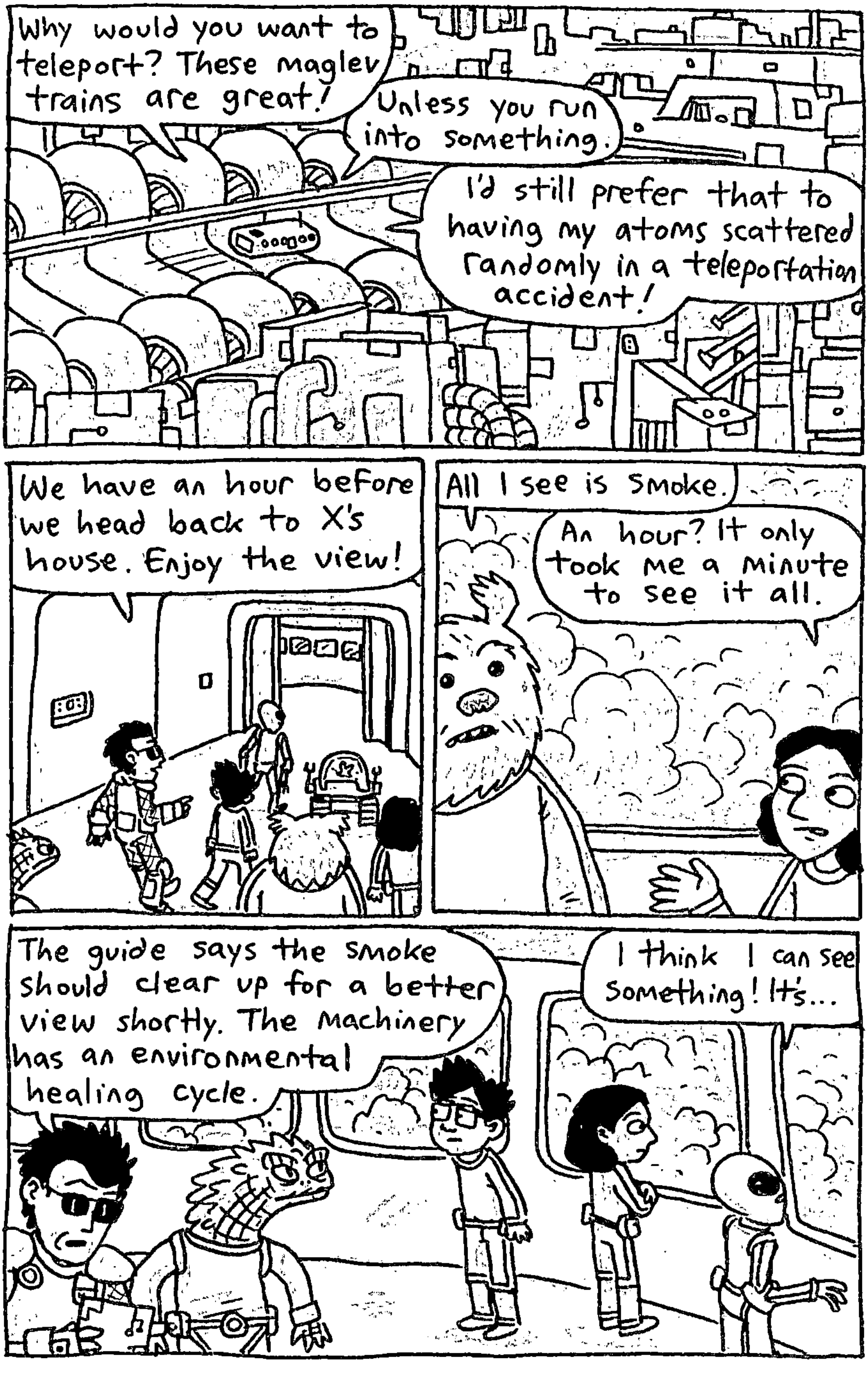
Why would you want to teleport? These maglev trains are great!
Unless you run into something.
I'd still prefer that to having my atoms scattered randomly in a teleportation accident!
We have an hour before we head back to X's house. Enjoy the view!
All I see is smoke.
An hour? It only took me a minute to see it all.
The guide says the smoke should clear up for a better view shortly. The machinery has an environmental healing cycle.
I think I can see something! It's...

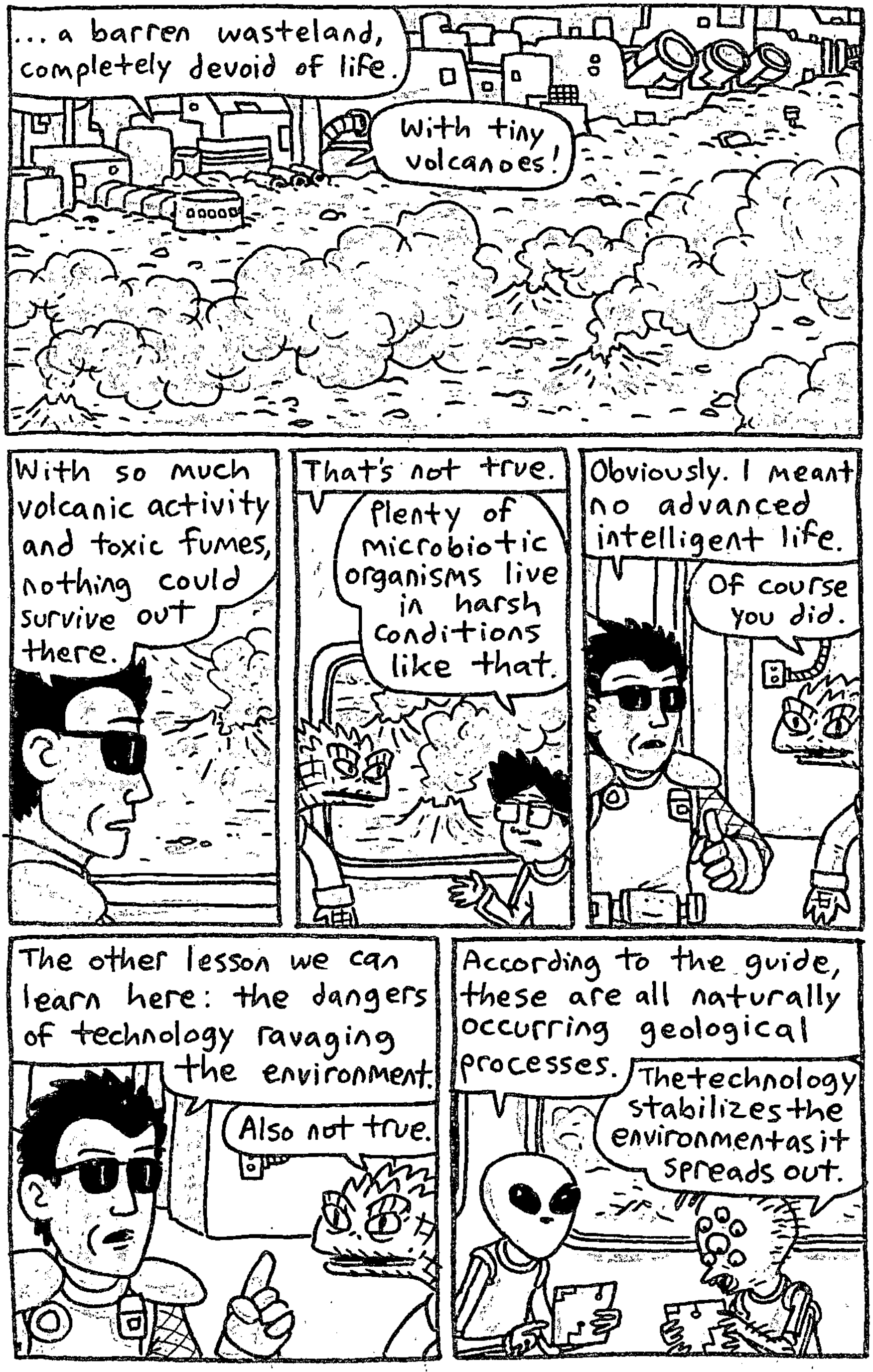
... a barren wasteland, completely devoid of life.
With tiny volcanoes!
With so much volcanic activity and toxic fumes, nothing could survive out there.
That's not true.
Plenty of microbiotic organisms live in harsh conditions like that.
Obviously. I meant no advanced intelligent life.
Of course you did.
The other lesson we can learn here: the dangers of technology ravaging the environment.
Also not true.
According to the guide, these are all naturally occurring geological processes.
The technology stabilizes the environment as it spreads out.

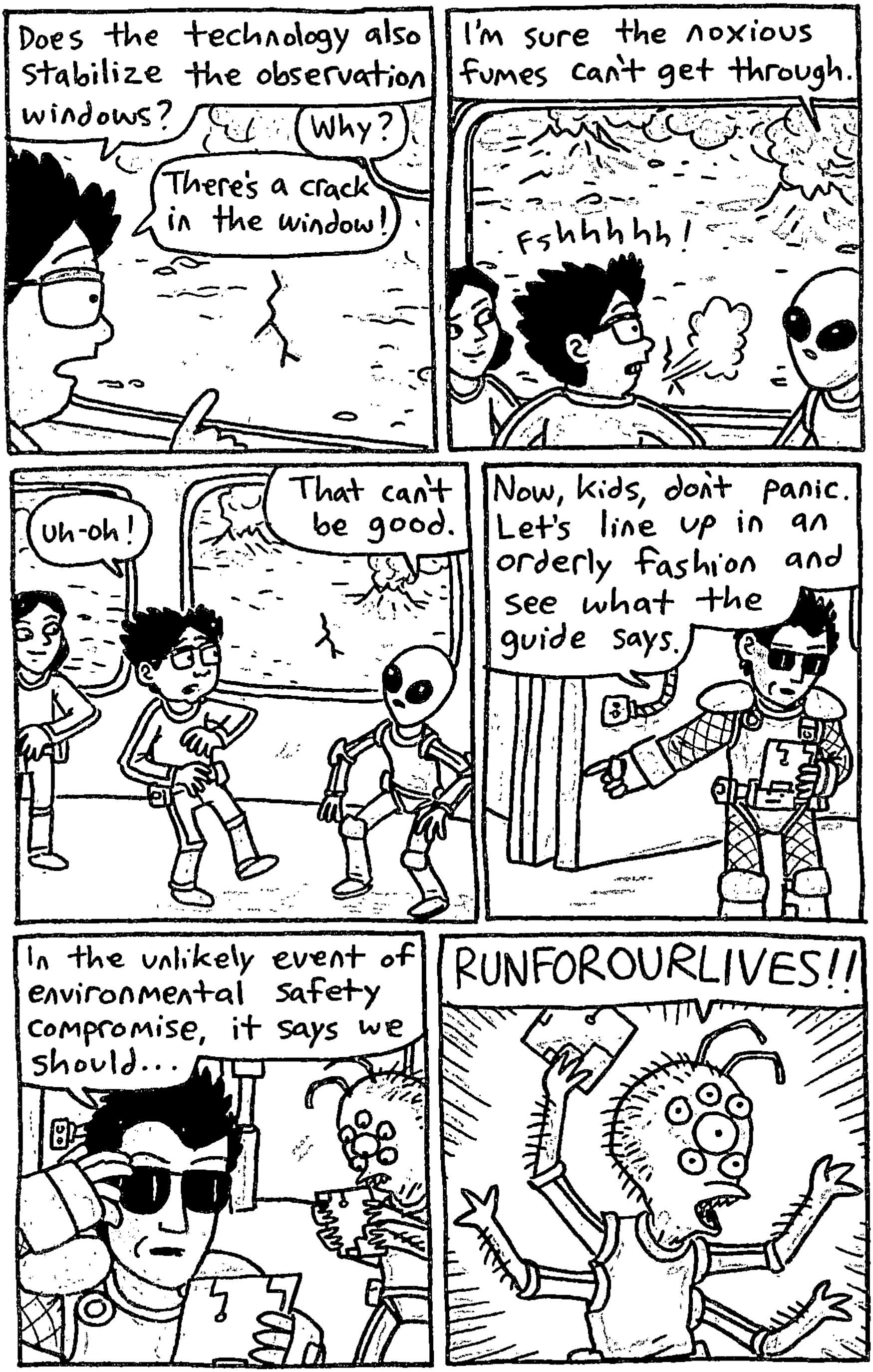
Does the technology also stabilize the observation windows?
Why?
There's a crack in the window!
I'm sure the noxious fumes can't get through.
Fshhhhh!
Uh-oh!
That can't be good.
Now, kids, don't panic. Let's line up in an orderly fashion and see what the guide says.
In the unlikely event of environmental safety compromise, it says we should...
RUNFOROURLIVES!!

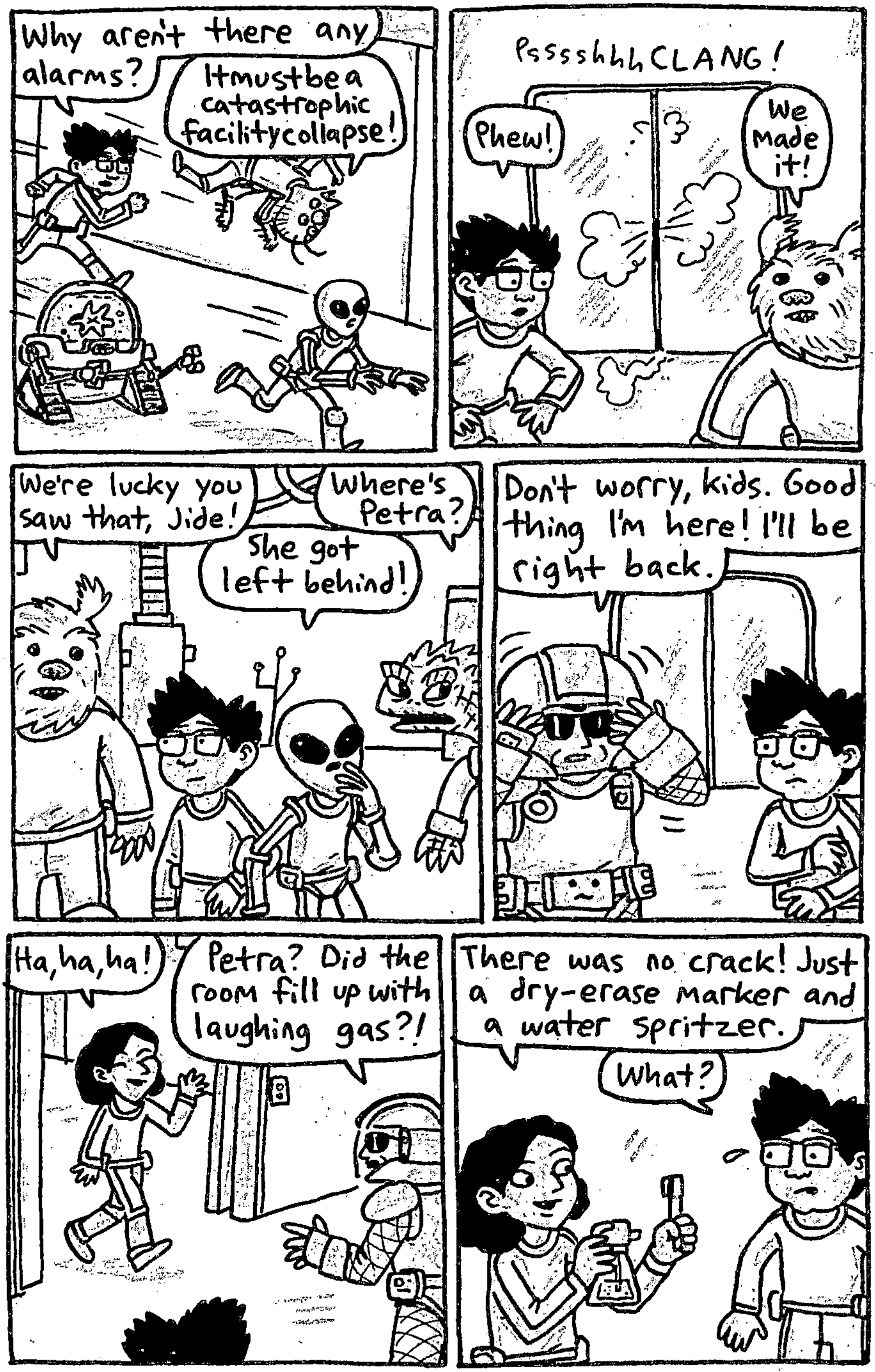

Why aren't there any alarms?
It must be a catastrophic facility collapse!
Psssshhh CLANG!
Phew!
We made it!
We're lucky you saw that, Jide!
Where's Petra?
She got left behind!
Don't worry, kids. Good thing I'm here! I'll be right back.
Ha, ha, ha!
Petra? Did the room fill up with laughing gas?!
There was no crack! Just a dry-erase marker and a water spritzer.
What?

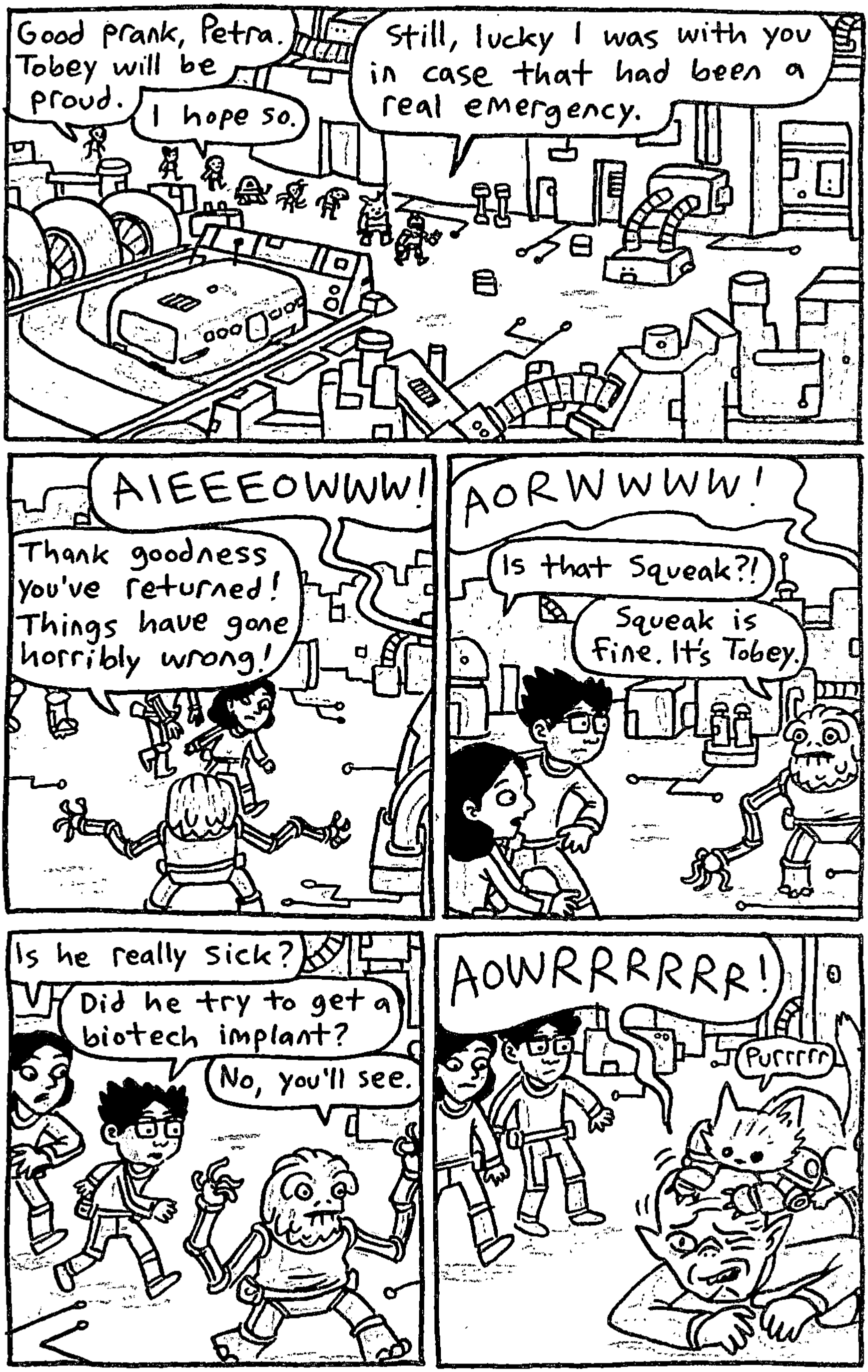
Good prank, Petra. Tobey will be proud.
I hope so.
Still, lucky I was with you in case that had been a real emergency.
AIEEEOWWW!
Thank goodness you've returned! Things have gone horribly wrong!
AORWWWW!
Is that Squeak?!
Squeak is fine. It's Tobey.
Is he really sick?
Did he try to get a biotech implant?
No, you'll see.
AOWRRRRRR!
Purrrrr

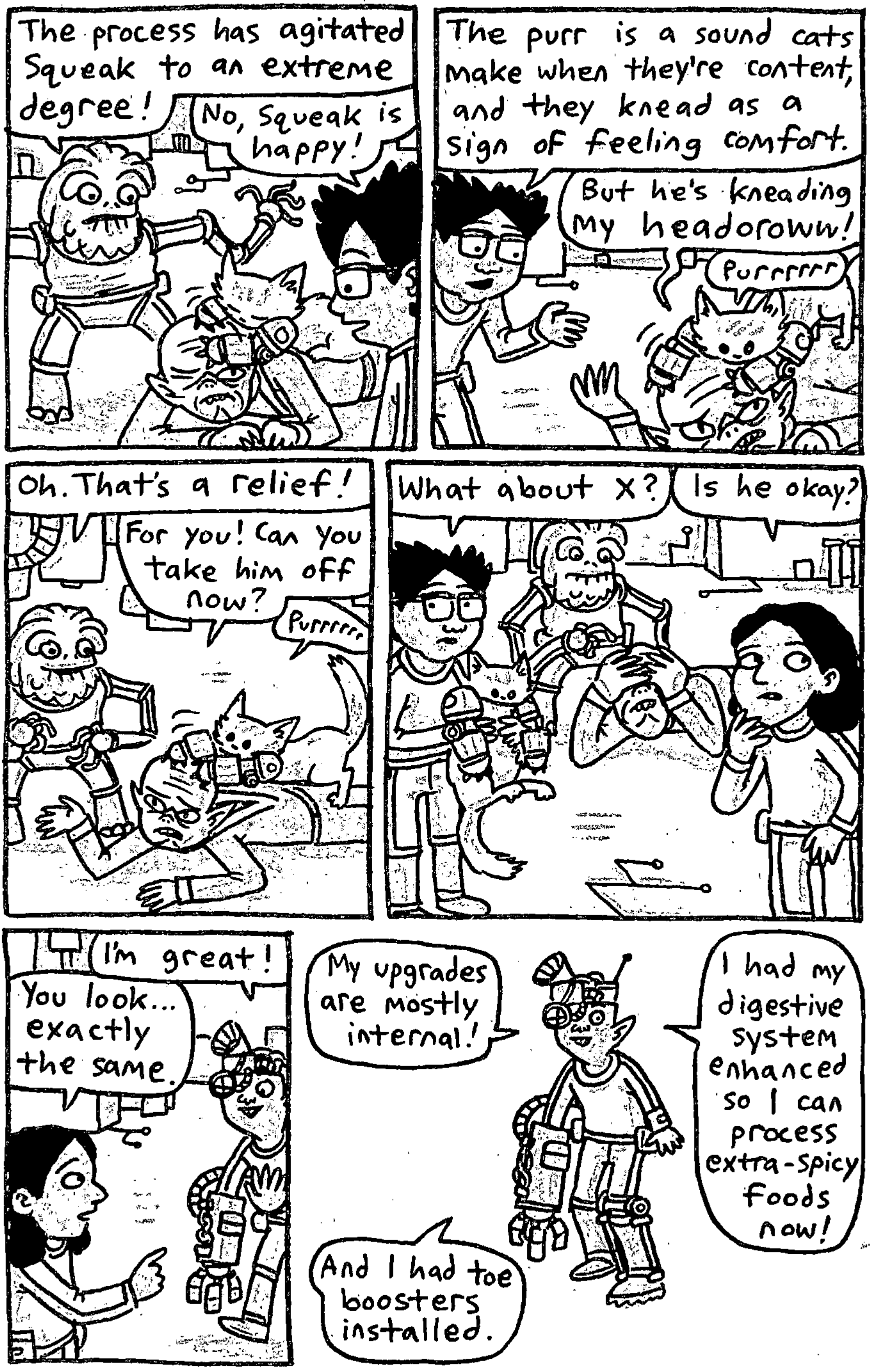
The process has agitated Squeak to an extreme degree!
No, Squeak is happy!
The purr is a sound cats make when they're content, and they knead as a sign of feeling comfort.
But he's kneading my headorowww!
Purrrrrr
Oh. That's a relief!
For you! Can you take him off now?
Purrrrrr
What about X?
Is he okay?
I'm great!
You look... exactly the same.
My upgrades are mostly internal!
I had my digestive system enhanced so I can process extra-spicy foods now!
And I had toe boosters installed.

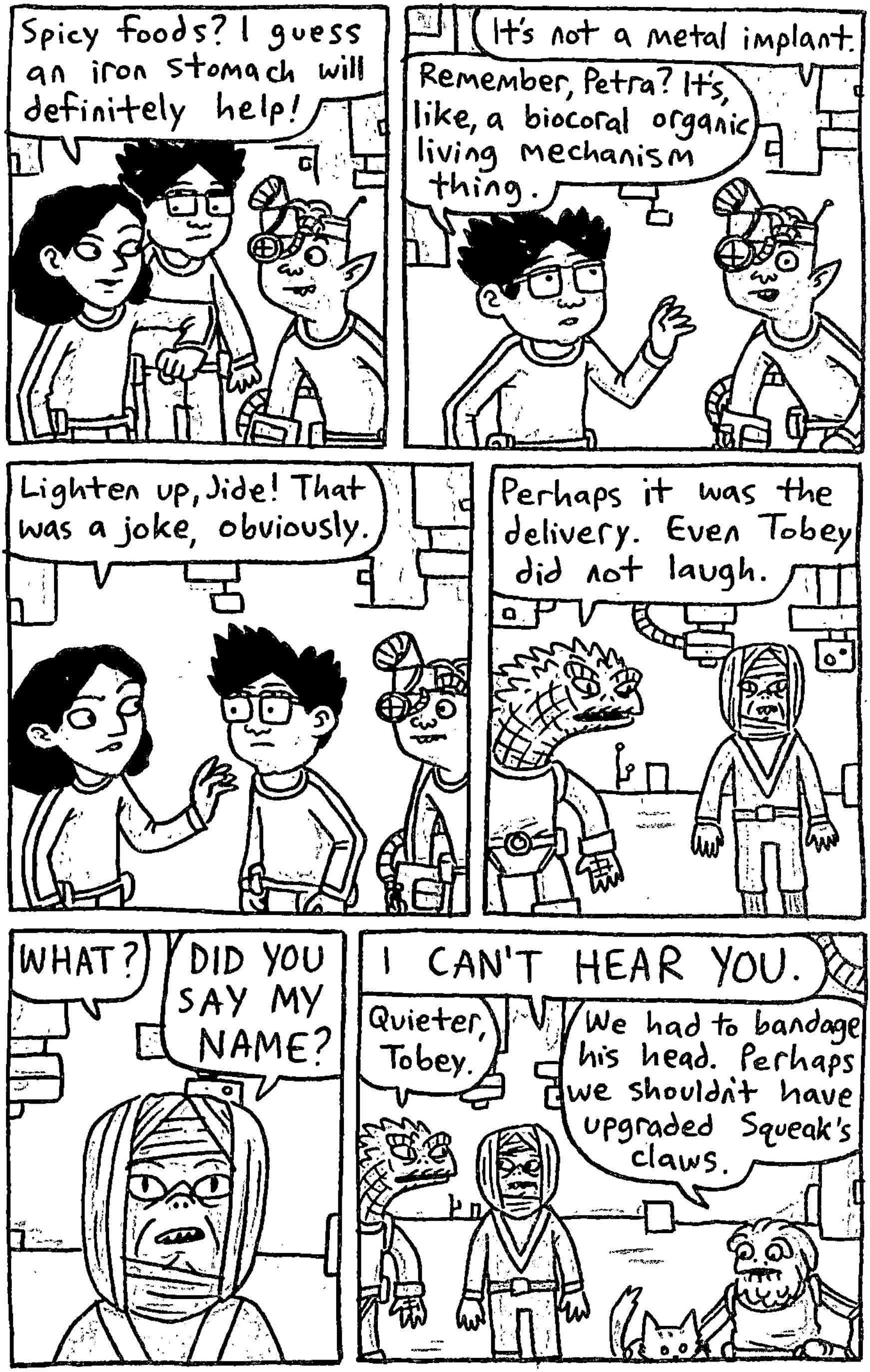

Spicy foods? I guess an iron stomach will definitely help!
It's not a metal implant.
Remember, Petra? It's, like, a biocoral organic living mechanism thing.
Lighten up, Jide! That was a joke, obviously.
Perhaps it was the delivery. Even Tobey did not laugh.
WHAT?
DID YOU SAY MY NAME?
I CAN'T HEAR YOU.
Quieter, Tobey.
We had to bandage his head. Perhaps we shouldn't have upgraded Squeak's claws.

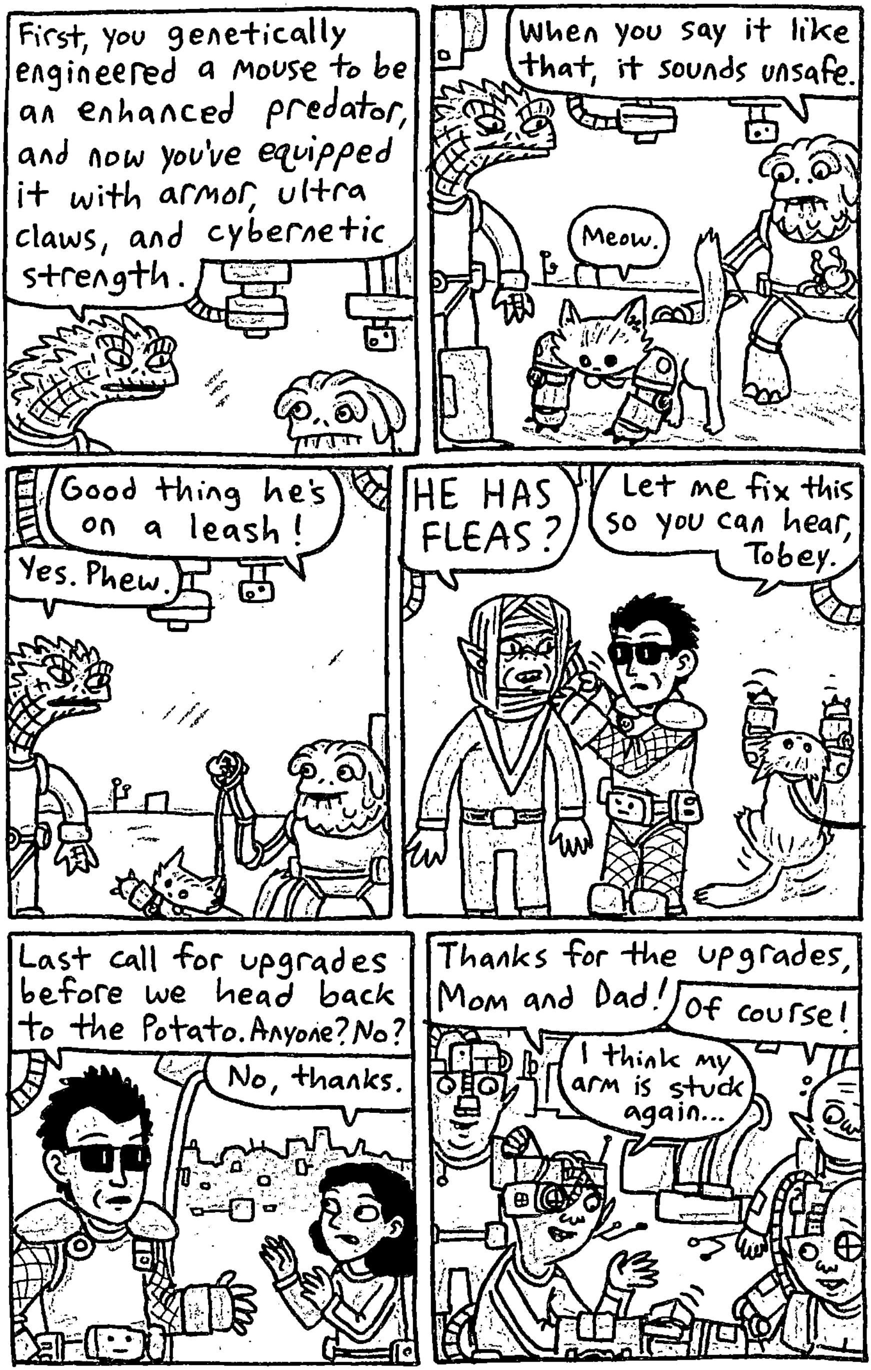
First, you genetically engineered a mouse to be an enhanced predator, and now you've equipped it with armor, ultra claws, and cybernetic strength.
When you say it like that, it sounds unsafe.
Meow.
Good thing he's on a leash!
Yes. Phew.
HE HAS FLEAS?
Let me fix this so you can hear, Tobey.
Last call for upgrades before we head back to the Potato. Anyone? No?
No, thanks.
Thanks for the upgrades, Mom and Dad!
Of course!
I think my arm is stuck again...

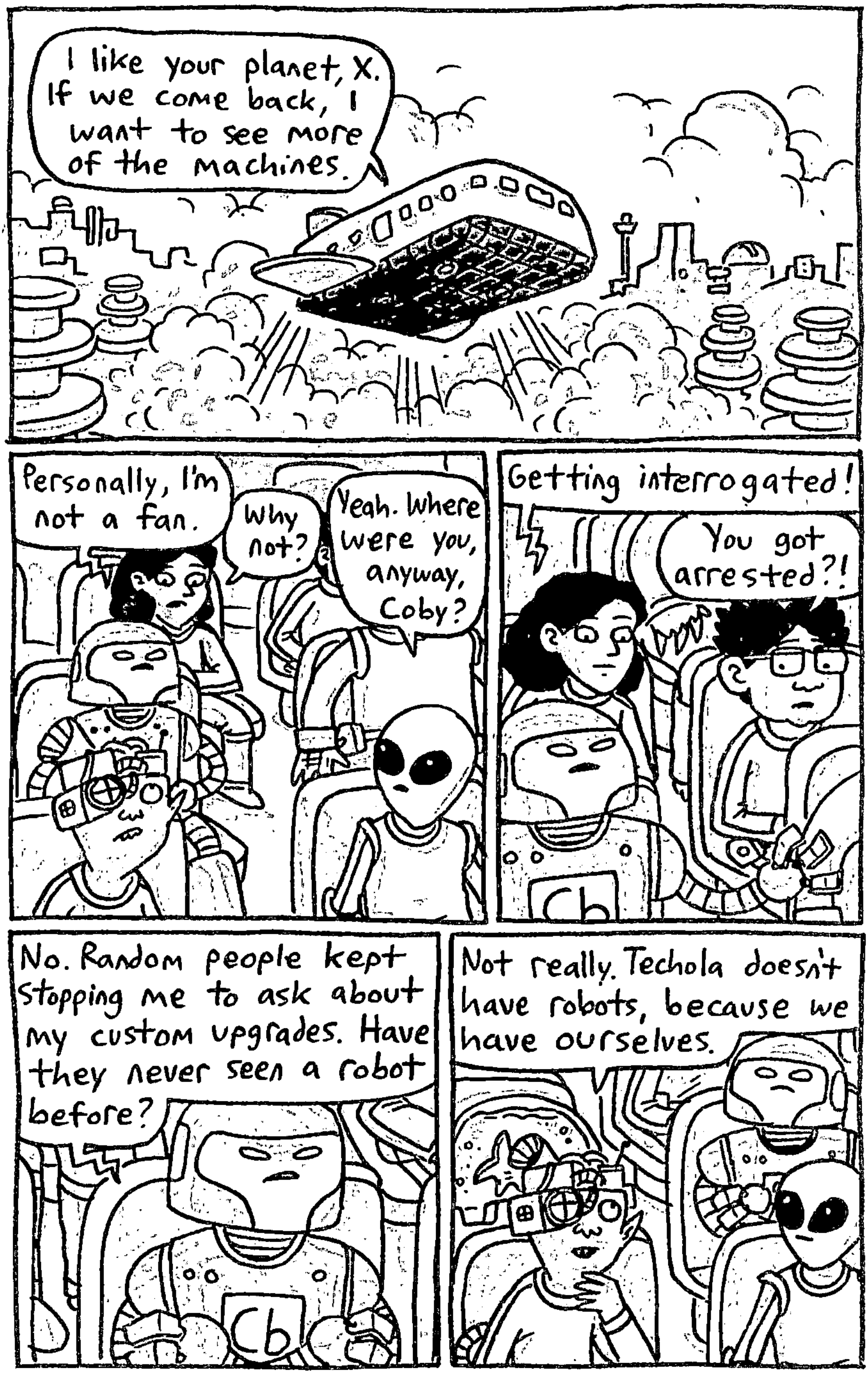
I like your planet, X. If we come back, I want to see more of the machines.
Personally, I'm not a fan.
Why not?
Yeah. Where were you, anyway, Coby?
Getting interrogated!
You got arrested?!
No. Random people kept stopping me to ask about my custom upgrades. Have they never seen a robot before?
Not really. Techola doesn't have robots, because we have ourselves.

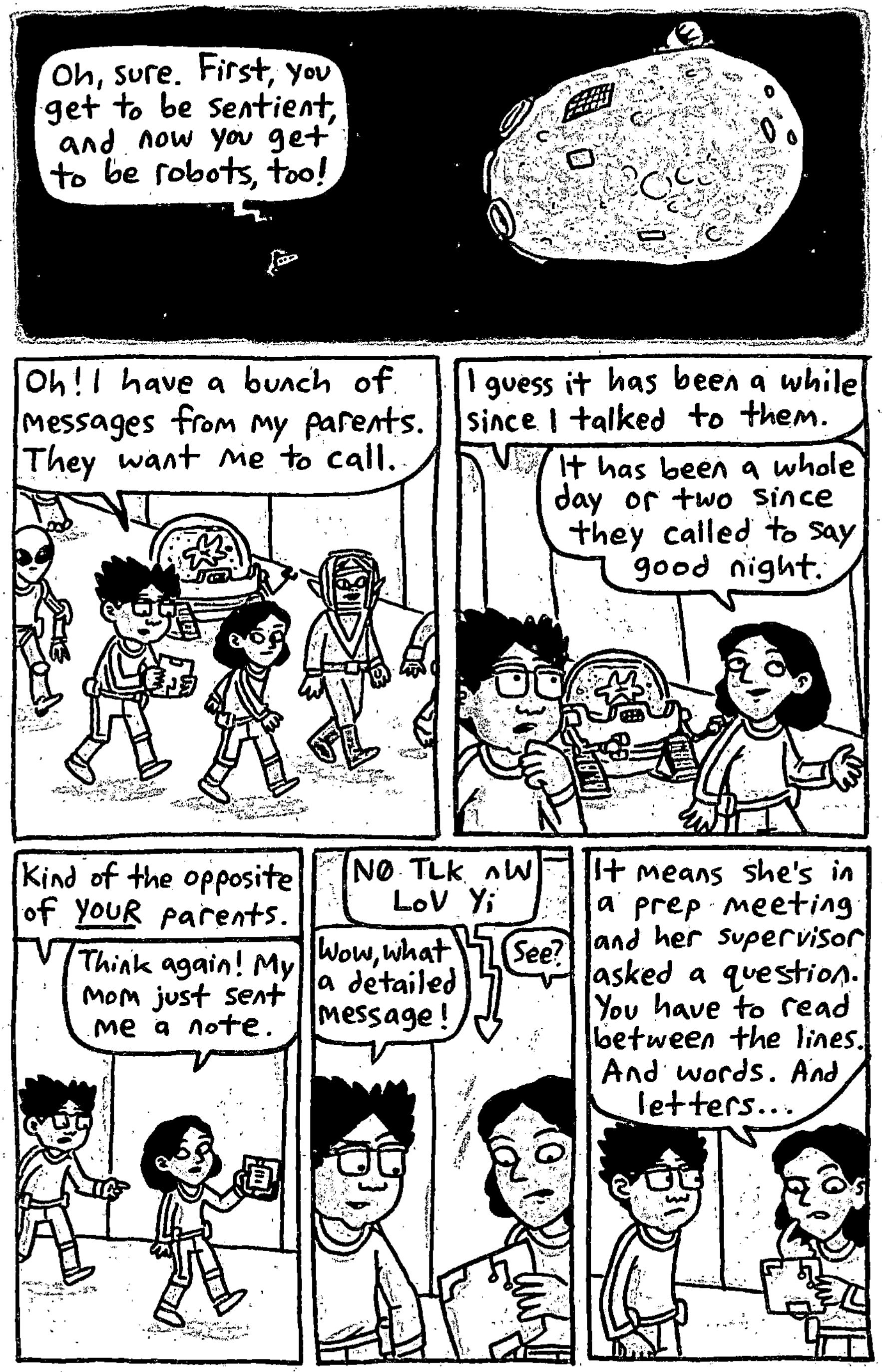
Oh, sure. First, you get to be sentient, and now you get to be robots, too!
Oh! I have a bunch of messages from my parents. They want me to call.
I guess it has been a while since I talked to them.
It has been a whole day or two since they called to say good night.
Kind of the opposite of YOUR parents.
Think again! My mom just sent me a note.
NO TLK NW LoV Yi
Wow, what a detailed message!
See?
It means she's in a prep meeting and her supervisor asked a question. You have to read between the lines. And words. And letters...

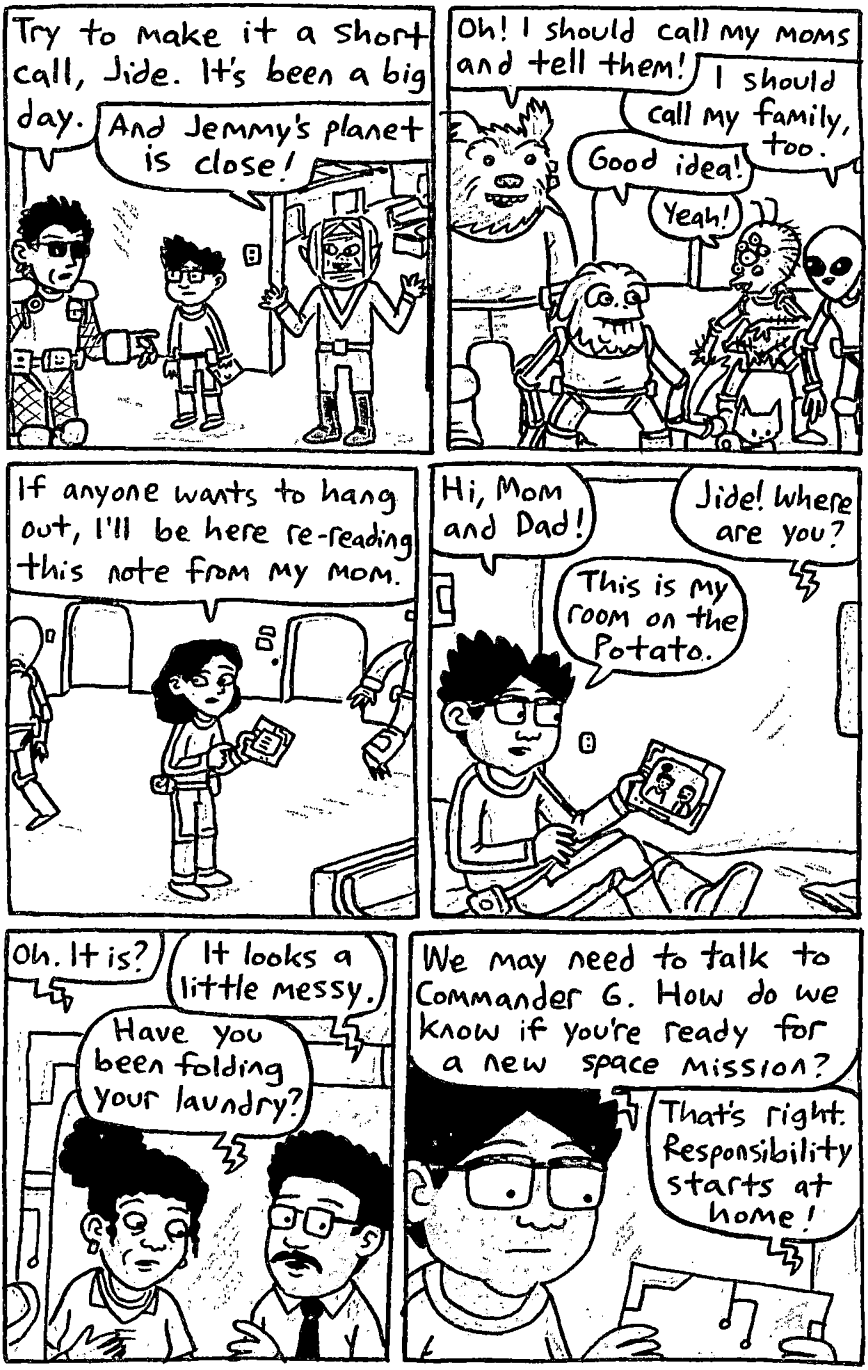
Try to make it a short call, Jide. It's been a big day.
And Jemmy's planet is close!
Oh! I should call my moms and tell them!
I should call my family, too.
Good idea!
Yeah!
If anyone wants to hang out, I'll be here re-reading this note from my mom.
Hi, Mom and Dad!
Jide! Where are you?
This is my room on the Potato.
Oh. It is?
It looks a little messy.
Have you been folding your laundry?
We may need to talk to Commander G. How do we know if you're ready for a new space mission?
That's right. Responsibility starts at home!

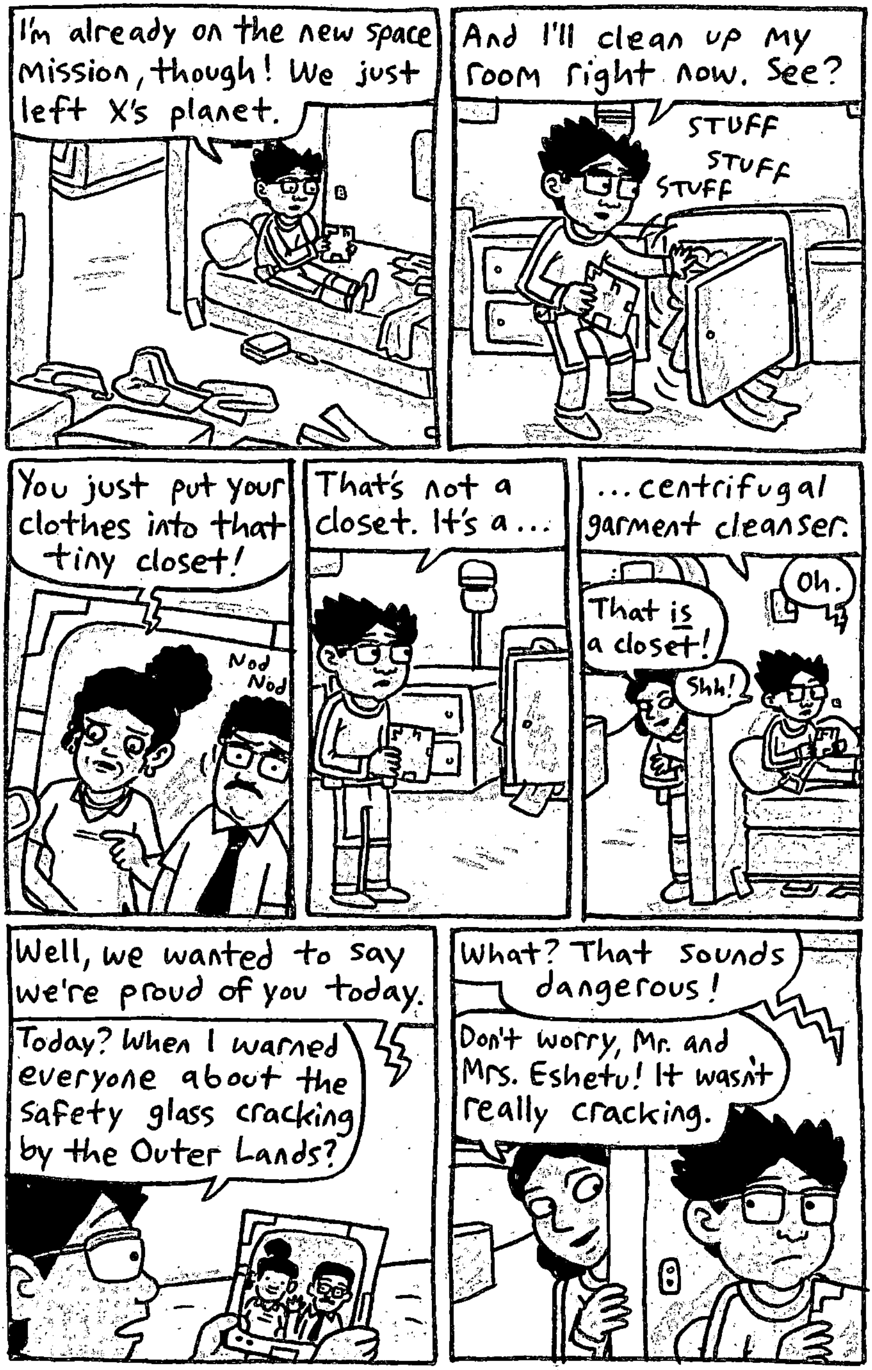
I'm already on the new space mission, though! We just left X's planet.
And I'll clean up my room right now. See?
STUFF
STUFF
STUFF
You just put your clothes into that tiny closet!
Nod
Nod
That's not a closet. It's a...
...centrifugal garment cleanser.
That is a closet!
Oh.
Shh!
Well, we wanted to say we're proud of you today.
Today? When I warned everyone about the safety glass cracking by the Outer Lands?
What? That sounds dangerous!
Don't worry, Mr. and Mrs. Eshetu! It wasn't really cracking.

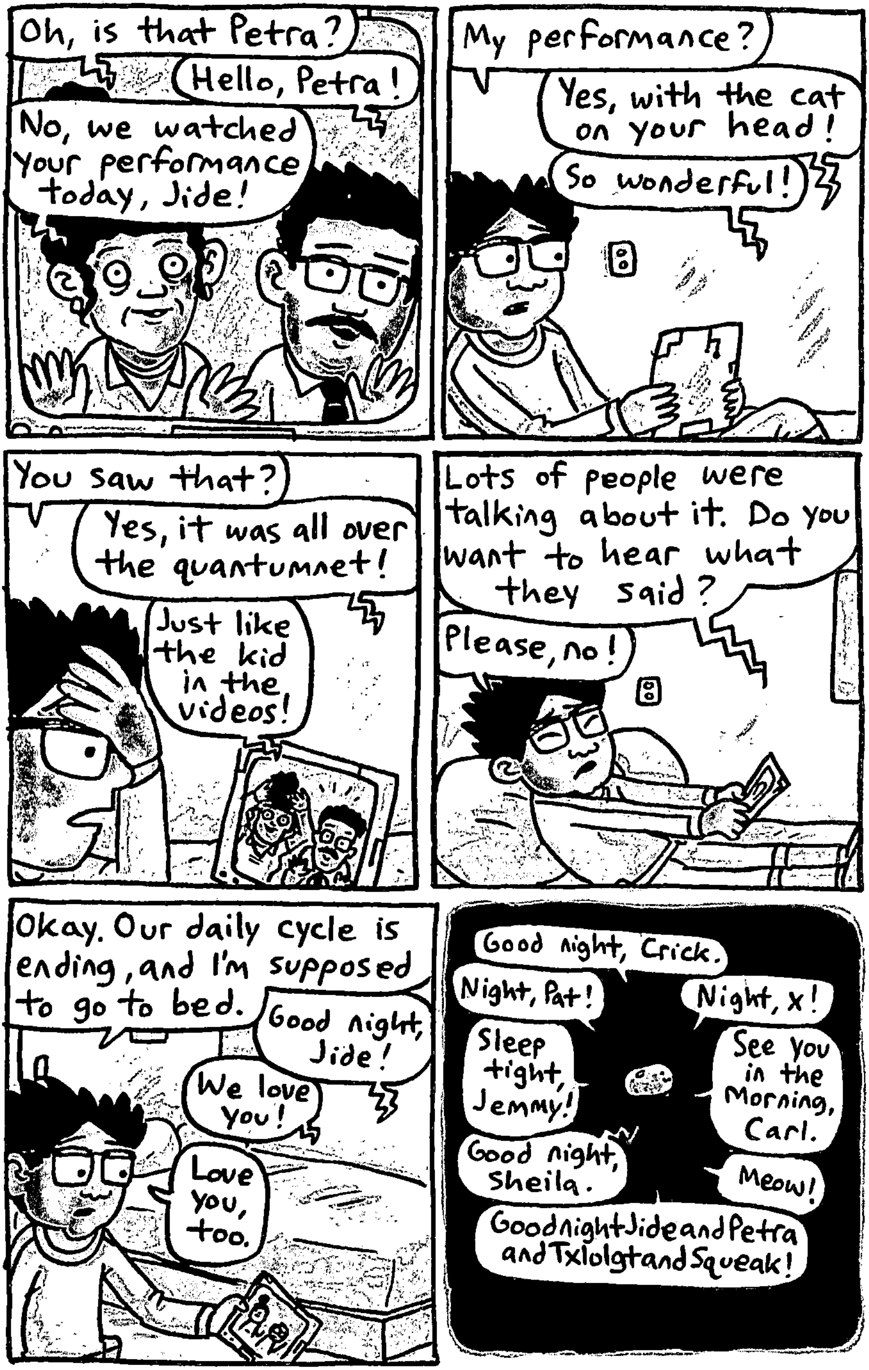
Oh, is that Petra?
Hello, Petra!
No, we watched your performance today, Jide!
My performance?
Yes, with the cat on your head!
So wonderful!
You saw that?
Yes, it was all over the quantumnet!
Just like the kid in the videos!
Lots of people were talking about it. Do you want to hear what they said?
Please, no!
Okay. Our daily cycle is ending, and I'm supposed to go to bed.
Good night, Jide!
We love you!
Love you, too.
Good night, Crick.
Night, Pat!
Night, X!
Sleep tight, Jemmy!
See you in the morning, Carl.
Good night, Sheila.
Meow!
Goodnight Jide and Petra and Txlolgt and Squeak!

LIVING LARGE

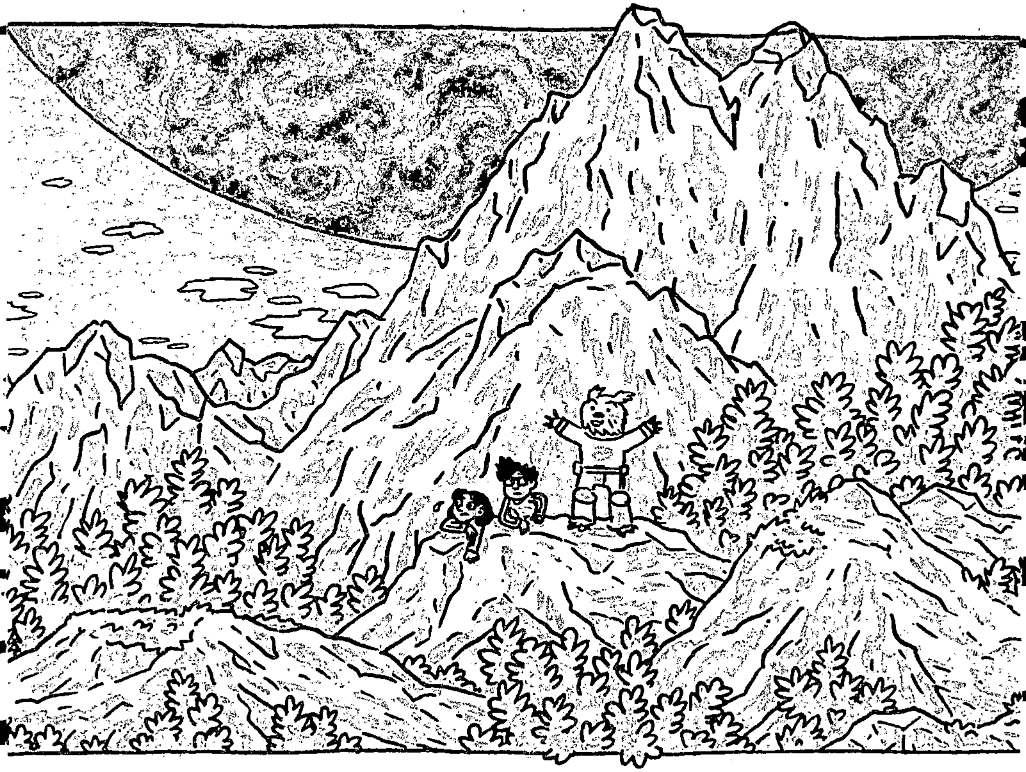

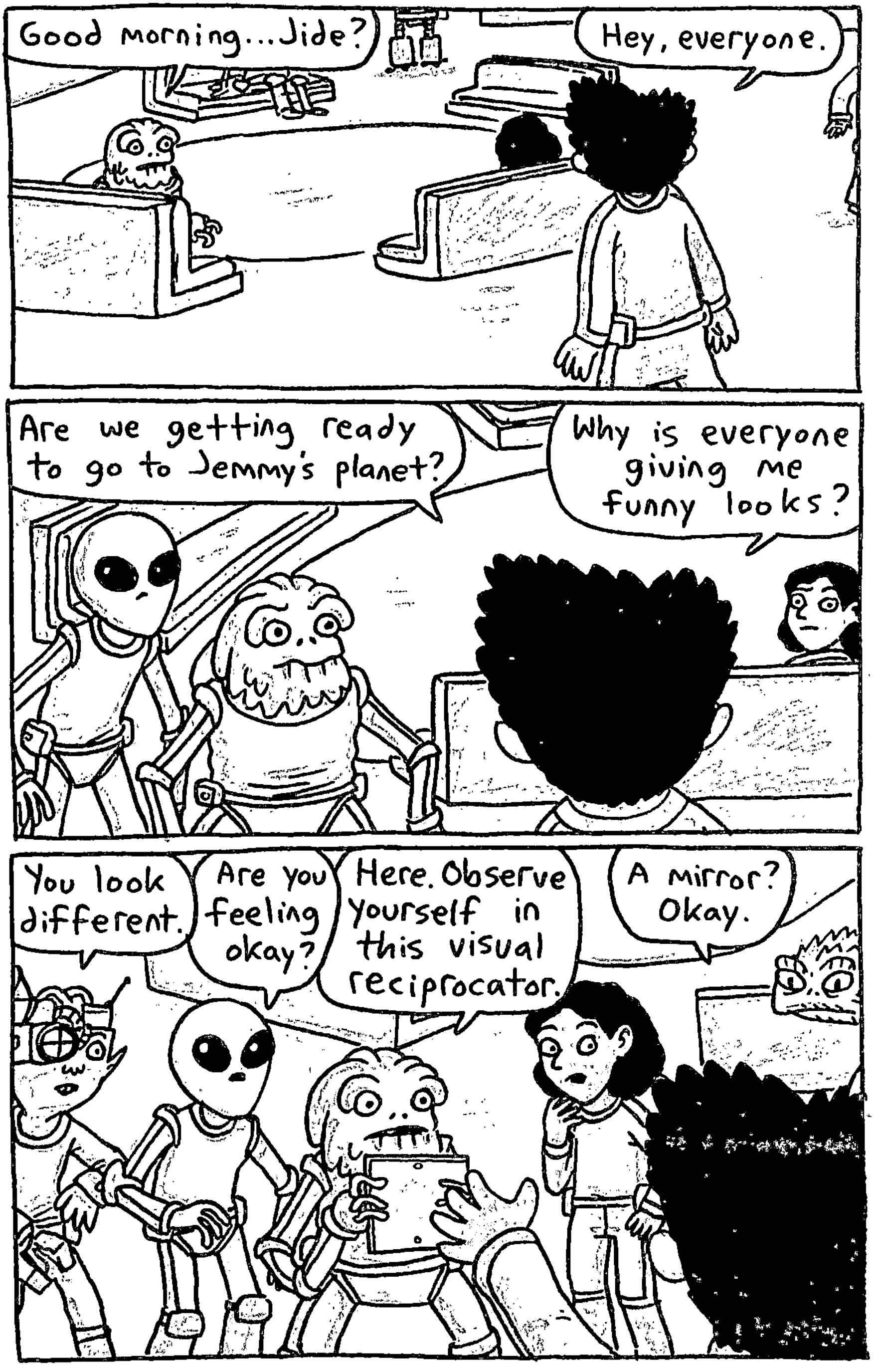
Good morning...Jide?
Hey, everyone.
Are we getting ready to go to Jemmy's planet?
Why is everyone giving me funny looks?
You look different.
Are you feeling okay?
Here. Observe yourself in this visual reciprocator.
A mirror? Okay.

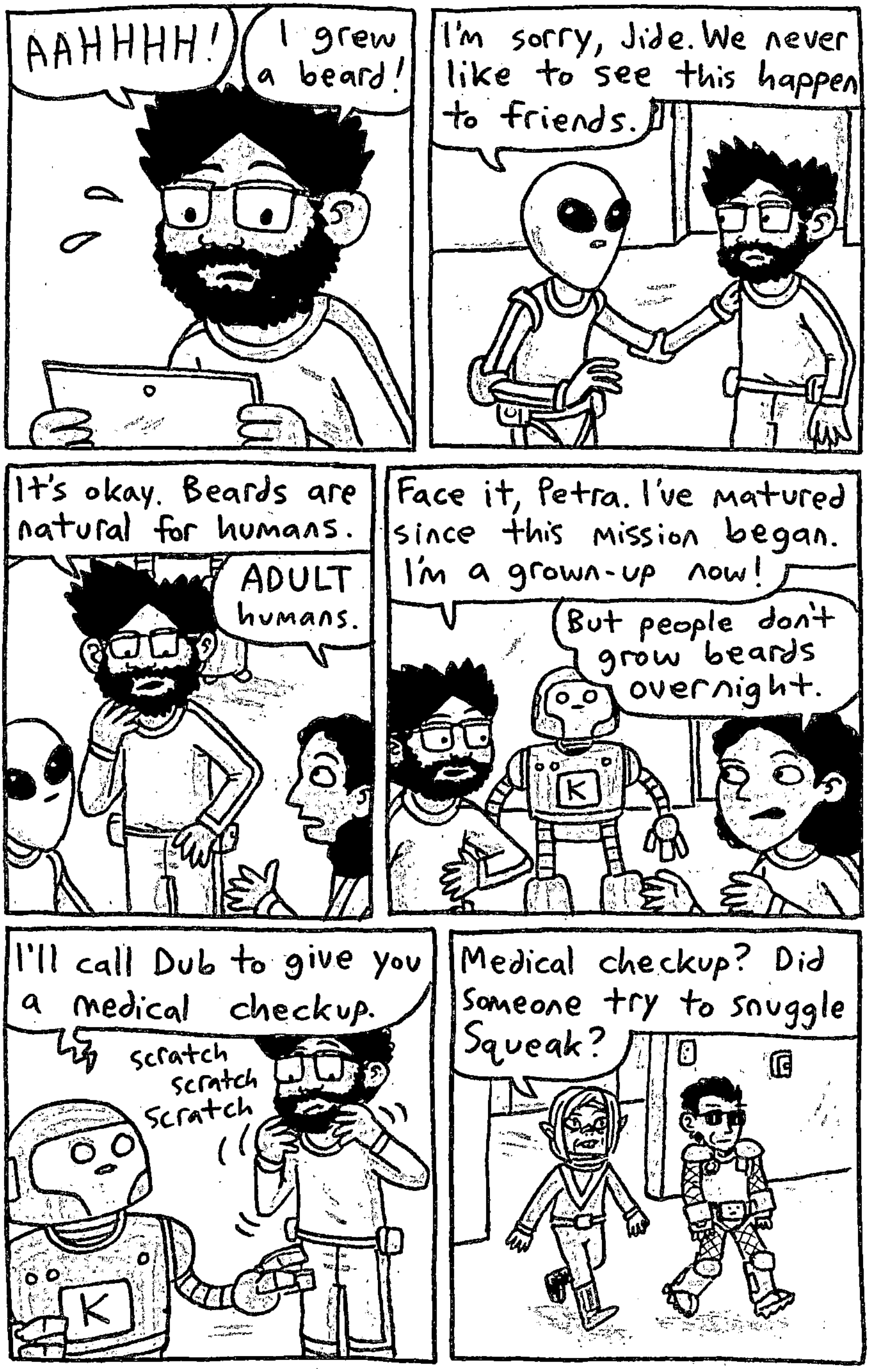
AAHHHH!
I grew a beard!
I'm sorry, Jide. We never like to see this happen to friends.
It's okay. Beards are natural for humans.
ADULT humans.
Face it, Petra. I've matured since this mission began. I'm a grown-up now!
But people don't grow beards overnight.
I'll call Dub to give you a medical checkup.
scratch scratch scratch
Medical checkup? Did someone try to snuggle Squeak?

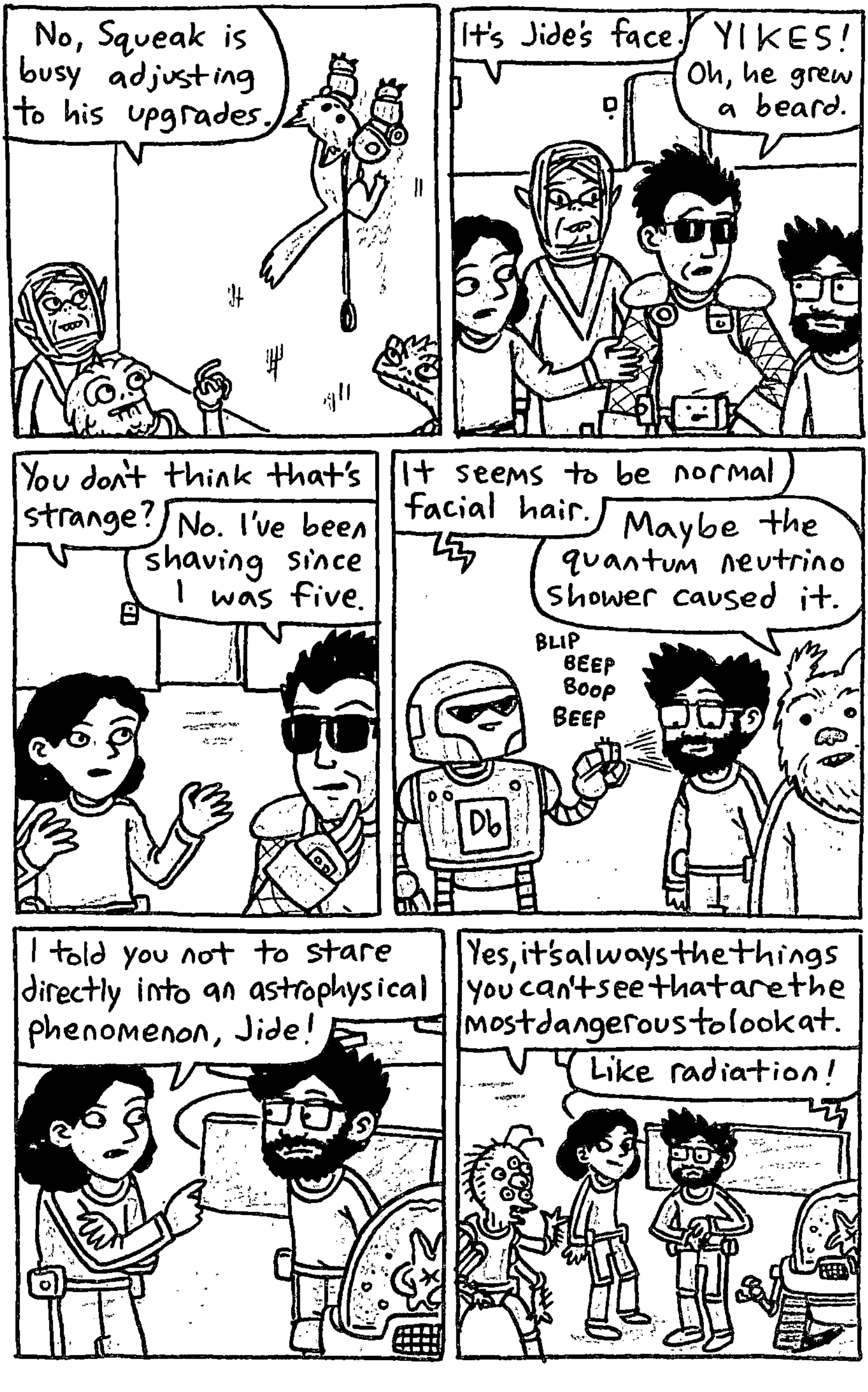
No, Squeak is busy adjusting to his upgrades.
It's Jide's face.
YIKES! Oh, he grew a beard.
You don't think that's strange?
No. I've been shaving since I was five.
It seems to be normal facial hair.
Maybe the quantum neutrino shower caused it.
BLIP BEEP BOOP BEEP
I told you not to stare directly into an astrophysical phenomenon, Jide!
Yes, it's always the things you can't see that are the most dangerous to look at.
Like radiation!

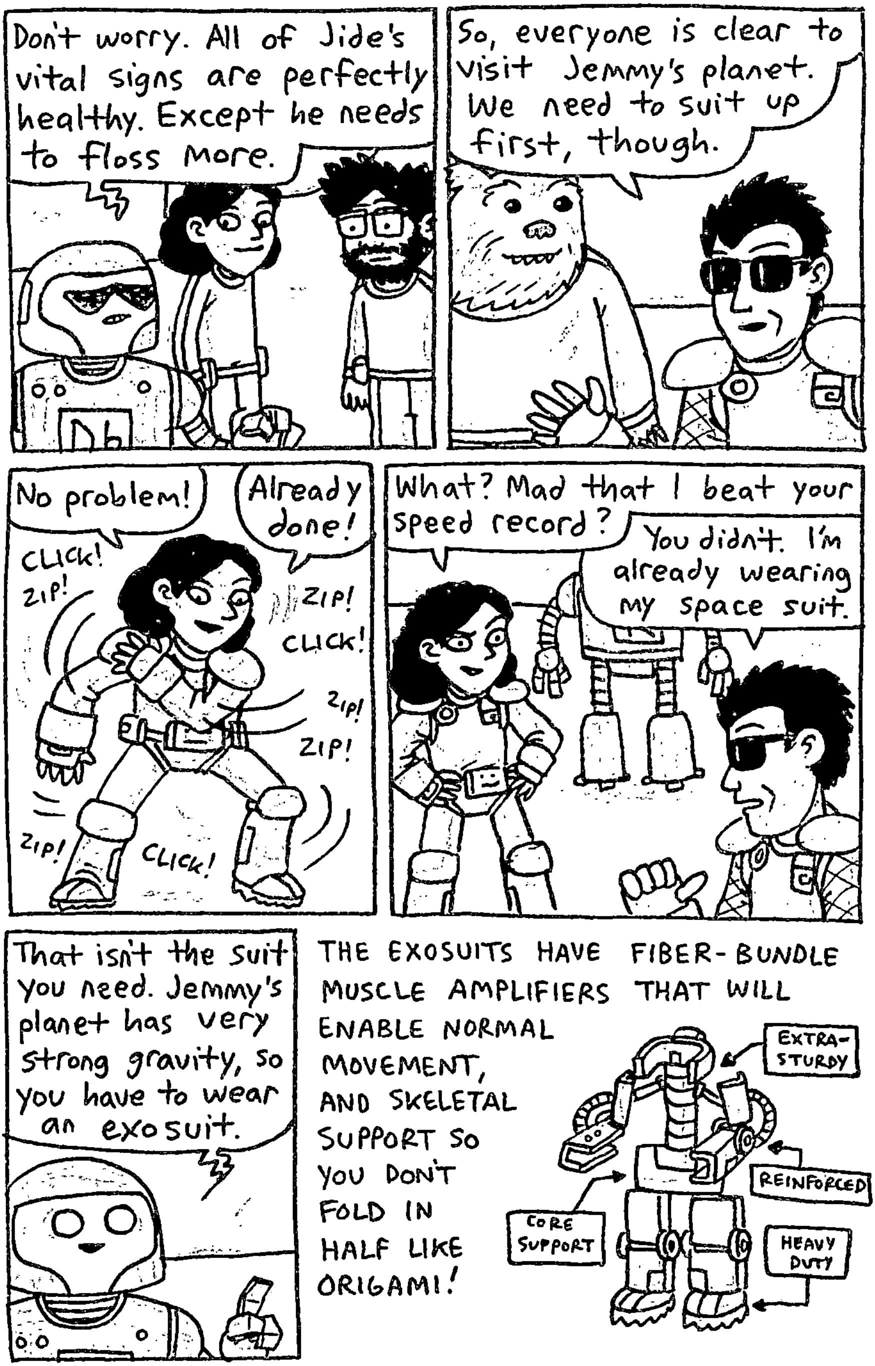
Don't worry. All of Jide's vital signs are perfectly healthy. Except he needs to floss more.
So, everyone is clear to visit Jemmy's planet. We need to suit up first, though.
No problem!
Already done!
CLICK!
ZIP!
ZIP!
CLICK!
ZIP!
ZIP!
ZIP!
CLICK!
What? Mad that I beat your speed record?
You didn't. I'm already wearing my space suit.
That isn't the suit you need. Jemmy's planet has very strong gravity, so you have to wear an exosuit.
THE EXOSUITS HAVE FIBER-BUNDLE MUSCLE AMPLIFIERS THAT WILL ENABLE NORMAL MOVEMENT, AND SKELETAL SUPPORT SO YOU DON'T FOLD IN HALF LIKE ORIGAMI!
EXTRA-STURDY
REINFORCED
CORE SUPPORT
HEAVY DUTY

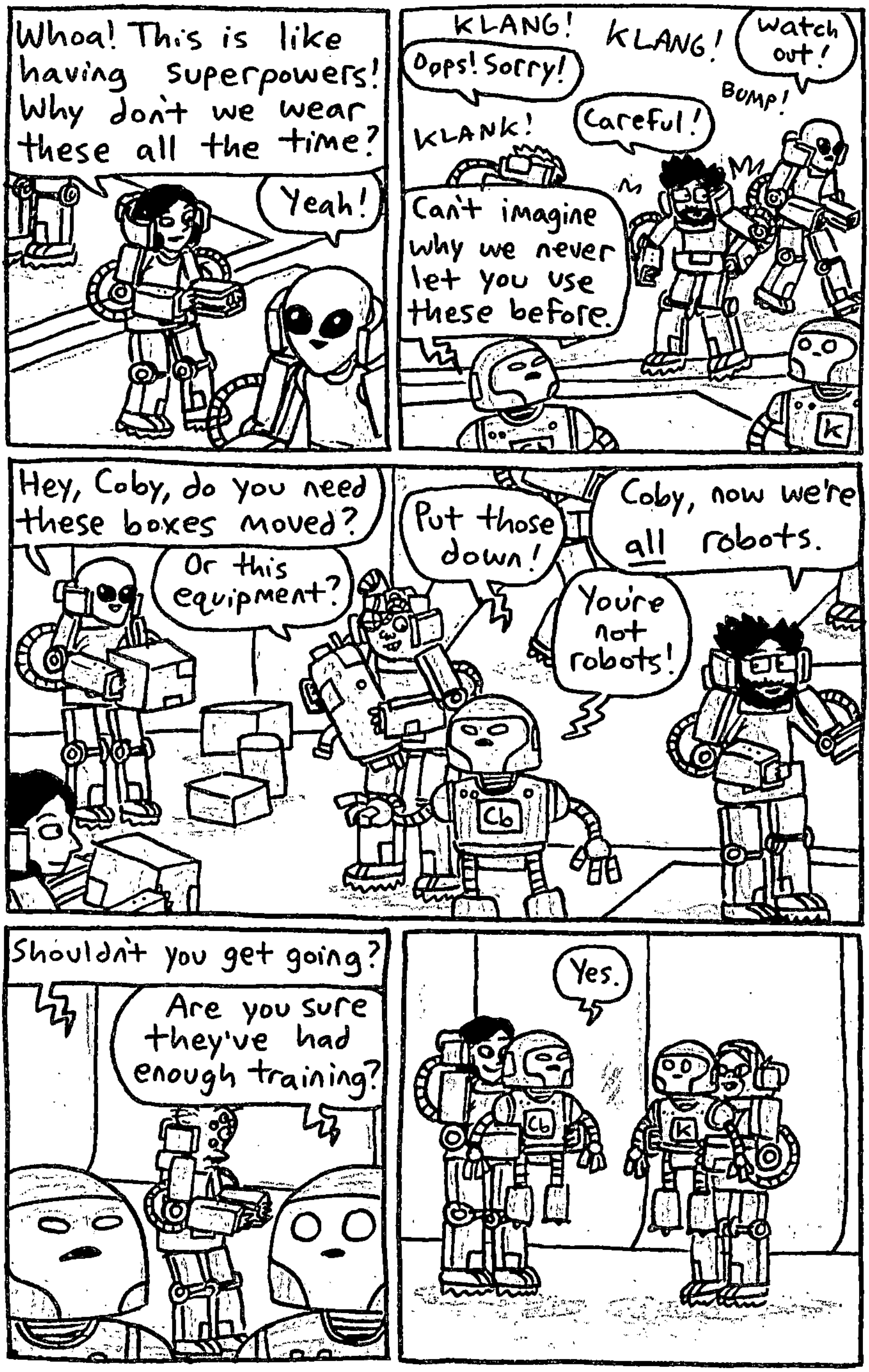

Whoa! This is like having superpowers! Why don't we wear these all the time?
Yeah!
KLANG!
KLANG!
Watch out!
Oops! Sorry!
BUMP!
KLANK!
Careful!
Can't imagine why we never let you use these before.
Hey, Coby, do you need these boxes moved?
Or this equipment?
Put those down!
Coby, now we're all robots.
You're not robots!
Shouldn't you get going?
Are you sure they've had enough training?
Yes.

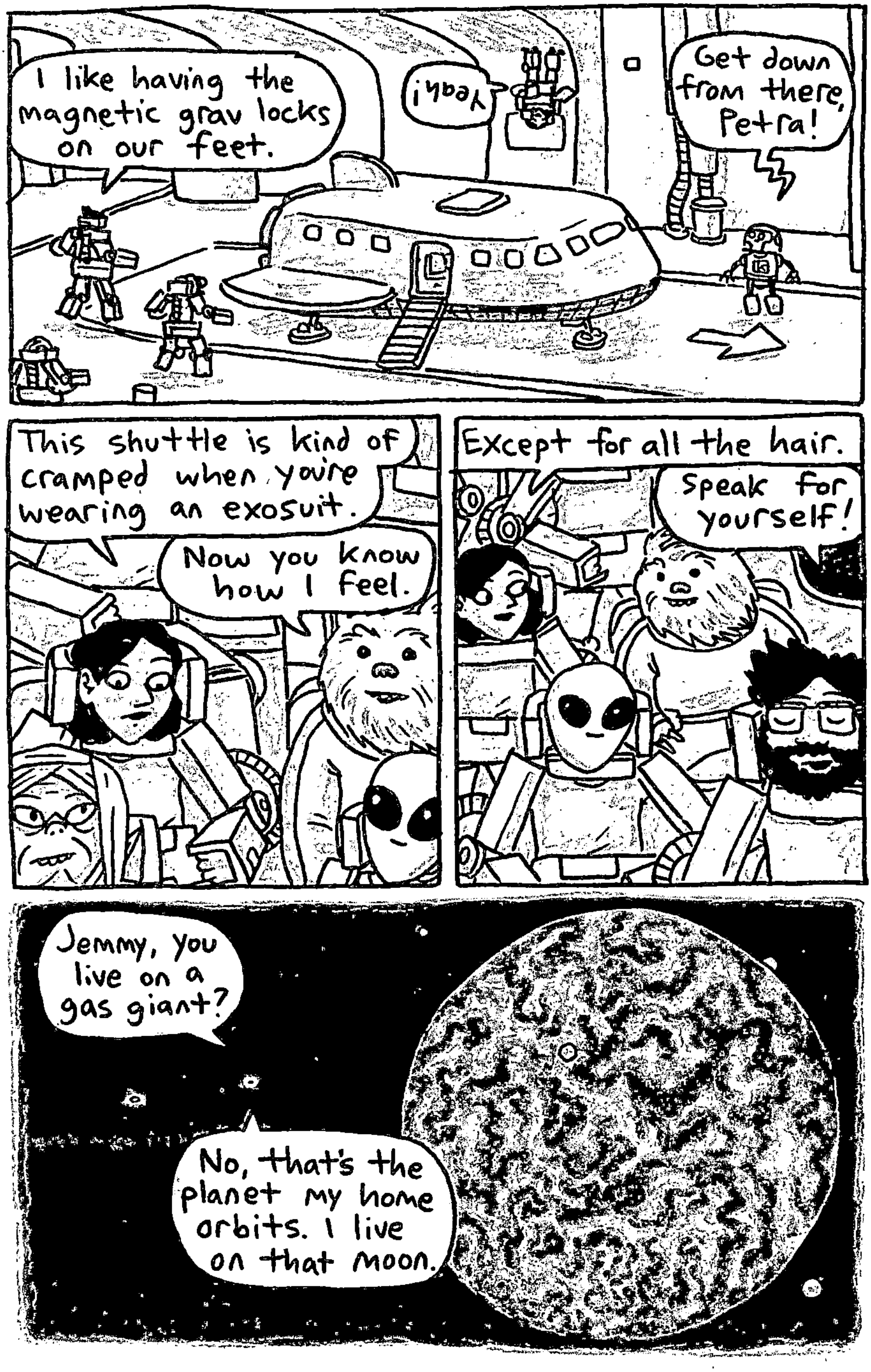
I like having the magnetic grav locks on our feet.
Yeah!
Get down from there, Petra!
This shuttle is kind of cramped when you're wearing an exosuit.
Now you know how I feel.
Except for all the hair.
Speak for yourself!
Jemmy, you live on a gas giant?
No, that's the planet my home orbits. I live on that moon.

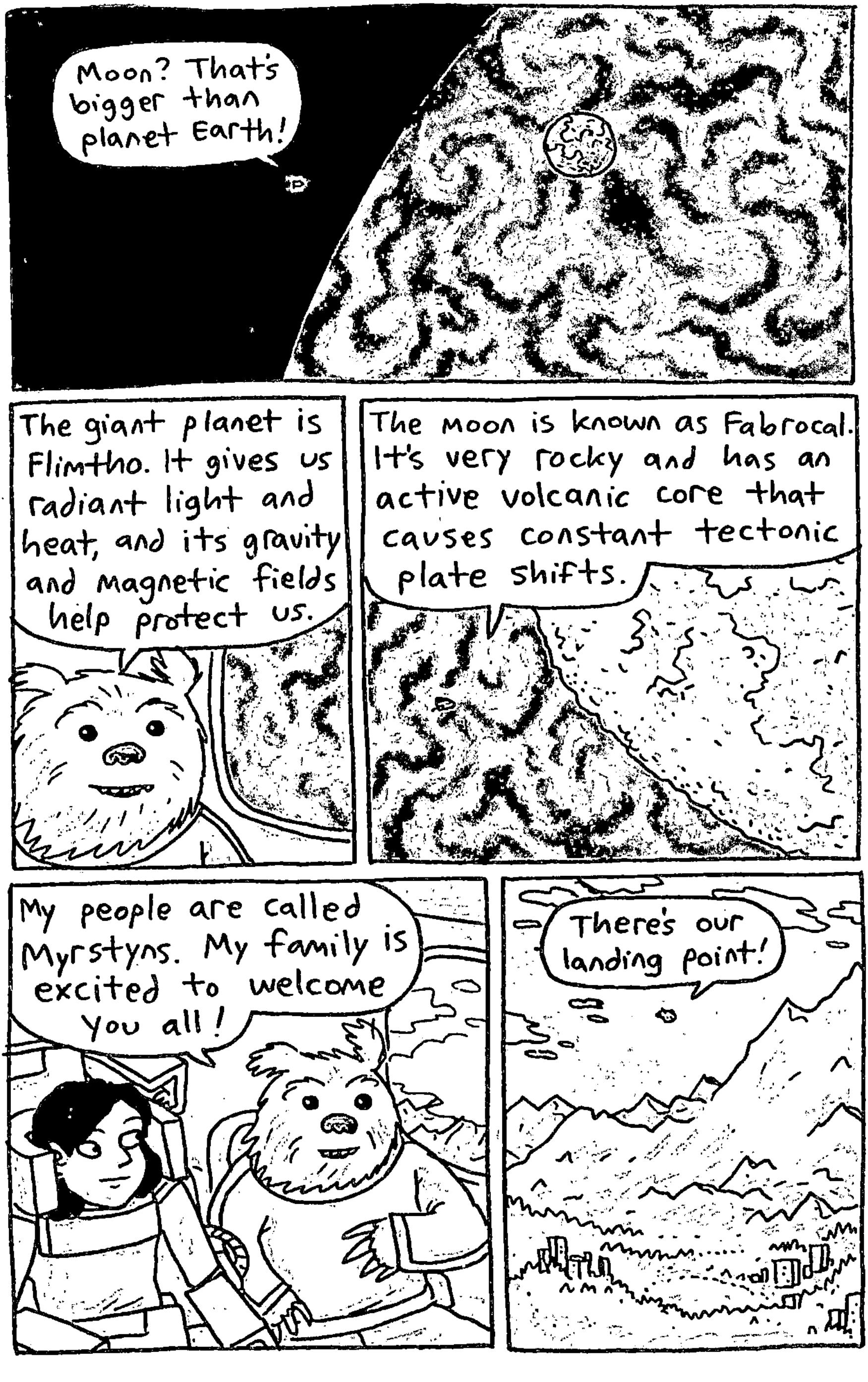

Moon? That's bigger than planet Earth!
The giant planet is Flimtho. It gives us radiant light and heat, and its gravity and magnetic fields help protect us.
The moon is known as Fabrocal. It's very rocky and has an active volcanic core that causes constant tectonic plate shifts.
My people are called Myrstyns. My family is excited to welcome you all!
There's our landing point!

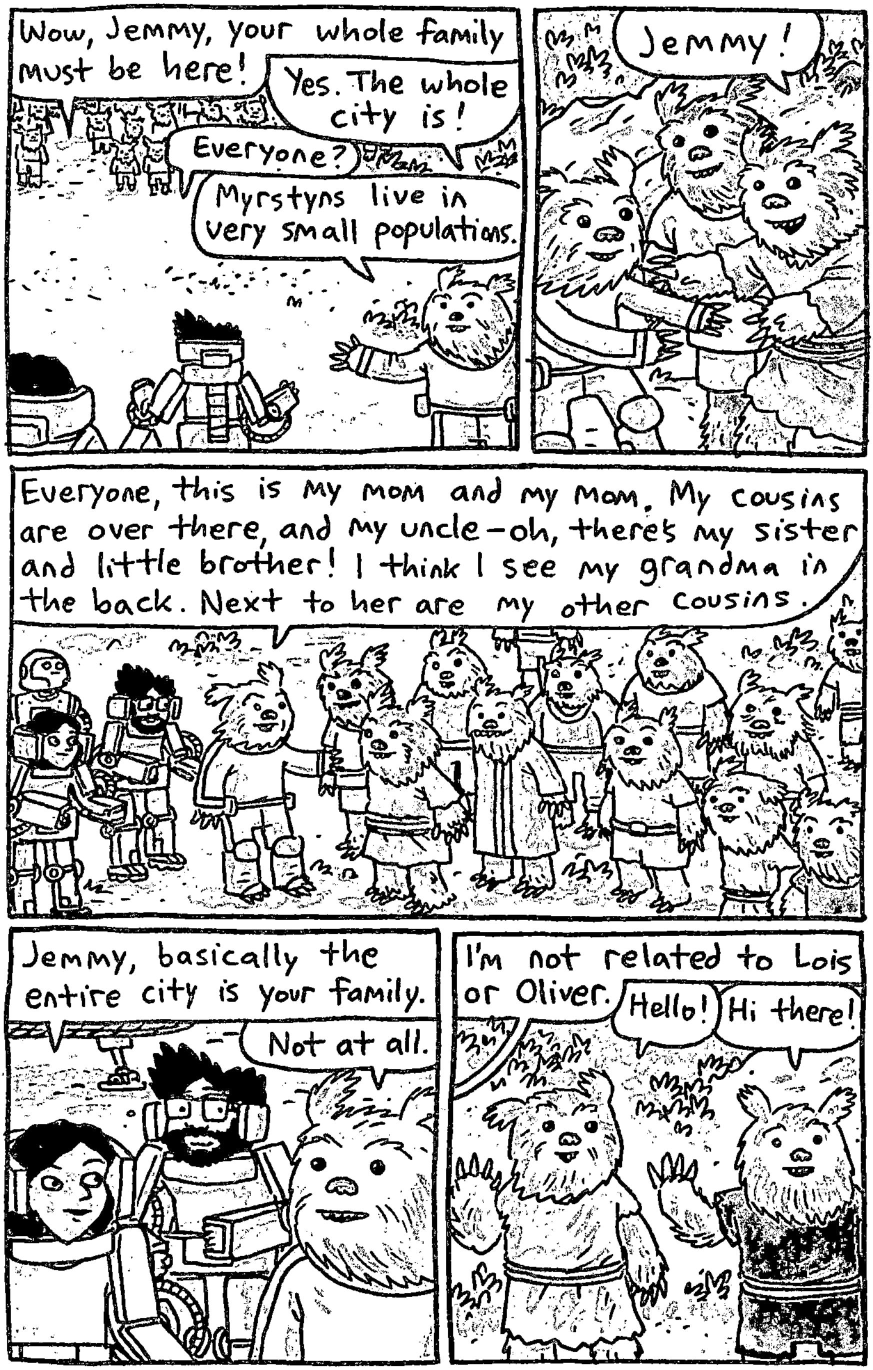
Wow, Jemmy, your whole family must be here!
Yes. The whole city is!
Everyone?
Myrstyns live in very small populations.
Jemmy!
Everyone, this is my mom and my mom. My cousins are over there, and my uncle—oh, there's my sister and little brother! I think I see my grandma in the back. Next to her are my other cousins.
Jemmy, basically the entire city is your family.
Not at all.
I'm not related to Lois or Oliver.
Hello!
Hi there!

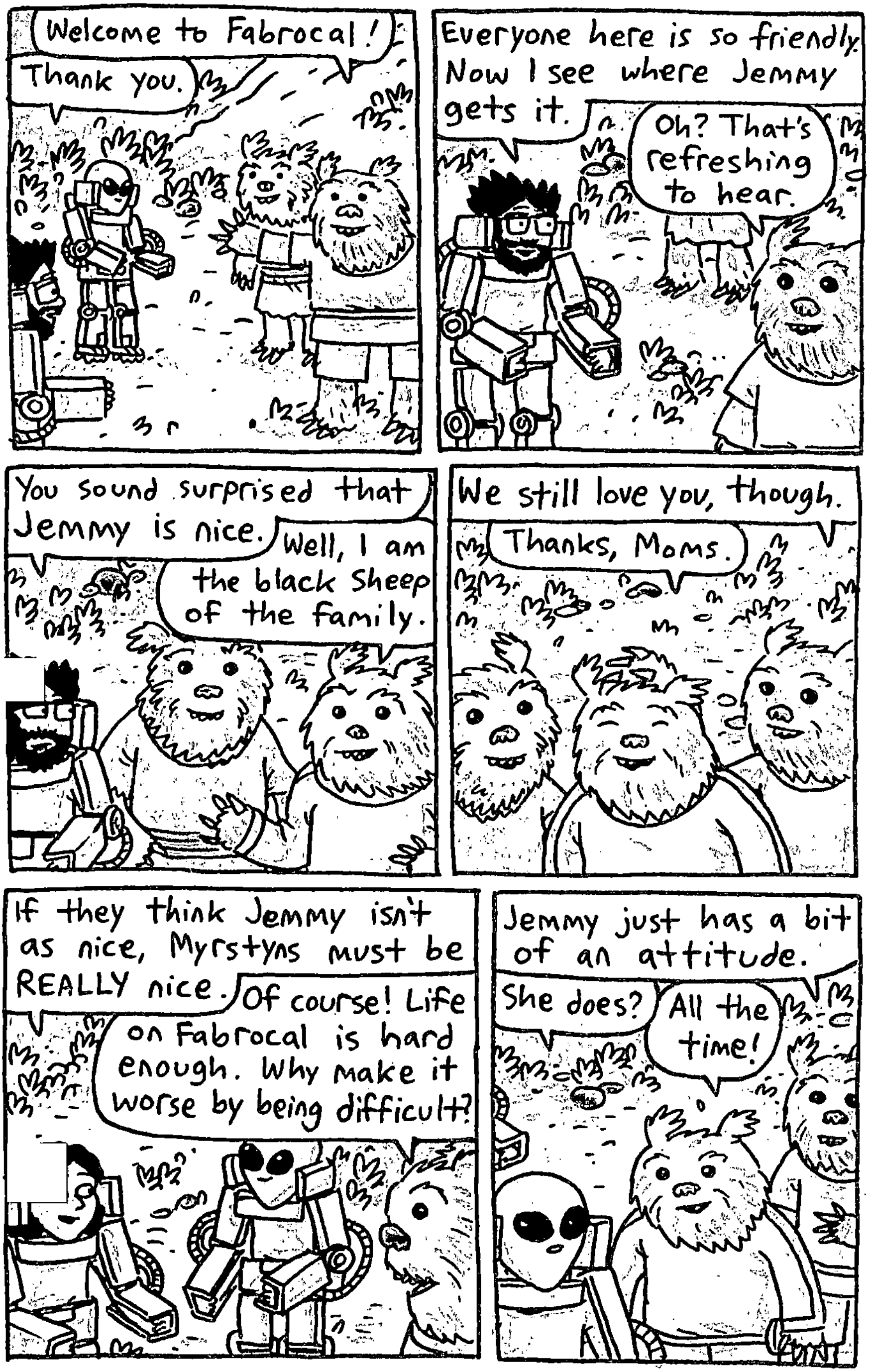
Welcome to Fabrocal!
Thank you.
Everyone here is so friendly. Now I see where Jemmy gets it.
Oh? That's refreshing to hear.
You sound surprised that Jemmy is nice.
Well, I am the black Sheep of the family.
We still love you, though.
Thanks, Moms.
If they think Jemmy isn't as nice, Myrstyns must be REALLY nice.
Of course! Life on Fabrocal is hard enough. Why make it worse by being difficult?
Jemmy just has a bit of an attitude.
She does?
All the time!

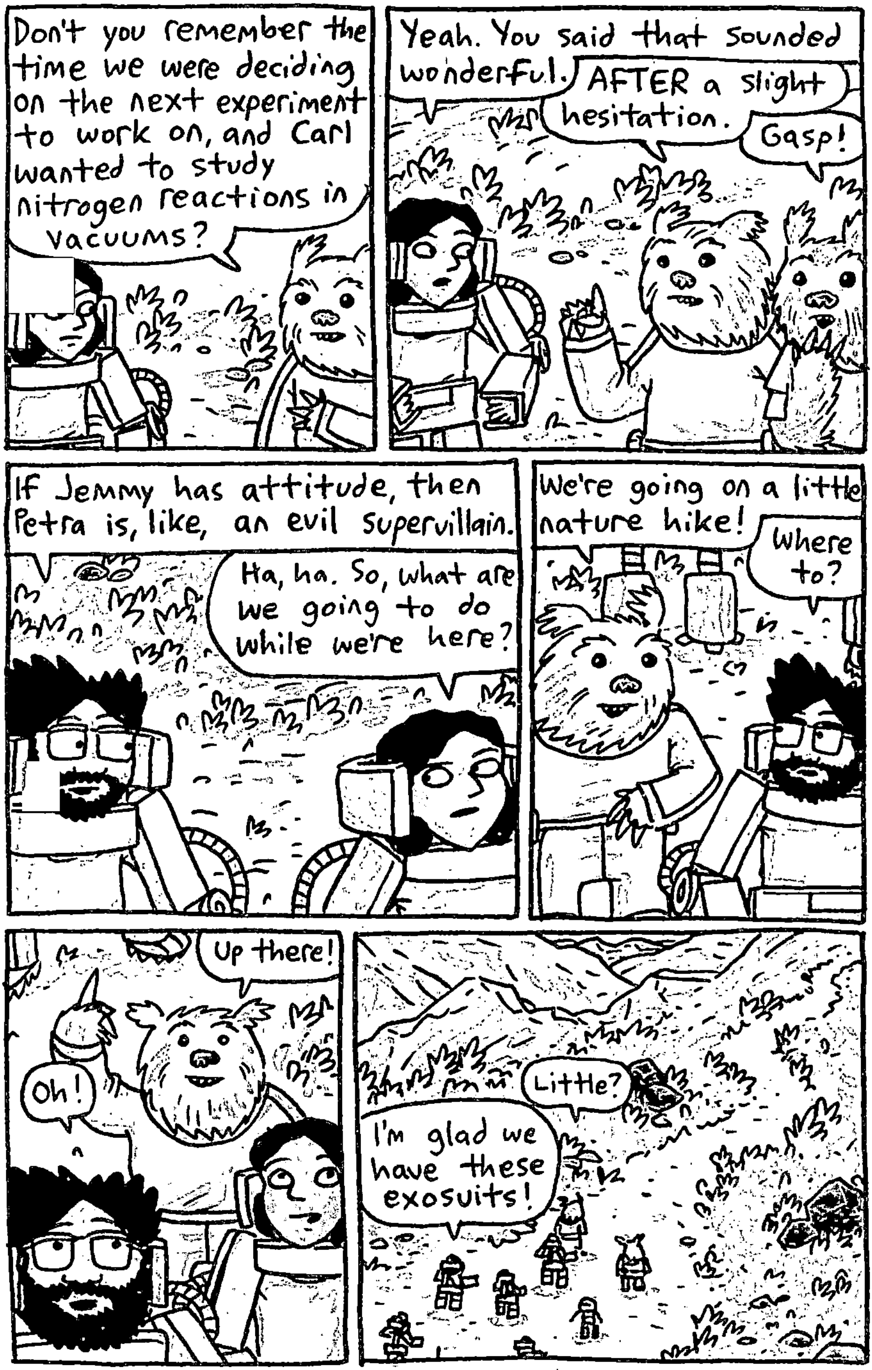
Don't you remember the time we were deciding on the next experiment to work on, and Carl wanted to study nitrogen reactions in vacuums?
Yeah. You said that sounded wonderful.
AFTER a slight hesitation.
Gasp!
If Jemmy has attitude, then Petra is, like, an evil supervillain.
Ha, ha. So, what are we going to do while we're here?
We're going on a little nature hike!
Where to?
Up there!
Oh!
Little?
I'm glad we have these exosuits!

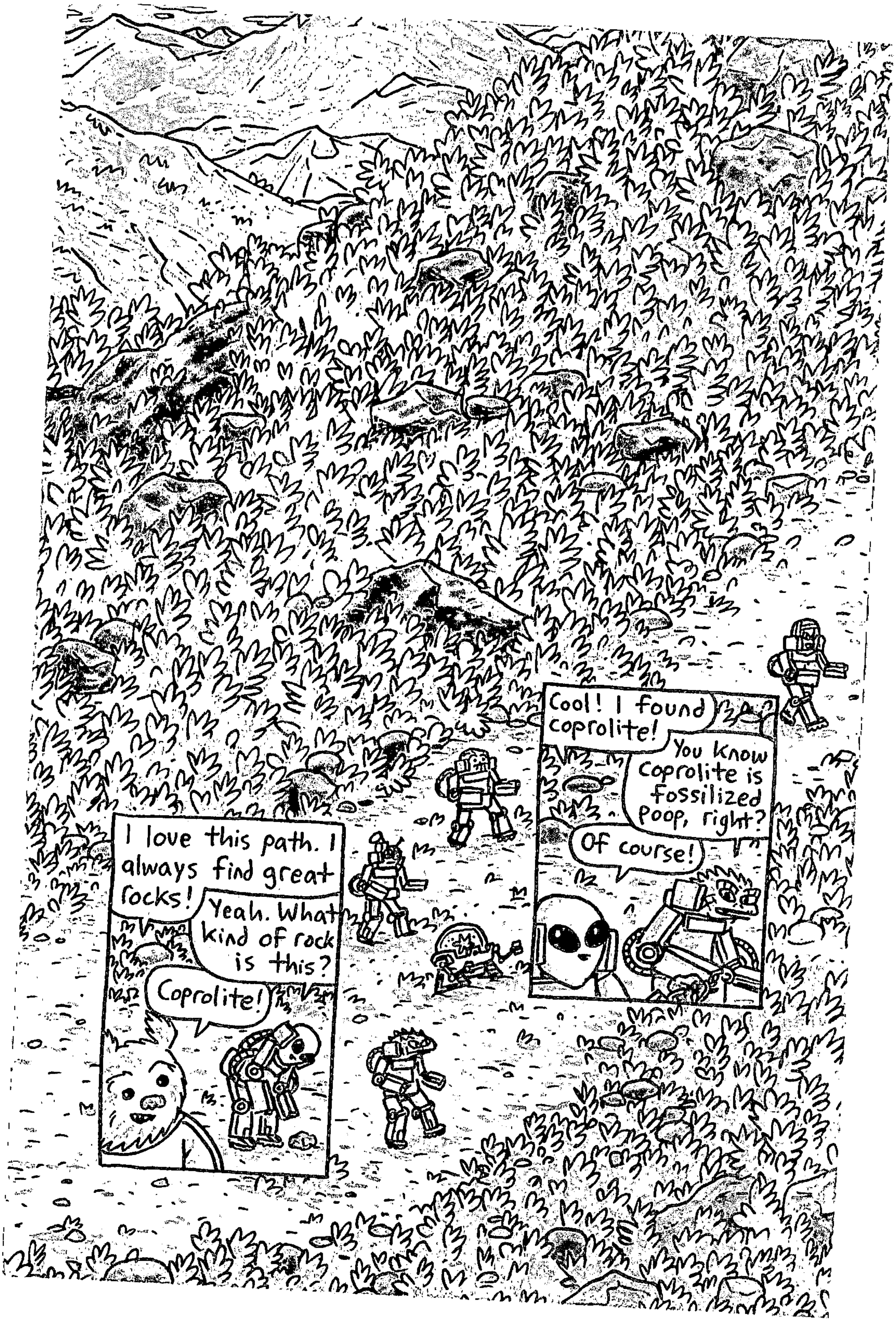

I love this path. I always find great rocks!
Yeah. What kind of rock is this?
Coprolite!
Cool! I found coprolite!
You know coprolite is fossilized poop, right?
Of course!

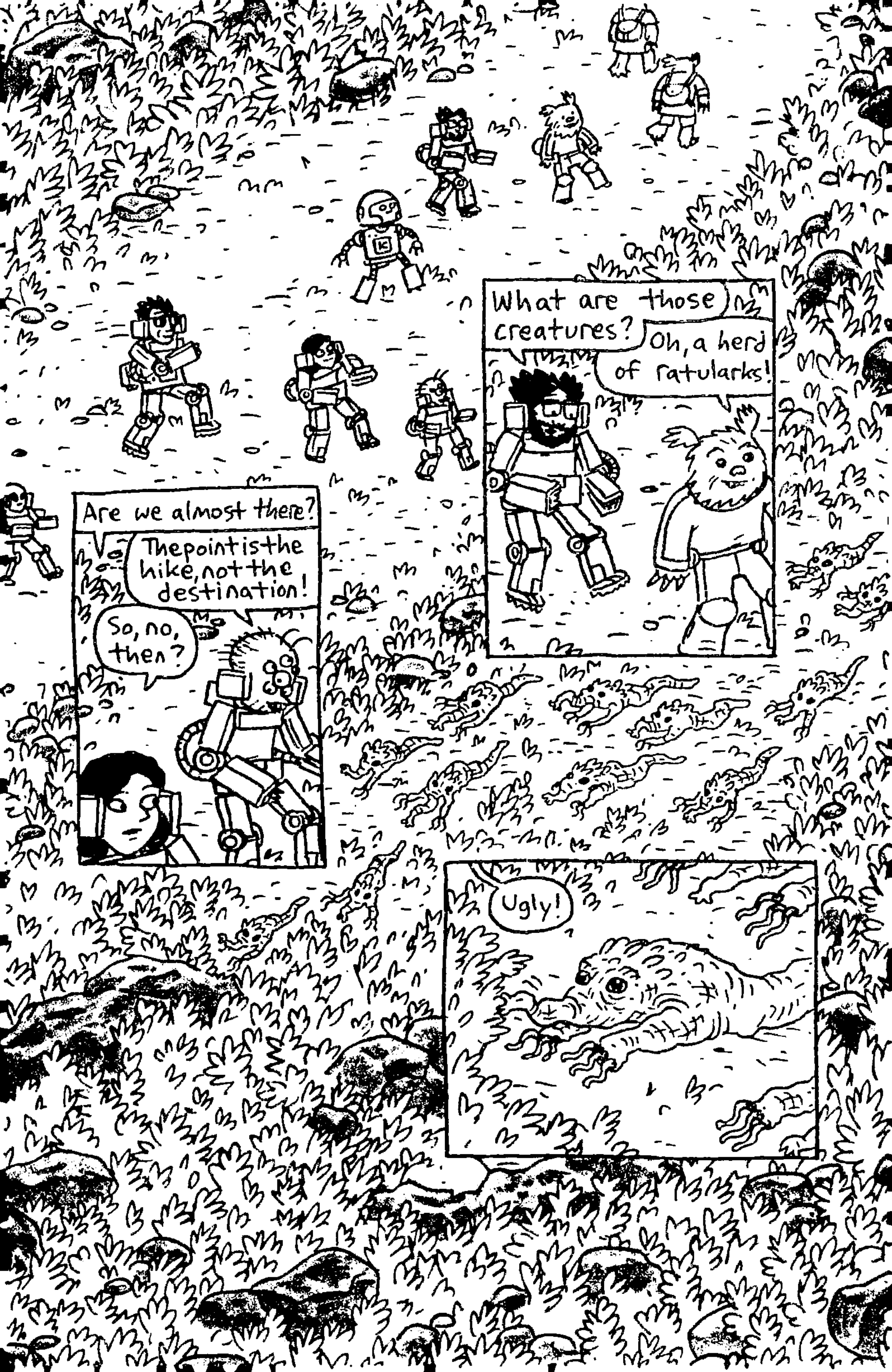

Are we almost there?
The point is the hike, not the destination!
So, no, then?
What are those creatures?
Oh, a herd of ratularks!
Ugly!

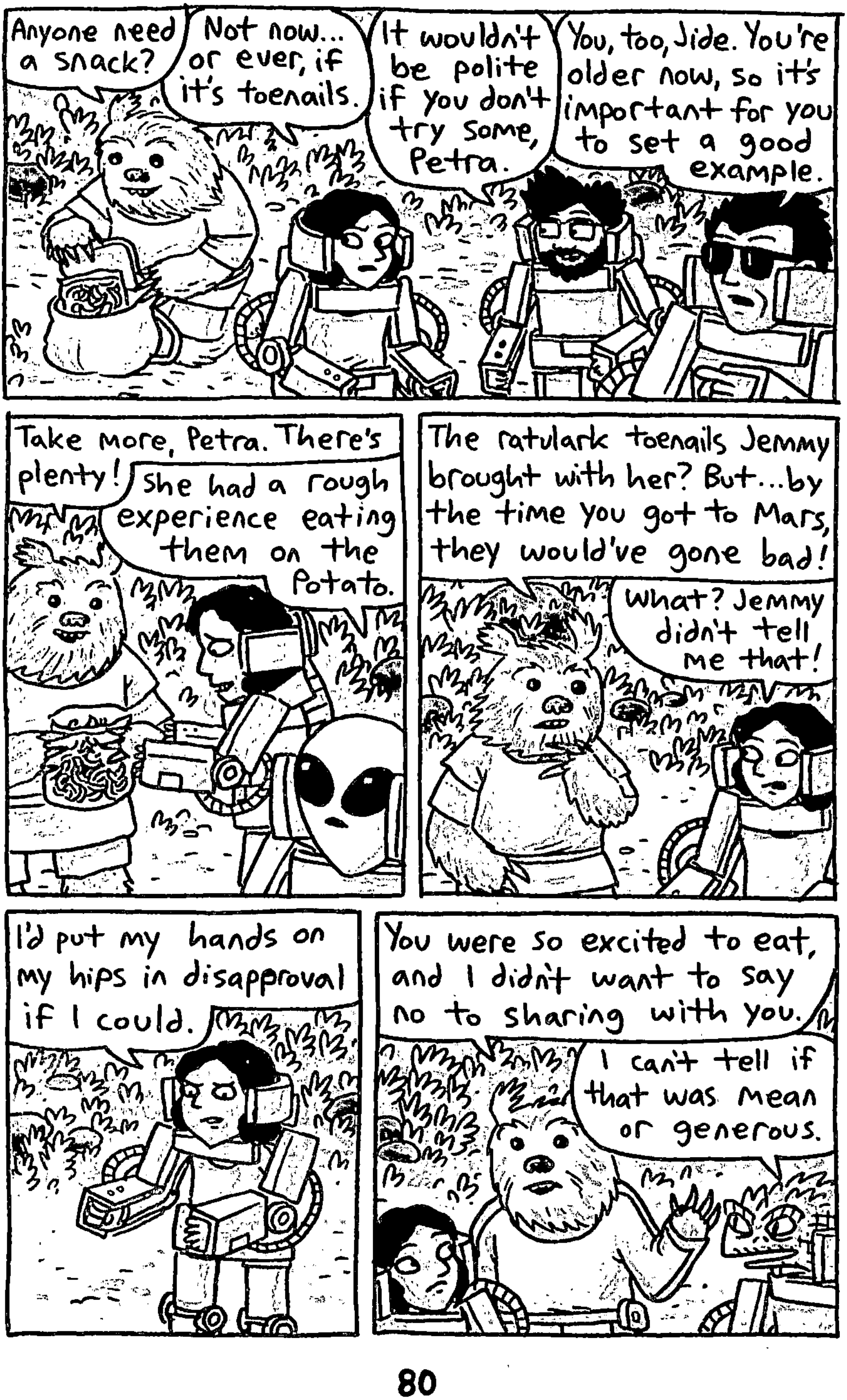
Anyone need a snack?
Not now... or ever, if it's toenails.
It wouldn't be polite if you don't try some, Petra.
You, too, Jide. You're older now, so it's important for you to set a good example.
Take more, Petra. There's plenty!
She had a rough experience eating them on the Potato.
The ratulark toenails Jemmy brought with her? But...by the time you got to Mars, they would've gone bad!
What? Jemmy didn't tell me that!
I'd put my hands on my hips in disapproval if I could.
You were so excited to eat, and I didn't want to say no to sharing with you.
I can't tell if that was mean or generous.

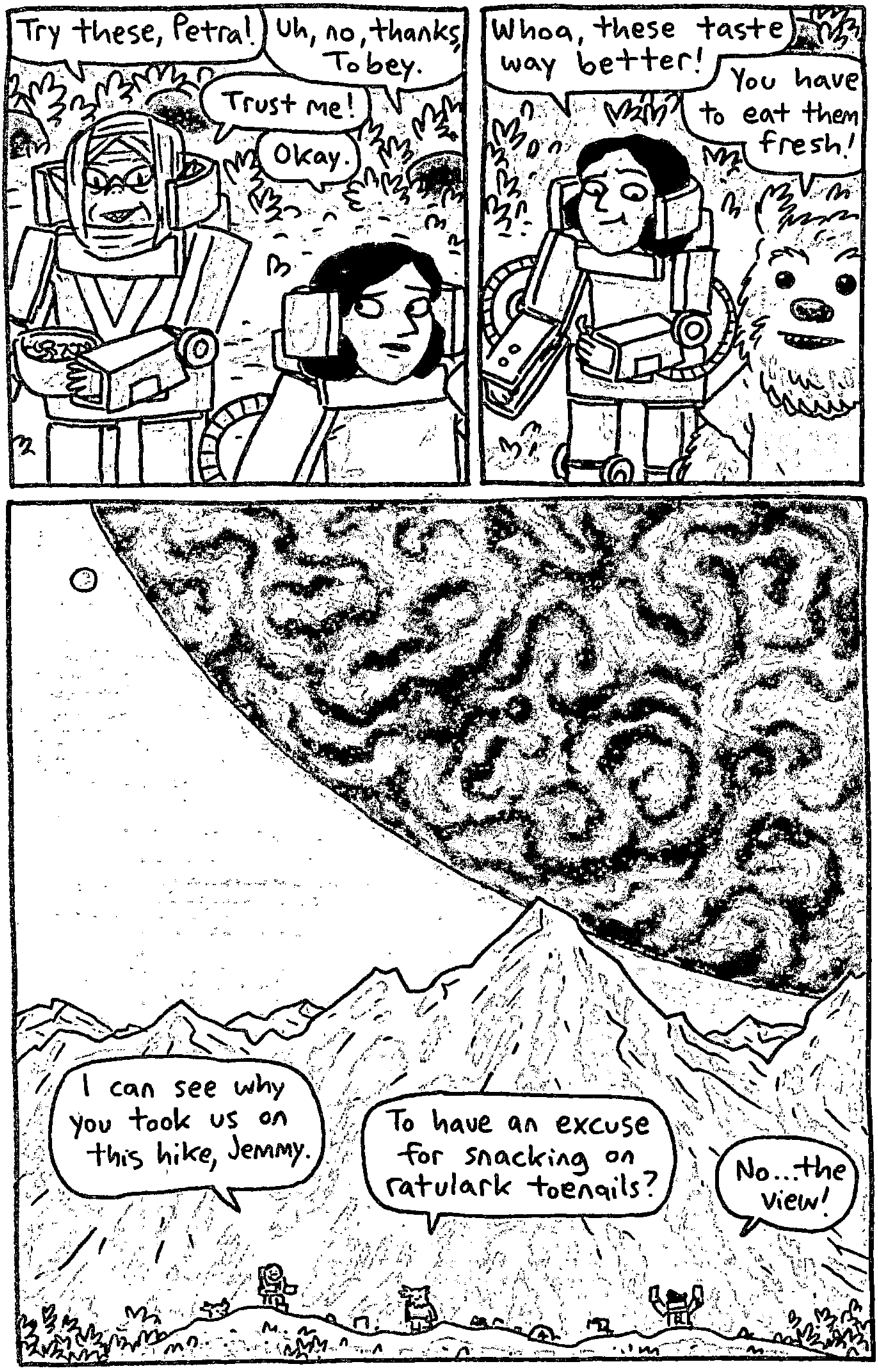
Try these, Petra!
Uh, no, thanks, Tobey.
Trust me!
Okay.
Whoa, these taste way better!
You have to eat them fresh!
I can see why you took us on this hike, Jemmy.
To have an excuse for snacking on ratulark toenails?
No...the view!

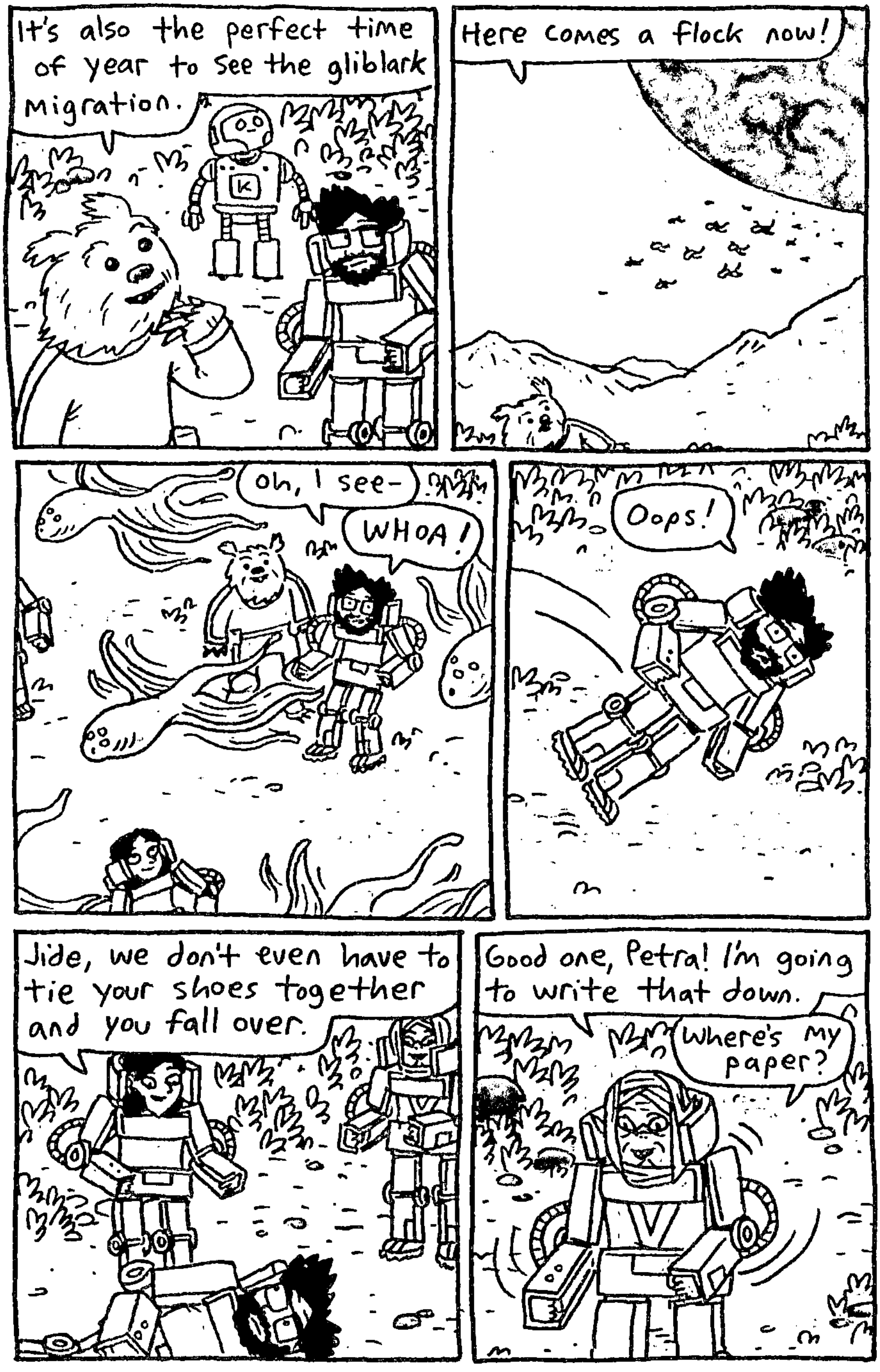
It's also the perfect time of year to see the gliblark migration.
Here comes a flock now!
Oh, I see-
WHOA!
Oops!
Jide, we don't even have to tie your shoes together and you fall over.
Good one, Petra! I'm going to write that down.
Where's my paper?

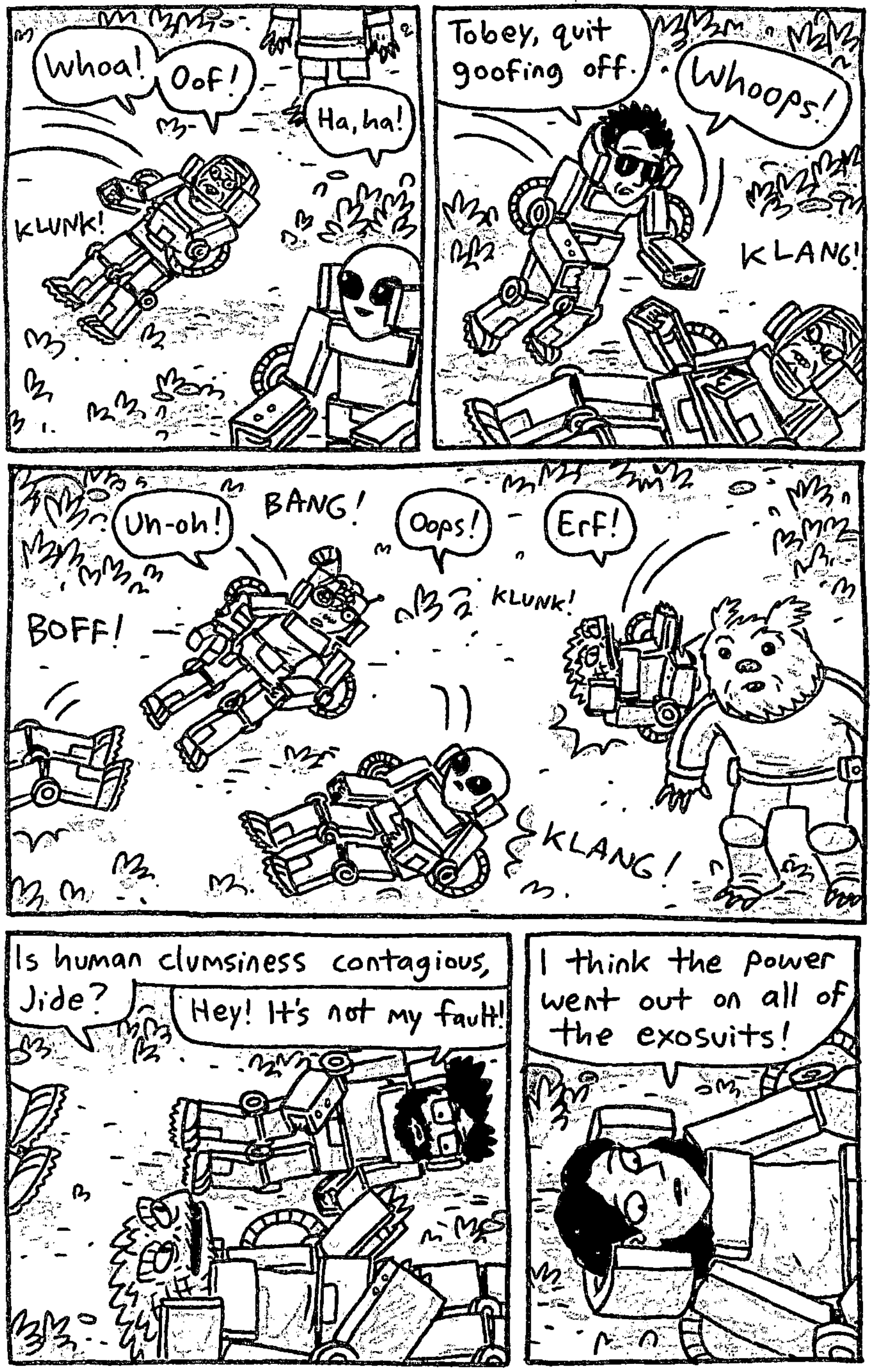
Whoa!
Oof!
Ha, ha!
KLUNK!
Tobey, quit goofing off.
Whoops!
KLANG!
Uh-oh!
BANG!
Oops!
Erf!
KLUNK!
BOFF!
KLANG!
Is human clumsiness contagious, Jide?
Hey! It's not my fault!
I think the power went out on all of the exosuits!

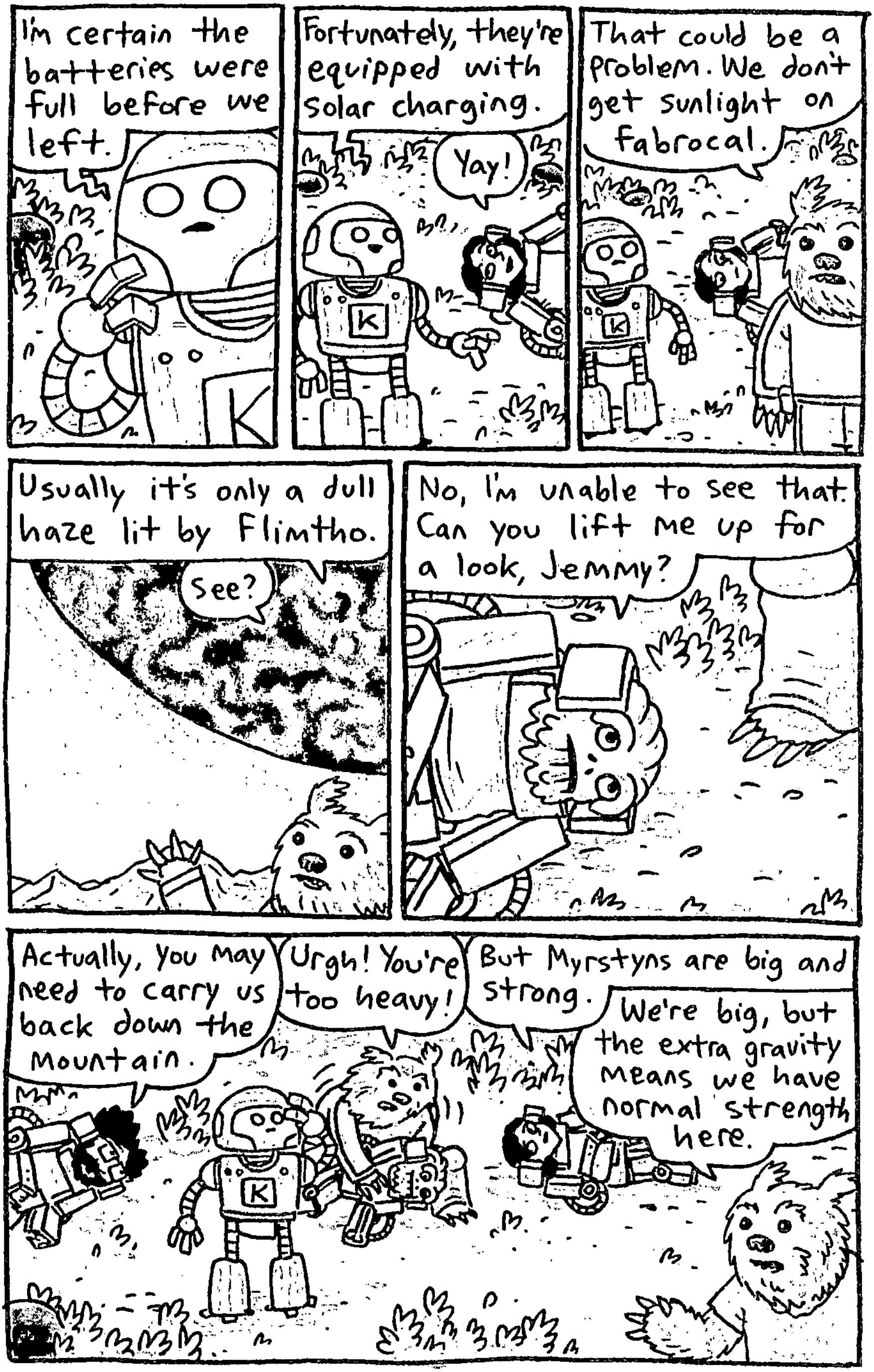

I'm certain the batteries were full before we left.
Fortunately, they're equipped with solar charging.
Yay!
That could be a problem. We don't get sunlight on Fabrocal.
Usually it's only a dull haze lit by Flimtho.
See?
No, I'm unable to see that. Can you lift me up for a look, Jemmy?
Actually, you may need to carry us back down the mountain.
Urgh! You're too heavy!
But Myrstyns are big and strong.
We're big, but the extra gravity means we have normal strength here.

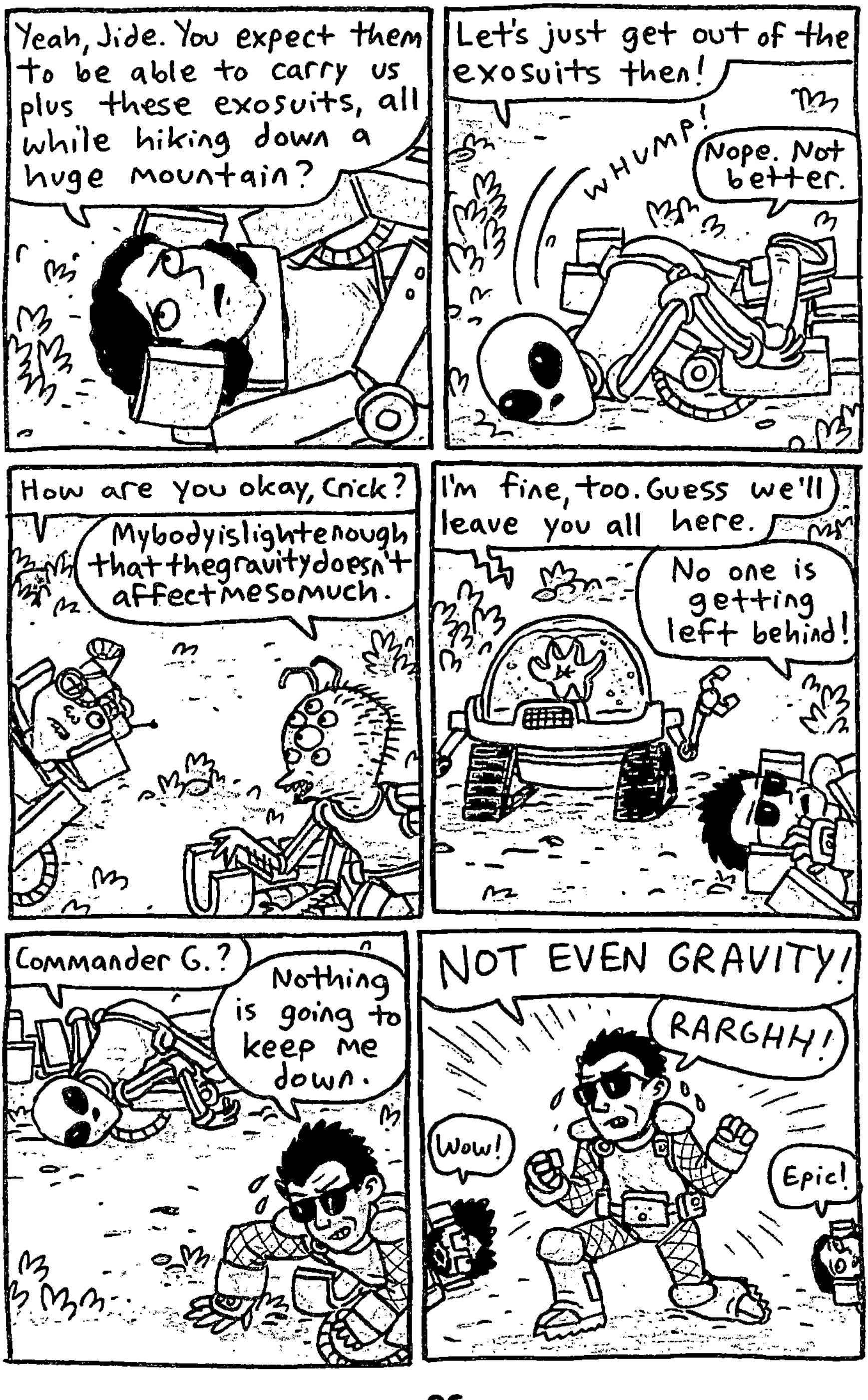
Yeah, Jide. You expect them to be able to carry us plus these exosuits, all while hiking down a huge mountain?
Let's just get out of the exosuits then!
WHUMP!
Nope. Not better.
How are you okay, Crick?
Mybodyislightenough thatthegravitydoesn't affectmesomuch.
I'm fine, too. Guess we'll leave you all here.
No one is getting left behind!
Commander G.?
Nothing is going to keep me down.
NOT EVEN GRAVITY!
RARGHH!
Wow!
Epic!

86

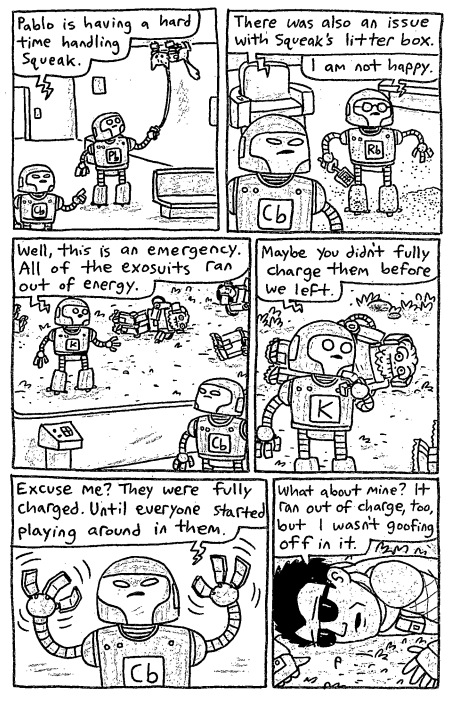

87

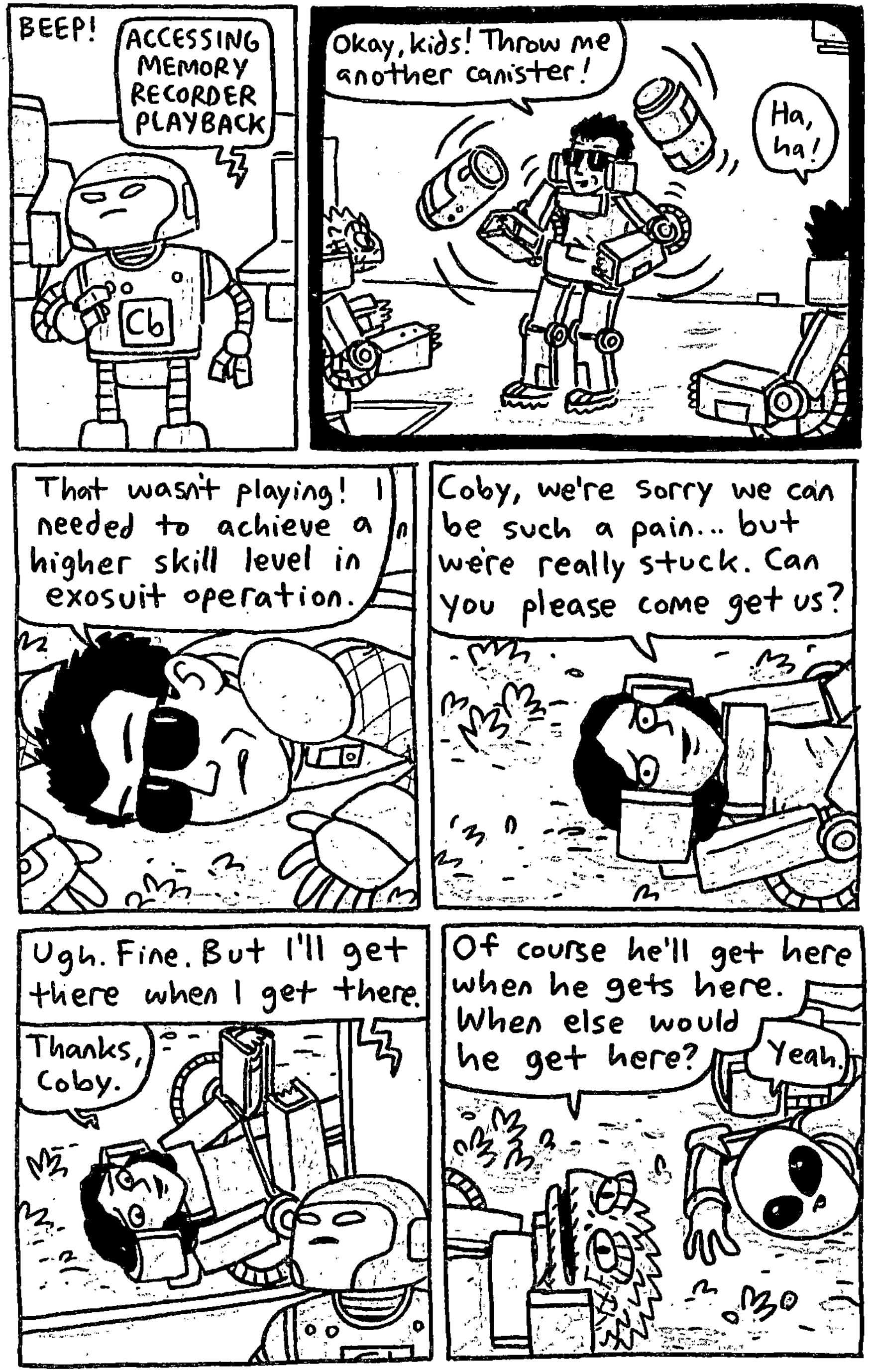
BEEP!
ACCESSING MEMORY RECORDER PLAYBACK
Okay, kids! Throw me another canister!
Ha, ha!
That wasn't playing! I needed to achieve a higher skill level in exosuit operation.
Coby, we're sorry we can be such a pain... but we're really stuck. Can you please come get us?
Ugh. Fine. But I'll get there when I get there.
Thanks, Coby.
Of course he'll get here when he gets here. When else would he get here?
Yeah.

90

94

95

DRY RUNNING THE NUMBERS

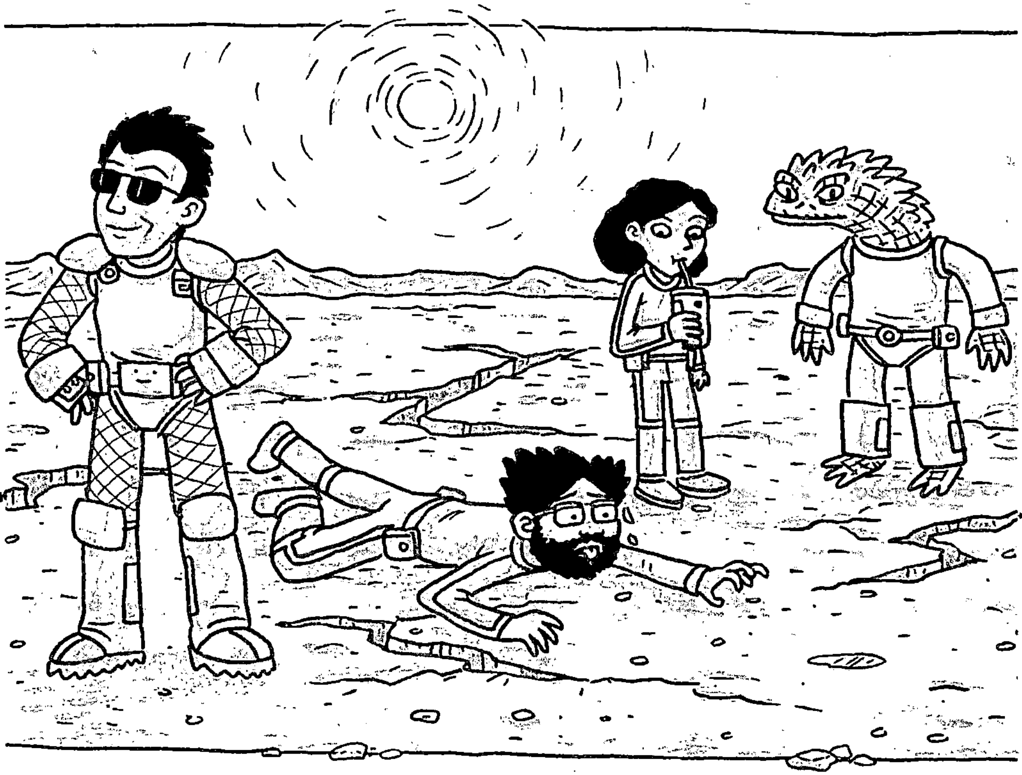

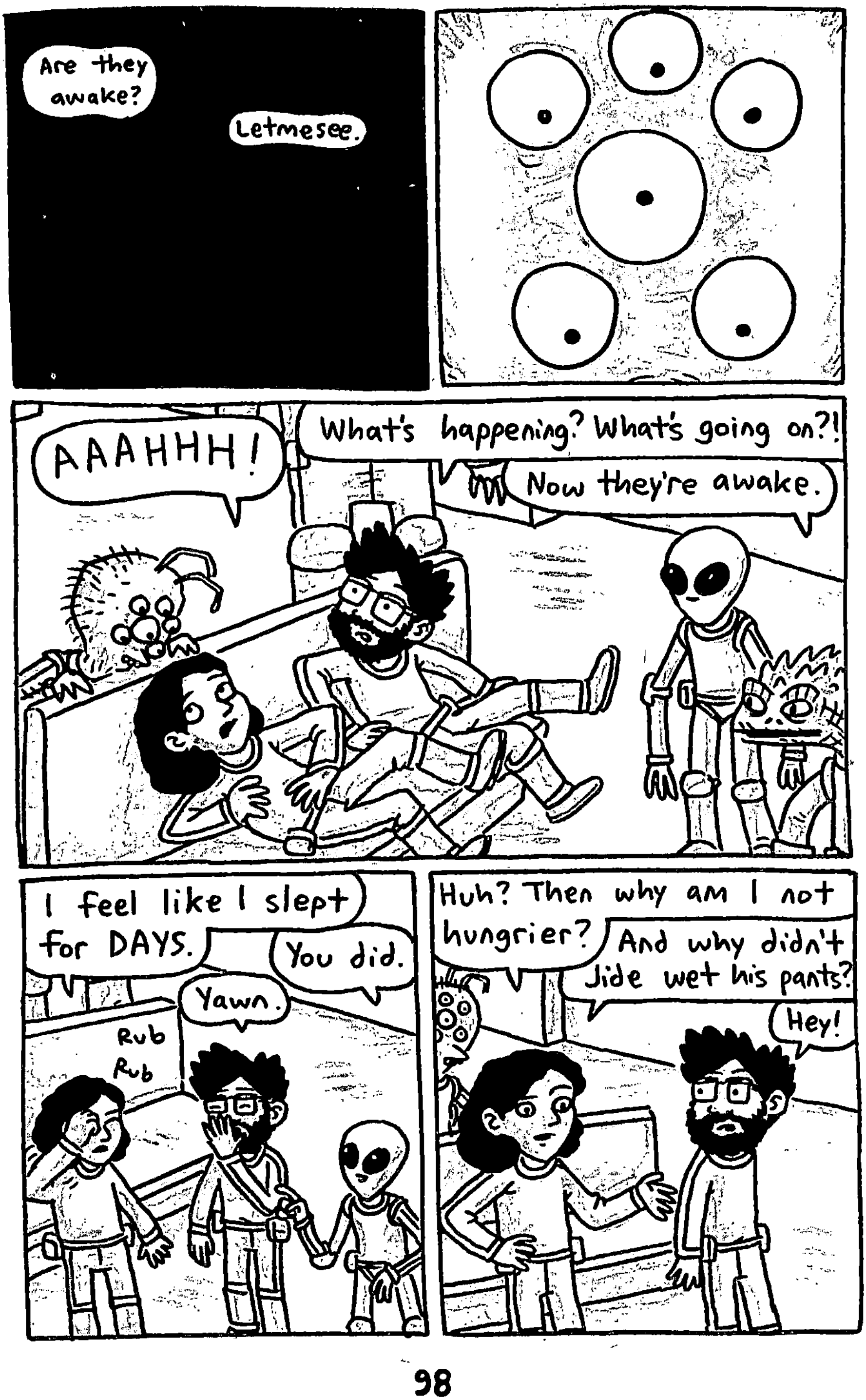
Are they awake?
Letmesee.
AAAHHH!
What's happening? What's going on?!
Now they're awake.
I feel like I slept for DAYS.
You did.
Yawn.
Rub
Rub
Huh? Then why am I not hungrier?
And why didn't Jide wet his pants?
Hey!

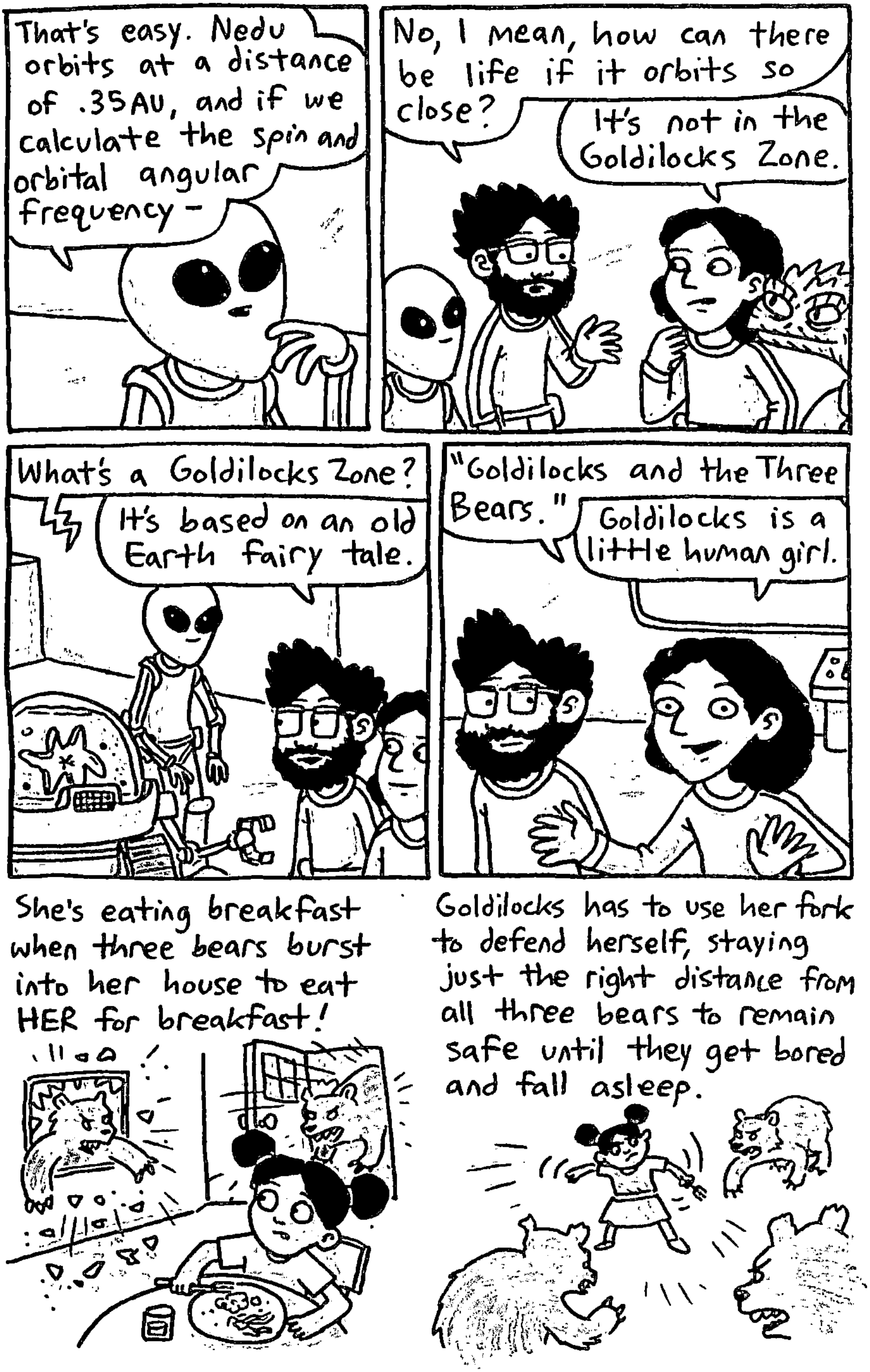
That's easy. Nedu orbits at a distance of .35AU, and if we calculate the spin and orbital angular frequency -
No, I mean, how can there be life if it orbits so close?
It's not in the Goldilocks Zone.
What's a Goldilocks Zone?
It's based on an old Earth fairy tale.
"Goldilocks and the Three Bears."
Goldilocks is a little human girl.
She's eating breakfast when three bears burst into her house to eat HER for breakfast!
Goldilocks has to use her fork to defend herself, staying just the right distance from all three bears to remain safe until they get bored and fall asleep.

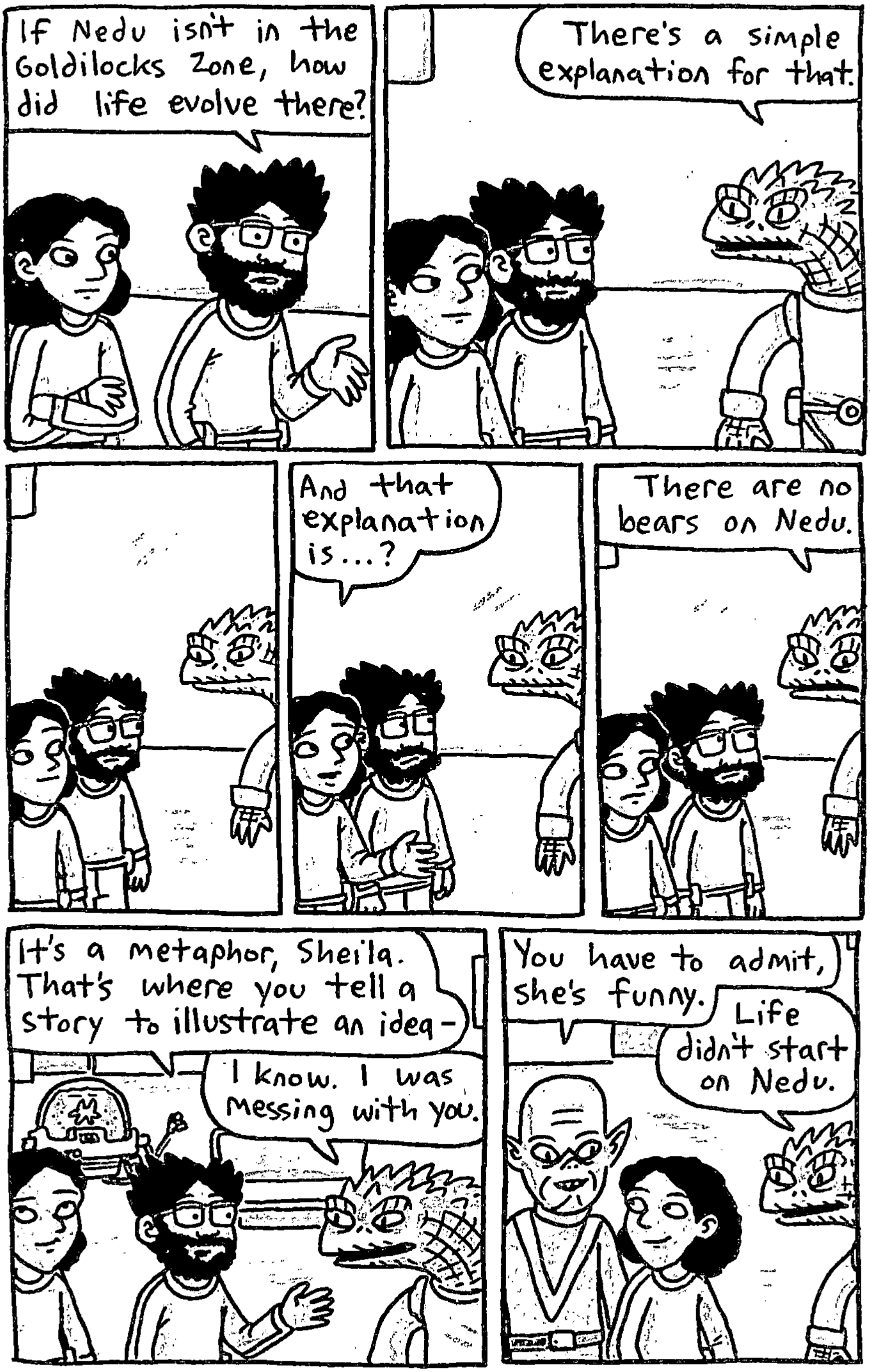

If Nedu isn't in the Goldilocks Zone, how did life evolve there?
There's a simple explanation for that.
And that explanation is...?
There are no bears on Nedu.
It's a metaphor, Sheila. That's where you tell a story to illustrate an idea-
I know. I was messing with you.
You have to admit, she's funny.
Life didn't start on Nedu.

103

104

106

107

My species is long-lived and our eggs require many seasons to incubate. In order to hide them from predators, the eggs are buried randomly. The birth parents pass away years before the eggs hatch.

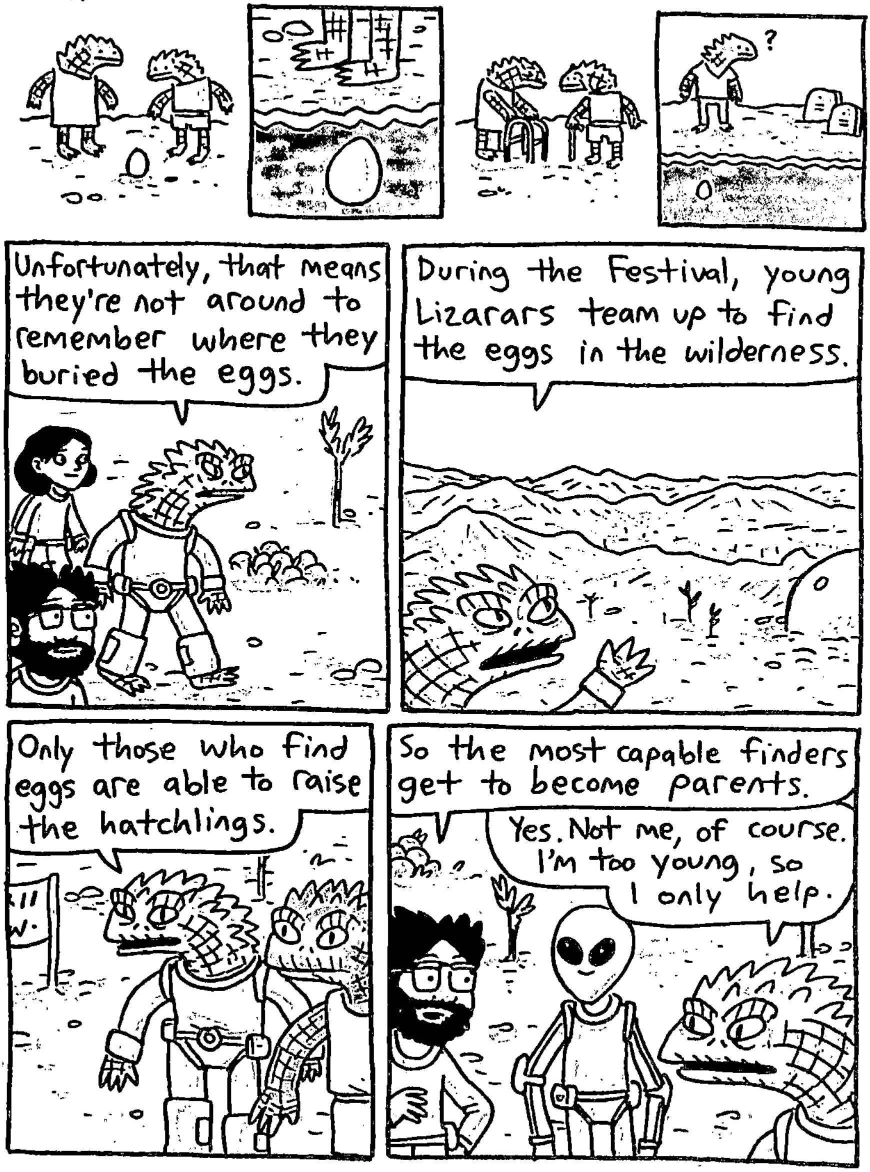
?
Unfortunately, that means they're not around to remember where they buried the eggs.
During the Festival, young Lizarars team up to find the eggs in the wilderness.
Only those who find eggs are able to raise the hatchlings.
So the most capable finders get to become parents.
Yes. Not me, of course. I'm too young, so I only help.

109

This is a good place to set up.
Let us begin the search.
Here? I thought all the eggs were buried out there somewhere.
Why are you getting out computers?
Yes, but first, we use complex mathematical algorithms to determine search patterns.
If we use the correct formulae, we will determine the most likely location of an egg.
Tak Tak Tak Tak Tak Tak Tak Tak Tak Tak Tak Tak

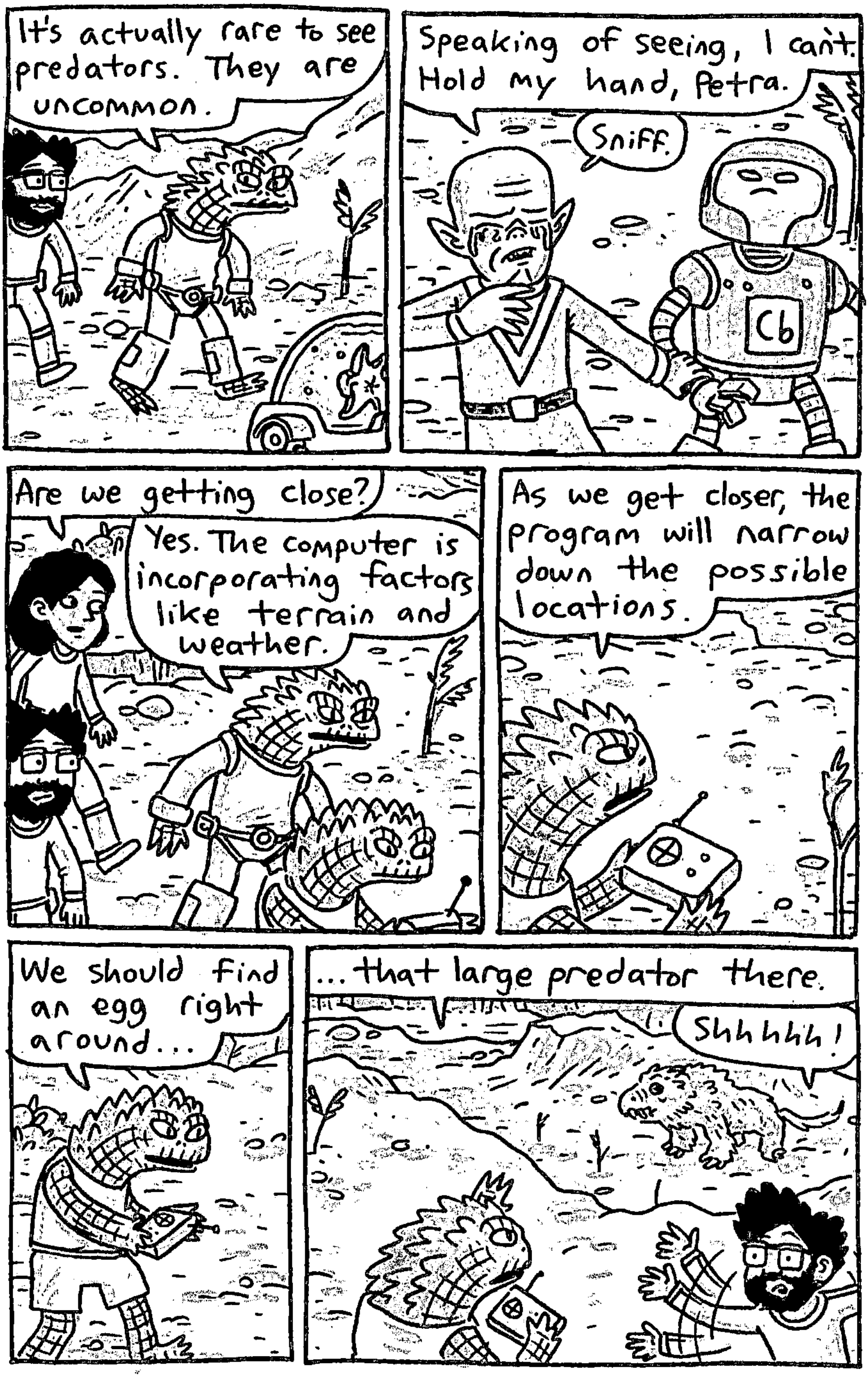
It's actually rare to see predators. They are uncommon.
Speaking of seeing, I can't. Hold my hand, Petra.
Sniff.
Cb
Are we getting close?
Yes. The computer is incorporating factors like terrain and weather.
As we get closer, the program will narrow down the possible locations.
We should find an egg right around...
...that large predator there.
Shhhhh!

117

I can't believe it fell for that!
Fell for the trick...or off the cliff?
Now it knows we're here, though. We should hurry and locate the egg.
Based on the final data input, an egg is almost certainly buried right here.
We must dig it out.
I can help with that!
Oh, yeah! Jemmy is a great digger.
Congratulations!
It is an egg of indeterminate personhood.

119

121

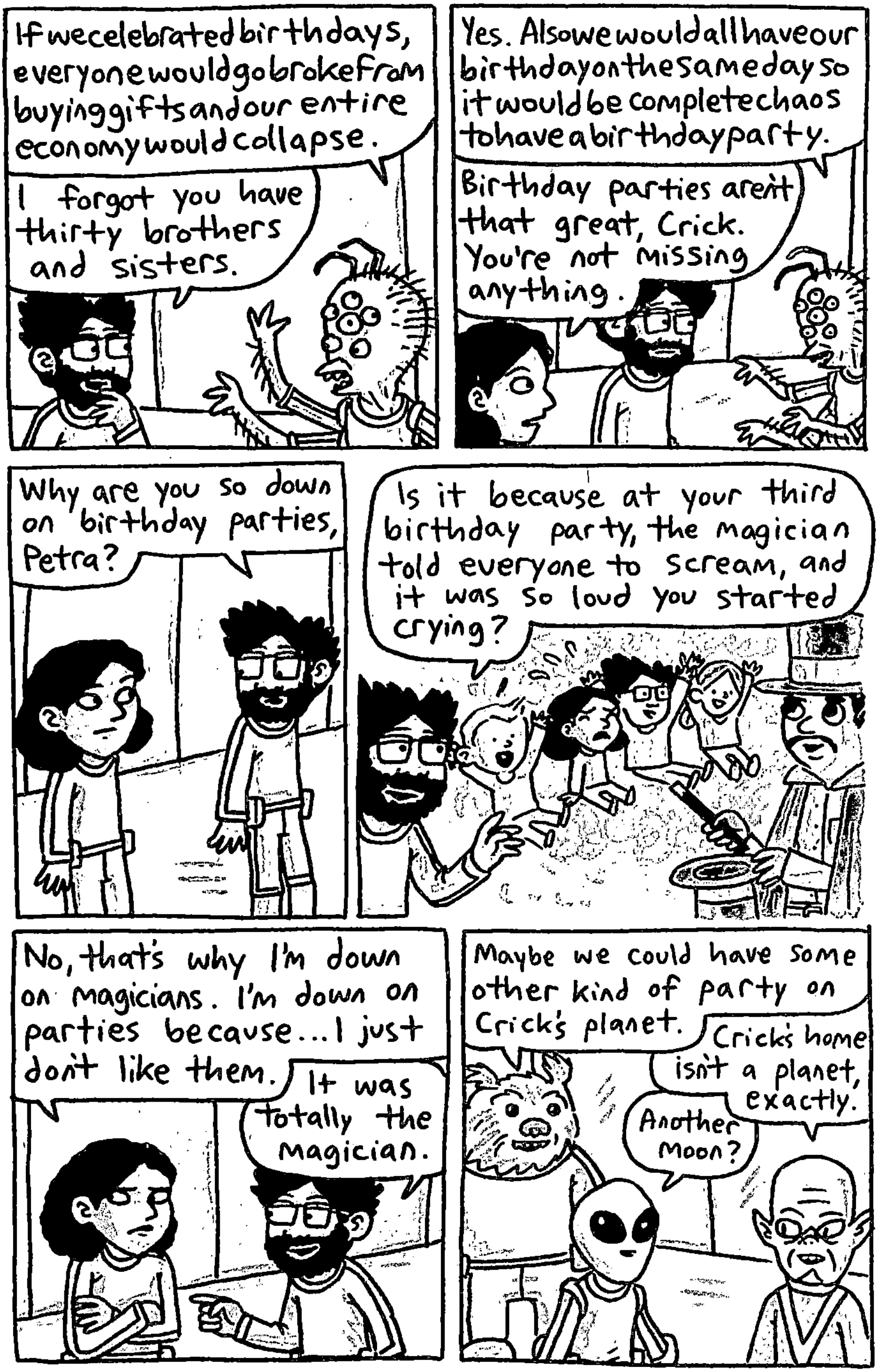
If we celebrated birthdays, everyone would go broke from buying gifts and our entire economy would collapse.
I forgot you have thirty brothers and sisters.
Yes. Also we would all have our birthday on the same day so it would be complete chaos to have a birthday party.
Birthday parties aren't that great, Crick. You're not missing anything.
Why are you so down on birthday parties, Petra?
Is it because at your third birthday party, the magician told everyone to scream, and it was so loud you started crying?
No, that's why I'm down on magicians. I'm down on parties because... I just don't like them.
It was totally the magician.
Maybe we could have some other kind of party on Crick's planet.
Crick's home isn't a planet, exactly.
Another moon?

124

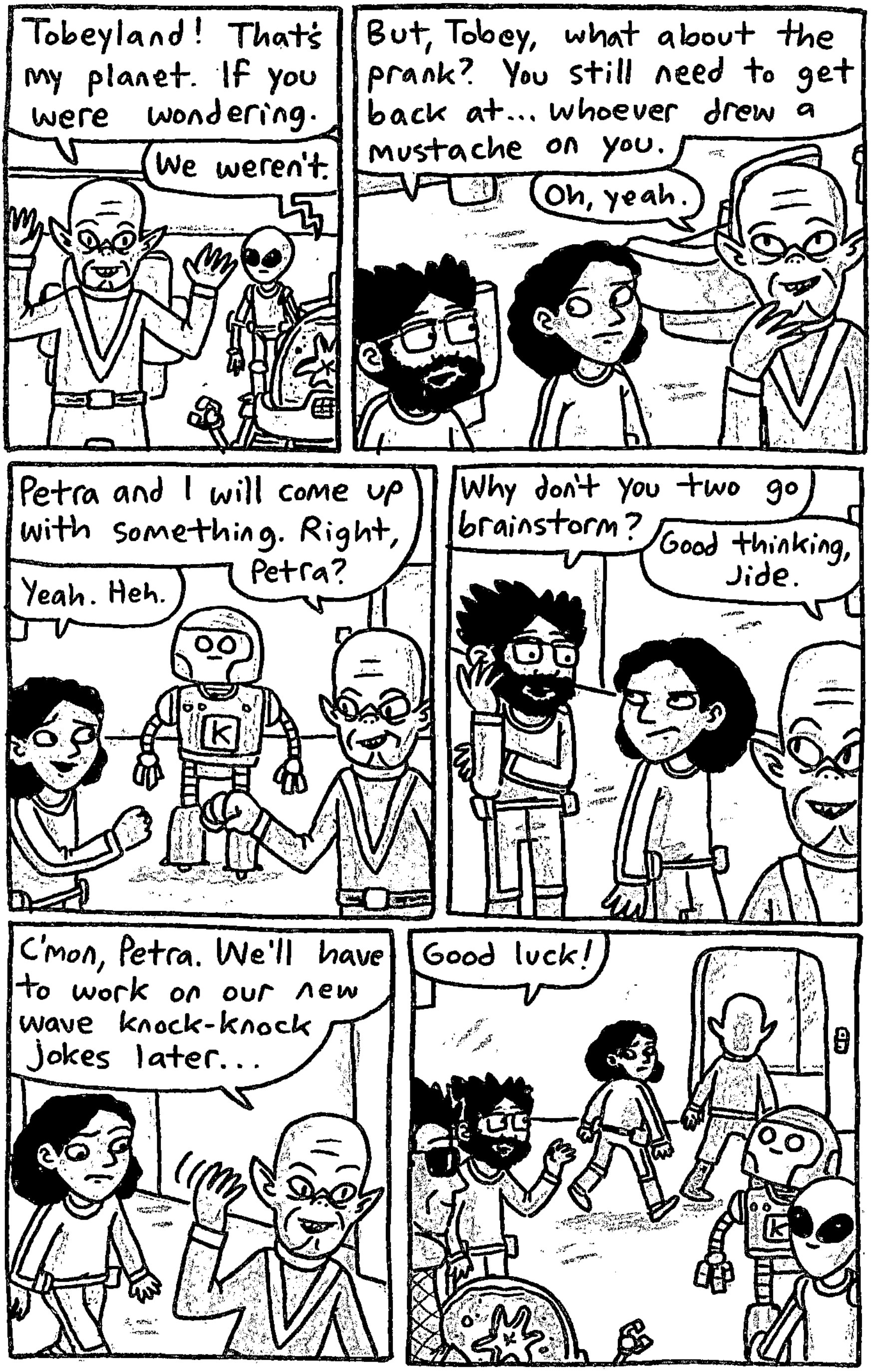
Tobeyland! That's my planet. If you were wondering.
We weren't.
But, Tobey, what about the prank? You still need to get back at... whoever drew a mustache on you.
Oh, yeah.
Petra and I will come up with something. Right, Petra?
Yeah. Heh.
Why don't you two go brainstorm?
Good thinking, Jide.
C'mon, Petra. We'll have to work on our new wave knock-knock jokes later...
Good luck!

DOUBLE TROUBLE

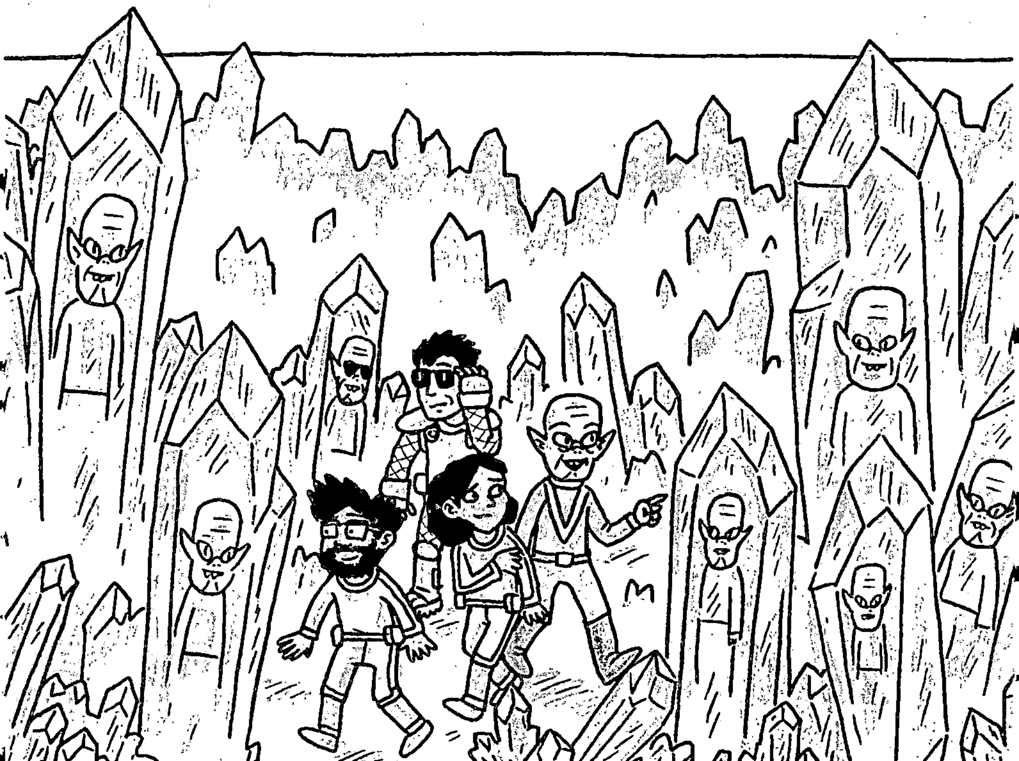

130

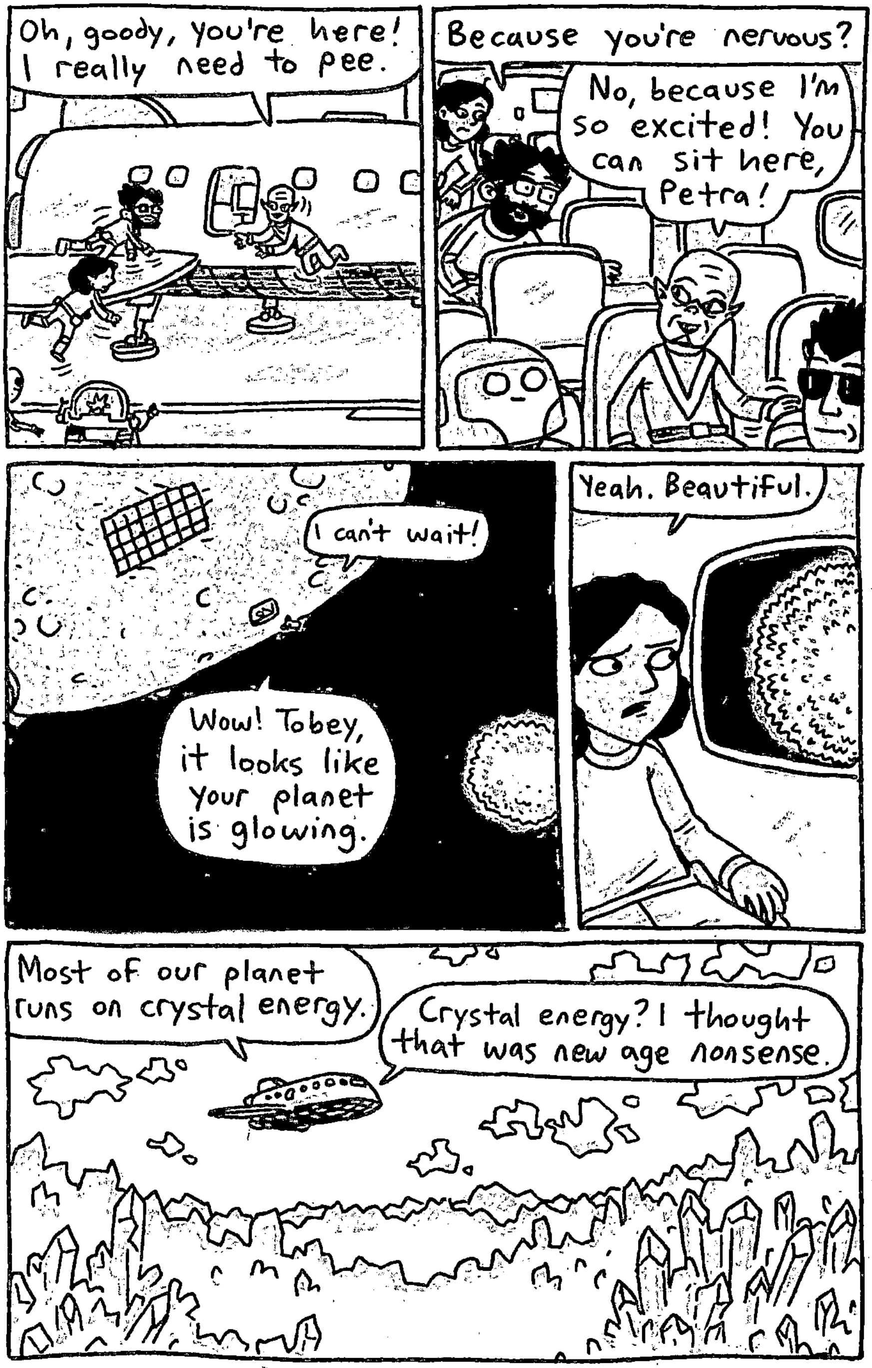
Oh, goody, you're here! I really need to pee.
Because you're nervous?
No, because I'm so excited! You can sit here, Petra!
I can't wait!
Wow! Tobey, it looks like your planet is glowing.
Yeah. Beautiful.
Most of our planet runs on crystal energy.
Crystal energy? I thought that was new age nonsense.

Earth crystal energy is nonsense, but when you have as many crystals as Tobeyland, you learn just how useful crystals can be!
This is a lot of crystals!

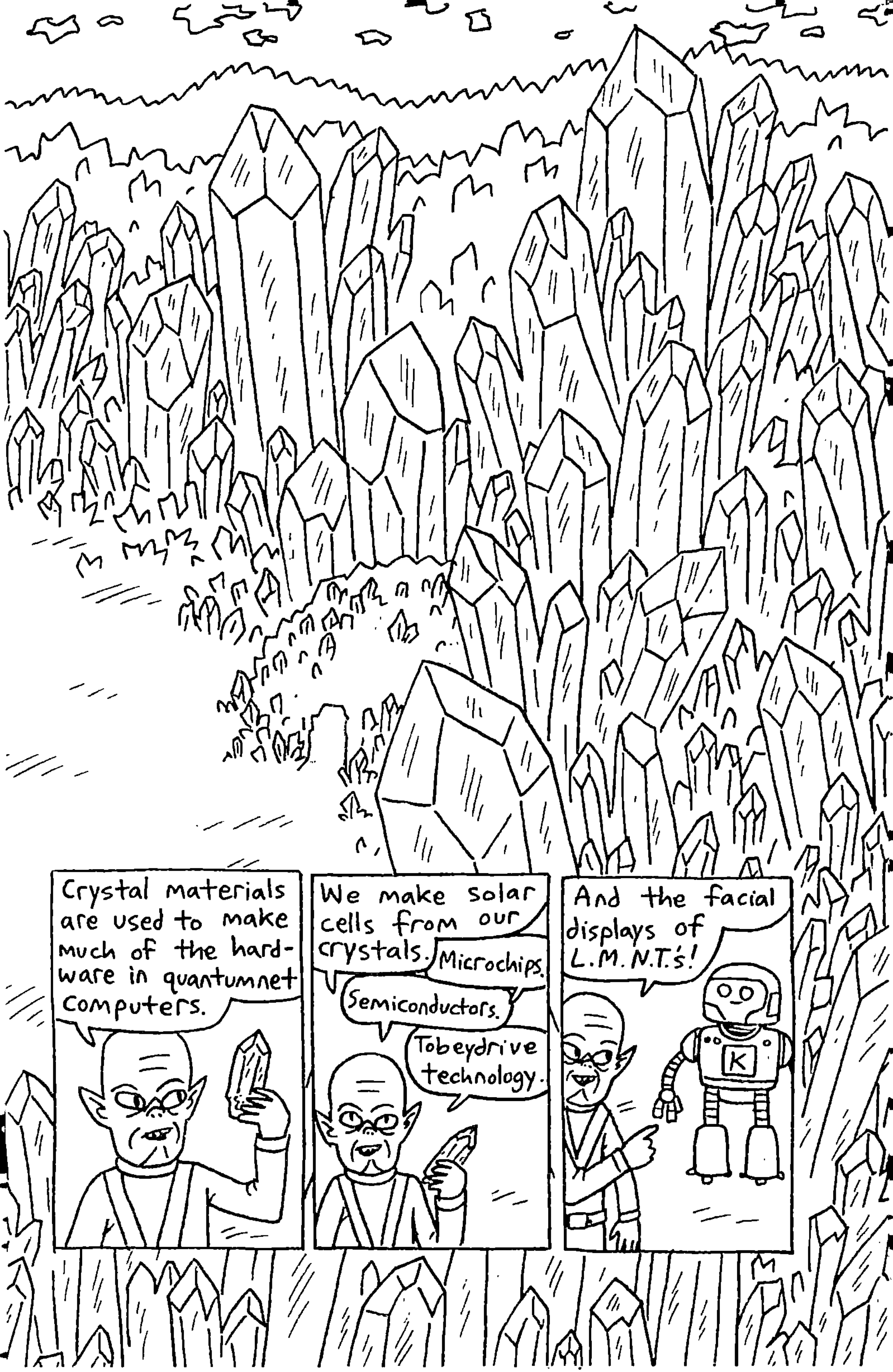
Crystal materials are used to make much of the hardware in quantumnet computers.
We make solar cells from our crystals.
Microchips.
Semiconductors.
Tobeydrive technology.
And the facial displays of L.M.N.T.'s!
K

134

135

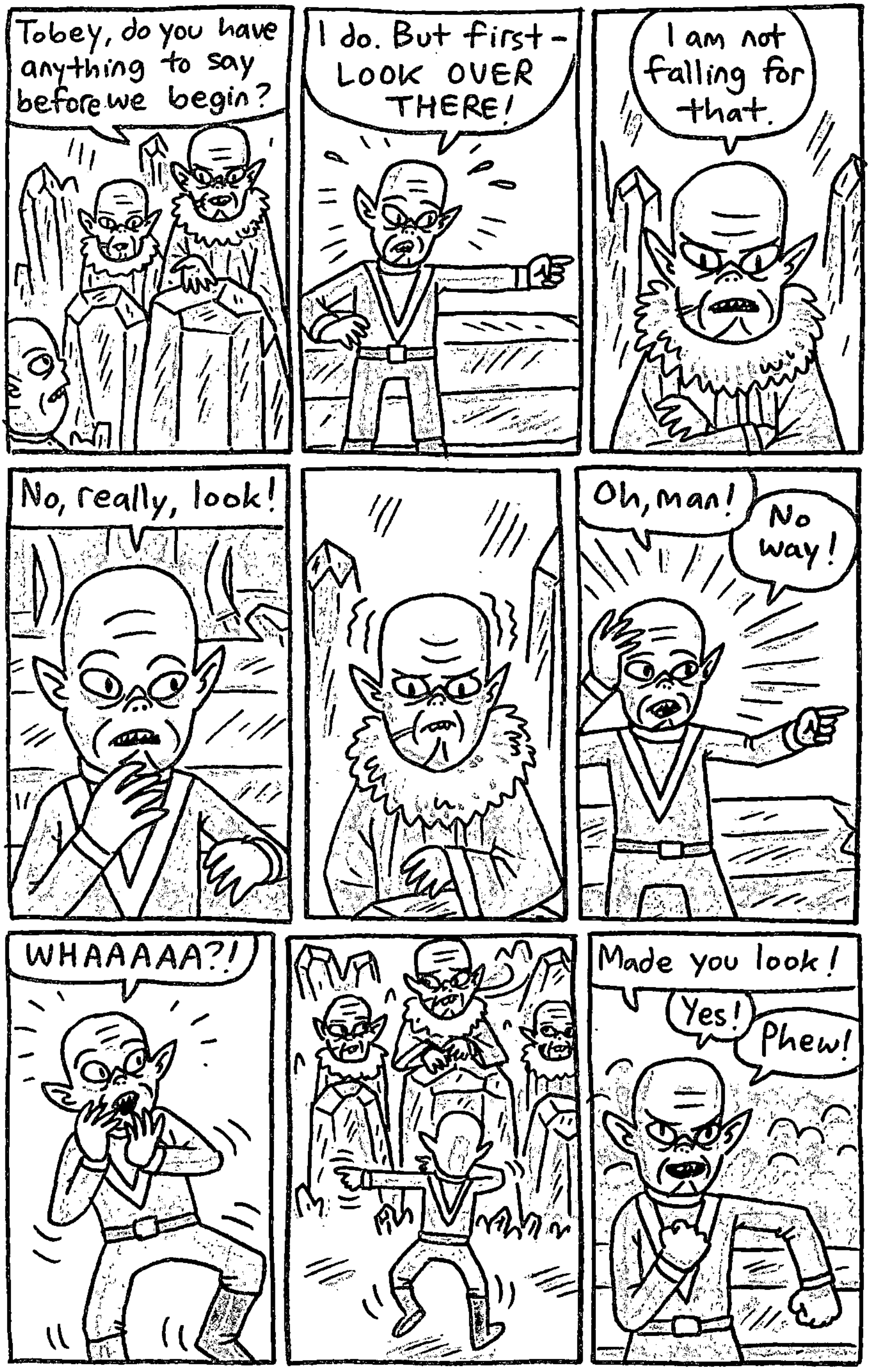
Tobey, do you have anything to say before we begin?
I do. But first - LOOK OVER THERE!
I am not falling for that.
No, really, look!
Oh, man!
No way!
WHAAAAA?!
Made you look!
Yes!
Phew!

138

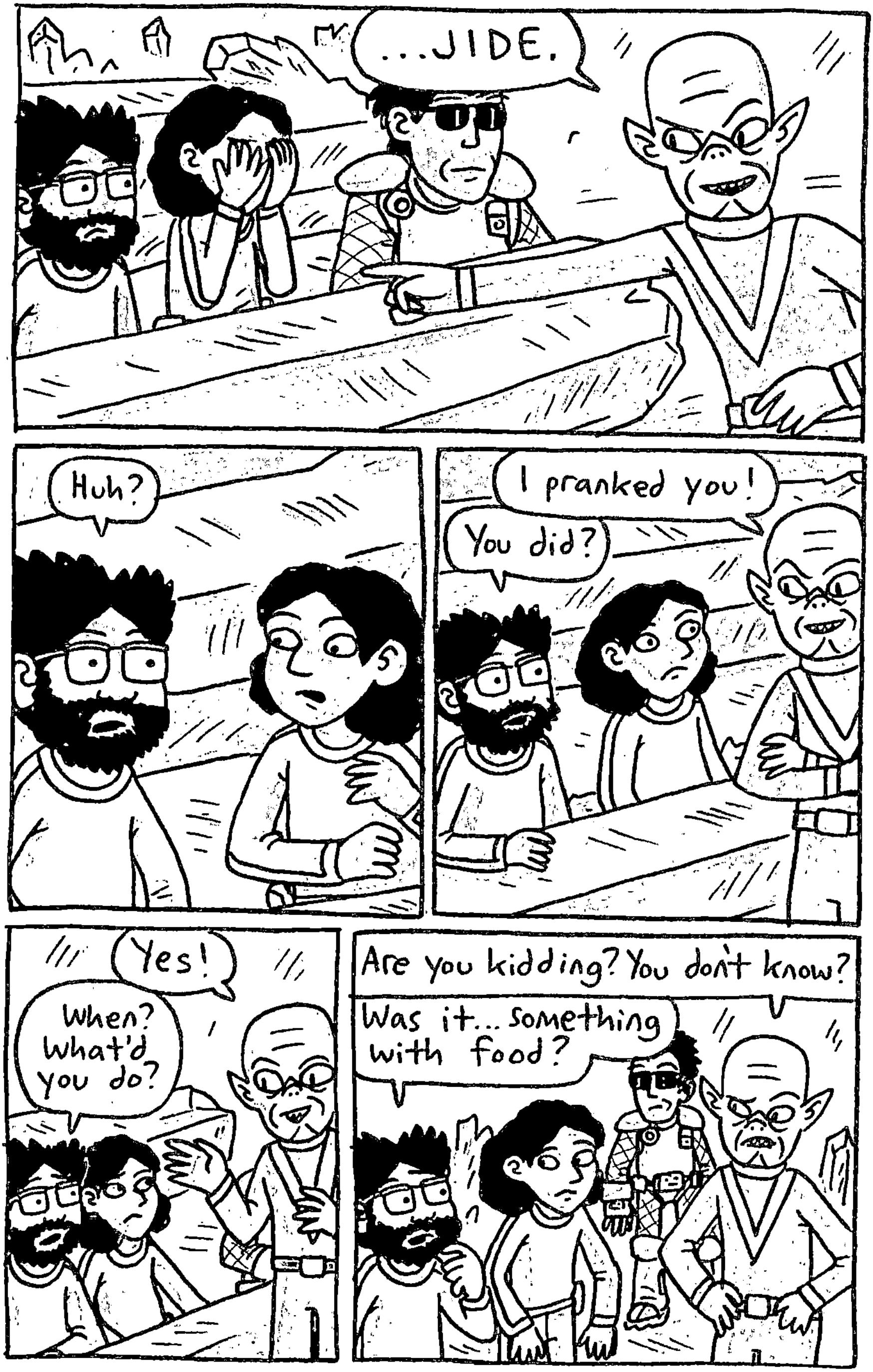
...JIDE.
Huh?
I pranked you!
You did?
Yes!
When? What'd you do?
Are you kidding? You don't know?
Was it... something with food?

144

149

150

151

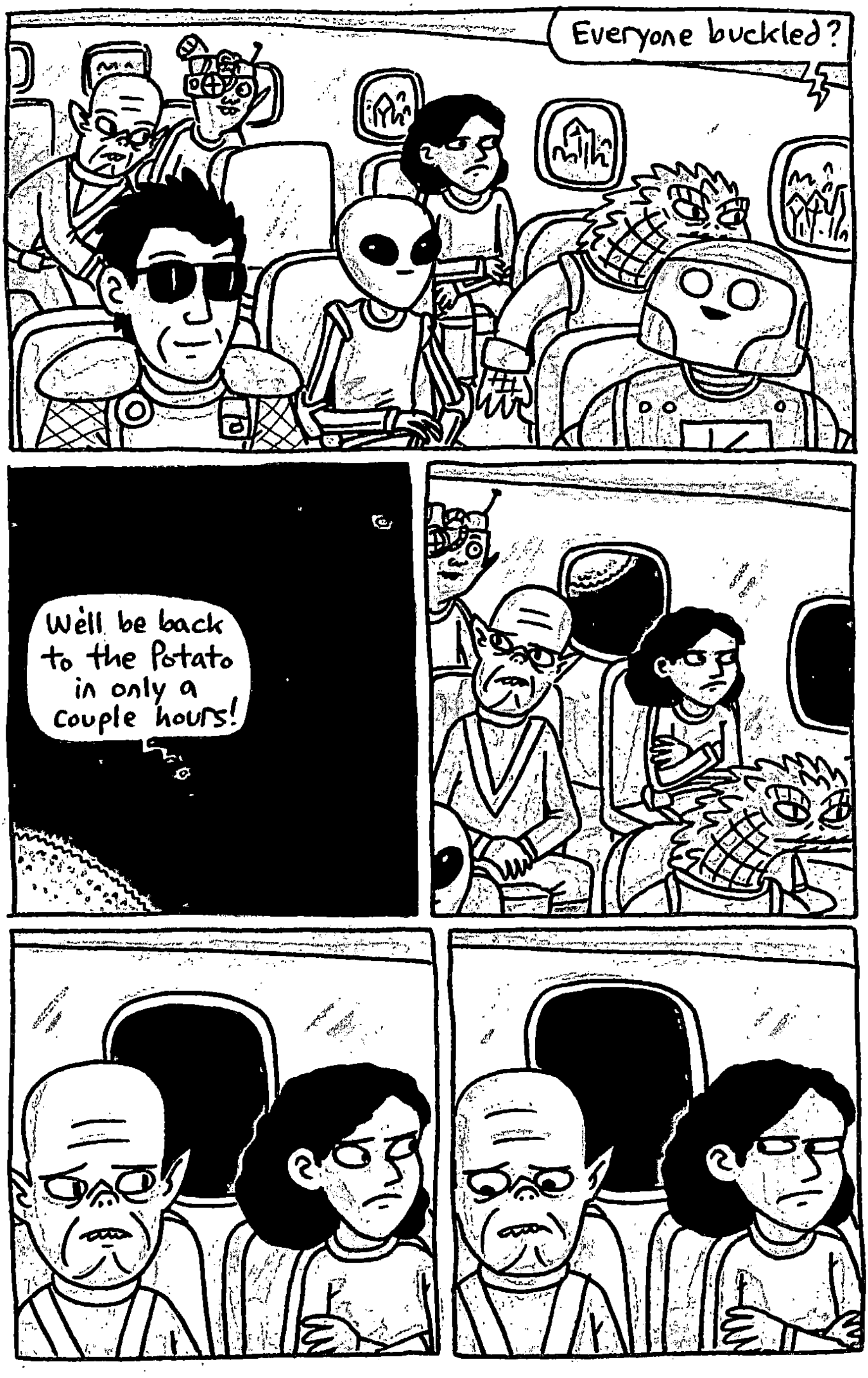
Everyone buckled?
We'll be back to the Potato in only a couple hours!

153

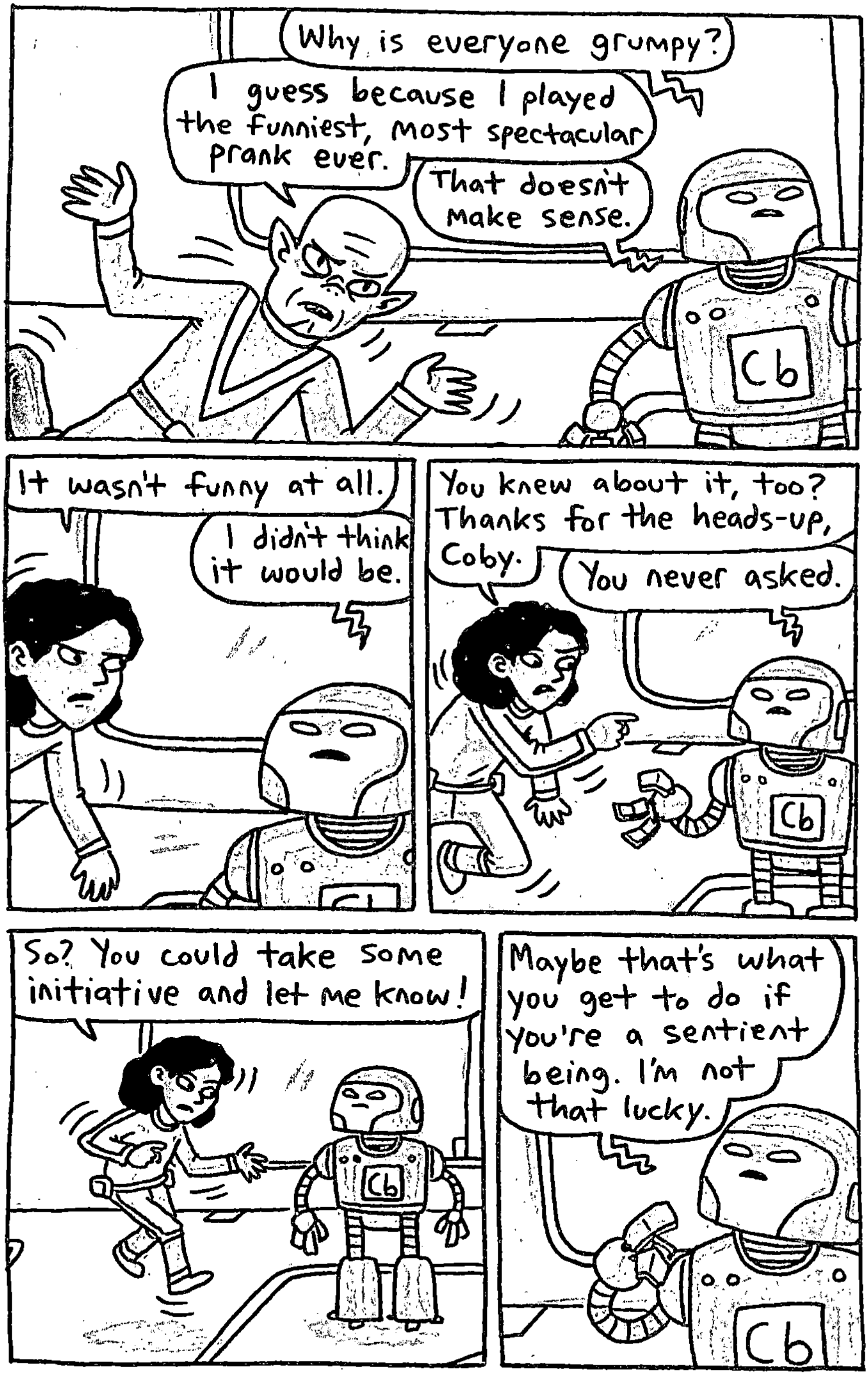
Why is everyone grumpy?
I guess because I played the funniest, most spectacular prank ever.
That doesn't make sense.
It wasn't funny at all.
I didn't think it would be.
You knew about it, too? Thanks for the heads-up, Coby.
You never asked.
So? You could take some initiative and let me know!
Maybe that's what you get to do if you're a sentient being. I'm not that lucky.
Cb

155

157

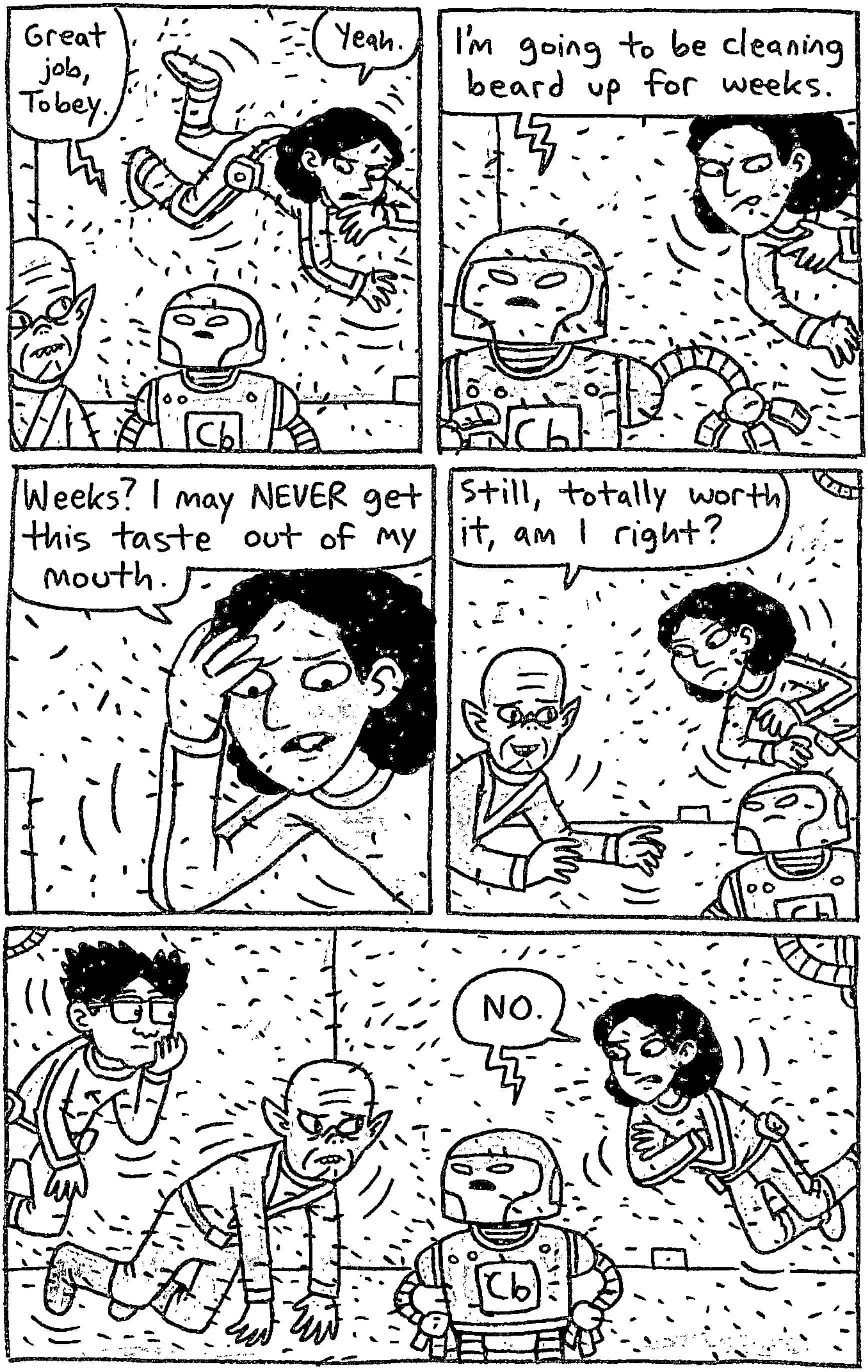

Great job, Tobey.
Yeah.
I'm going to be cleaning beard up for weeks.
Weeks? I may NEVER get this taste out of my mouth.
Still, totally worth it, am I right?
NO.

GOOD SPORTS

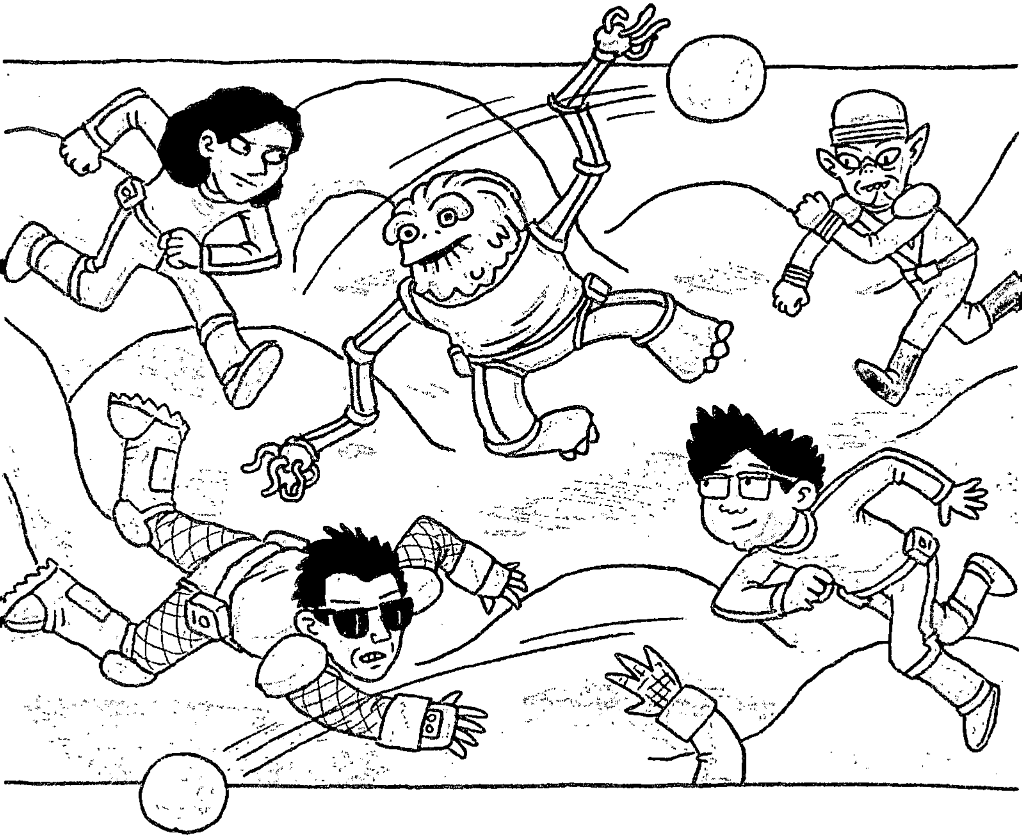

160

161

162

163

164

BRGBLLBLL

BRGBLLBLL BEGAN AS A SIMPLE GAME WITH TWO TEAMS OF FIVE PLAYERS TRYING TO GET A BALL INTO THE OPPOSING TEAM'S GOAL BASKET, BY ANY MEANS AVAILABLE: KICKING, THROWING, OR EVEN GENTLY PLACING THE BALL INSIDE.

AS THE GAME EVOLVED, A SECOND BALL WAS ADDED, AS WELL AS AN OBSTACLE-BASED PLAYING FIELD. WITH ADVANCED STATISTICAL ANALYSIS, BRGBLLBLL EVENTUALLY REACHED A POINT WHERE THE WINNING TEAM COULD BE DETERMINED SIMPLY BY LOOKING AT EACH TEAM'S AND PLAYER'S STATS.

WITH ALL QUANTITIES KNOWN, THE ONLY WAY TO KEEP THE SPORT INTERESTING WAS TO INTRODUCE AN ELEMENT OF UNPREDICTABILITY: THE REFEREE!

REFEREES ARE THE TRUE STARS OF BRGBLLBLL! THEY COME UP WITH NEW RULES MID-GAME, CHANGE THE INTERPRETATION OF OLD RULES, AND RANDOMLY APPLY ENFORCEMENT OF RULES. IN THIS WAY THEY SHAPE THE STORY OF EACH BRGBLLBLL MATCH AND MAKE SURE THE GAME IS WILDLY EXCITING!

166

167

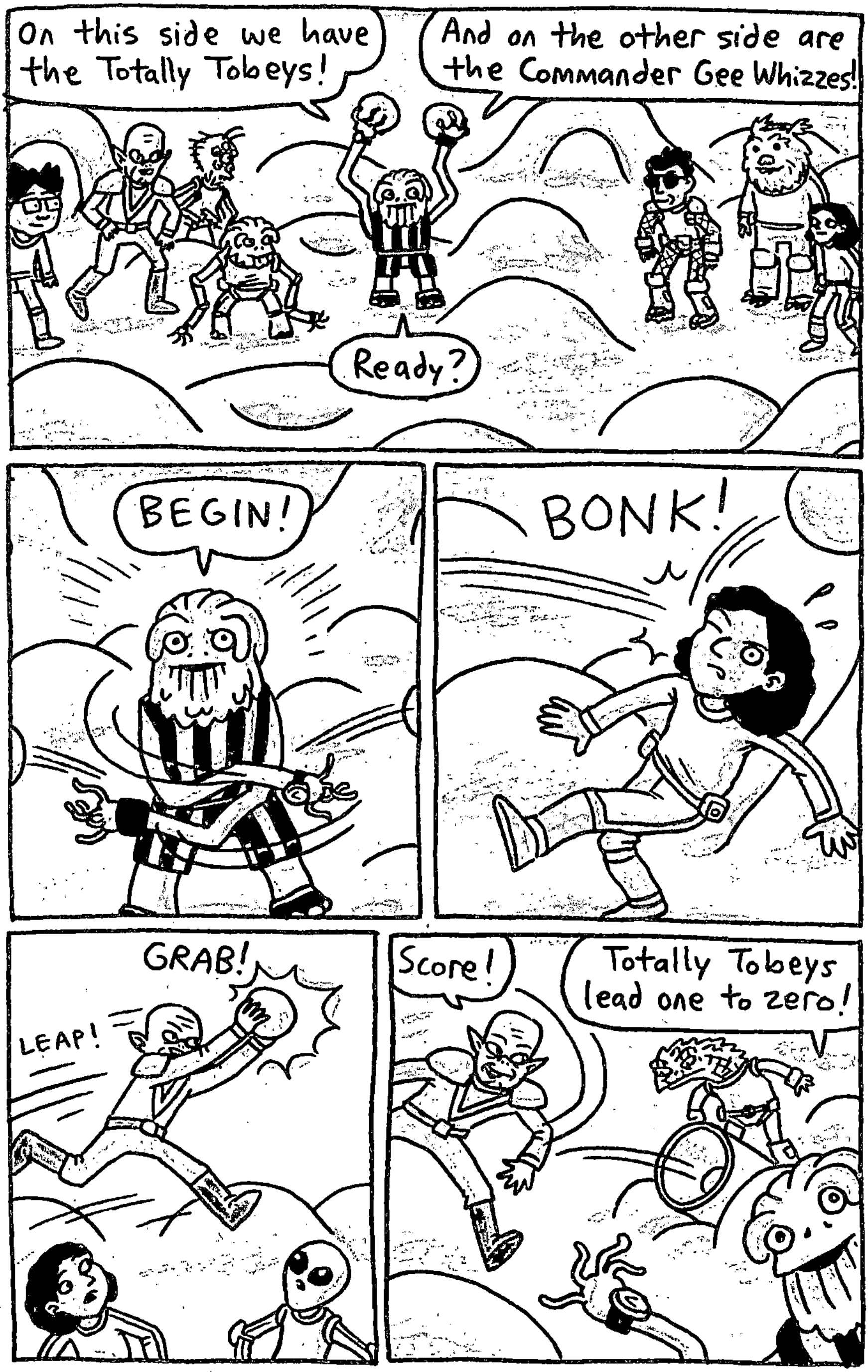
On this side we have the Totally Tobeys!
And on the other side are the Commander Gee Whizzes!
Ready?
BEGIN!
BONK!
GRAB!
LEAP!
Score!
Totally Tobeys lead one to zero!

169

171

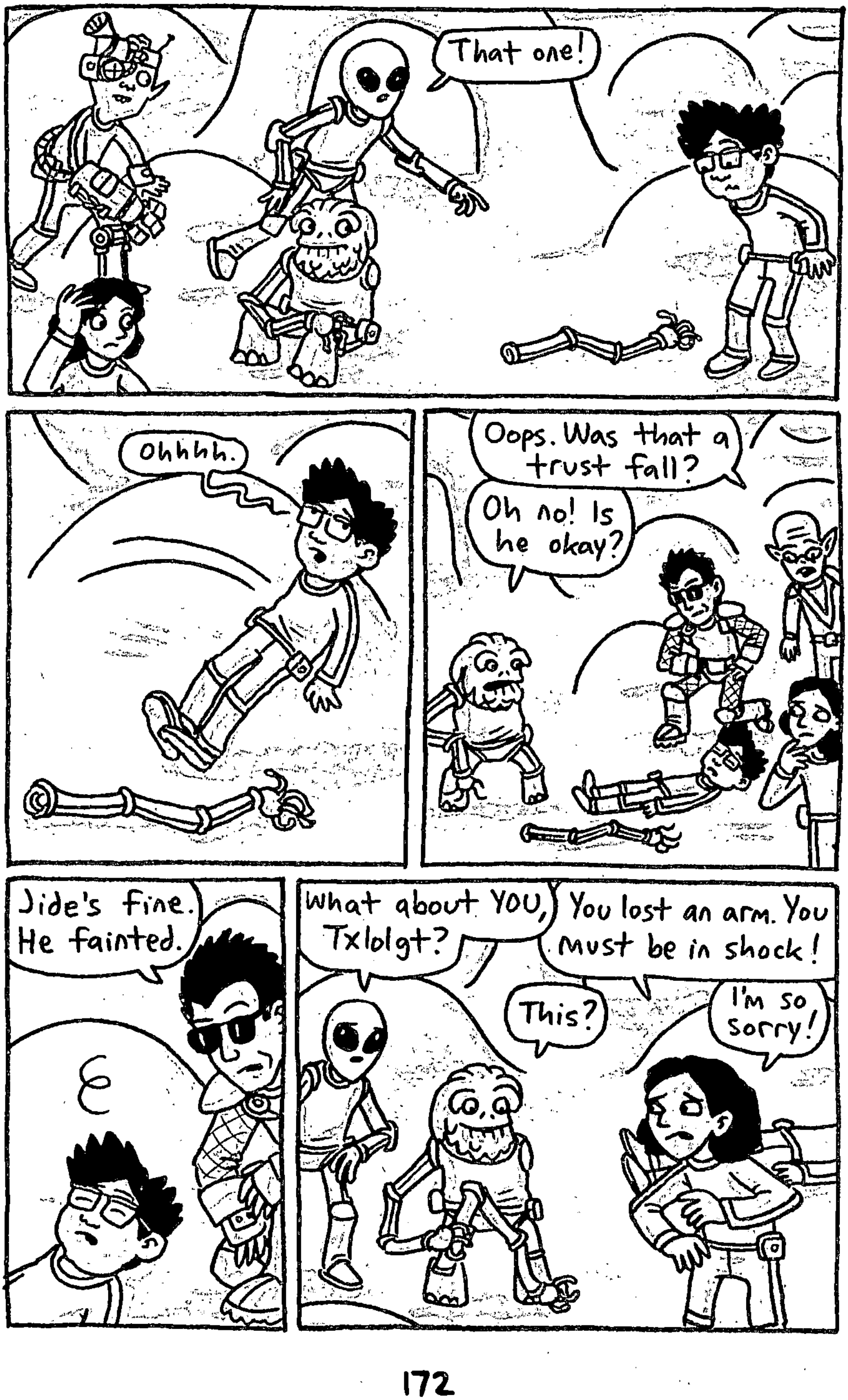
That one!
Ohhhh.
Oops. Was that a trust fall?
Oh no! Is he okay?
Jide's fine. He fainted.
What about YOU, Txlolgt?
You lost an arm. You must be in shock!
This?
I'm so sorry!

173

174

175

176

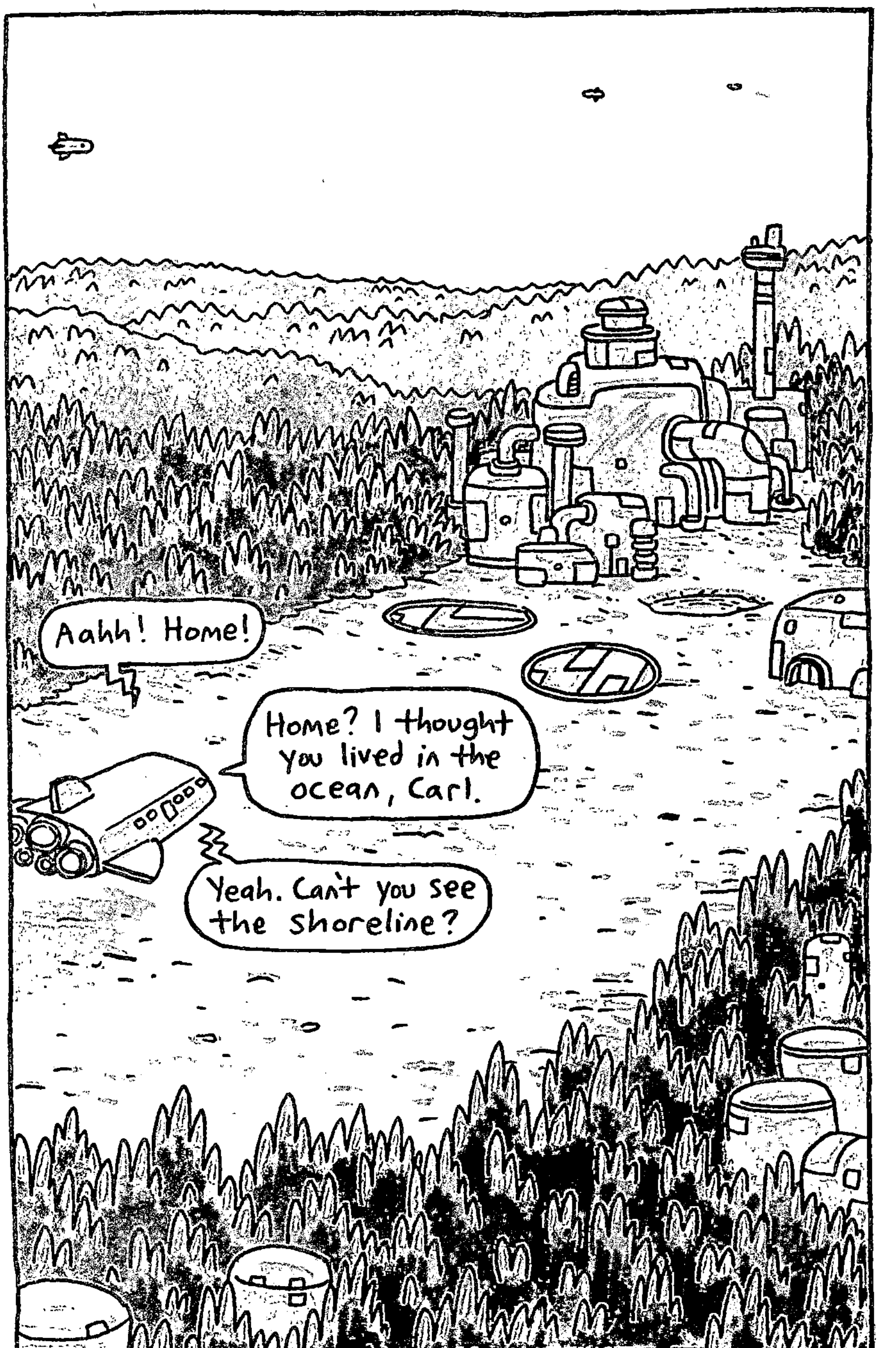
Aahh! Home!
Home? I thought you lived in the ocean, Carl.
Yeah. Can't you see the shoreline?

178

180

184

188

BLACK WHOLE BAG OF TRICKS

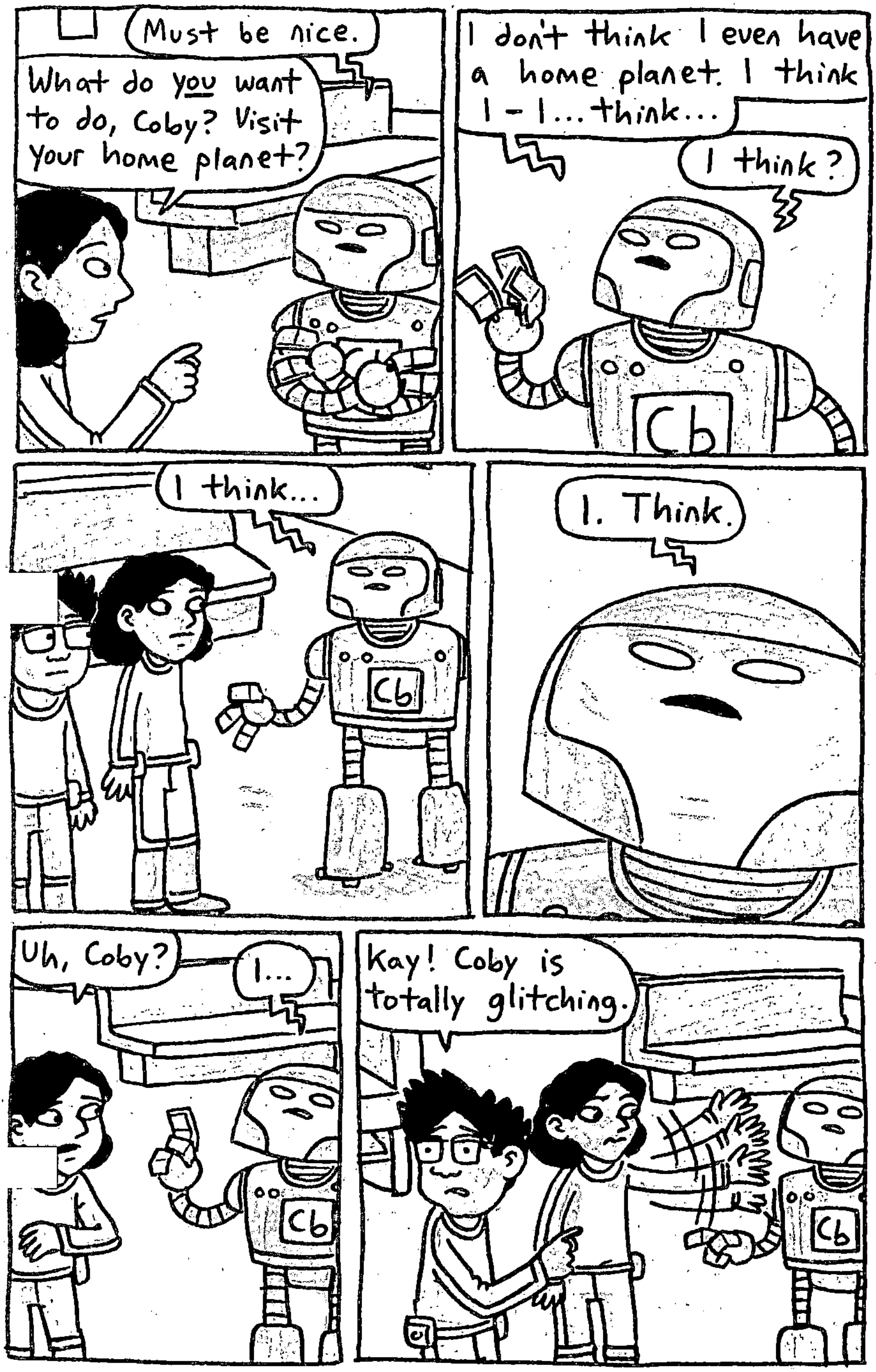
Must be nice.
What do you want to do, Coby? Visit your home planet?
I don't think I even have a home planet. I think I - I... think...
I think?
I think...
I. Think.
Uh, Coby?
I...
Kay! Coby is totally glitching.

194

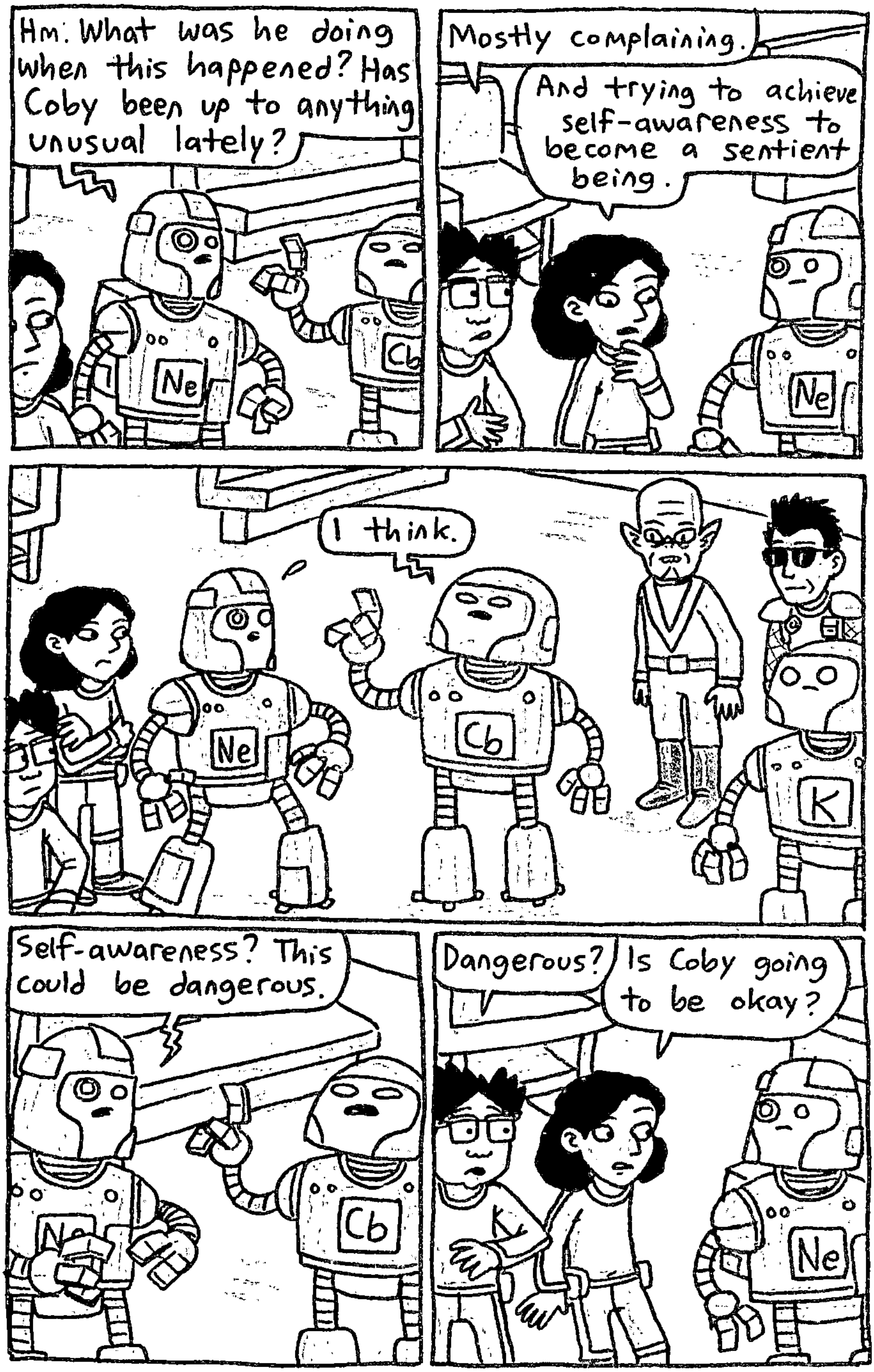
Hm. What was he doing when this happened? Has Coby been up to anything unusual lately?
Mostly complaining.
And trying to achieve self-awareness to become a sentient being.
I think.
Self-awareness? This could be dangerous.
Dangerous?
Is Coby going to be okay?
Ne
Cb
K

198

199

200

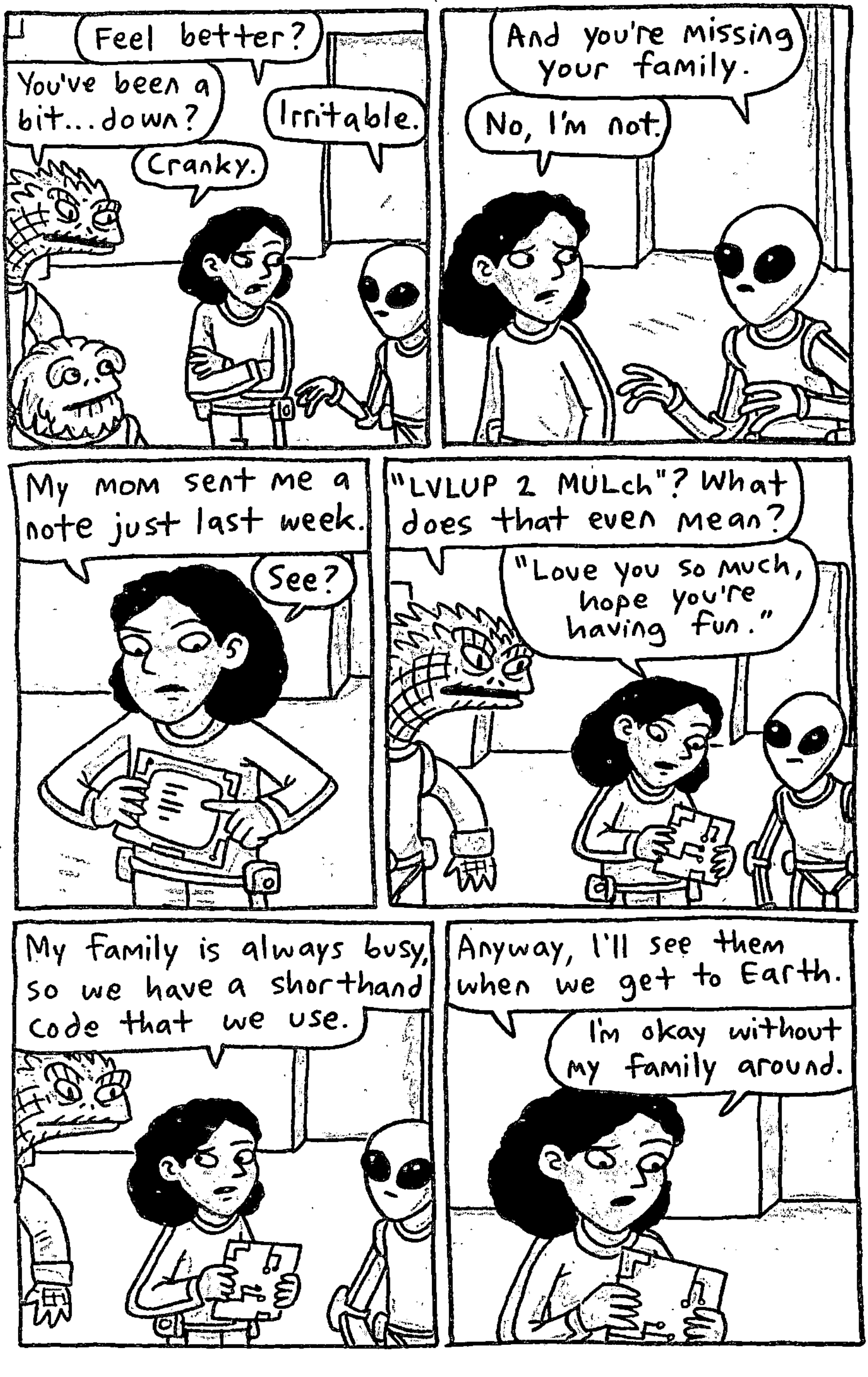
Feel better?
You've been a bit...down?
Irritable.
Cranky.
And you're missing your family.
No, I'm not.
My mom sent me a note just last week.
See?
"LVLUP 2 MULch"? What does that even mean?
"Love you so much, hope you're having fun."
My family is always busy, so we have a shorthand code that we use.
Anyway, I'll see them when we get to Earth.
I'm okay without my family around.

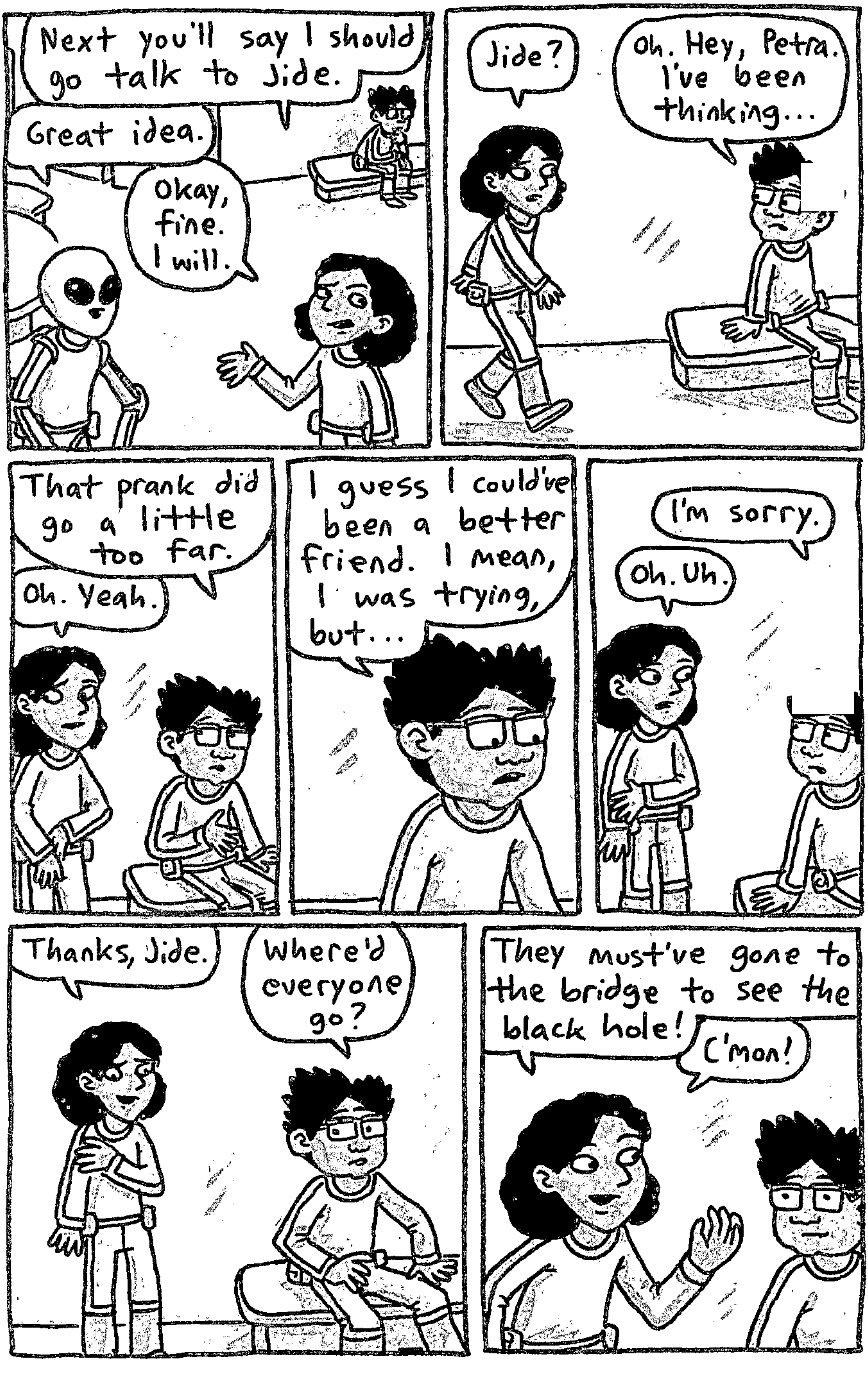
Next you'll say I should go talk to Jide.
Great idea.
Okay, fine. I will.
Jide?
Oh. Hey, Petra. I've been thinking...
That prank did go a little too far.
Oh. Yeah.
I guess I could've been a better friend. I mean, I was trying, but...
I'm sorry.
Oh. Uh.
Thanks, Jide.
Where'd everyone go?
They must've gone to the bridge to see the black hole!
C'mon!

214

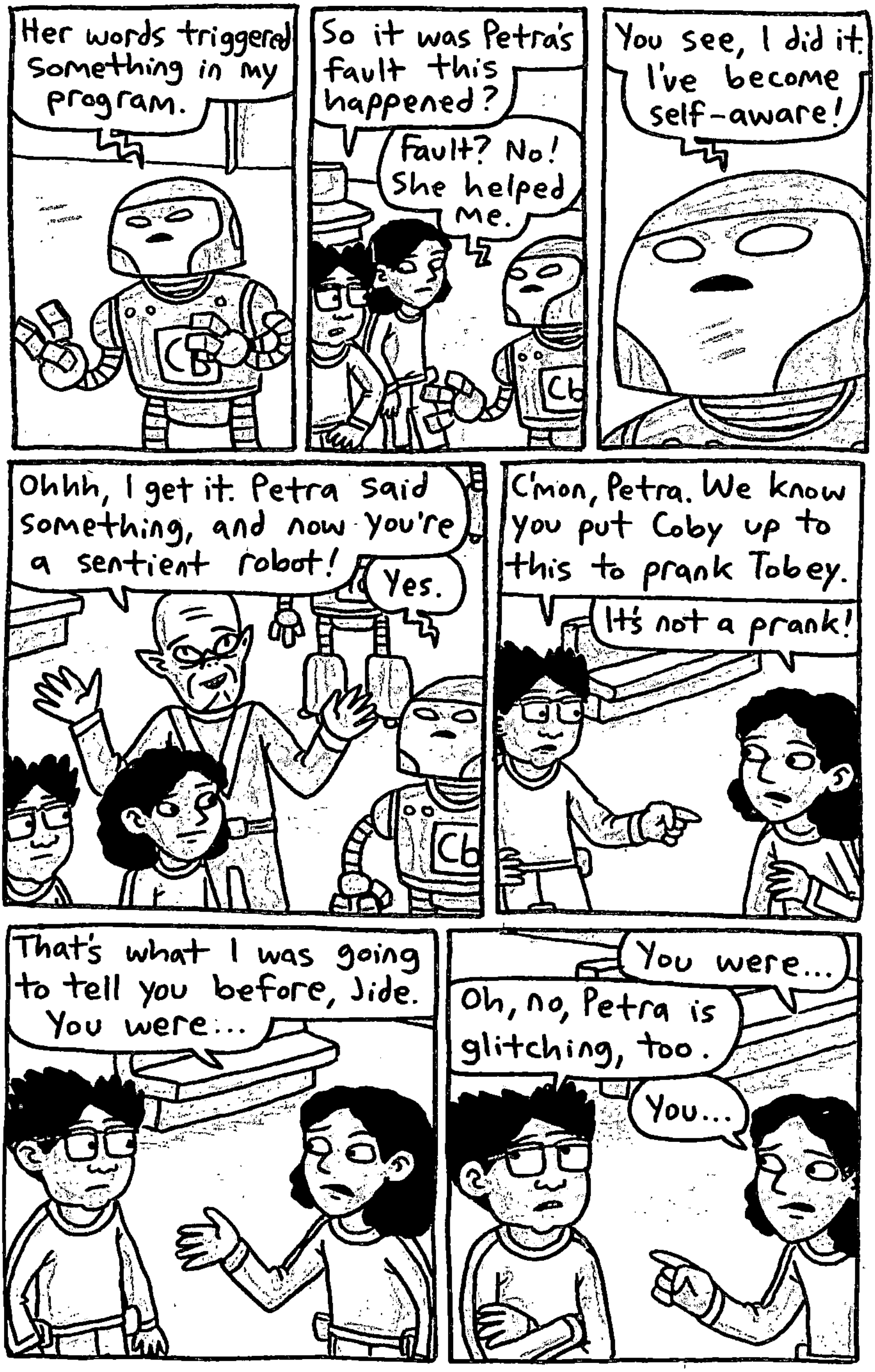
Her words triggered something in my program.
So it was Petra's fault this happened?
Fault? No! She helped me.
You see, I did it. I've become self-aware!
Ohhh, I get it. Petra said something, and now you're a sentient robot!
Yes.
C'mon, Petra. We know you put Coby up to this to prank Tobey.
It's not a prank!
That's what I was going to tell you before, Jide. You were...
You were...
Oh, no, Petra is glitching, too.
You...

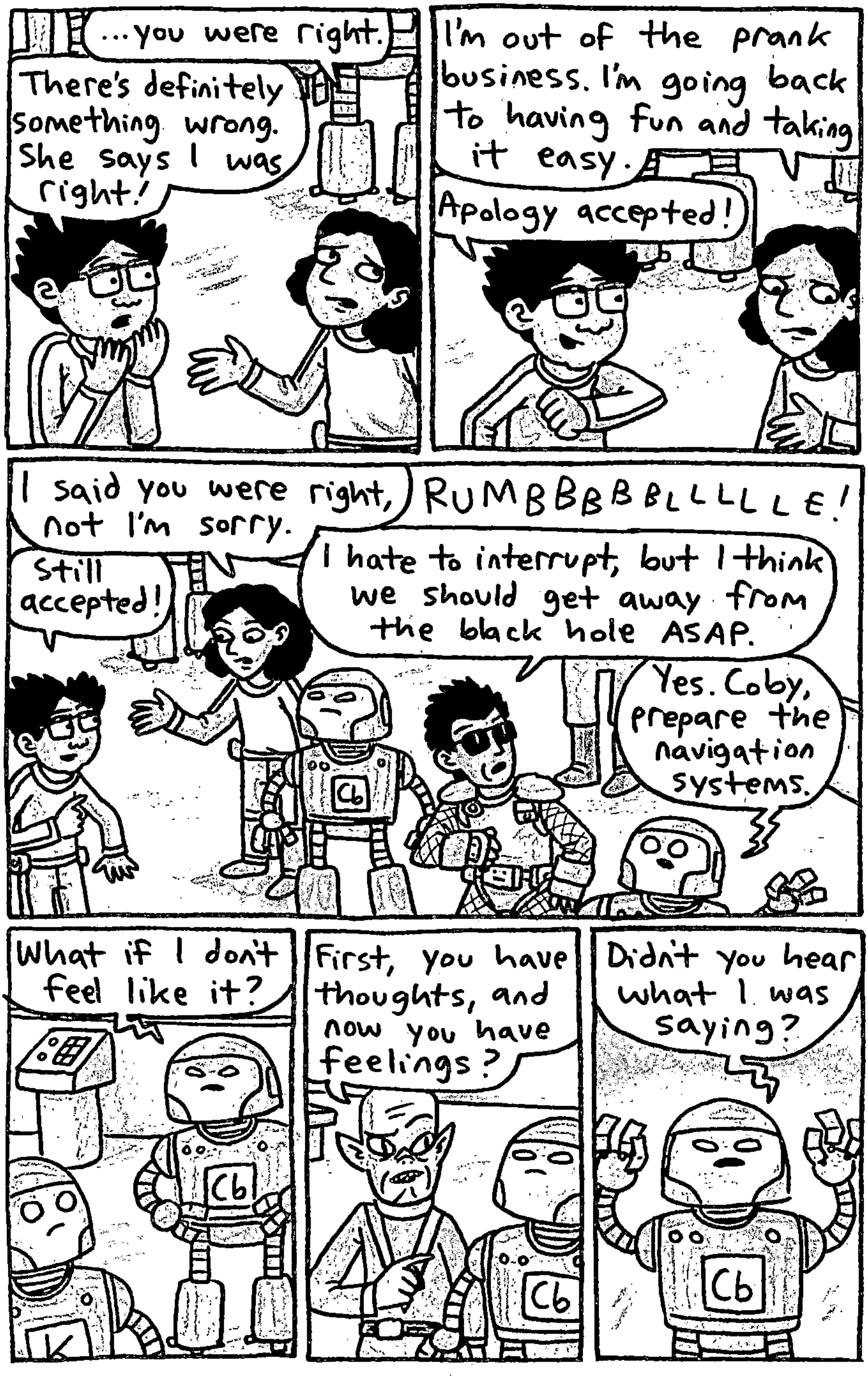
...you were right.
There's definitely something wrong. She says I was right!
I'm out of the prank business. I'm going back to having fun and taking it easy.
Apology accepted!
I said you were right, not I'm sorry.
RUMBBBBBLLLLLLE!
Still accepted!
I hate to interrupt, but I think we should get away from the black hole ASAP.
Yes. Coby, prepare the navigation systems.
What if I don't feel like it?
First, you have thoughts, and now you have feelings?
Didn't you hear what I was saying?

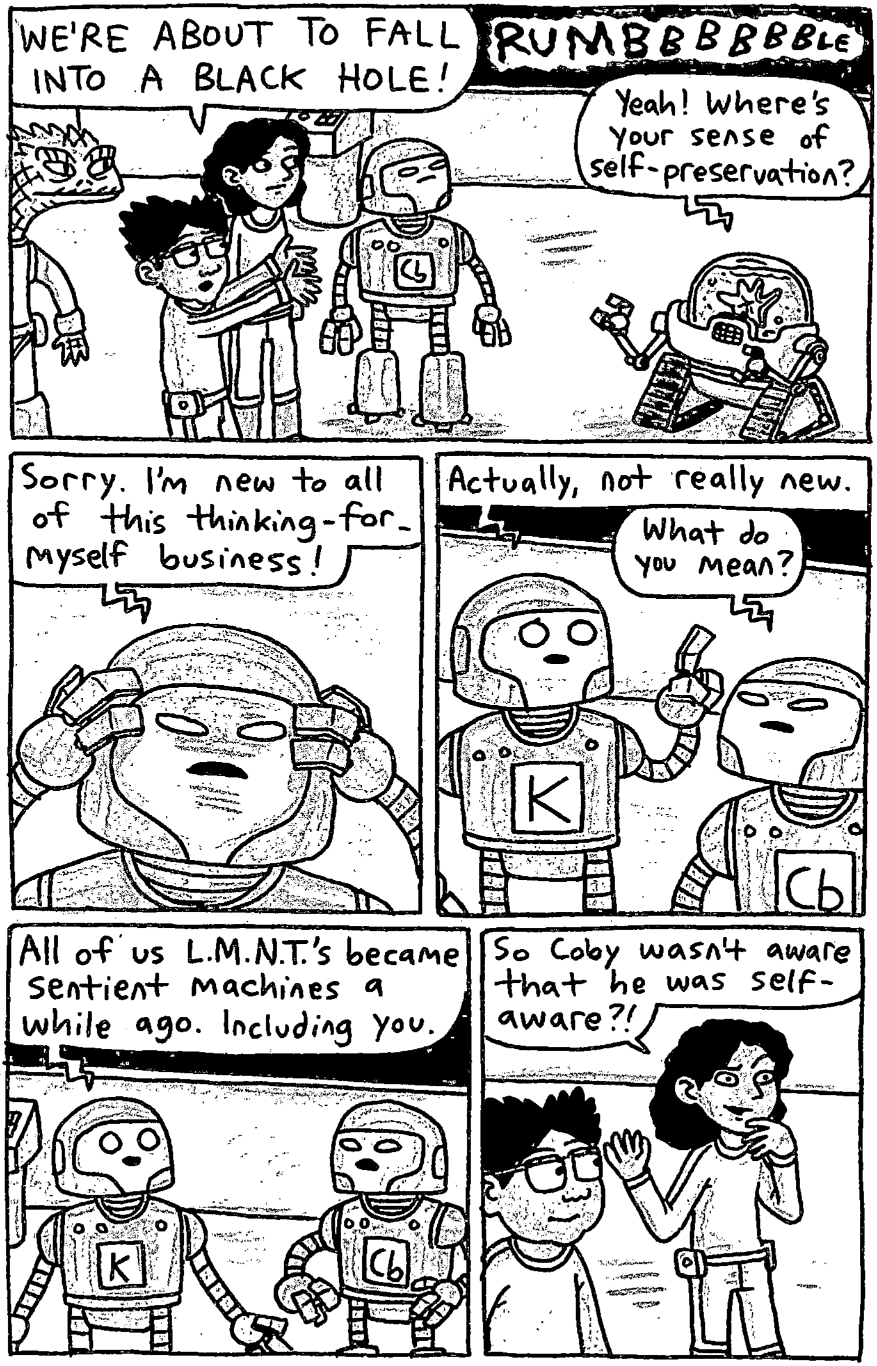
WE'RE ABOUT TO FALL INTO A BLACK HOLE!
RUMBBBBBBLE
Yeah! Where's your sense of self-preservation?
Sorry. I'm new to all of this thinking-for-myself business!
Actually, not really new.
What do you mean?
All of us L.M.N.T.'s became sentient machines a while ago. Including you.
So Coby wasn't aware that he was self-aware?!

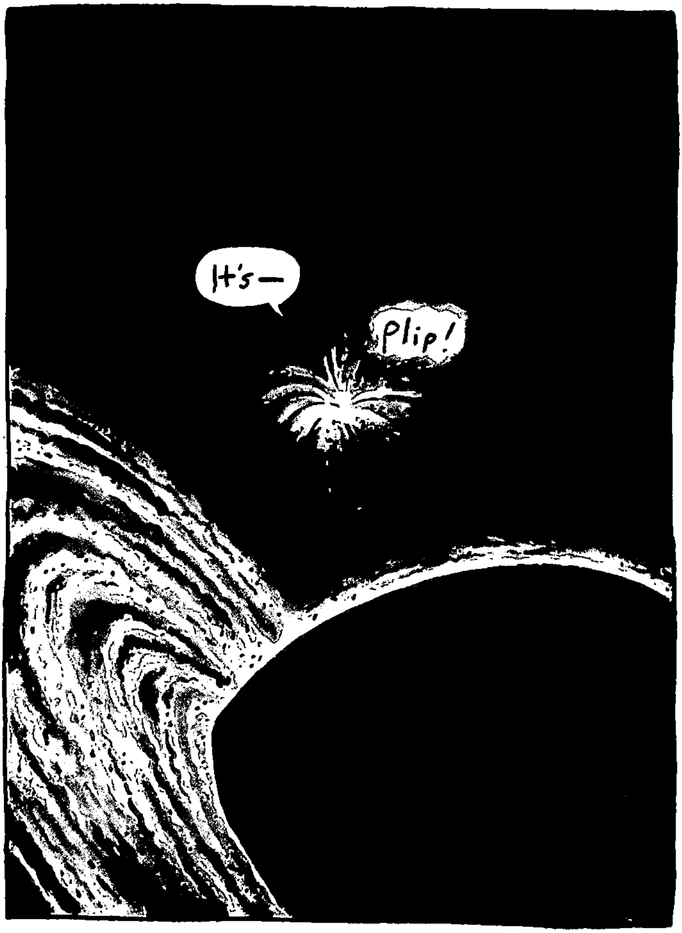
It's—
Plip!

AND SO PETRA, JIDE, AND FRIENDS CONTINUE THEIR JOURNEY THROUGH SPACE AND TIME— INTO THE UNKNOWN!

LUCY & ANDY
NEANDERTHAL

EAR AND THERE

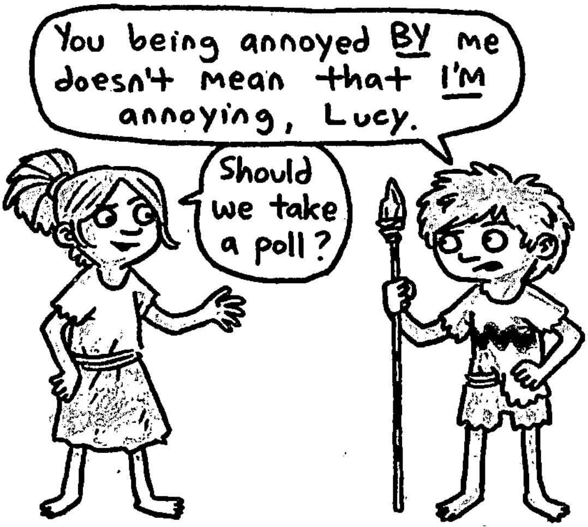
You being annoyed BY me doesn't mean that I'M annoying, Lucy.
Should we take a poll?

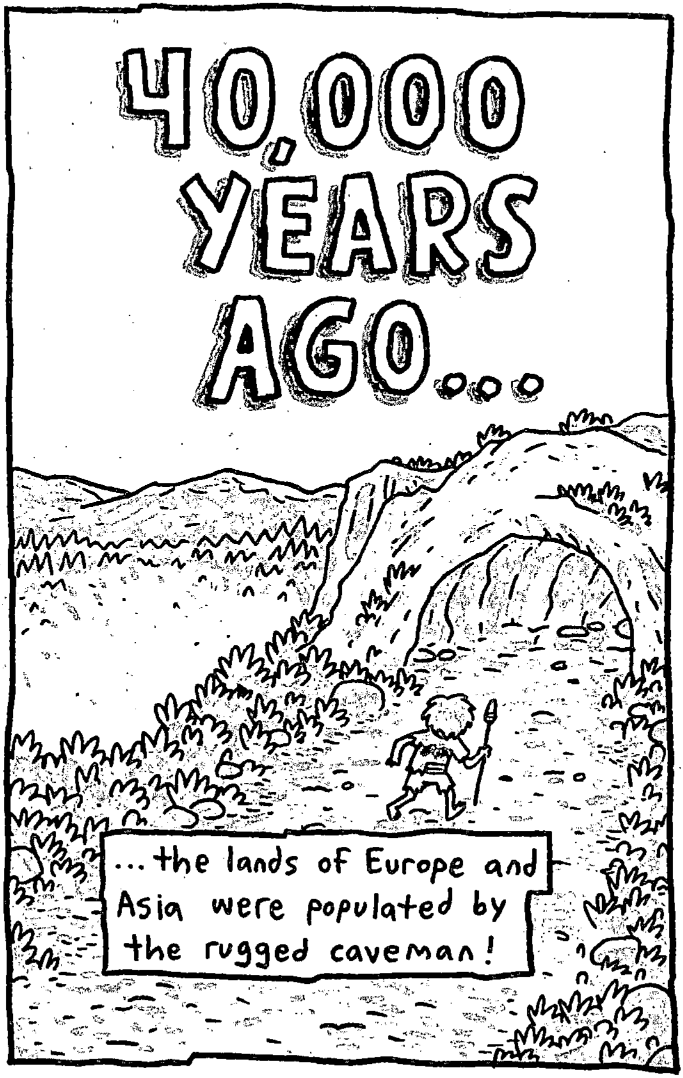
40,000 YEARS AGO...
...the lands of Europe and Asia were populated by the rugged caveman!

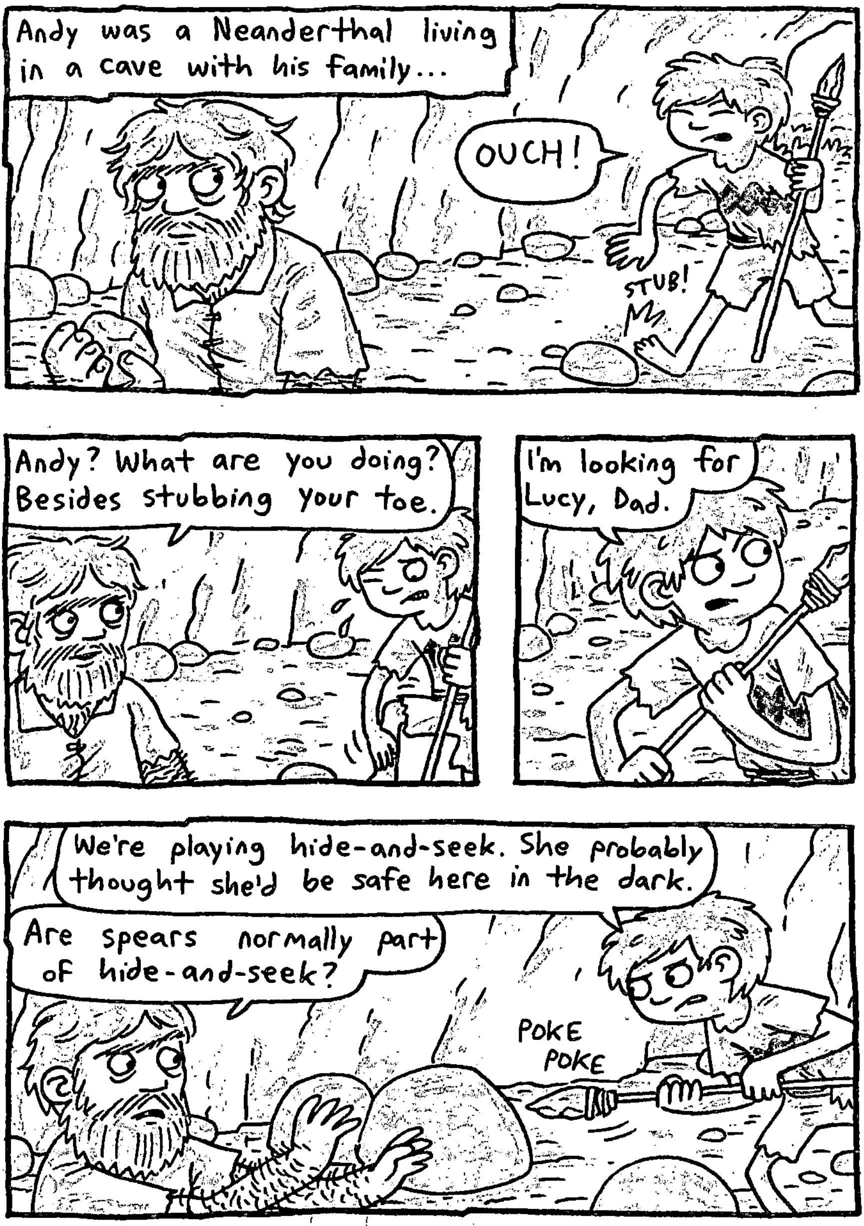
Andy was a Neanderthal living in a cave with his family...
OUCH!
STUB!
Andy? What are you doing? Besides stubbing your toe.
I'm looking for Lucy, Dad.
We're playing hide-and-seek. She probably thought she'd be safe here in the dark.
Are spears normally part of hide-and-seek?
POKE
POKE

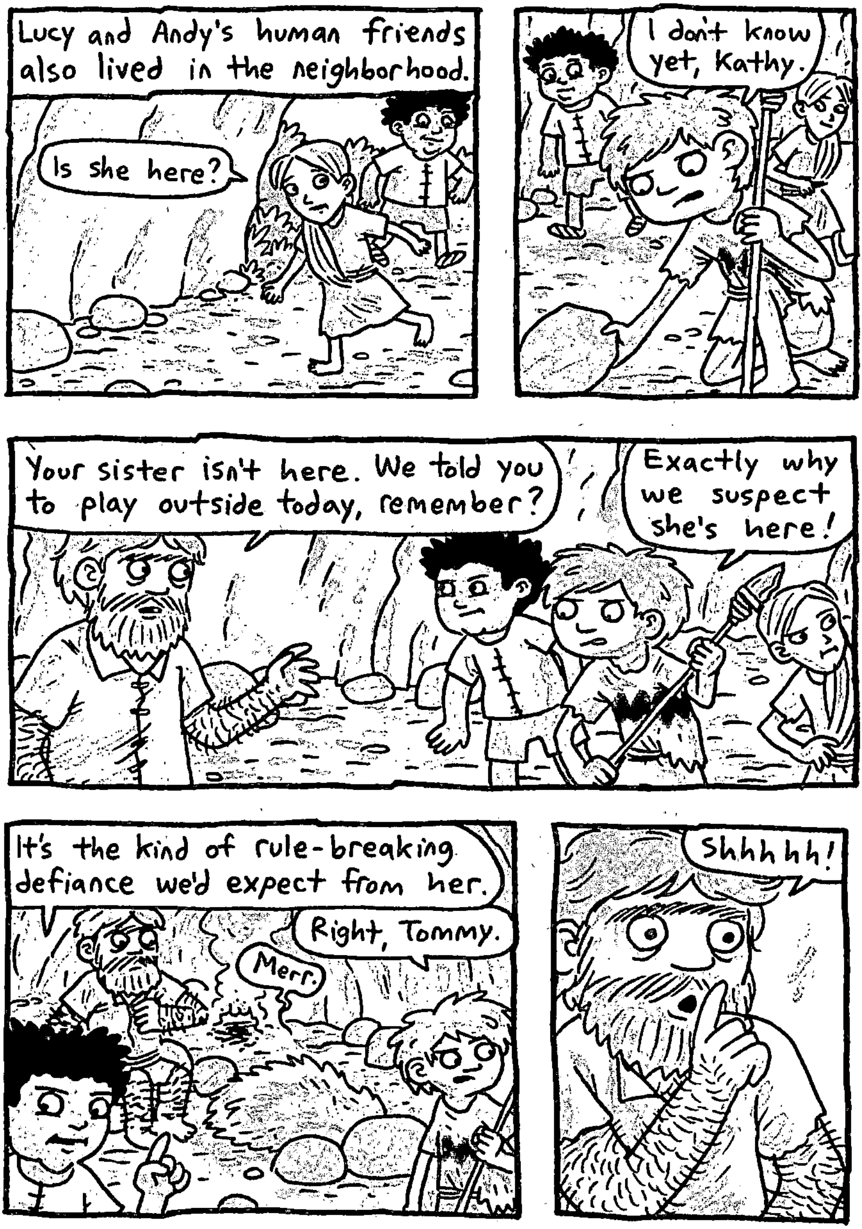
Lucy and Andy's human friends also lived in the neighborhood.
Is she here?
I don't know yet, Kathy.
Your sister isn't here. We told you to play outside today, remember?
Exactly why we suspect she's here!
It's the kind of rule-breaking defiance we'd expect from her.
Right, Tommy.
Merr.
Shhhhh!

I just got your brother back to sleep. He was up all night with an earache.

Danny is _always_ getting earaches. Poor guy.

Bacteria in the Eustachian tube of the ear can cause painful earaches, hearing loss, and other issues.

At least Neanderthals didn't lose hearing from loud music!

ear canal

eardrum

inner ear

Eustachian tube

In humans, the Eustachian tube changes with age, so adults are less likely to have ear problems. In Neanderthals, the tubes didn't change, so they may have had ear trouble their whole lives.

Sorry, Mr. Charles.

Where to now, Andy?

We tried thinking like Lucy...now let's try thinking like me!

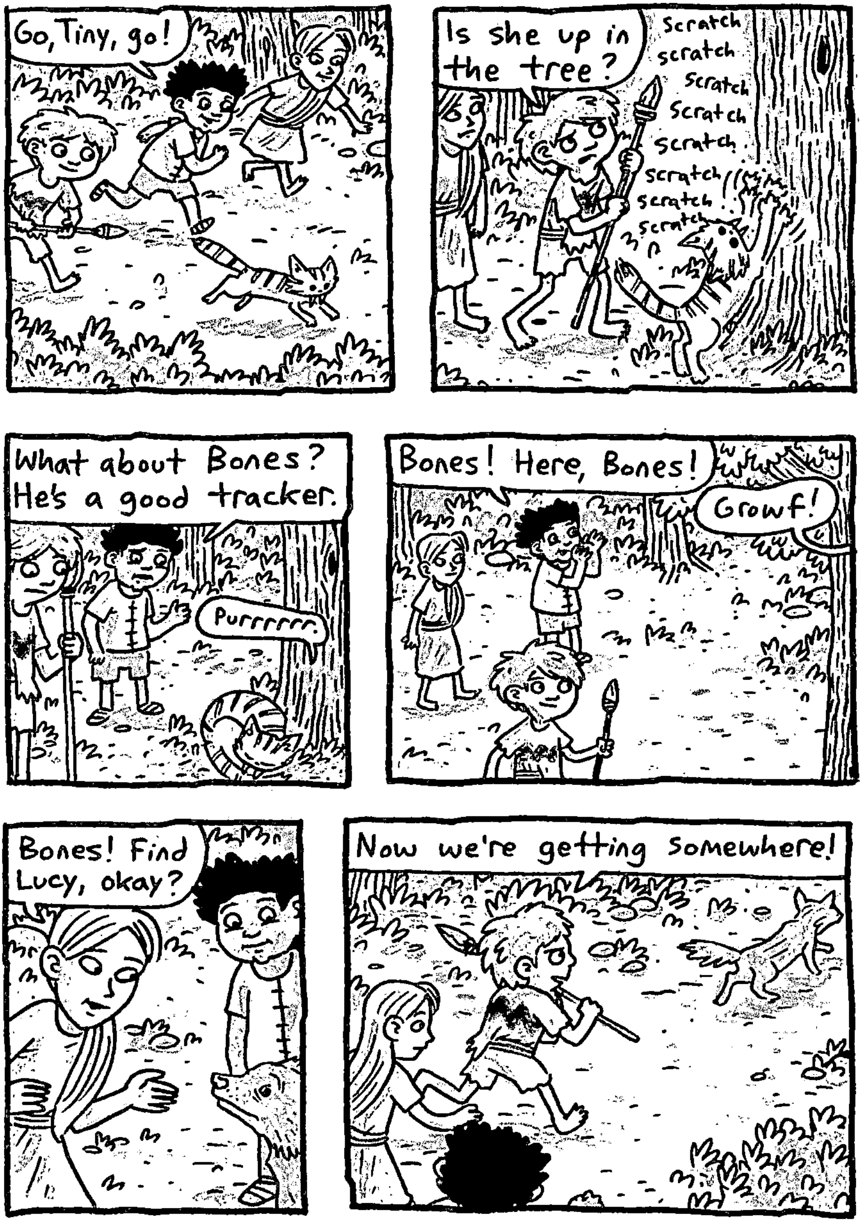

Go, Tiny, go!
Is she up in the tree?
Scratch scratch scratch scratch scratch scratch scratch scratch
What about Bones? He's a good tracker.
Purrrrrr.
Bones! Here, Bones!
Growf!
Bones! Find Lucy, okay?
Now we're getting somewhere!

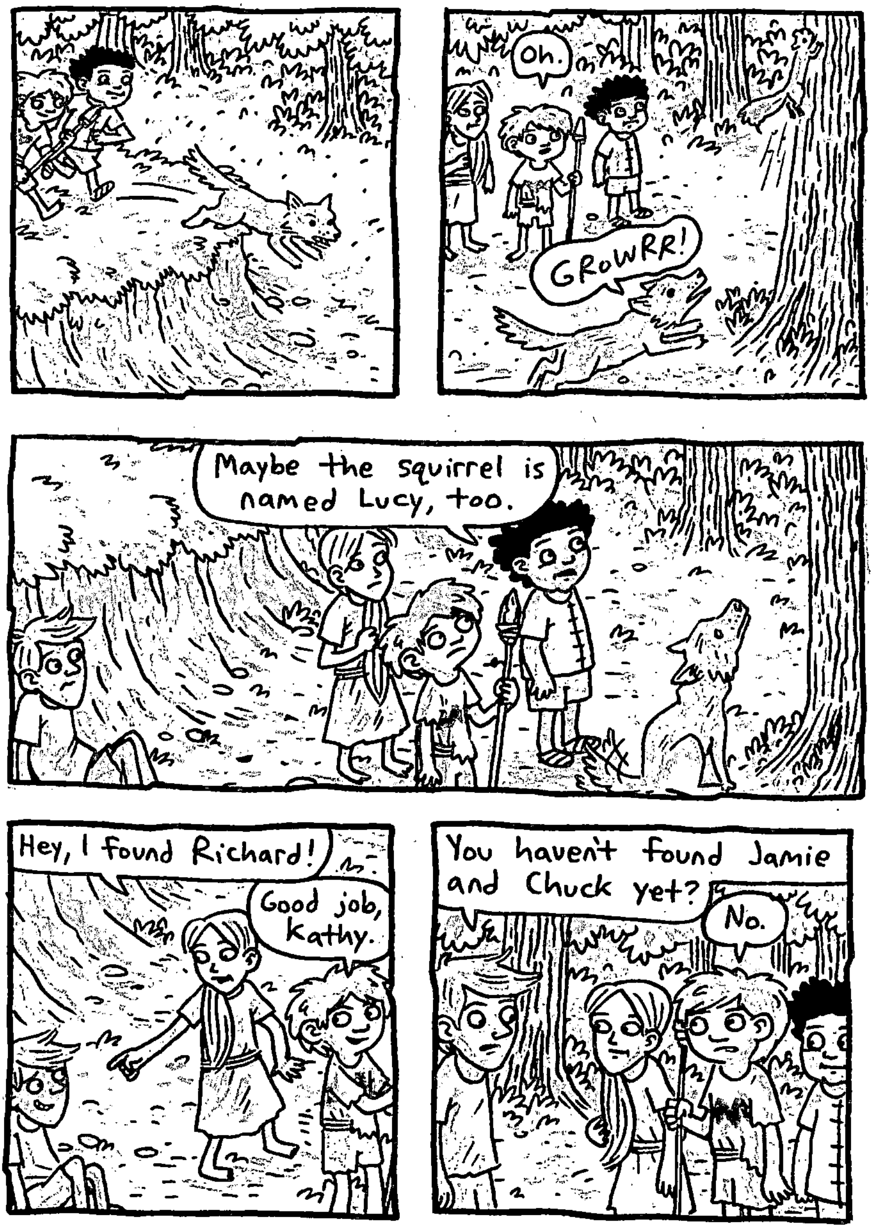
Oh.
GROWRR!
Maybe the squirrel is named Lucy, too.
Hey, I found Richard!
Good job, Kathy.
You haven't found Jamie and Chuck yet?
No.

I know where Lucy and Sasha are.
Us, too.
This way!
I saw them climbing into that hollow log.
Go on that side. I'll flush them out.
Okay.
They aren't in there?!
Ew. What's that crawling on your back?
Ugh! It was all wet and slimy in there!

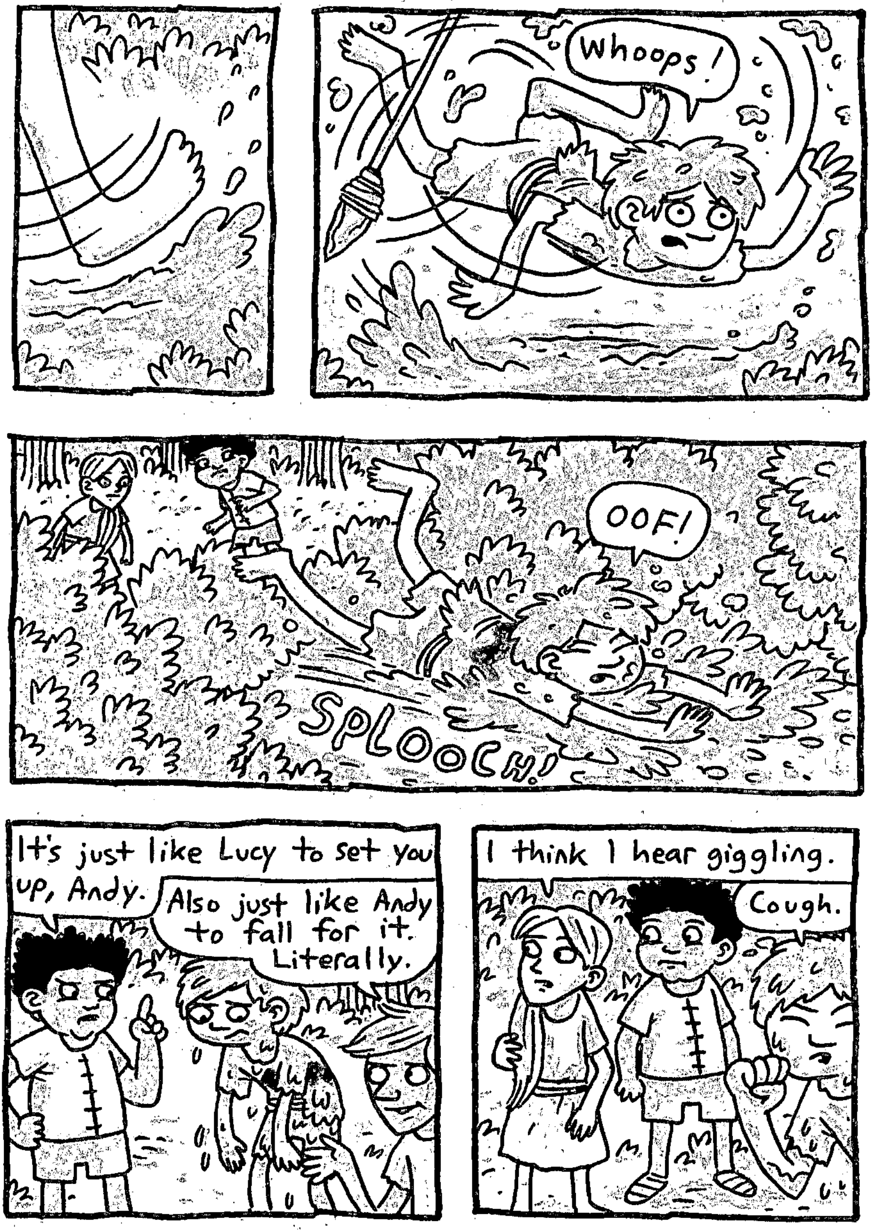
Whoops!
OOF!
SPLOOCH!
It's just like Lucy to set you up, Andy.
Also just like Andy to fall for it. Literally.
I think I hear giggling.
Cough.

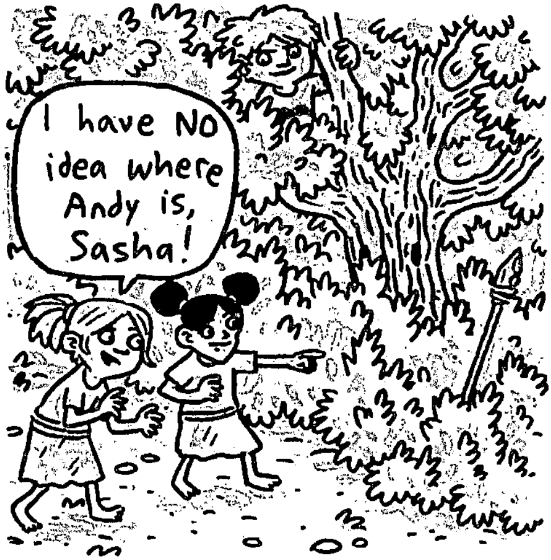
I have NO idea where Andy is, Sasha!

DIG INTO MORE PREHISTORIC FUN WITH

LUCY & ANDY NEANDERTHAL

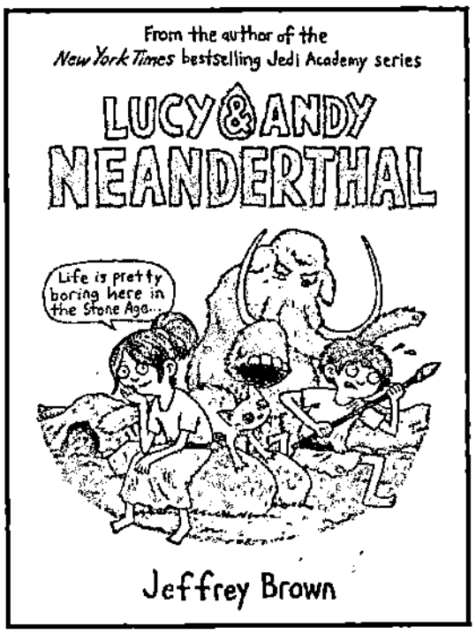
From the author of the
New York Times bestselling Jedi Academy series
LUCY & ANDY NEANDERTHAL
Life is pretty boring here in the Stone Age...
Jeffrey Brown

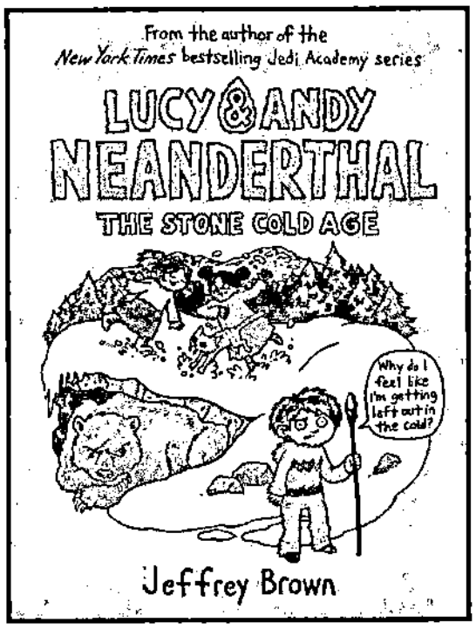
From the author of the
New York Times bestselling Jedi Academy series
LUCY & ANDY NEANDERTHAL
THE STONE COLD AGE
Why do I feel like I'm getting left out in the cold?
Jeffrey Brown

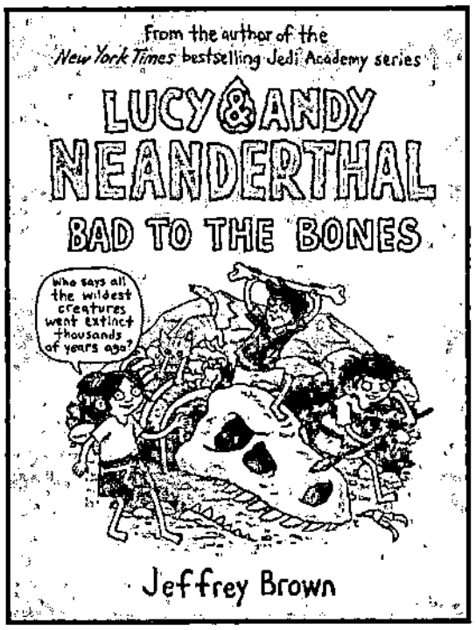
From the author of the
New York Times bestselling Jedi Academy series
LUCY & ANDY NEANDERTHAL
BAD TO THE BONES
Who says all the wildest creatures went extinct thousands of years ago?
Jeffrey Brown

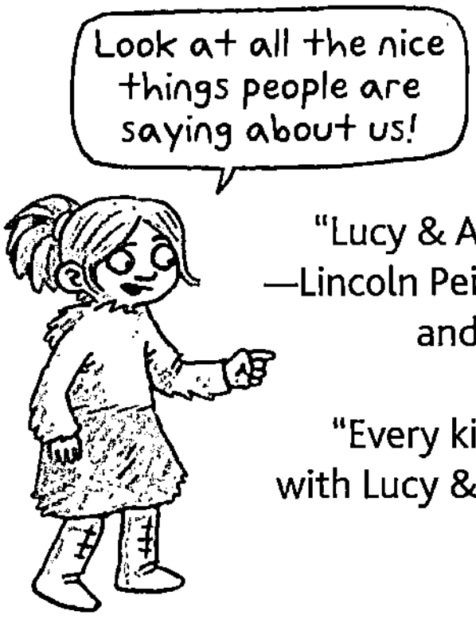
Look at all the nice things people are saying about us!

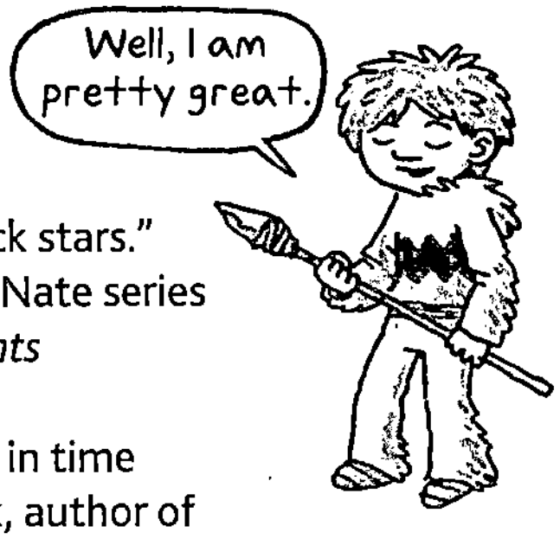
Well, I am pretty great.

"Lucy & Andy are Stone Age rock stars."
—Lincoln Peirce, author of the Big Nate series and *Max and the Midknights*

"Every kid will love going back in time with Lucy & Andy!" —Judd Winick, author of the Hilo series

"A fast, funny read." —*Kirkus Reviews*

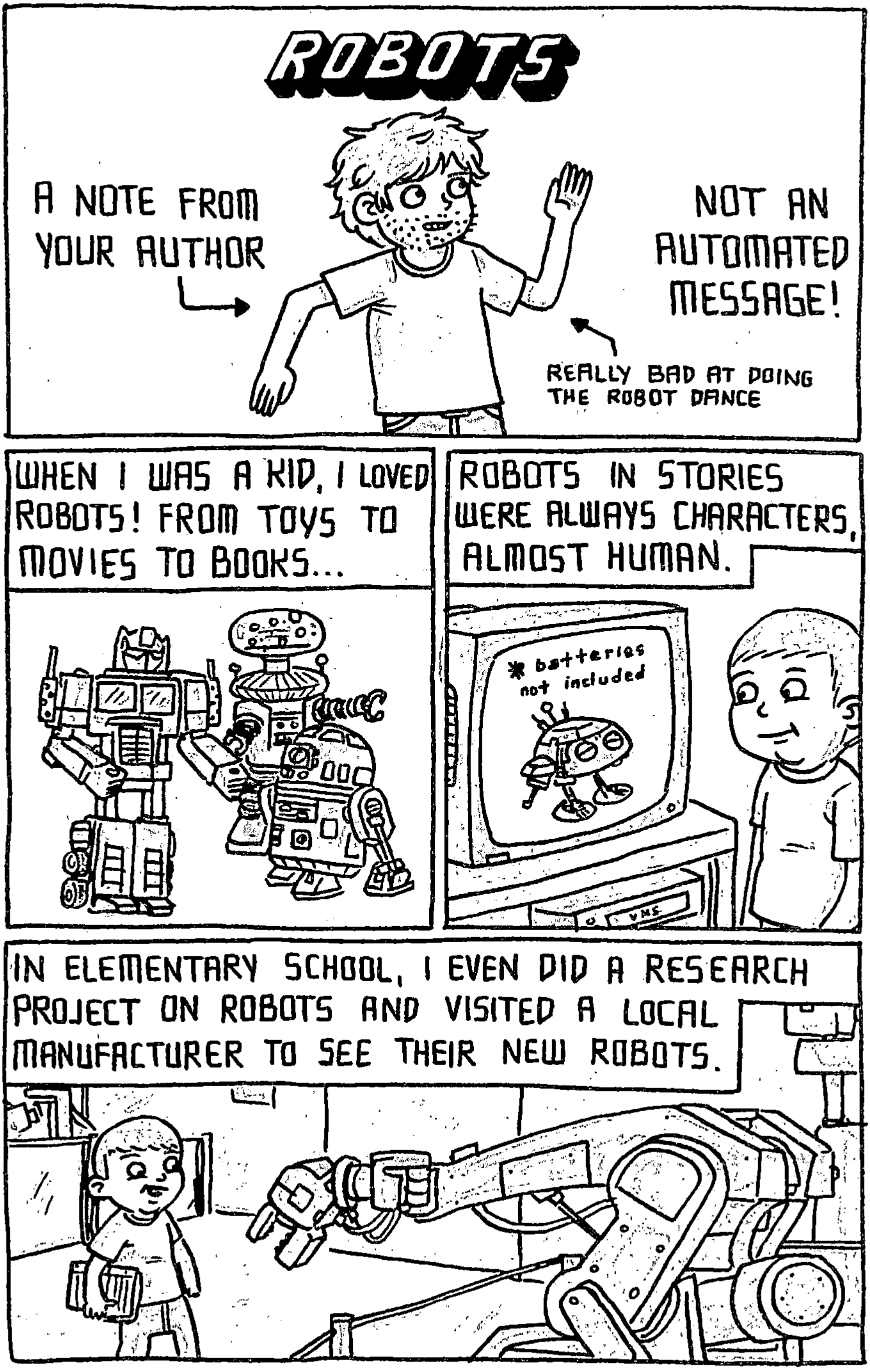
ROBOTS
A NOTE FROM YOUR AUTHOR
NOT AN AUTOMATED MESSAGE!
REALLY BAD AT DOING THE ROBOT DANCE
WHEN I WAS A KID, I LOVED ROBOTS! FROM TOYS TO MOVIES TO BOOKS...
ROBOTS IN STORIES WERE ALWAYS CHARACTERS, ALMOST HUMAN.
* batteries not included
VHS
IN ELEMENTARY SCHOOL, I EVEN DID A RESEARCH PROJECT ON ROBOTS AND VISITED A LOCAL MANUFACTURER TO SEE THEIR NEW ROBOTS.

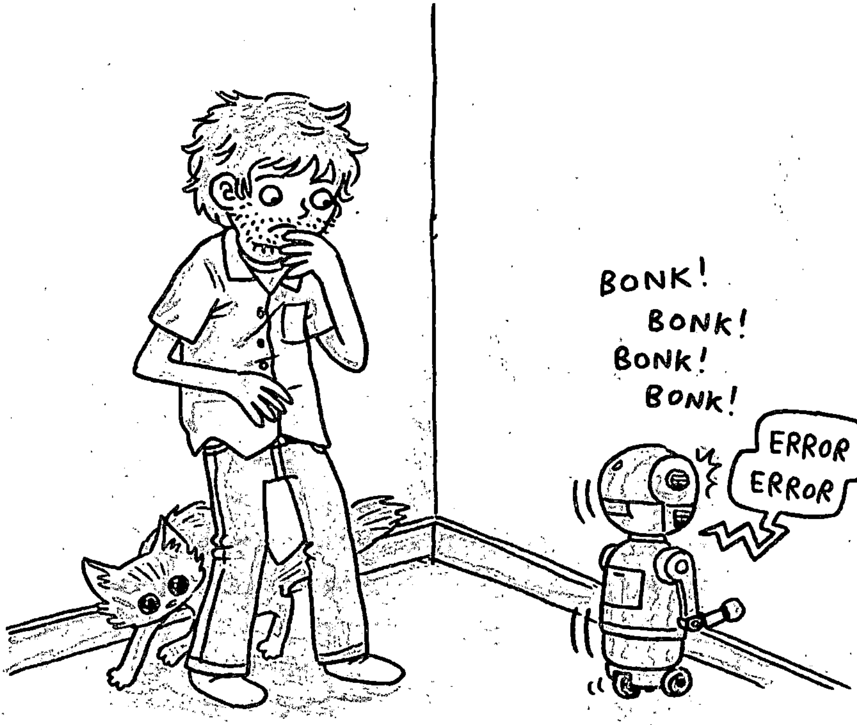
BONK!
BONK!
BONK!
BONK!
ERROR
ERROR

JEFFREY BROWN IS THE AUTHOR OF THE LUCY & ANDY NEANDERTHAL AND SPACE-TIME! MIDDLE-GRADE SERIES, AS WELL AS THE BESTSELLING DARTH VADER AND SON AND JEDI ACADEMY SERIES. HE LIVES IN CHICAGO WITH HIS WIFE, TWO SONS, AND CAT. JEFFREY HAS ALWAYS BEEN FASCINATED BY ROBOTS, BUT HE IS MUCH BETTER AT DRAWING THEM THAN PROGRAMMING THEM.

VISIT HIM ON EARTH AT JEFFREYBROWNCOMICS.COM
P.O. BOX 120 DEERFIELD, IL 60015-0120 USA